A DAY LIKE ANY OTHER

A DAY LIKE ANY OTHER

TOM OLIVA

Ballast Books, LLC
www.ballastbooks.com

Copyright © 2025 by Tom Oliva

All rights reserved. No part of this book may be reproduced in any form or by any electronic or mechanical means, including information storage and retrieval systems, without permission in writing from the publisher, except by reviewers, who may quote brief passages in a review.

ISBN 978-1-964934-27-3 (Hardcover)
ISBN 978-1-964934-28-0 (Paperback)
ISBN 978-1-964934-29-7 (Ebook)

Printed in the United States of America

Published by Ballast Books
www.ballastbooks.com

For more information, bulk orders, appearances, or speaking requests, please email: info@ballastbooks.com

PREFACE

THIS BOOK IN no way represents the beliefs, political extremes, or hysterical demonstrations of any group, party, or organization whatsoever. What it does represent is the worst-case scenario of a very possible natural catastrophe. It represents only the fact that there live among us those who have sworn an oath to the US Constitution, the essence of our republic, and, by extension, the citizens of these United States. You may not know who they are if you pass them on the street or move in next door to one of them, but rest assured that in dire times, when the need is great, they will be the ones to come forward and fulfill their oath—for the good of all.

MILITARY OATH OF ENLISTMENT

ENLISTED

"I, *(state your name)*, do solemnly swear *(or affirm)* that I will support and defend the Constitution of the United States against all enemies, foreign and domestic; that I will bear true faith and allegiance to the same; and that I will obey the orders of the president of the United States and the orders of the officers appointed over me, according to regulations and the Uniform Code of Military Justice, so help me God."

OFFICER

"I, *(state your name)*, having been appointed an officer in the *(military branch)* of the United States, as indicated above in the grade of _____ do solemnly swear *(or affirm)* that I will support and defend the Constitution of the United States against all enemies, foreign or domestic; that I will bear true faith and allegiance to the same; that I take this obligation freely, without any mental reservation or purpose of evasion; and that I will well and faithfully discharge the duties of the office upon which I am about to enter, so help me God."

"The secret to happiness is freedom . . . and the secret to freedom is courage."

THUCYDIDES

CHAPTER 1

WASHINGTON, DC

He was supposed to be sleeping. However, sleep seemed impossible given what he knew about the events about to unfold. He didn't dare look at the clock; he knew it had to be at least three o'clock in the morning. How long had they said it would take? "Science advisors"—they didn't have a clue what to expect. He scoffed audibly, causing his wife to stir. He wasn't permitted to tell her anything about the present situation. He felt his stomach turn slightly at the thought of how upset she was going to be when she found out what he knew—and that he hadn't said one word of it to her. He knew his staff wouldn't have been too upset if he had brought her into the loop. He was more afraid of someone else.

A man whom, until three days ago, he had only met casually at a couple of fundraisers. He was someone he knew stood firmly in his camp—a loyal supporter and a very generous contributor—though he could not remember the man's name... if he had ever known it to begin with. The relationship had changed drastically the same day he had first met with his science team concerning the coming event. He was still amazed at how this person had known everything about to unfold, and yet, he had only just learned of it himself a few hours before. The fact that this man had somehow managed, with the help of his own NASA director, to corral him into a private meeting at NASA headquarters, of all places, following a classified briefing was mind-blowing all on its own.

"How could my best scientists not see this coming, yet you act as if you've known for months?" he had asked the man in disbelief. The answer he had received had given him a chill, and, even now, he felt sick when he recalled the meeting.

"Who do you think really controls all those satellites and fancy devices, those supercomputers and high-tech gizmos?" the man had said. He had sat stunned that this person would dare to speak with such arrogance to him. Did he not know who he was?

"I control all those things! Me and my people! And if you know what's good for you and your family, you'll do what I tell you! Shit is about to hit the fan, sonny, and it's time you understand who's really running things!"

At that point, the old man had handed him a satellite phone and said, "If it rings, answer it."

"Who the hell *are* you?" he had asked the mysterious old man in disbelief.

"You can call me Mr. X," the man had answered as he turned to leave.

That had ended their first and only face-to-face meeting.

As if on cue, the phone started ringing, nearly stopping his heart. But it wasn't the satellite phone—it was the bedroom phone. He didn't allow it to finish even one ring, snatching it from its cradle and swinging his legs out to stand all in one motion.

"Yes?" he answered as calmly as he could.

"It's time, Mr. President," the voice on the other end responded.

"I'll be right down," President Keller replied. "So it begins," he muttered to himself as he began to dress.

CHAPTER 2

THE SUBURBS NORTH OF PHILADELPHIA, PENNSYLVANIA

IT WAS ALWAYS the same, every night for weeks. There was a frightened child wailing, although he could never tell if it was a boy or a girl. From somewhere behind him, he heard a *boom!* There was a deafening blast and a wave of heat. He turned to look but saw only his wife and children standing and staring at him. Not speaking, not moving—only watching, seemingly waiting for him to do something. He began to ask them what they were waiting for, but just as he opened his mouth—*boom!* There was another blast, this time from above him. He looked up but saw only the sun—except the sun, he realized, was getting closer. Fast. He could feel the heat; it was burning him! He tried to shield his face, but it was too hot. He tried to scream, but he had no voice. As smoke began to rise off his body, he suddenly found himself standing at the foot of a massive building constructed of what looked like white marble. This could have been a majestic piece of architecture one sees in photographs, but instead it more so resembled a scorched medieval fortress just after it'd been assaulted by some foe.

There seemed to have once been a meticulously manicured landscape, but that was no more. It was instead replaced by a barren wasteland of smoldering earth and debris, cratered and blasted—the site of some horrific battle. He heard a voice calling him from somewhere nearby. He couldn't see who it was through the smoke, but the voice sounded familiar. He started to run this way and that way, but he couldn't find the person calling him. The voice ceased, and he stopped running, breathless. He felt as though someone was behind him and turned quickly, as if to surprise them before they could get away. He turned and was then amazed, becoming frozen with disbelief.

It was his father, his face filthy from the battle that had obviously just been fought here. He recognized this as the voice that had been calling to him. His heart filled with joy at the sight of him, but before he could speak, his father looked him in the eyes with a stare so powerfully intense that he was once again stunned into immobility. His father said only one word, raising his hand and pointing his index finger directly at his stunned audience.

"Soon."

"DAD!!" he shouted, sitting straight up in bed, breathless. His wife stretched out beside him. He realized he was safe. He lay back down and exhaled forcefully, but not before flipping over his sweat-soaked pillow. He sighed deeply and noted the time on the clock. As always, it was 3:33 a.m.

"The same dream again, Andy?" his wife asked, repositioning sleepily.

"Yeah, same as before," he answered, staring at the ceiling. "Always the same."

With concern in her voice, she asked, "Maybe it's time to go talk to the VA about this?"

"I'm not goin' to the VA, for Christ's sake! Give it a rest!"

Andy was not only freaked out by this recurrent dream but also irritated by his wife, who was once again implying he had a problem. He did not feel as though he had post-traumatic stress disorder, nor did he feel there was any reason to feel that way. He had been on the receiving end of quite a bit of indirect fire—rockets and mortars, mostly, and some RPGs. He had never fired a shot in anger, and the only extent of his exposure to direct combat was having to direct the sanitizing of blood-soaked aircraft interiors after medevac missions. He felt fine and couldn't understand why this was happening to him.

"Well, do something so we can both get some sleep sometime soon!" Her displeasure was obvious, though she did not raise her voice or change her tone.

As he turned over to attempt to sleep again, he wondered, *What the hell could it mean?*

CHAPTER 3

WASHINGTON, DC

President William Keller had been elected two years earlier on the platform of renewing job growth and evening the playing field for all Americans. He would keep America out of the rest of the world's affairs and make the ultra-rich pay their fair share. He would end poverty and reduce the military's wasteful spending. He presented the same story some politicians had been peddling for decades. The nation was ripe for it, and it worked. Americans, weary of war and international strife, would buy the narrative hook, line, and sinker and hope the smiling fool in the television commercial would follow through on his promises.

As it turned out, he succeeded only in drawing down the military, which was easy for his kind. Nothing much else changed, as politically driven promises usually resulted in little more than more politics. A large American military footprint still remained in the Middle East, only now it was stretched farther due to the draw downs. A stagnant economy, skyrocketing unemployment, the nation divided along every political fault line possible. It was the status quo, just the way politicians liked it.

It wouldn't be long before President Keller learned that everything he believed in was a lie, smoke and mirrors to conceal the "man behind the curtain"—a group of super-secret, ultra-powerful mega-rich that ran everyone and everything, including him. His mysterious visitor had made that clear, but he had been getting the feeling for some time prior that someone, somewhere other than the White House, was pulling the strings. And now he found himself about to preside over what was possibly the greatest natural disaster to strike humankind since the Great Flood. Things hadn't turned out at all like he had planned.

Keller had mindlessly taken the satellite phone from Mr. X and, at the urging of NASA's Director Morris, hadn't handed it directly to his Secret Service detail.

"Please, Mr. President, you must do what he says. They have my children under surveillance. They drugged my son in his own home and sent me the video of them threatening him with a knife while he was unconscious. He woke up on his couch hours later with no recollection of what had happened," Morris had told him.

Keller had done his best to assuage the increasingly agitated Morris that he would get to the bottom of this "Mr. X" and keep Morris and his family safe. Morris had been horrified at the thought, pleading with Keller to just play along. Keller had agreed but wasn't convinced, thinking, *I'm the most powerful man on the planet. No one bullies me.*

Upon returning to the White House, Keller had gone directly to the Oval Office, determined to dispose of the Mr. X matter immediately. He called for the head of his Secret Service detail to meet him there, as he needed to focus his energy on the coming crisis. He wasn't about to let some old man threaten him, no matter how insistent Morris was. As Keller moved to settle in behind the Resolute desk, he noticed a file marked "Classified, POTUS Eyes Only" on the seat of the chair. Opening the file as he sat, he saw a handwritten cover sheet for a thick stack of papers and photographs that stated, "Mr. President, you will find enclosed all the reason you need to choose the winning team." Keller's heart sank as he flipped through the pages before him—sworn affidavits from all of his cabinet members testifying that Keller and the administration had known about the coming disaster for months and did nothing. The file was complete with official-looking scientific data and photographs of the sun that Keller had zero understanding of but that troubled him deeply. It was clear to Keller that the affidavits were forgeries. There was no way they were real since he and his entire staff had just learned of the impending doom. Or was there? Had they known?

His fear and doubt over the idea that his own people were setting him up was replaced with horror as he began looking through the photographs. There was photo after photo of his children playing on the White House lawn, or at the beach, or at a dozen other locations. Keller felt true fear when he came to photo after photo of his twin daughters sleeping in their beds inside this very building. Keller sat staring at the photos, sweat forming on his forehead. The room felt very small, and Keller felt as though the walls were actually getting closer.

Bzzzz-bzzzz-bzzzz. The satellite phone in his jacket pocket scared Keller half to death, startling him back into reality.

He answered with a confused "Hello?"

"I assume you've seen enough of the file I sent over." Mr. X's voice sounded matter of fact.

"Who the hell do you think you are? You think you're going to scare me with some photoshopped pictures and fake testimonies from my own people? You've got it all wrong!"

"Perhaps the affidavits are fakes, perhaps not, but I assure you without a doubt that the pictures are real. What's also real is that the planet is about to be struck with a great cataclysm. You have to decide if you want to be part of what comes after or become just another tragic casualty like so many others are doomed to become."

The call went silent, but Keller sat still, the words of Mr. X ringing in his ears.

Moments later, Special Agent Billings entered and said, "You wanted to see me, sir?"

Keller thought for a moment, putting the phone back into his jacket pocket. "No, no, never mind, thank you. I'm sorry to have bothered you."

That had been three days ago, and now the day was upon him. As he dressed quickly, he noticed the First Lady watching him.

"Hey," he said, buttoning his shirt.

"Hey," she replied, sitting up.

"Did the phone wake you? I'm sorry," he said sincerely.

"Of course the phone woke me. That damn thing is worse than the alarm clock. I jump out of my skin every time it rings after ten. What's going on? The Middle East again?"

"No, but I wish it was," he said, almost smiling.

"Now I'm worried!" she said, cocking her head to one side and looking concerned.

"It's really bad. It's so bad that I can't even say anything to you. I shouldn't even be saying anything now."

"But you're going to, right?" she asked, although it wasn't really a question.

"It's the sun," he answered. "The scientists aren't sure to what extent the damage will be."

"What? Wait—damage? What's going on?" she replied. He had her full attention now.

"Hurry up and get dressed. You're coming with me." He figured he had already let the cat out of the bag, and he wasn't going to keep her away now. There's no way she'd roll over and go back to sleep after that kind of bombshell. "They need me in the Situation Room. It's about to start."

CHAPTER 4

THE SUBURBS NORTH OF PHILADELPHIA

It was a toss-up. What was more annoying: the kids arguing about whose turn it was to feed the dog or the alarm clock buzzing away on its third snooze, sounding annoyed that Andrew wasn't up yet? Or perhaps getting up and going to a job he truly hated was the real annoyance. No matter. He was already late, and even though the little voice in his head kept saying, *Call out today; you really need to call out today,* he ignored it as he shut off the alarm and dragged himself to the shower. It was a day like any other, and he needed to get on with it.

Andrew Lemon, like most Americans that morning, was simply living the American dream. He had a good job that paid well. He had retired a year ago from the US Marine Corps after twenty-two years of service as a Gunnery Sergeant. With two tours in Iraq and two tours in Afghanistan, he had done his duty to his country and was now moving on to the next phase of his life as a civilian. His wife of eighteen years, Melissa, had stood by him through all of his deployments, and their relationship was as strong as ever. They still truly loved one another after all this time. They had two children—a son, David, age sixteen, and a daughter, Kathryn, age thirteen. Along with his marriage, they were the true joys of his life. With another combat deployment looming, he had opted to retire rather than put his family through another eight months of angst with Daddy in harm's way.

Andy was a fourth-generation American of Italian descent, though his name didn't suggest it. When his great-grandparents arrived in the country, a mix-up at Ellis Island had forever turned the ancient family name of Limongi into Lemon. It wasn't uncommon for customs inspectors at Ellis Island to mutilate difficult-to-pronounce ethnic names into something more Americanized.

Most times, the immigrants didn't discover this issue until much later in the process due to the language barrier, and once they understood the error, they figured it wasn't worth the hassle. They were just happy to be in the United States, so they moved on with their new "American" names. So just like that, Antonio Limongi had become Anthony Lemon. Andrew's grandfather used to say, with his hands in the air and his shoulders shrugging, "America give us a lemon, so we make lemonade!" It was a running family joke that was just a matter of fact. They were the Lemons.

His great-grandfather had come to this country with ten dollars in his pocket, a pregnant wife, and a dream to start a better life. He worked hard at several odd jobs before finding steady work at the local grocer in their Brooklyn neighborhood. Well-liked by the owner as his hardest worker, eventually he was brought on as a business partner. Anthony Lemon, his wife Marcella, and their two sons, Anthony Jr. and Michael, were a turn-of-the-century American success story.

When the US entered World War II, Michael Lemon signed up to serve in the US Marine Corps before they could draft him into the Army. He deployed to the Pacific and served as a private in the Second Marine Division. He fought and was wounded on the Pacific island of Saipan. He returned home and took over the family grocery business from his father. He married and had two sons, David and Peter.

David followed in his father's footsteps and joined the US Marine Corps before he could be drafted. He deployed to Vietnam and was wounded at the siege of Khe Sanh in 1968. He returned home after recovering from severe injuries, but instead of taking over the family business—a career his brother gladly undertook—David decided to go to college and earn a degree in criminal justice. Soon after graduation, he joined the NYPD.

After joining the NYPD, David married his high school sweetheart, Anntonella "Ann" Rengazzi. She often teased David, saying, "What kind of Italian is named David Lemon? You're not Italian. Someone just told you that, right?" David's usual reply was to shrug his shoulders, raise his hands, and say, "Easy there, Mrs. Lemon" while feigning anger.

Ann and David followed the family tradition and had two sons: first Andrew, and then Anthony eighteen months later. Soon after Anthony's birth, David accepted a job as a Nassau County police officer and moved the family out to the suburbs, being the first of the family to do the unthinkable and leave Brooklyn.

It was in this setting that Andrew grew up—in a close-knit family of war heroes, Italian traditions, and close family ties. Going to Brooklyn for holidays and family occasions was not to be missed. While it was always an adventure to visit Brooklyn, with its old-style rowhomes and old-world atmosphere, David knew that Andrew preferred the neatly manicured lawns with trees and shrubs that were a commonplace landscape out on Long Island. Life was good.

By the start of Andrew's junior year of high school, he had already decided to join the Marine Corps like his father and grandfather before him. He ignored his father's life-long advice to never join the Marines. He always told him, "If you go into the service, join the Air Force or the Navy. They got it good." What David really meant, though he never actually said it directly, was, "Join the Air Force or the Navy, and you'll live longer." David had seen and experienced combat at its worst, and he didn't want his sons to go through the hell he and his father had been through.

At seventeen, Andrew brought home a US Marine Corps recruiter so that David and Ann could sign the underage release form for him to enter the delayed entry program, which meant enlisting a year before he actually left for boot camp. It was with mixed feelings that David took this turn of events and his son's decision to do the exact opposite of what he had told him. David was filled with a father's pride but also full of apprehension over this decision. He knew Andrew could handle it; he just didn't know what the world would have in store for his son. David was incredibly relieved to find out that Andrew would be guaranteed a Military Operational Specialty (MOS) in aviation. He knew that an MOS in aviation would spare him the hard life of a ground-pounding grunt and the ever-present specter of a sudden and violent death.

Many times in Vietnam, David had watched from the jungle floor as helicopters and jets flew overhead. He always imagined the comfortable accommodations those guys returned to every night. But in reality, he was only slightly jealous of those lucky bastards. He understood war and knew that no one ever really had it easy, nor was anyone completely safe.

David had gained enormous respect for those flyers on one fateful day while surrounded during the siege of Khe Sanh in 1968. He saw how they braved the storms of enemy fire in order to bring in supplies for the Marines and evacuate the wounded. After being wounded by a North Vietnamese rocket explosion, David left the besieged airfield on a Marine Corps UH-1 Huey helicopter. In most cases, the wounded were taken to the airfield for evacuation, which wasn't any safer. Through the haze of being blown up and receiving a morphine injection from the Corpsman, he remembered the sound of the Huey coming in to get him. He also distinctly remembered the eruption of enemy fire from the hillside opposite his position. He would be forever grateful for those pilots and the enlisted crewmen in that Huey.

David's injuries had been severe enough to require immediate evacuation. Fortunately for him, the portion of the perimeter where he had happened to be was just a few yards from a flat spot the pilots were familiar with. The bird that would carry him from the battlefield seemed to appear from nowhere. In reality, it had just dropped a load of supplies to another unit farther down the perimeter. It had flown in at treetop level and dropped into the landing zone (LZ) at such speed that David had no doubt it would crash right on top of him. He remembered thinking, *Oh great, the medevac bird is going to kill me!*

The pilot flared the helicopter's tail at the last moment, hovered briefly, then settled on its skids. The crew chief was out before the bird had fully settled, waving toward the group surrounding David and preparing to carry his litter to the bird. As another burst of green tracers ripped the air overhead, the crewman started waving more vigorously while shouting something into his helmet-mounted microphone, undoubtedly informing the pilots what they already knew—that the LZ was hot and getting hotter. As David's buddies were loading him onto the deck of the Huey, more rockets started landing dangerously close.

The crew chief wasted no time in giving the pilots the OK to take off while still strapping David down to the floor with a cargo strap. David couldn't hear, but he was sure the crew chief, a short man with a thick mustache and a set of corporal stripes painted on his helmet, said, "Ready in the back." Corporal Crew Chief had said it with such calm that David wondered if he knew he was at Khe Sanh in a hot LZ. The bird immediately lifted off and started forward in the same instant. As they were flying no more than five feet off the ground, David could see the heads of his litter bearers still dashing back to the safety of the trench line. He could also see the muzzle flashes in the jungle all pointed at him. Taking fire from what seemed like all directions and feeling very naked strapped to the deck of that metal coffin, David thought momentarily, *Put me back on the ground where it's safe!* Regardless, the crewmen were busy manning their .30-caliber machine guns, showering him with spent casings as they raked the tree line covering their egress. They were busy and would not have heard him anyway had he made such a request. Nor would they entertain returning to that death trap just because he was scared shitless.

A few moments later, which seemed like an eternity to David, the Huey found some clean air free from enemy fire, and the corporal crew chief turned and crouched down, shouting so David could hear over the rotors and engine noise, "Today's your lucky day, bro!"

It was a very lucky day for all of them. Bullet holes riddled the aircraft. The copilot's windshield was shot out, David could see daylight through the overhead, and there was something hot leaking on him, which he learned later was hydraulic fluid.

David could not hear what they were saying but saw the crew engaged in some kind of banter that must have been funny. They were all laughing and lighting cigarettes, the adrenaline rush still evident in their eyes. As the bird raced further and further from Khe Sanh, David could see the airfield at the center of Khe Sanh's perimeter—or what he assumed was the airfield—shrouded in what looked like a giant storm cloud. He knew it was a cloud of dust from the constant pounding the complex received daily.

As the fear started to subside and the morphine started really kicking in, the more he felt like he might actually make it out of there. David realized that these Marines had flown into that mess and put themselves in great danger to rescue him. He felt a humbleness like never before that he would never feel again in his life. They didn't know him, but they had come in and gotten him anyway.

It was at this point in the story, the one time he told it, that David started becoming emotional. "The courage," he said as his voice started to crack.

Ann quickly shuffled Andrew and Anthony, who at the time were still preteens, into another room, telling them, "Daddy needs a minute."

David's respect for the wing had been earned in the harshest of realities that day, and he was proud his son would now be a part of that legacy.

David did not talk about his time in Vietnam. He would recount this story only *once* for his sons. It was strictly by sheer circumstance that the story got out. A rare afternoon of drinking Jack Daniels with his brother had loosened his tongue and brought back the memory.

David died twelve months after Andrew had graduated from recruit training at Parris Island. Andrew had known that something was wrong in the months before his dad's passing, but neither David nor Ann had said a word about his sickness. In hindsight, it was a clear case of Agent Orange exposure. Unfortunately, he wasn't diagnosed with mantle cell lymphoma until he had reached stage IV. It took almost forty years to show up but didn't take long to take him out. Andrew's parents hadn't wanted to worry him.

As they laid his father to rest, Andrew's mind returned to his father's words: "The courage."

Eighteen months later, Andrew's mom died, everyone agreed, from a broken heart.

Andrew Lemon was the son of a cop/Vietnam vet, the grandson of a World War II survivor of the Pacific theater, and the great-grandson of an immigrant. He was an heir to the American dream. His family had come from Europe with nothing and had flourished.

Andrew was a career Marine. He had traveled the world, met Melissa—the girl of his dreams—and started a family. He had risen through the ranks to Gunnery Sergeant and served his country in Iraq and Afghanistan with pride. He had retired approximately twelve months earlier and had never been so miserable in his entire life. The words "I love the Corps" never entered his mind until after he was out. Until then, it was just his profession, but now he missed it, and there was no going back.

Little did he know that the previous twelve months were but a respite from the chaos and uncertainty he had grown accustomed to in the Corps. Events were closing in on him, and the cruel future that awaited would leave him longing for the mundane repetition of the rat race he detested.

CHAPTER 5

THE SUBURBS NORTH OF PHILADELPHIA

Andrew felt his blood pressure rising as he approached the kitchen. The conversation concerning who should feed the dog had apparently continued while he was in the shower. The little voice in his head once again suggested calling out from work. *You really need to stay home today, Andy.* Andy thought, *Hmm, I should, but not today though—too much to do*, talking himself out of it. He entered the kitchen as his son explained what a burden feeding the dog had been on him and how Kathryn always got out of doing it because, supposedly, it took her longer to get ready.

"I'm a girl! It takes longer, stupid!" Kathryn replied.

"Don't call me stupid, stupid!" said David with a sneer. "You're up there dillydallying and wasting time because you know Mom will make me do it," he added, waving his hand toward his mother, who sat at the counter nearby watching the show.

"Mom, explain to him how it takes us longer to get ready in the morning," Kathryn said, turning to her mother, attempting to gain an ally in the argument.

No longer able to pretend to be invisible, Melissa had been drawn into their imbecilic conversation and thus forced to comment. As she began to speak, Andrew entered the kitchen, essentially bailing her out of throwing gas on the fire as she usually did in these situations.

"Just part of being the mom," she would say as both offspring stormed off angrily.

"How about this!" Andrew started, perturbed. "I'll feed the dog if you guys go clean up what comes out the other end!" He gestured toward the backyard.

"Dad!" scoffed David, squinting in disgust.

"Ewwww!" cried Kathryn.

Melissa snickered. She had always admired his way with words. He had caught her eye the first moment she saw him all those years ago when she was in college. He walked into the room strong and confident, tan and handsome.

15

Who's that? she wondered. He wasn't one of the usual college boys who attended those parties, either pimple-faced and shy or handsome and arrogant, as if every girl wanted to be with them. It was apparent that he and his companions weren't students.

She learned they were Marines from the air station when one of her sorority sisters greeted one of them with a hug and introduced them by saying, "Hey everyone! This is my cousin Ray and his buddies from the base. Make yourselves at home guys."

That was the beginning. It didn't take long for him to notice her looking at him. She was a black-haired beauty with big dark eyes, gentle features, and an infectious smile. He was instantly smitten. She had known immediately that her father, a surgeon, would never approve. He viewed the military with distrust. He remained a hippie to this day. But love is love, and here they were all these years later, in domestic bliss, enduring moronic arguments over canine eating and bathroom habits.

"I'm glad you're amused," Andy said, turning toward his wife, squinting with his hands on his hips.

She was as beautiful as the first time he had seen her all those years ago. Her eyes sparkled in the morning light, and she was beautiful—even without makeup, her hair a mess, and wearing an old flannel pajama top. She was still his little college girl whom all the other Marines envied him for.

"How did your dumb ass manage to score a supermodel, Lemon?" they would tease.

"Ya know, no girl can resist the Italian stallion," he would reply, grinning from ear to ear. But in truth, he knew he was way out of his league and how lucky he really was.

"Now here's what's going to happen. David, feed the friggin' dog. Now!" Andrew said, pointing at his son. Turning to his daughter, he said, "Kathryn, you feed the dog tomorrow. It's not that difficult, people!"

The ensuing explosion of protest and dismay was instant and sustained. Andrew couldn't quite make out what either of his children were saying as they were both speaking at the same time—neither, it seemed, pausing to breathe. His already ill mood started moving into that place that could only be described as ugly. That hot temper inherited from generations of Italians was about to emerge.

Melissa, seeing that the show was over and that things were about to move to a different level, intervened. "OK! Dad has spoken. Now get moving, both of you—you're going to be late."

David reluctantly went to the garage to feed the dog, muttering something about fairness. Kathryn sneered at her brother and squinted at Andrew as she left to finish getting ready for school.

"You're in a fine mood this morning," Melissa said after the kids were gone. "Maybe you should just call out. There's no need to contaminate the rest of the world with that attitude."

Andrew's head was still spinning from the verbal tsunami that his children had just inflicted upon him. He was with it enough, however, to realize that at this point, the only member of the family who wasn't giving him a hard time was Gomer, their black Lab and the subject of all the discourse and angst. Gomer, up until a few moments ago, was focused solely on the chipmunk darting back and forth across the deck, just outside the sliding doors off the kitchen.

Gomer had been acquired at about the same time Andy had retired. The kids had talked him into it under the premise of a dog being a good retirement gift, when, in reality, they just wanted a dog. Andy hadn't fought them on it; they had earned it. Since they had endured their dad's absence on four combat deployments, it was the least he could do for them.

Andy had insisted on naming him Gomer after the comical television character Gomer Pyle. Andy had said, "If we're gonna have a dog, it's gonna be a jarhead like me." Though Gomer Pyle the television character was far from being anything remotely close to a squared-away Marine, Andy felt the name was fitting for a puppy. Gomer Pyle Lemon was just over a year old now. He was a full-grown dog but still a puppy at heart. He came over to greet Andy, his attention free now that the chipmunk had gone on to bigger and better things.

"Yeah, you and me buddy, we gotta stick together against these humans," Andy said, looking at his wife with raised eyebrows.

Just then, David returned looking irritated, carrying a bowl of dog food that he unceremoniously deposited in front of Gomer, who wasn't the least bit interested.

David guffawed audibly, "He doesn't even want it!"

Andy started to stand up from scratching Gomer's neck to express his displeasure with his son's attitude, but Melissa beat him to the punch. "Thank you. Now go finish getting ready."

David left the room, giving his dad one last sassy-eyed look. Once again, Melissa beat Andy to the punch. "Go, you're already late!"

Melissa turned to Andy, who was still staring in the direction his son had just departed, nodding with a negative expression. "You know, these are your children, not your Marines!" she said, with her usual raised brow. It wasn't the first time he had heard this lecture. "They're not Lance Corporals to be bossed around by the all-powerful Gunny." Of course, she was correct, but old habits die hard, and Andy was just at the beginning of being Mr. Lemon and had yet to let go of the self formerly known as Gunny Lemon.

"That boy needs to check his attitude!" Andy said, not willing to give up so easily.

"His attitude is normal—he's a teenager. Get over it!" Melissa shot back, once again completely correct.

"It's not so much to ask them to feed the damn dog," Andy said, wanting the last word.

"No, it's not, but when you come at them like that, already in a bad mood, it's like throwing gas on a fire," Melissa added.

"Whatever," Andy replied, still contemplating just going back to bed.

"By the way, you need to take them to school," Melissa added, half under her breath, before turning away.

"Wait... what?" Andy said, snapping out of his going-back-to-bed fantasy.

"They both procrastinated on projects that are due today, so they are finishing them as we speak and missing the bus in the process. So you need to take them. Because, as I told you last night, my car won't start," Melissa said, pouring a cup of coffee.

So much for going back to bed, he thought, reaching for his cell phone. He would be late, at the very least, and would need to let them know at the salt mine. Of course, he didn't really work in a salt mine—he just preferred calling it that. He considered it toiling at a slave wage. It was a long way from the Marine Corps. Everyone kept telling him, "This is just how it is on the outside," which didn't make him feel any better. He missed the Corps and realized just how much he loved it only after getting out. The old saying "You don't know what you've got till it's gone" was never so true than in this situation for Andy. There was no going back though. He had made his decision, and he had to see it through to whatever end.

CHAPTER 6

WASHINGTON, DC

THE SITUATION ROOM was packed full. Everyone that could be there was there. Normally, the Situation Room was a subdued conference room, never more unruly than the occasional argument over some policy decision or perhaps a football score before a meeting got started. This morning, pandemonium had taken over.

All of the Joint Chiefs of Staff were present. Secretaries of the Departments of State, Defense, Homeland Security, and Energy were also present, along with the CIA, FBI, FAA, and FEMA directors, all of whom brought at least one high-level aide. It was chaos. It seemed like everyone was talking at once. Some were looking at laptop screens on the Situation Room's conference table. Others were on the phone, presumably talking with personnel who were monitoring conditions in the field. President Keller and the First Lady stood watching the chaos in stunned amazement. Neither of them was prepared for such utter confusion. Then, just as they were sure everyone was talking at once, the room went silent.

General John Mattlin, chairman of the Joint Chiefs, had noticed the Kellers standing in the doorway looking confused and shouted, "Good morning, Mr. President." At this, the room had fallen silent, and all heads had turned toward the doorway where the First Couple stood holding hands, staring like two deer in oncoming headlights just before an eighteen-wheeler's impact. "Good morning, ma'am," the general added in a softer tone once the room was silent.

"Good morning, General," she answered uneasily, elbowing her husband to snap him out of his stupefied state.

"Good morning... good morning, everyone," he answered quickly at his wife's prompting. He felt very uncomfortable saying such a thing as "good morning" today. It had been predicted to be anything but good. "Where are we, people? What's going on? How much time do we have left?" he asked, taking his seat at the head of the table. He had recovered from his earlier moment of confusion and was now ready to be briefed.

The normal seating protocol was disregarded given the present situation and the overcrowded nature of the room. Those that were near a seat took one; the rest stood. Dr. Norman Detweiler, the Chief Science Advisor to the President, moved to the front of the conference room to stand beside the giant screen that, at the moment, had a picture of the sun on it. It was obviously the first slide of a PowerPoint presentation of Dr. Detweiler's briefing.

The president turned to his chief of staff and asked, "Is everyone present?"

"Yes, Mr. President. The vice president is with us via video conference from NORAD in Cheyenne Mountain. Otherwise, everyone with a need to know is in this room."

A need to know. That had troubled him since this thing began. It had been agreed that putting out news of this magnitude to the general population may create a panic and cause a catastrophe all on its own, even if the solar event proved not to be as severe as feared. The president's mysterious visitor had made it crystal clear that this was to remain undisclosed to all but those absolutely necessary.

"Hey, Frank! How's the weather there?" the president said, addressing the vice president.

"I wouldn't know, Will. I'm inside a mountain," the vice president replied jokingly via the video monitor to the left of the president.

Vice President Franklin Goodwin was known for his quick wit and his ability to charm even the most hostile of political opponents. He was a short, round-faced man with a ruddy complexion, more resembling a midwestern farmer rather than a Washington politician. He was, in fact, a very formidable opponent and had only lost the presidential primary by the very slimmest of margins. Some felt President Keller had stolen the nomination from him and that that was the reason he was chosen to be vice president.

He and President Keller had become close friends since the primary season, and the president respected his input and opinions on issues and policy decisions. He was wishing at this moment, on the eve of destruction, that he had told his friend about his meeting with Mr. X.

"OK, Frank, fair enough," Keller replied with a chuckle. *Leave it to Frank to make me laugh at a time like this,* he thought.

"Please proceed, Doctor," the president said, speaking directly to the skinny man at the podium who could only be a scientist, stereotypically so.

A DAY LIKE ANY OTHER

"Hello, everyone," Dr. Detweiler said, adjusting the laptop directly in front of him on the briefer's podium. Dr. Norman Detweiler—MIT professor of nuclear engineering, Harvard graduate, Nobel Prize recipient, and advisor to the president of the United States—looked as though he hadn't slept in days, and he hadn't. Since NASA's notification three days ago, he hadn't slept a wink. He had gathered the best minds in science from around the country. They had pored over all the data and finally confirmed NASA's preliminary data and predictions. He was troubled not only by the pending event and the potential catastrophe it could bring but also by the burning question of why NASA, with all its technology, could only give three days' warning.

"As you all know," he began, "three days ago, NASA satellites monitoring solar activity detected coronal mass ejections larger than we have seen in modern history. While coronal mass events are normal and occur every day, this event has an imminent intersection with Earth in approximately four hours, as previously projected."

There was a collective audible gasp at that statement. Everyone in the room had already been given this news, but hearing it again was no less of a shock than hearing it for the first time. They had all hoped that NASA's calculations were wrong and that life could just go on as usual without any further drama. The absolute reality of it, now confirmed, was crushing.

President Keller asked what no one else would. "So there is no change from the original calculations? We're going to take this one on the chin?"

"I'm afraid so, Mr. President. We've run the computer models nonstop since getting the initial report, and they have all come back with the same results. Earth is about to experience something it hasn't seen since the 1859 Carrington event.

"As we all know"—he had already briefed everyone present when this all started, but he felt he should go over it again, as this was the first time they were all together in the same room at the same time—"in 1859, the telegraph communications failed, operators were injured by the sudden surge of electricity, and telegraph equipment caught fire. If what's about to hit us is as intense as the 1859 event, we are looking at a total breakdown of the power grid at the very least. It is unclear if motorized vehicles will be affected. Some research says yes, other research says no. We won't be sure until it hits us. Also, there is some concern that this much energy hitting Earth all at once could affect the weather, as well as possibly create seismic activity."

"Dr. Detweiler." This is where President Keller had to chime in—he couldn't understand how these big brains, as he called them, didn't know what to expect. "There are a lot of 'ifs' in your briefing. It seems as though you and your team have no idea what we should expect." He was irritated, and it showed.

"Ah, well, yes, Mr. President..." The scientist knew this would be coming from at least one of the assembled directors. "The truth is that we don't really know. The 1859 event was well documented, but they obviously didn't have the sort of data collection and documentation we have today." He was exhausted and in no mood for a politician's attempt to throw him under the bus, as if he was supposed to predict the future. It showed in the tone of his voice. "In 1859, within hours of an amateur astronomer by the name of Richard Carrington witnessing dark spots on the sun, all hell began to break loose with the telegraph system. All over the planet, witnesses reported colorful auroras so bright in the night sky that birds began to chirp and people began to rise and start their daily chores. At least this time, we got three days' advanced notice thanks to our highly developed technology."

The room was silent. The president and the scientist were locked in a death stare.

It was the vice president, sensing the tension all the way out in Colorado under a mountain, who broke the silence. "Well then, Dr. Detweiler, how have we used that extended time of three days? What have we done to prepare, other than ship ME off to a hole in the ground?"

The room breathed again. The scientist shuffled his papers, composing himself. The president leaned back in his chair, and the First Lady touched his arm. He took her hand.

"That's a very good question, Mr. Vice President," Detweiler responded, now more composed. "Due to the sensitive nature of this matter, the many unknowns, and the potential for civil unrest, it was decided to take steps that were subtle enough to go unnoticed by the general population or to be passed off as a drill or training exercises."

"Yes, I know, Doctor. We left the bulk of the human population in the dark for their own good." The vice president was adamantly against this tactic but had succumbed to the president's insistence that they play it this way. "So, what DID we do?"

Detweiler really did not like politicians. "What we did was order all naval vessels to sea. It is our hope that they may be minimally affected by The Event if they are at sea, away from the power grid and on their own power. They will shut down all systems just before the effect hits them in order to, hopefully, prevent the damaging effect of the power surges."

"Wait a minute," said the FEMA director, Paul Whiting, a fat, little man who seemed to always be out of breath. "A power surge? Hell, I have surge protectors all over my office and my house—they won't stop the damage? Isn't that what they're for? You mean to tell me the Navy needs to shut its ships off to prevent power surge damage?"

Dr. Detweiler stood before them, amazed. All this had been in the brief they had received. The world as they knew it was potentially coming to an end, and this idiot hadn't bothered to read the briefing report. He decided that he disliked political appointees even *more* than he disliked politicians.

"Well, Mr. Whiting, the surge protectors presently available to the public and to the military, for that matter, are not designed to withstand this kind of surge. All the energy is front-loaded here. It will pass any kind of shut-off mechanism before it even has a chance to sense the increase. As far as shutting off an entire ship . . . well, once again, we just don't know and wouldn't want to take that chance." Unable to resist, he added, "This information was in your briefing report."

Whiting turned beet red and said sheepishly, "Thank you, Doctor."

Without acknowledging the "thank you," Detweiler continued, "We have put all nuclear power plants on alert for an imminent emergency shutdown drill evaluation. We basically told them that we are coming and to be ready. They will have staff sleeping on their desks until we call it off. It's cruel for us to do it this way, but given the potential ramifications of even one catastrophic meltdown, they will just have to deal with it."

Everyone nodded in agreement with his last statement. A nuclear meltdown would be very bad.

"All intercontinental missile silos are, at this moment, in the middle of a lockdown drill," Detweiler continued, ignoring the nodding baboons around the table. "This drill simulates a massive enemy attack that has destroyed the power grid. They are all on battery power, isolated from any connection to outside power lines or any part of the grid. These batteries are also shielded in what's known as a Faraday cage, which protects them from bursts of electromagnetic energy."

Military planners had long known that an electromagnetic pulse would threaten their ability to launch a counterstrike on the attacker. Thus, they took great measures to protect the missile silos and their deadly contents.

"We have positioned Navy ships at various points along the projected path of 'The Event,' as we are calling it. These ships will be the first indicators of how severe this is going to be." Detweiler paused for a moment here, looking up at his audience. "They are our canaries in the coal mine. If we can't reestablish contact with them after they power back up after The Event passes, we'll know it's going to be bad."

It appeared to Dr. Detweiler that all present in the room began to sweat at that moment. These were people at the highest levels of power, and the complete lack of control made them uncomfortable, to say the least.

"Air travel is also a major area of concern. The FBI and the FAA both have a plan for keeping air travel grounded during the time frame of The Event. I will defer to the FBI and FAA directors to give the details on this area of the briefing," Detweiler said, nodding toward the president.

"Thank you, Doctor," said a mountain of a man with a full head of silver hair and the face of a baby. FAA Director David Hughes was a former Air Force bomber pilot who had been recruited into the FAA after leaving active duty while still a young man. He had worked his way to the top and was truly honored to be part of what he felt was the finest agency in the entire federal government. "With the help of the FBI, we've put a halt to all takeoffs and ordered all airborne aircraft to land before 0700 hours Eastern Standard Time. As we speak, the skies are becoming empty, the likes of which we haven't seen since September 11, 2001." Director Hughes then nodded toward the man seated next to him.

Taking his cue, FBI Director Robert Cummings stood as Director Hughes took a seat. Robert Cummings was a no-nonsense type of person in everything he did. He had started his career as a patrolman in downtown Baltimore. Through hard work and ambition, he now found himself as the first Black FBI Director in American history. He was respected by all and trusted to always tell it like it is, regardless of the political winds and ramifications. It was said that his integrity was impeccable, which said a lot in Washington, DC.

"What we've done," Cummings began without pleasantries, "is issue a warning about an imminent attack on the air traffic control computers by a terrorist group with a sophisticated computer virus. All airports are to suspend flight operations until further notice by order of the FBI. The foreign FAA counterparts around the world will receive the threat warning as well and suspend flight operations, of course, at least for any flights heading this way. If The Event passes without incident, we will issue an all-clear order, and everyone can go about their business."

FAA Director Hughes picked up here with, "Being that the continental US is going to experience The Event first, there is no reason to include any other countries in the threat warning at this time. As Director Cummings stated, if The Event moves on without incident, then everyone goes on about their business. If not, it will be clear enough that no one should be flying anything. Let's hope that's not the case."

"Let's hope not," Detweiler said. "Beyond that, all we can do is monitor the situation as it unfolds. Any further preparation would raise suspicion and possibly expose the whole thing. That call was above my pay grade. Are there any questions?"

He felt more could have been done to put FEMA assets in place, as well as bring the military to a higher state of alert, but he had been aggressively overruled by President Keller. He still wasn't sure why the president had been so angry when discussing preparations. It was very *not* like William Keller to become so upset so easily.

The secretary of state was the first to raise her hand with a question.

"Yes, Madam Secretary?" Detweiler had been raised to respect a lady, even if she was a political appointee.

Secretary of State Amanda Carson was a tall, slender woman with shocking red hair. A career bureaucrat, she was known as the Viking bitch of the State Department for the intensity with which she pushed herself and her subordinates. More than a few careers had been destroyed by her climb to the top. She was a stark contrast to FEMA Director Whiting, seated next to her, still looking a little flushed from Dr. Detweiler's earlier dressing-down.

"Thank you, Dr. Detweiler," she began. "I have read through the briefing report, and I still have a problem with the level of secrecy we are imposing on ourselves here."

"Amanda—" the president interrupted her.

"No, Will," she said, raising her hand in his direction. They were getting a glimpse of the Viking bitch. "I can understand the need for secrecy to prevent a panic, but I really think we're going too far here. Not to mention that by not informing our allies, we're putting ourselves in a very difficult position. Keeping the news of the possible end of the world as we know it away from those who have stood with us over the years is going to cause irreparable damage to long-standing alliances. And I'm the one who's going to have to explain it to all of them, thank you very much."

"Amanda—" Keller tried again to chime in.

"Not to mention"—she had a lot to say and would be heard out—"that we are hanging the entire population out to dry with not even the same kind of warnings we would issue for a snowstorm or a hurricane. History is going to look very badly on us if this turns out to be as bad as the good doctor and his eggheads are predicting!" She paused, turning to Detweiler. "No offense to you or your eggheads, Doctor."

"None taken, Madam Secretary," Detweiler replied, nodding his head. He liked her style—maybe all political appointees weren't so bad.

"Amanda, please," President Keller began. "None of us are happy about the need to keep this so hushed up. We've been over this—a panic would be just as bad as The Event itself. As far as the allies go, you know as well as I do that they can't keep a secret any better than we can. That's why only a handful of people outside this room know anything about it, and most of them are with the vice president inside a mountain. It's just something we're going to have to deal with after this thing rolls through and we have a better idea of what exactly we're dealing with."

The reality was that he had also wanted to inform the allies, if not the entire globe, as well as issue some kind of warning. Even if it wasn't the actual truth, at least people would have had an opportunity to somewhat prepare. He had been given a very stern admonishment to do nothing of the sort from Mr. X.

"I know, I know. It's just not sitting well with me. I'm sorry," Amanda Carson replied, looking toward Dr. Detweiler.

Keller knew everyone was as upset as he was at the way things were playing out. He also knew it was going to fall on him if it went badly. There was no more use in fretting over it. With the hour now upon them, they had only to hold on for the ride.

"It's understandable, Amanda," he said with compassion. "How long until the first vessel feels the effect, Doctor?" They needed to move on. Time was short, and all these decisions had been made already.

"The first ship is the USS *Elrod*, a frigate out of Norfolk, Virginia, positioned approximately here, mid-Atlantic," Detweiler answered, bringing up on the screen behind him a map of the entire North Atlantic from North America to Europe. The graphic zoomed in on a ship-shaped icon with the latitude and longitude of its position displayed.

"The *Elrod* will be shutting down in five minutes. We have voice communication with them until then," Detweiler said, gesturing to a naval officer wearing a communications headset seated at a laptop terminal nearby.

"Yes, sir. I'll put them on speaker." Taking his cue, the officer clicked his mouse and spoke into his headset-mounted microphone. "You're on with the Situation Room, *Elrod*."

"Good morning, Mr. President. Captain Willard J. Thompson and USS *Elrod* at your service!" said the upbeat voice from the Situation Room's speakers.

"Good morning, Captain!" replied Keller. "It looks like you have the honor of being our canary in the coal mine, as Dr. Detweiler has so eloquently described you."

"Well, I guess it's all part of the job, Mr. President," Captain Thompson said, laughing. "We'll do our best to keep you posted on what we're experiencing." There was more static coming through on the transmission now. "We are going to be shutting down all systems in two minutes, Mr. President. We will reestablish communications as soon as we have everything back up and running."

"OK, Captain. We'll be here. Good luck and thank you!" President Keller responded in as upbeat a tone as he could.

"Aye aye, sir!" was Captain Thompson's only response—he had business to attend to.

With that, the officer in the Situation Room shut off the speakers and pointed to a countdown clock in the upper right-hand corner of the world map graphic on the big screen. It was counting down from one minute.

A nervous voice from the gaggle of aides gathered in the back of the room said what they were all thinking.

"Here we go."

Everyone in the room grunted, exhaled, or shifted nervously in their seat.

As the clock ticked down to zero, blinked several times, and began ticking back up to mark the time passed since the USS *Elrod* was overtaken by The Event, all present silently stared at the big screen. The vice president was the first to speak, shattering the silence and nearly causing at least three coronary arrests.

"How long until Elrod gets back to us?"

"Approximately twenty minutes, Mr. Vice President. They will start turning on non-essential equipment first to see if it's safe to start turning on more critical systems once they have an idea of what's going on. All we can really do at this point is wait," Detweiler concluded. He took his seat, exhaling forcefully.

CHAPTER 7

THE SUBURBS NORTH OF PHILADELPHIA

THE MORNING WAS quickly slipping away. At this rate, it was going to take him all day just to get his kids dropped off at school. He was beyond irritated with the two of them. Both had taken their time doing their projects. David had some kind of research project on the sun and Kathryn had a book report to finish—neither of which seemed so difficult that they would require last-minute finishing. *That woman is way too easy on these kids!* he thought, referring to Melissa. *Not to mention, what teacher on Earth would give project assignments due the first week of October? School just started, for Christ's sake!*

He had them both captive in the car now. Neither spoke. They knew the first one of them to make a noise would be the one to bear the brunt of their dad's frustration—frustration that was building every passing minute. The morning rush hour traffic was only adding to the pressure cooker that was Andy's brain. The only sound was the morning talk radio program Andy had tuned into permanently in his pickup truck—or so it seemed to his children, who didn't dare complain about it today given his present mood.

The host was going on about something to do with all air travel being grounded and questioning how this could happen based only on the possibility of a cyberattack.

"In this day and age, with all our technology and all our sophisticated government counterespionage and spy-tech programs, do you mean to tell me the government can't prevent this without screwing up air travel?!" the host was ranting. "Sure, they have no problem hacking our emails, or tapping our phones, or tracking our movements! But this! Oh nooooo, shut down air travel! Makes me sick to think—"

At that, the radio went silent. In fact, the truck had shut off. Andy instinctively reached down and turned the ignition key, and the truck restarted after three tries. *Now what the hell was that?* he thought.

Andy looked at his son in the passenger seat quizzically, who looked at him with the same expression.

"Maybe they cut him off," Andy said, half joking. "Not allowed to have too much emotion these days, ya know!"

David grunted and shrugged, pushing the preset buttons, thankful he could put something else on without having to complain about it as usual, which would usually result in his dad putting on bagpipes music. "My truck, my music," Andy would say.

"Now what!" Andy said, throwing his hands up. The traffic light was out, and no one was moving. Andy glanced at the clock that was just blinking and thought, *If traffic doesn't get moving, the kids and I are going to be very late.* "Come on guys, figure it out, someone go!" he said to the windshield.

"How 'bout that!" Andy said as cars started navigating the intersection. He, however, had yet to move, and when people started getting out of their cars ahead of him, he once again became concerned. "My God!" was all he said, getting out to see what was going on.

David, still scanning channels, said, "Nothing will tune in."

His father slammed the driver's-side door, obviously irritated.

"Whatever," David mumbled, continuing to scan.

Andy looked ahead and saw the hood up on the car three ahead of his.

The driver told the gathering crowd, "It just stopped running. All the gauges pegged, I heard a pop, and then it just died."

"Wonderful," Andy said under his breath. As if on cue, Andy suddenly became aware of someone screaming behind him. He turned to see a car several back from his engulfed in flames.

"Holy shit," Andy barked. "Stay in the truck!" he shouted at his children as he turned to run toward the burning vehicle.

It was some sort of hybrid, he recognized, and the whole rear end where the batteries were stored was engulfed in flames. There were already two men pulling the occupants out—a young mother and her two small children. Andy arrived at the passenger side just in time to be handed a toddler, whom he took and ran away from the burning vehicle with. The child was unharmed following Andy's quick examination on the lawn of some poor homeowner, whose front yard was now bedlam. The child was wailing at the top of its lungs. Andy quickly realized that this was the child from his dream. He stood there staring blankly as the child's mother and sibling arrived along with the Good Samaritans who had rescued them. Her car was now fully engulfed.

On the verge of hysterics, all she could say was, "It just caught on fire. We were on fire."

Andy, having returned the wailing child—who was now sobbing and hyperventilating—to its near-hysterical mother, was reaching for his cell phone to call 911 when he heard someone saying that his cell phone was dead. Andy saw a man in a business suit with a cell phone in his hand, shaking his head to the man next him who was now checking his cell. Andy quickly got his phone from his pocket, only to find that his phone was also dead.

"What the hell is going on here this morning?" Andy asked the men trying to calm the woman whose car was now a raging inferno. People were driving on sidewalks and lawns to try and get their vehicles far enough away lest they catch on fire as well. A woman who had pulled her SUV up on the lawn near Andy said that her cell had just cut out about the same time the traffic light had died.

"I guess we're all gonna be late this morning!" laughed one of the men nearby.

They all chuckled. Even the woman with the burning car grinned at that, beginning to realize that she and her children were safe.

The ground began to tremble under their feet. Faces that had been chuckling moments before were once again turned to concern bordering on panic. It was an earthquake!

The shaking was over quickly, but it had been a strong shake. Andy had experienced strong shakers during his time stationed in Arizona and California. But he was in the suburbs north of Philadelphia—they didn't have earthquakes here, did they? Today they did!

Simultaneous to the earthquake was a loud *boom!* The transformer above them exploded in a blast of blue-green light, showering everyone with sparks. Then the next one down the line exploded, then the next and the next. Transformers were exploding everywhere; the flashes could be seen against the morning sky. A power line had caught on fire, engulfing a tree in flames. The scene was quickly turning surreal.

Someone yelled, "Oh my God, look!" They were pointing down the street at a geyser of water shooting up into the air like some kind of giant fountain. People were now in full-blown panic mode. Any one of the morning's events on its own would be easily dealt with by the population at large, but as a whole, it was too much all at once. People were running in all directions, with some getting back into their vehicles and others either abandoning or forgetting that they had vehicles and just running, presumably back home.

A DAY LIKE ANY OTHER

Andy was running back to the truck where his now extremely anxious children were both shouting at him.

"What the hell is going on?" shouted David, looking worried.

Kathryn had jumped into the driver's seat. She yelled directly into Andy's face, "Daddy, what was that?"

"It was an earthquake, sweetheart—happens all the time, nothing to worry about!" Andy replied so quickly as to sound like a single word, climbing into the driver's seat and sliding his daughter's small frame over with his body as if she wasn't even there.

"Nothing good!" was his reply to David as he put the truck into drive and angled it to pull a U-turn back toward home and away from the geyser ahead. He maneuvered the truck across several lawns and though a hedge to avoid the burning car that was no longer the most interesting thing that had happened that morning.

"We need to get home," Andy said calmly, maneuvering back onto the pavement and now pointed in the right direction. His mind was far from calm. He was oblivious to the pandemonium unfolding around him, though he was still able to avoid several near-collisions with other vehicles and running townsfolk. He was preoccupied with the wailing child who had been, up until a few minutes ago, a vision from a bad dream. And with the fact that his dream came true at the onset of what was obviously some sort of natural disaster. What about the rest of the dream? The child was only the beginning. What the hell was going on here? His mind was racing.

"We need to get home," he repeated calmly.

ANDY PULLED INTO his driveway with a huge sigh of relief. On the way home, they had seen two other cars on fire, three conked out with their confused drivers standing nearby, a four-car pileup at an otherwise quiet intersection, and a half-collapsed storefront that was obviously a result of the earthquake. It was madness to a level he had never seen before in his life.

As Andy started to get out of the car, the radio suddenly came back to life.

"Are we back, are we back?" It was the voice he recognized to be the morning talk radio host who had been cut off earlier.

"OK, hey everyone, Tommy Rye the Talk Radio Guy here. We are back and will stay with you as long as possible. Apparently, we have experienced some kind of power surge that knocked out power to the entire neighborhood here in Center City—with an earthquake as a kicker to make things a little more interesting!" He was trying not to sound worried, but it wasn't working. "All of a sudden, the lights went super bright. Some exploded, then everything went dark. The backup power that was supposed to kick in automatically didn't, and maintenance guys say the relays were melted. We're on the backup to the backup generators right now, thanks to our building maintenance guys working a few miracles on the fly. There are extension cords all over the place, so let's hope the fire marshal doesn't stop by today. You should have seen the crew here scrambling to get us back on air. Great job, guys!"

Just then, Melissa came walking out of the house and over to the truck, still in her robe. Half bent to one side, looking at the three of them sitting in the truck in the driveway, she obviously didn't understand why they weren't coming into the house or at least getting out of the truck.

"What are you guys doing?" she asked as Andy rolled his window down. "The power is out, by the way. I barely got done with my shower. Did you feel that earthquake? Crazy, huh!"

"Wait, listen!" Andy said, cupping his hand around his ear, then pointing to the radio.

"Hold on. Our ever-diligent production staff is informing me that the whole city is out, and we can expect the emergency broadcast system to start broadcasting anytime now." His crew was feeding him information now. "How did we come by this? Someone from the mayor's office? All the phones and email are out, cell phone service too. What'd they do—run over here from city hall? They did? I was kidding!" The host was starting to calm down a little, getting back into his more believable brand of humor.

"This is a big deal, Andy," Melissa said, nodding. "My God! Are you guys OK?"

"Mom! You should have seen it!" David started excitedly. "There were cars exploding and water shooting up like you see in the movies! It was crazy! People were freaking out!"

"Mom!" Kathryn started, talking over her brother. "Daddy saved a baby and drove through someone's hedges and across lawns! Dirt was flying everywhere, and people were running! What's going on, Mom?" Kathryn was on the cusp of womanhood, but at times like this, she was still mommy's little girl.

"Oh my God, is it that bad?" Melissa asked Andy. "You saved a baby?"

"Shhh, listen!" Andy was still listening to the radio. There would be time to revisit the morning's events later, but he needed more information right now.

A DAY LIKE ANY OTHER

Baaa-baaa-baaa! It was the emergency broadcast system.

"All residents are to find shelter and remain in place until further notice. Do not attempt to repair any electrical infrastructure. Avoid travel except for absolute necessities. More information will be communicated as it becomes available."

Baaa-baaa-baaa!

"That's it!" The host was back on. "Wow. Like I said, folks, we will stay on as long as possible. We are running on a diesel generator right now, so as long as we have fuel, we will be here. Based on that message from emergency broadcasting, I don't have a warm and fuzzy feeling that the authorities have any idea what's going either."

Andy had heard enough.

"OK, listen," he said, snapping into Gunny mode. "David, go get the Water-Bob from the basement and start filling it up in the downstairs bathtub." He had purchased the one-hundred-gallon water storage device after one of the blackouts they had had the previous year.

"Kathryn," he said, turning to his daughter, "go dig the solar-powered radio out of the camping gear and set it up somewhere in the sunlight. We can't sit in the truck all day."

"Melissa—" he started, but she cut him off.

"Wait! Before you start giving me orders, tell me what the hell you guys saw out there!" she said, holding her hand up in front of her.

"Go get dressed. We have to go stock up on food right now. I'll tell you on the way!"

"It's that bad, Andy?" she answered as he shuffled her toward the house.

"I hope not, but it doesn't look very good. All hell is breaking loose. People are starting to act crazy already!"

CHAPTER 8

WASHINGTON, DC

NO ONE WAS speaking. Aides had been coming and going, exchanging whispered conversations with their respective bosses and then dashing off again to carry out their instructions. President Keller sat at the end of the table, massaging his temples. He hadn't moved since taking his seat so many hours ago. All the cabinet members were still present, all in various states of disrepair.

After contact had been lost with the first picket ship, it was never restored. Subsequently, one by one, all the other picket ships had failed to reestablish contact. At 0733 hours local time, the effect had struck the East Coast of the United States. The Situation Room had gone dark, and a few minutes later, the whole building had shaken violently, toppling the briefer podium right out from in front of Detweiler.

The First Lady had left immediately following the earthquake to go check on the children. After what had seemed like hours, though it had only been enough time for the White House maintenance staff to connect power output cables to the massive generators that now provided energy to the entire building, the power came back on. The battery-powered emergency lights that had been their only illumination turned off. Though the power had been restored, they were still out of contact with everyone outside the White House. Their only source of information as to what the effects of The Event had been were the fragmented reports from the staffers who had been running in and out.

All the computers were on and running, but the streams of data they had been providing were now gone. Their operators sat and stared, waiting for information to come running through the door as if it were the 1800s again.

President Keller, who had stopped rubbing his temples, now sat with both palms flat on the table, looking across the room at Dr. Detweiler, who sat on the floor scribbling on a notepad and leaning back against the podium that was now returned to its upright position. His smashed laptop lay upon it, having not survived its impact with the floor during the earthquake. The president couldn't stand it anymore; he had been as patient as possible for as long as he could.

"It's been over three hours, people!" he yelled, pounding both fists on the table. "We have had people running in and out of here, bringing what I am assuming is information! So one of you needs to start telling me something right now!"

FEMA Director Whiting was the first to speak up; he knew it would have to be him to start off the bad news.

"Mr. President, as you know, reports are coming in only as fast as a person can run out to talk face-to-face with someone on the street and return here. What we know so far isn't much. The only reports we are getting are from the DC metro area. All phone service, including cellular, is totally shut down. Power is out for the entire city.

"Traffic is backed up everywhere. It's a total mess. Any vehicles that were running just turned off, and some—mostly hybrids—burst into flames. Most vehicles restarted fine; some did not. But with the power grid down, there are no traffic lights, so no one is going anywhere anyway, at least not in any organized manner. Needless to say, it's complete chaos. People are abandoning their vehicles, and others are driving on sidewalks—it's a free-for-all. Some of our aides who are out running down info are riding bikes to get through the gridlock."

"Wait," Keller interrupted, "why some cars and not others?"

"I have no idea. Perhaps Dr. Detweiler can answer that one," Whiting said, passing the buck.

"Doctor?" Keller asked, fully aware that Dr. Detweiler wasn't paying the least bit of attention.

Detweiler realized that everyone was looking at him and looked up from scribbling.

"I'm sorry, what?"

"The cars shut off. Some blew up, some restarted fine, and some didn't. Why?" Keller was irritated but not surprised.

Detweiler was visibly exhausted.

"Oh, right," he said, putting down the pad. "There's no telling. Too many factors to consider: the amount of metal used in construction, the positioning of electromagnetic-sensitive devices, the quality of the wiring, dumb luck. It's hard to say at this point. It's going to take decades of studying this thing to even begin to understand what just happened." The president started rubbing his temples again. That wasn't what he wanted to hear, but he had a feeling that he was going to get a lot of that today. They needed to prepare a statement and would have to say something besides "We have no idea."

"Please continue, Mr. Whiting," Keller said, exasperated.

"Right," Whiting continued. "As I said, communications are down completely. The only thing that is still working are handheld radios, the walkie-talkie ones like the police use—that is, as long as they weren't on their charging stations when the power surge rolled through and destroyed the circuits. In fact, anything that was plugged into a wall socket is now useless—computers, appliances, TVs, everything. Some even caught on fire."

"Whiting," Keller interrupted again, "I'm sitting here looking at computers running just fine. Why these and not any others?"

Detweiler was tuned in now and answered without being prompted.

"This room was designed to withstand an electromagnetic pulse attack by an enemy—basically, if a nuclear weapon exploded in the atmosphere, creating much the same effects we are seeing now from the present event, just on a much smaller scale. This room and all its wiring are shielded to protect all the electronics within it. Corporate mainframes, NASA, FBI, CIA, the Defense Department, and pretty much all the major government mainframes are protected in a similar manner. So all our important data should be safe, including all the data NASA collected just prior to warning us that this was coming."

It had been bothering him why there had been such a short time frame to react in. He felt that he had only been given partial data and that his requests for more were never responded to. Something wasn't right, and he wanted to get to the bottom of it.

"So I assure you that I will figure out why; I just need more than three days to do it."

Keller leaned forward in his chair, clasped his hands together, and spoke slowly.

"Dr. Detweiler, I don't think we need to be concerning ourselves with that right now. We need to focus on what we are going to do to get our nation through this difficult time." What he really wanted to say was, *I wouldn't do that if I were you; you may find something that could get you killed.*

He leaned back in his chair and nodded to Whiting to continue, but in his mind, he thought, *Detweiler is going to be a problem if he digs too deeply. We'll have to keep an eye on him.*

A DAY LIKE ANY OTHER

Director Whiting continued, "Any backup generator that was hardwired into the grid was fried immediately. Hospitals, radio stations, and fire and police stations only have power right now if they have a backup to the backup—basically the generator they would use to keep things running if their main backup were getting refueled or repaired. It's not a pretty picture. Those will only run as long as they get fuel, and it's only a matter of time before that becomes a problem due to delivery issues."

Removing his glasses and looking around the room, he concluded with, "The bottom line is that we are attempting to get assets out to deal with this mess here in DC. We are assuming that local municipalities around the country are doing the same, as they would with any disaster. The Joint Chiefs have issued orders to have troops assist when requested—whenever we establish communications with them again, that is. There are no satellite communications either, I should add, so everything is going to have to be relayed somehow or delivered by Pony Express. Not being permitted to front load any preparations has put us at a huge disadvantage here, Will. It's biting us in the ass, and it's only going to get worse."

He'd gone there. He was feeling the stress of the impossible situation he had been handed, and as any true politician would, he was setting up to start the blame game.

"Thank you, Mr. Whiting."

Keller ignored the shot Whiting just took at the decision to keep things quiet. *Whiting could become a problem as well. Better keep an eye on him too.*

The best thing Keller had heard from the entire briefing was that the satellites were out. Perhaps he wouldn't be hearing from Mr. X anymore. That would be a big relief. This was going to be difficult enough without some mysterious outsider calling the shots and making things harder on him.

"If that's all you have for me people, then we are in really bad shape—way worse than anyone expected," Keller began, sounding grim. "We are going to have to tell people something. We are going to have to get some sense of how much damage was inflicted, and we are going to have to provide relief wherever possible."

He felt something vibrate in his pocket. It was the satellite phone, as if on cue. Did Mr. X read minds too? His heart sank. His hope that he was done hearing from Mr. X was nothing more than a fantasy.

He ignored it and continued, "I don't care what it takes. If you all need to get out there on bicycles to make things happen, then that's what I expect you to do. Let's meet back here at 6:00 p.m., since all of us sitting here staring at each other serves no purpose. Maybe by then we will have more information to work with. And if anyone hears from the vice president, come find me. I'll want to talk to him immediately."

He was mentally exhausted, exasperated, and, quite honestly, scared to death. He did his best not to let it show.

"We will get through this. We just need to get through these first hours. Once we get a better idea of what's going on, we will be in a better position to do our jobs. Thank you, everyone. I'll see you this evening. If anyone needs me, you know where to find me. Good luck, and everyone, please be careful."

As cabinet members began filtering out, Keller noticed that Whiting had sweat through his shirt and looked as if he would be physically ill.

"You OK, Paul?" Keller asked sincerely.

"No, I'm not OK, Will!" Whiting snapped. "We really screwed ourselves this time. We are blind—blind! We have no idea what's going on, we have no assets in place, and we have no relief supplies pre-positioned! We are hoping, *hoping*, that local municipalities will make a difference, but they have limited capabilities. They won't be able to do much outside of the first few hours!"

It was an obvious meltdown, but who could blame him? He was the FEMA director, and there was nothing he could do to manage the present emergency.

"And when things go completely to shit, who do you think is going to be blamed?" Whiting paused, looking Keller in the eyes. "Me! That's who! It's going to be my head that rolls!"

"Paul!" Keller was sorry he asked. "Please calm down. We are all in this together. No one is going to get singled out."

Keller didn't really believe that. He said what he had to. He was a politician, and in politics, the truth didn't matter.

"Now go get some fresh air, have a look around, and we will all talk again later," Keller said, grasping Whiting's shoulder. "We'll get through this."

"I'm sorry, Will," Whiting said, calming down a bit. "I'm sorry, you're right. It's been a tough morning. We'll talk again later."

"That's the spirit!" Keller replied, exiting the Situation Room, headed for the Oval Office. The satellite phone had been vibrating through the whole exchange with Whiting, and he needed to find somewhere private to answer it.

A DAY LIKE ANY OTHER

KELLER ARRIVED AT the Oval Office a few minutes later. On the way, Special Agent Ryan Billings, the head of his Secret Service detail, briefed him on the status of White House security. He informed him that if needed, Marine One would be flown over from Quantico if the president wished to do a flyover of the city to see the damage for himself. Keller was surprised that such a thing was possible given the grim state of affairs he was just briefed on.

"Are the aircraft flyable?" he had asked.

Billings told him that it appeared that they were, but the maintenance folks were checking all the systems thoroughly to be sure. They should be getting the thumbs-up soon.

Billings told the president that, initially, one of his agents was sent down to assess the situation but got stuck behind a bottleneck of wrecked vehicles about halfway there. It was there that he received a radio transmission from the detail at Quantico and relayed the initial reports back up to the White House. He told the president that the poor guy was told to stay put and keep relaying messages and any other reports.

Keller thanked Billings as he was closing the door to the Oval Office and thought, *That was the best thing I've heard all morning. Very resourceful. Way to think on the fly and make things happen. Maybe I should make Billings the FEMA director.*

The door had no sooner clicked shut when the satellite phone began to vibrate again. *This is worse than an obsessive girlfriend,* Keller thought, getting the phone out of his pocket.

"My God! I was in a briefing! Do you expect me to just say, 'Excuse me, everyone. I have a call I need to take' right after we were just informed that all the phones are out? Gimme a break!" Keller answered, none too polite.

"Well, now," the voice on the other end started. "Are we feeling a little pressure, Mr. President?" Mr. X said sarcastically.

"What do you think? You have all the answers, right?" Keller answered with disdain.

"I usually have most of the answers, my boy, but where you're concerned, I do indeed have all the answers," Mr. X answered, sounding more serious. "For instance, that mess of a FEMA director, Whiting. He's in way over his head. That little tantrum he threw after the briefing was pathetic. I must say that you handled it well. I guess that's why we picked you for the job. Mark my words, he is going to have to go sooner or later, and when he does, we have a plan for that, too."

"Hey, wait a minute! How would you know that? That just happened in the Situation Room! That's a secure facility!"

Keller was shocked. There is no way Mr. X could have known that unless had had been there in the room. There was no way.

Mr. X was laughing at him. "You poor boy. You really think there's anything that we don't have access to? We watched the whole briefing; we've been watching all day. Very amusing, I must say. You and your band of merry morons, fretting and wringing your hands there all day. Hell, I'm watching you right now. Don't look so stunned. Do you really think we would set our front man free to run amok without being properly monitored?"

Keller was standing there in the Oval Office, his mouth agape, feeling very naked. For the first time in his life, he felt truly afraid.

"I suppose you have my bedroom bugged as well," he said incredulously.

"If we thought we'd see anything interesting there, we would, or maybe we have. No matter, you'll figure it out eventually. That's not why I called."

"Why did you call?" The anger was back in Keller's voice.

"You are going to have to deal with that scientist. If he starts digging too much, he will figure out the truth, and if that gets out, you, my friend, will probably be sent to the gallows. And none of us wants that. That would hinder our plans, and I suppose you wouldn't find it very agreeable either."

Keller was stunned and afraid again, like a mouse being toyed with by a cat.

"What is the truth anyway? Since it's my ass on the line here, apparently, I think I have a right to know!"

"Well, I suppose it doesn't matter now that it's all over. We knew the sun was going to blast us weeks ago. Our people noticed a pattern forming, and we took action to get prepared."

Keller couldn't believe what he was hearing.

"And you didn't bother to fill the rest of us in? You son of a bitch!"

"No! We didn't!" Mr. X didn't hesitate with his response. "If we had let the word out, everyone else on Earth would have been trying to get themselves prepared as well, and, quite frankly, that would have hindered us in our preparations. We needed all of you little worker bees to keep on buzzing along as if everything was just fine. To be honest, some of us didn't want to say anything and just let the cards fall where they may. Others and I felt that it was necessary to have someone on the ground—on the inside—to help usher in the new order we would create. That's you, my boy. So now you know."

"So you just let who knows how many people die because you didn't want to be inconvenienced?" Keller said, sincerely appalled.

"You just don't get it, do you?" Mr. X said slowly. "There are a lot more people who are going to die. That's part of the plan. A broken, despaired populace is much easier to rule. Besides, there were too many people to keep under control anyway. A lot more are going to die—you need to understand that. This is the great culling of the herd we have been waiting for for a very long time. You know as well as I do, Mr. President, that one can never let a crisis go to waste."

Mr. X. had had enough, and it was time to set Keller straight again.

"Now, you listen, and listen carefully. Word of this gets out, and they will be coming for you, not me, so you will do exactly what you are told. And I am telling you to deal with that scientist or I will. Got it? You can either be the leader of a new world, or you can be dead."

Keller stood in shocked silence. He was the one now sweating through his shirt.

"Do you hear me, Keller?" Mr. X asked, as an adult would ask a child.

"I hear you," Keller answered in a whisper.

"Good," Mr. X replied, then hung up.

Keller was left all alone with his thoughts. He went and sat at his desk, feeling like he wanted to run away, but he knew there was nowhere to run. As a lifelong politician, the idea of unlimited power at the head of a new, all-powerful government had its appeal. The deaths of the untold thousands of people who would be a part of that were difficult for him to stomach. His life had been threatened. He could probably deal with that—at this point, death would be a relief. Was his family at risk? He couldn't deal with that. Mr. X hadn't said.

What am I going to do now? he thought, staring blankly across the room.

CHAPTER 9

THE SUBURBS NORTH OF PHILADELPHIA

Andy was in crisis mode. He had dealt with many crises in his day, but never one of this magnitude. No one had come out and said how bad it actually was. He just felt it in his bones that shit was hitting the fan. He knew it. Unlike any other crisis he had dealt with in his days in the Corps, this one directly concerned his family's safety and welfare. He hoped he was overreacting, but he wasn't going to take any chances.

He had caught Melissa up on the events of his and the kids' morning drive, and she was now quickly getting dressed. Andy was headed for the basement to take inventory of their food stocks. They had learned from experiencing hurricanes in North Carolina, snowstorms in Pennsylvania, and assorted power outages everywhere they had lived that having extra food and water on hand was always a good idea. He wanted to take stock and run to the store as soon as possible to beef up their supplies. There was no telling how long the power would be out.

He heard the water running and assumed it was David filling the Water-Bob. *Good,* he thought.

Kathryn was on her way up from the basement as Andy was on his way down. She held up the solar-powered radio like a trophy as she passed.

"Good girl!" Andy said as he passed. "Go find a sunny spot."

"I *knooow*," Kathryn answered, slightly annoyed and handing off the flashlight she had used to hunt through the camping gear.

Andy immediately noticed upon arriving in the basement that they were woefully short on bottled water. They could use the water David was storing for cooking and washing, but Andy didn't want to drink out of a giant rubber bag if he didn't have to. They had a large stock of dried and canned beans, canned meat and tuna, several cases of canned beef stew, and a good stock of pasta and rice. He felt somewhat relieved but still felt it was worth heading back out into the chaos. *Can't be too prepared,* he thought.

As he turned to head back upstairs, he cast the flashlight beam onto the safe standing in the corner across the basement. *Not right now,* he thought. There were other things to do first. He hoped he wouldn't have to arm himself and that this was just another inconvenience to get through.

Andy arrived at the top of the stairs exactly at the same time Melissa was arriving from the bedroom, nearly knocking him back down the stairs and her into the doorframe.

"Oh, hey!" she said, "How are we lookin'?"

"Pretty good! I want to get more water, at least, and whatever else we can grab," Andy replied. "How much cash do you have?"

He figured the days of using credit cards for everything were on hold for a while.

"A hundred or so," Melissa answered. "Is that enough?"

"Gonna have to be," Andy answered honestly. There was no getting any more cash until the power came back. From what he had seen on the failed drive to the school, he figured the power was out all over the area, not just in this neighborhood.

"Daaaad!" It was David calling from the bathroom.

"What's up?" Andy called back.

"Is this full enough?" replied David.

"If you're ready, get Kathryn and go get in the truck. We're heading over to the wholesale place," Andy told his wife as he headed toward the bathroom.

"Yes, sir," Melissa answered.

She didn't like it when he gave orders, but this was different. She had a feeling this wasn't just another power outage, and she knew her husband, though far from perfect, was in his element in a crisis, and she was happy to be with his program for now.

Andy entered the bathroom and saw that the WaterBob was nearly full. It filled the tub like some giant bloated slug and looked as if it would burst at any second. *That's great!* he thought, feeling some relief from the fact that they'd have a backup water supply.

"How's it goin'?" he asked his son, who was crouched next to the tube.

"Is this full enough?" David asked. "The water is slowing down."

The water pressure was dropping off quickly.

"Yeah, that's good," Andy said, not wanting to contaminate what they had already with whatever may be left in the pipes.

As he had feared, the earthquake had broken their water main somewhere upstream. He had hoped the geyser they had seen earlier was on some other circuit, but they were not so lucky. He figured that with the sixty gallons they had in the hot water heater and what was now safely stored in the Water-Bob, they had over 160 gallons of water. *That should be enough for a while,* he thought to himself.

"Cap it off. Good job, bud. Come on, we're heading out to get some stuff," Andy told David, grabbing his shoulder and giving it a squeeze.

He loved his kids and was proud of them. Given what they had been through this morning, they were both real troopers.

"You ready to venture out into chaos again?" Andy asked jokingly.

"Sure, why not!" David said. "It's cool running over crap."

"Ha ha, it was kind of fun," Andy answered. "Let's hope things have settled down some from before."

He hoped, but he doubted it. People were starting to panic. He had reservations about taking his family out into the chaos, but he didn't want to leave them home without him either.

ANDY AND DAVID arrived at the truck. The girls already had the radio on. The morning radio host was still on and sounding even more agitated than before.

"What's the word?" Andy asked, climbing into the driver's seat.

"This is really bad, Andy!" Melissa answered. "Power is out all over the place, the earthquake broke water and gas lines, and buildings have collapsed. They're saying overpasses may be unstable and to stay put until further notice."

"Lovely," Andy said, backing out onto the street. "Here we go on another adventure, kids!"

A monotone "Yaaay" came from the back seat.

"Maybe we shouldn't be going out right now," Melissa said, concerned.

"It's only going to get worse as the day goes on and people start realizing all they have in the house is ice cream and potato chips," Andy said as they turned onto the main road.

The scene was just as they had left it earlier. A broken-down car was partially blocking their lane, and vehicles were veering into the oncoming lane, creating a bottleneck and slowing traffic to a crawl. *The store is only a mile away. Shouldn't be too long as long as we keep moving,* Andy thought. Andy wanted no part of a regular supermarket, and Wholesale World was the nearest bulk warehouse around. He was always amused by how all the bread, eggs, and milk would sell out right before a big snowstorm. He would joke, "I guess everyone is counting on French toast to sustain them through the storm."

At the next intersection, they came upon the first police officer they had seen all day, directing traffic through the intersection. Three houses down from the corner, the fire department was attempting to douse a burning house.

"What do you suppose started that, Dad?" David asked from the back seat.

"A busted gas line, maybe," Andy answered, unsure.

People were out of their houses all along the route, talking in small groups and comparing experiences, as humans do. Some were watching the fire department at work, while others were running to get into their vehicles. *They have the same idea we do, probably. Good thing we're going now,* Andy thought.

Andy pulled into the parking lot and immediately knew they had been correct in heading out when they did. The parking lot was packed solid. He didn't bother looking for a parking spot; he saw others already parking wherever there was room. It had been just over two hours since the lights went out, and things were getting desperate already. The exploding transformers, or maybe the earthquake, had probably pushed people past their limits.

Andy pulled the truck up over the curb into a grassy area behind another pickup truck and said, "This spot looks good."

People were hurriedly heading toward the front doors as others were heading back to their vehicles, carts and flatbeds loaded with goods of all kinds. Andy was taking stock of what they had purchased—bread, canned goods, pasta, and water, for the most part. It was water Andy had come for, and he was hoping that Wholesale World wouldn't run out. He stepped up his pace.

The parking lot was nothing compared to the pandemonium that met them once they entered the front doors. The checkout lines were backed up ten people deep. The cashiers were doing their best to get customers checked out, but without power, their systems were obviously overwhelmed. The lighting was from the dirty skylights high above and portable light units that were powered by small generators running somewhere outside, the extension cords stretched across the floor all going in the same direction.

David found a flatbed cart and pulled up next to his dad with a nod. Andy turned to the girls behind him.

"Everyone stay close."

As they turned the corner into the aisle where the water was kept, Andy's worst fear had been realized. The aisle was packed with people jostling for positions to get to the skids of water that the store employees had brought down from the higher tiers. One man elbowed another in the face, and the man who was elbowed came back at the elbow thrower, who was of a lighter build, and sent him tumbling into a woman and another man. *Things are going to shit in a hurry,* Andy thought.

"This isn't going to work," he said out loud.

"What?" Melissa asked over the din.

From the front of the store, a manager began speaking with a megaphone.

"Attention, Wholesale World shoppers. Due to the current power outage, we are unable to process anything other than cash transactions. Please, cash transactions only."

Who would try to use a credit card in a power outage? Andy thought.

His question was answered as the noise level elevated. Apparently, a lot of people thought they would use their plastic and were not very happy. He could hear one man yelling that he had no cash and had no food at home, and what was he supposed to do? Others started joining in the argument. The manager could be heard explaining the obvious: if the power is out and the phones are out, then there is no way to run credit or debit through. It was too late—no one was hearing him, and some had begun leaving, goods in hand, causing more chaos. Those in line started heading toward the exit with their unpaid items in hand. Andy felt time running out. They needed to get out of there. The brawl in the water aisle had turned into a full melee. People were grabbing at cases of water and wrenching their bodies back and forth as if they had just recovered a rebound in a basketball game. Andy thought, *This is worse than Black Friday brawls.* Just then, Andy saw someone scaling the shelving tiers, ignoring the store employee yelling for him to get down. Andy saw that the man was climbing toward several more skids of water that were two levels up and knew that this wasn't going to be pretty. He also saw this as his opportunity.

"David!" Andy said, grabbing his son around the shoulders. "Did you see all those extension cords plugged into the light units?"

"Yeah, I saw those," David replied.

"I need you to follow those outside!" Andy said, handing David the keys to the truck. "Then bring the truck around, as close to that exit as possible, OK?"

David took the keys apprehensively and said, "Dad! I don't have my license!"

"I know, buddy! I don't think that matters today!" Andy answered, looking at the chaos going on around them. "I need you to do this, OK?"

A DAY LIKE ANY OTHER

"OK, I can do it, Dad!" David said, turning to go track down where the power cables exited the store.

"Wait! Where's he going?" Melissa asked. "Why does he have the keys? Andrew, what are you doing?"

"We need to get out of here, but we need to leave with what we came for!" Andy began. "He's going to meet us by another exit. I need you and Kate to go find an aisle that's not hosting a fistfight and get as much of whatever you think will keep long term without refrigeration. Get back here as quickly as you can!"

"Uh, OK!" Melissa answered. "What are you gonna do?"

"I'm gonna get the water," Andy answered, directing her attention to the climber, who was now trying to tear through the plastic shrink-wrap.

"Oh God, be careful!" Melissa answered as she took Kathryn's hand to go search for a less combative aisle.

Andy watched them disappear into the chaos and thought, *I hope that was a good idea.* When he turned, he saw that the climber was through the plastic and preparing to drop a case of water down to who Andy thought must be the man's wife. A small crowd started to gather to see what was about to happen. He could feel the desperation around him and knew he didn't want the same scene as the aisle he had just come from. He approached the group that was gathering.

"Look! I don't want to fight you people for a few cases of water! So let's do this together. You start throwing cases down," Andy said, pointing to the climber who was still holding the first case of bottled water, not wanting to drop it into what probably looked to him like a school of hungry sharks.

"We'll catch 'em and stack them on the flatbeds. I have a back door we can get out of, but we'll have to work fast! OK?" Andy asked, looking around at his newly formed working party.

They all nodded, and at that, another man began climbing up to help the climber. Quickly, cases of water began dropping down, and the flatbeds started filling up. About the time the last case was airborne, Melissa and Kathryn arrived back from their foraging. Melissa was carrying four cases of canned soup, and Kathryn was bear-hugging a fifty-pound bag of rice.

"Those are my girls!" Andy yelled over the din.

"OK! Let's get out of here!" Andy yelled to the group. "We may have to fight our way out. You and you!" Andy said, pointing to the two largest men present. "You're on either side of the flatbeds as we exit; you keep anyone from grabbing our water. The rest of you just keep the flatbeds moving!"

One man nodded, and the other said, "You got it!"

"OK! Follow me!"

As they left the relative quiet of their aisle, they were immediately noticed by some of the water brawlers, who started to head toward this new stockpile. Andy's crew of water thieves were determined, however. They rolled through like a freight train. An entire skid of water is heavy, and with several people pushing, it was a freight train. Most people had enough sense to get out of the way. Some moved when Andy yelled for them to move. Those who thought they could grab a case and run got stiff-armed by one of the big dudes, knocking them down (or at least out of the way). Anyone who got past Andy and the two big dudes lead blocking simply bounced off the mass of bottled water, unable to grab hold of it.

They had followed the power cables to a propped-open fire exit, but unable to slow their momentum, the bottled-water express ended its run by crashing into the exit and spilling a good amount of its contents through the open doorway, the other flatbeds crashing into the first. It was a flatbed pile-up that in any other circumstances would have been hilarious to witness.

Andy turned to one of his big dudes and said, "Couldn't have planned that any better!"

The big dude answered with, "I love it when a plan comes together!"

Andy didn't have to say another word. His crew was already throwing the remaining cases out the open door. Melissa and Kathryn were loading their loot into the truck, which Andy noticed had a large scrape down the rear quarter panel.

David was running up saying, "Dad, it wasn't my fault—people are being crazy!"

Andy wasn't concerned with the damage, "Never mind that! Just start loading water!"

As they began driving away, Andy wondered if it would have been worth it to go back in again for another load of rice and soup. But then he began to feel guilty for having just looted several cases of water, some soup, and a bag of rice. Looking around at his family, he thought, *Gotta do what ya gotta do. I guess only time will tell if I overreacted or not.*

"Well, that was nuts," Andy said to his family as they turned out of the parking lot toward home.

His family just sat in silent agreement.

A DAY LIKE ANY OTHER

I hope we don't have to do that again, Andy thought as he drove. He would if he had to, though. This was his family, and he would do whatever it took to keep them safe and secure.

"Whatever it takes," he said under his breath.

CHAPTER 10

WASHINGTON, DC

THE HOURS HAD ticked laboriously by. Washington, DC, had been rocked by an aftershock that had sent people, who were already on edge, spilling out into the streets. President Keller had spent only ninety minutes in the residence with his wife and children. The First Lady had been with him through the initial event effect. She quickly departed once the earthquake hit to check on their twin daughters, Abigail and Aimee, who were five years old. He spent the rest of the long day alternating between the Situation Room, where the occasional tidbit of information would trickle in, and the Oval Office, where he would sit staring at the satellite phone, fretting over his dilemma.

His daughters had been extremely excited to tell him all about how all the things in their room had fallen down during the earthquake. They wanted to know if he had been the one to turn the lights back on. Keller listened and played along like any good dad would with his little girls. The First Lady, however, could see through the act and knew things were not going well. He filled her in as best he could when the girls were distracted, but in the end, he really didn't have much to say.

"There's a lot of confusion right now," he told her honestly.

The First Lady, Joyce Bitford-Keller, married William Keller twelve years ago as a matter of course. She was a daughter of high society, and William Keller was a young aspiring politician. They were a perfect match. Though her family enjoyed extreme wealth, her parents put on a "for the people" facade that endeared them to the political left. Thus, their financial dealings (and misdealing) were overlooked. They were clearly members of the ultra-rich yet were accepted by the community organizer crowd.

Theirs was as close to an arranged marriage as one could come in twenty-first-century America. They knew deep down that this was the case but went along with it anyway, playing their parts in the show that was modern politics and power. As the next generation of the political, industrial, and financial elite, they knew what was expected of them. In time, they came to love one another, as people thrown together often do.

She was comfortable and accepted in that world but also independent enough to pursue her own endeavors—at times, against the family's wishes. Her African tour in the Peace Corps soon after graduating from Yale was a good example. More recently as First Lady, she had undertaken a campaign to fight teen pregnancy in the inner cities, a touchy subject for her husband's political party, especially when she teamed up with churches to implement her program.

Over the years, she had proven she was far more than a trophy wife. She had a toughness she had cultivated all on her own through self-imposed adventures. It had served her well in her life, and she was passing it on to her twin daughters. She was a good mom, and her girls were her greatest source of pride. As First Lady, she smiled when she was supposed to smile and supported her husband as she was expected, but she still longed for the adventures of her youth, far away from the world she had grown up in.

Her father would tell her often, "We are the elite; we are expected to behave a certain way." Then he would laugh and add, "Well, at least when the peasants are watching!" She never bought into that, but she also never had the strength to push away from it. Now she found herself married to the most powerful man in the world in the middle of potentially the greatest crisis to face mankind in the modern age. *What can I do?* she wondered to herself.

PRESIDENT KELLER TOOK his seat in the Situation Room; the entire cabinet had reassembled.

Gone were the many aides and cronies; only the heads of the various departments and administrative offices were present. All looked haggard and tired, faces drawn and somber. Keller had received fragmentary reports all day and already knew things were not going well, but by the looks on the faces before him, he knew the big picture was far worse than anyone had expected.

"Alright," Keller started, "I'm glad to see you all back safely. What are we looking at? What are we doing?"

Dr. Detweiler stood and moved back to his podium. "Well, Mr. President," Detweiler began, "we are in a world of shit."

The statement startled only Keller. Everyone else just sat staring straight ahead—they all knew it already; Detweiler had just said it in his own special way.

Recovering, Keller said, "Can you elaborate, please, Doctor?"

"It's not pretty," Detweiler began. "We were able to reestablish contact with the ships by relaying messages from ship to ship, station to station. They all started back up without issue once The Event passed on and are standing by for further orders. All the communications satellites—military and civilian, classified and unclassified—are offline, and we don't know if they will ever come back online again. For all we know, they're falling out of orbit as we speak. The entire power grid is down. Let me say that again. The ENTIRE power grid is down.

"It was the same everywhere. First, the power went out. Then, any vehicle that was running immediately shut off, bursting into flames. Then, power transformers started exploding—to be precise, every transformer exploded—and some power lines caught fire. Power transfer stations exploded, then melted. The nuclear power stations all report that they are intact in spite of the earthquakes. They could theoretically begin operations, but with the grid down, they would have no way of delivering the power they were producing. Quite honestly, we need to just leave them shut down for now. The last thing we need is a nuclear incident to deal with on top of everything else. To summarize, the power grid is down indefinitely—maybe for months, maybe for years."

None of the staff were moving; they just sat and stared straight ahead. Keller looked around at each of them.

"Well, who does have power?"

"That's a very short list," Detweiler answered, bowing his head. "As we feared, anything that was connected to the grid when The Event rolled through was damaged, even if it wasn't turned on. The only power being generated out there right now is from portable generators or backup systems that were independent of the power grid at the time of exposure. Those assets are going to hospitals first. Some police and fire departments have these as well, and so do a few radio stations, which we are trying to use to get information out to the public. These small power units are by no means capable of running entire buildings, so only essential systems are being powered right now."

"Well, that's a bit of good news, isn't it?" Keller said, trying to find anything positive.

"Well," Detweiler started, shaking his head slowly from side to side, "it would be. But keeping fuel supplied to all these generators is going to become extremely difficult given the amount of damage sustained by the road network. The earthquakes have severely damaged roads, bridges, and tunnels, to the point where collapses have been reported and others have been shut down for fear of collapse. Getting anything delivered —food, fuel, medical supplies—is going to be a major challenge. Not to mention, those backup generators only deliver a fraction of the power the grid normally provides. Even those with power only have partial capabilities. It's not a pretty picture out there."

At that, Paul Whiting, the FEMA director, spoke up. "Right now, we are making contact with all our offices around the country with instructions to use whatever assets they have at their disposal to assist local and state governments as best they can. I've asked the Joint Chiefs to issue the same orders to their local commanders around the country, and they have agreed. All the governors we've talked to are already calling up National Guard assets, but that's proving difficult given the lack of electricity."

"So what you're telling me is that state and local governments are on their own for now?" Keller said, leaning forward.

"Yes, sir, pretty much, for now," Whiting answered, looking away from the president.

Keller sat back in his chair, looking pale and deflated. He realized at that moment that he was helpless to directly assist anyone outside of the Washington metro area. The helplessness went against his being. It didn't sit well with him, and he knew Mr. X, who he now knew was secretly attending this meeting, wouldn't be pleased either.

"OK, Paul," Keller said, trying to find something encouraging to say. "Keep me posted as things develop and do what you can with what you've got."

Whiting nodded, looking on the edge of a nervous breakdown.

"Have we talked to any of our allies? How did the rest of the planet fair? Better than us, I hope," Keller asked the room.

Secretary of State Amanda Carson stood and began to speak.

"We were able to speak with our Canadian and Mexican counterparts via radio relay. It's the only way anyone is communicating, other than some ham radio operators who were able to get their equipment repaired quickly. They have been proving useful as well. Anyway, they were hit just as hard as we were. Once The Event struck and our worst fears were realized, we immediately began trying to get the word out to whomever we could via monitor ships. Once we had reestablished contact with them, that is.

"We've heard nothing from the Russians or the Chinese, or anywhere in Asia for that matter, as well as nothing at all from the Southern Hemisphere. The distances are too great right now given the limited extent of our capabilities. The Europeans were pretty upset that we sat on this information but thanked us, reluctantly, for the warning. It'll still be several hours before they get hit, but from what Detweiler has said, they can expect the same as we got."

Carson paused, then added, "They are going to want an explanation when this thing settles down."

"We'll deal with that when the time comes, Amanda," Keller said. The Europeans were the least of his worries. "How are people taking it?"

"Reports from the field range from total chaos to stunned disbelief," Whiting replied weakly. "It's only going to get worse. The supermarkets were cleaned out in hours; you can't even find a loaf of bread out there right now. And there's no telling when they will get restocked. Hospitals are overflowing with patients, dealing with everything from building collapses to car accidents, heart attacks, and burns from exploding electrical equipment. They're running on diminished power, so a lot of their equipment and machines are useless."

Keller sat staring at Whiting, wondering if he was actually having some sort of medical emergency himself. Confident he wasn't, Keller spoke.

"We are going to have to make a statement and tell people what we know and ask them for calm. I know it's been a long day already, but we need to come up with something that I can deliver as soon as possible."

He had barely finished his sentence when he felt the satellite phone vibrating in his pocket. *Seriously?* Keller thought to himself.

"OK, everyone," Keller continued, "let's take five, then get back to it. Thank you, everyone. You all have done an amazing job today. Just one more task, and then we can try to get some rest," Keller said, standing. He needed to answer the phone.

"One more thing Mr. President." It was General Mattlin. "We still haven't heard from the vice president or anyone else at NORAD."

In all the excitement, Keller had forgotten about the vice president.

"Nothing?" Keller asked, getting up from his chair.

"No, sir, nothing," Mattlin replied.

"I'm sure he's fine. He's in a mountain, what could happen?" Keller said, leaving the room.

Everyone present was somewhat stunned by the abruptness with which Keller had ended the meeting, and the nonchalant nature of his response to the news of the vice president's failure to reestablish communication was troubling. The staff members chalked it up to stress as they began to prepare a public statement. They were all ready for this day to be over.

A DAY LIKE ANY OTHER

FBI Director Cummings got up and headed for the coffee pot. Dr. Detweiler joined him there moments later.

"Hey, Bob, can I talk to you for a minute in the hallway?" he said, almost in a whisper.

Surprised by Detweiler's sudden appearance beside him, Cummings said, "Ah, sure Norm. What's up?"

"Not here," Detweiler said, gesturing toward the door with his head. "Something's not right."

"That's an understatement today, Norman," Cummings said as Detweiler herded him out the door and into the hallway.

"Shhhh!"

ARRIVING BACK IN the Oval Office somewhat out of breath, Keller answered the satellite phone, irritated.

"You cannot keep calling like this while I am in a meeting! Sooner or later, one of them is going to hear this thing vibrating. Frankly, I'm surprised they haven't already!"

Ignoring Keller's tirade, Mr. X replied calmly, "I don't know what you plan on saying in this statement of yours, but you will NOT admit any knowledge of the impending disaster whatsoever. Is that clear, Keller?"

President Keller detested this Mr. X more than he had ever detested anyone before in his life. This man's total disrespect for him as president was infuriating. His threats, his complete disregard for protocol, and his constant degrading and insulting of Keller were really getting under his skin, which was very thin on a good day. Keller lashed out.

"Look, you will address me as Mr. President or President Keller! I don't care who you think you are or what you think you have over me. I am the president of the United States, and you will show me the respect afforded that office. And as for my statement, I will deliver whatever information my staff and I agree should be delivered to the American people! Am I making myself clear, Mr. X?"

"You are the narcissist they say you are, William Keller," Mr. X replied calmly. "Fine. If you need a demonstration of what I think I can do, then you shall have your demonstration."

With that, the call ended, and Keller was left to wonder, *Demonstration?*

A moment later, the lights suddenly went dark, and Keller could hear groans of dismay coming from the other side of his office door as those who hadn't already rushed home reacted to the outage.

A moment after that, the satellite phone buzzed again. Keller hit the answer button.

Before he could say a word, Mr. X said, "Do you want your electricity back, William?"

Keller felt a mix of extreme anger and extreme panic. *How did he do that?* Keller thought.

"Who are you?"

"I'm the man you work for, Mr. President," Mr. X said sarcastically. "Do you want your electricity back?" he asked again.

Infuriated, Keller replied, as calmly as possible, "Yes."

"I thought so," Mr. X replied. "So let's be clear then. You will say nothing to indicate any prior knowledge of the impending disaster whatsoever. Is that clear? Do you understand?"

"I understand," Keller answered flatly.

With that, the power came back on, and Keller could hear cheers and clapping from the other side of his door.

"Don't test me again, Keller," Mr. X said sternly, like a parent would speak to a child. "Next time it won't be the power that disappears."

"What the hell does that mean?" Keller replied.

"Do what I tell you, and you won't have to find out," said Mr. X. "And you're going to have to deal with that poor fellow from FEMA; he doesn't look well. That department isn't able to handle this. We planned it that way. I'm sending you our man—he's going to handle things when you shut down FEMA."

"What? Shut down FEMA? The way you planned it? Sending a man? What are you talking about?" Keller said, his mind swimming in confusion and stress.

"You'll see," Mr. X said snidely. "And that scientist is going to be big trouble. He hustled the FBI director out of your meeting pretty much as soon as you left. I wonder what they could be talking about, William. You need to find out. Regardless, your Dr. Detweiler is bringing about his own demise. The question is, who is he going to take with him?"

The call ended. This was all getting overwhelming for Keller. He wanted to find a hole to hide in. He wished he was missing inside a mountain with the vice president. He tried to put it all out of his mind as he headed back down to the Situation Room to work on their official statement.

As he turned the corner toward the Situation Room, he thought, *How did we come to this, and how are we going to get out of it?*

As he entered the room, he said, as upbeat as he could muster, "OK, everyone, let's get this done!"

Taking his seat again, Keller looked across at Detweiler, who was staring straight at him. Keller turned his gaze to FBI Director Cummings, who was staring straight through the wall across from him.

Keller remembered what Mr. X had said. *Your Dr. Detweiler is bringing about his own demise. The question is, who is he going to take with him?* It rang in Keller's ears like alarm bells. Mr. X was correct, but Detweiler wasn't going to take William Keller with him.

No, not William Keller, Keller thought as the meeting began.

CHAPTER 11

THE SUBURBS NORTH OF PHILADELPHIA

*M*Y FELLOW AMERICANS. *I come to you tonight in this hour of great tumult and catastrophe to assure you that the federal government, in cooperation with state and local governments, is doing the utmost possible to secure safety and ensure the basic needs of those affected by this natural event. The armed forces have been put on alert to assist in humanitarian efforts and rescue missions where requested. The Federal Emergency Management Agency is working tirelessly to assess and assist the areas hit hardest.*

I ask all Americans to please remain calm in this challenging time. I ask for cooperation with law enforcement and emergency services. I ask that citizens, with the exception of emergency services and medical professionals, stay in their homes to await further instructions from local officials whenever possible. I ask that emergency services and medical professionals please report to their places of employment. I also ask all National Guard personnel and military reservists to report to their commands to assist in relief efforts. All military leaves are hereby canceled, and service members should make their best efforts to return to their duty station. In the event this is not possible, they are to report to the nearest military headquarters for further instructions and assignments.

From what we know at this time the earth was struck by a massive solar flare. It was a direct hit of the worst possible magnitude. The electrical outages, mechanical failures, and seismic activities are all a result of this solar event. The best minds in science are at this time studying all available data to devise the best possible course of action in getting basic utilities back online as quickly as possible.

In the days that follow, we will all face challenges. If we all work together in good faith and trust in one another, we will get through this difficult time. We will overcome and carry on as Americans always do. God bless you all, and God bless the United States of America.

Signed, President William S. Keller

A DAY LIKE ANY OTHER

"Well, there ya have it," said Tommy Rye the Talk Radio Guy.

He had been on all day, and Andy and his family had been listening since getting home from their shopping trip-turned-looting trip. The station had been getting reports from sources around the area and passing them on to listeners. None of the other radio stations had come back on the air, so this was the only show in town. Tommy Rye had just finished reading the president's official statement, received via radio relay through Philadelphia-area FEMA headquarters.

"The sun got us good today, folks. It would seem the big brains down in DC had no idea this was on its way. Seems hard to believe, but that's a conversation for another day. Right now, we need to get through this together. I'll be back here tomorrow morning at eight. Well, at least that's the plan. We have staff out scouring the area for diesel fuel for the generator. Everyone who lives outside Center City has headed for home and won't be back till further notice. As you all know, I live here in the city, so you're stuck with me until the gas runs out. Not the way I'd dreamed about being the biggest show in town. Stay safe out there everyone. Good luck, and God bless. This is Tommy Rye the Talk Radio Guy signing off."

With that, the radio went quiet. Everything was quiet. The entire neighborhood was silent but for a siren somewhere far off in the distance. Andy and Melissa looked at one another, but it was Melissa who spoke first.

"I never thought silence could be so creepy."

"Yeah, it's one thing in the mountains," Andy replied, "but there's something just not right about it in the city."

"Daddy, he never said when the power is coming back on," said Kathryn, still trying to tune the radio to a different station.

"You noticed that too, huh?" Andy replied. "That's because he doesn't know. This has never happened before."

"It takes them a week to get it fixed after a hurricane or an ice storm," David said, chiming in on the conversation from the other room.

"David's right," Andy said, looking at the pile of stolen water and canned goods that as of this moment he no longer felt guilty about taking. "I don't think the power is coming back for a very long time. Things are going to get very interesting around here."

"More interesting than this morning?" Melissa asked sarcastically.

Andy had seen more than a couple of third-world countries and knew how rough those cultures were. Americans were not prepared to live rough; they were too dependent on modern amenities. He knew the mayhem they had witnessed earlier was only the beginning. Looking into his wife's eyes, he saw that she was as concerned as he was. He knew that together, he and his family would be OK. Others he was not so sure about, and that was what concerned him the most. What threat were desperate, hungry people going to pose to his family? He had stolen water and canned goods knowing full well it was wrong, and as a member of the military, he was expected to always hold himself to a higher standard. Yet he had done it and felt OK about it now.

What would happen next? They didn't even have all the details of what exactly had happened, nor the complete extent of the damage. What could the government do to help three hundred million citizens? He had family in New York, and Melissa had family in another part of Pennsylvania. How did they fare? Would he ever know? Winter was coming. He knew they were not prepared for a winter without modern conveniences. Looking out the window at the rapidly growing darkness, he thought for a moment how the day had started. He chuckled to himself and thought, *Well, Andy, you were sick of that grind anyway.*

"Way more interesting than this morning, my dear," Andy said finally. "We are in for a wild ride, I think."

AT THAT SAME time in Washington, DC, President Keller was standing staring out the window of the Oval Office at the fading light, something he had done countless times before. Except this evening, the city grew dark with the setting sun. No streetlights came on, no office lights. No lights at all. The lights on the White House grounds were diminished, but he could still see that security had donned body armor and rifles and had taken up positions of equal intervals along the fence line. He had sent his cabinet members home and told them to return in the morning, provided their families were safe and secure.

The discussion about how much detail about when and what they knew about The Event to include in their official statement had become heated. Dr. Detweiler and others wanted more of both and had argued vigorously. FEMA Director Whiting had insisted that the fewer people who knew, the better off everyone would be; the road ahead was going to get hard enough without an angry citizenry. In the end, Keller had to side with Whiting, not only because he agreed with him but because that was what Mr. X had insisted upon.

A DAY LIKE ANY OTHER

Only a few minutes earlier, he had received word that the vice president was missing following an explosion in the NORAD control center. The situation there was extremely confusing. All the highest-ranking officers and officials were present in that control center at the time of the mysterious blast. Keller couldn't help but think Mr. X and his "people" had something to do with that. Keller started feeling angry at the thought that his friend and vice president had been assassinated. *I'd call that bastard Mr. X and ask him if I could.* Could he? He'd never given it a thought before. As he began reaching in his pocket for the satellite phone, there was a knock on the door. He put aside his anger for the moment.

"Come in."

It was the NASA director, Dr. Gregory Morris, and a tall, well-built man who Keller assumed was one of Dr. Morris's assistants, though he didn't have the look of a scientist. All had agreed that it was more important that Morris monitor The Event from NASA headquarters rather than the Situation Room during the countdown—especially given that the last time Dr. Morris and Dr. Detweiler had been in the same room, they had nearly come to blows over the level of secrecy NASA was imposing even on Detweiler himself. Keller presumed Morris had come to brief him now that Detweiler had left.

"Whatcha got, Greg?" Keller said, greeting his NASA director and gesturing the two men toward the couches to sit.

"Hello, Mr. President," Dr. Morris replied, shaking his boss's hand.

Keller couldn't help but notice the clammy handshake Dr. Morris had just bestowed upon him. Dr. Morris was a stereotypical scientist. Obsessed with details and fascinated with mysteries of the universe, he had been a NASA employee ever since graduating from MIT some thirty years ago. The usually vibrant and upbeat man looked as if he had seen a ghost. He was pale and frail looking. Something other than the day's events was bothering him. Keller turned his attention to the stranger who had accompanied the doctor.

"William, this is Howard Sykes," Morris said, turning even whiter than when he had entered the room.

Keller, still looking at Dr. Morris and wondering if the man was going to vomit on the carpet, reached his hand toward Sykes.

Sykes took the president's hand in a crushing handshake that made Keller forget about Morris for the moment.

"Mr. President, it's a pleasure," said Sykes, looking directly into Keller's eyes. Keller was now sure this man was no scientist.

"What brings you by, Greg?" he said.

"It's Detweiler," Morris said, nodding his head slowly from side to side. "Right before The Event, someone on his staff accessed the NASA mainframe. Information was downloaded, but we don't know for sure how much."

Keller was only slightly surprised and actually almost let out a snicker. Detweiler had gotten the best of them; he was tenacious when he set his mind to something.

Becoming more serious, Keller asked, "Well, how do you know it was him?"

"It was him!" Morris was livid. "He's been after me for days to get more access. You and I both know that's not possible. Now who knows what he's got—and more importantly, what he's going to do with it!"

Keller had never seen Dr. Morris so angry, and he thought at this moment that Morris would strangle Detweiler if he were in the room.

"I'll talk to him, Greg. I'll get him to delete the data or something. Just please calm down. You're going to give yourself a stroke."

Morris sat back in his seat with a sigh and looked at Sykes.

Sykes, who had been listening to Morris's tirade, emotionless, sat forward slightly and said, "Maybe you should go get a drink or something, Dr. Morris. Let me have a chat with the president—what a privilege after all, to be in the Oval Office."

Sykes's grin gave him away. Keller thought, *Sykes doesn't work for Morris. Morris works for Sykes.*

Dr. Morris leapt to his feet and said, "Yes, a drink. I need a drink." He looked relieved.

He was dismissed and was now happily leaving. He didn't want to be around for what was going to happen next—that was obvious.

Morris left, closing the door behind him. President Keller was the first to speak.

"Who are you?" he asked Sykes, who was now smiling at him.

"He's a good man. Brilliant!" Sykes said, tilting his head toward the door Morris had just exited. "He's had a hell of a day. What a day, huh, Mr. President?"

"Who are you?" Keller asked again, more agitated.

"I'm afraid the time is over for talking to Detweiler, Mr. President," Sykes said calmly. "He's dragged the FBI director into this now. Not very good for any of us, now, is it?"

Keller's jaw dropped. He couldn't hide his shock.

A DAY LIKE ANY OTHER

"Don't look so surprised, Mr. President," Sykes said, reaching into his pocket and pulling out a satellite phone identical to the one Keller had been tormented by as of late. "It would seem we have a mutual friend."

Keller felt sick and imagined he looked the part as he felt the blood leave his face.

"Who are you?" Keller asked, much weaker than before.

"Through us, kings rule, Mr. President," Sykes said calmly, looking straight through the president. "Now here is what we are going to do."

As Sykes began to lay out the plan Keller was expected to execute, Keller knew from this moment on that he would be nothing but a pawn in whatever these people had planned. He sat and listened, feeling very empty and alone. These people were in charge. *How did this happen?* he wondered.

CHAPTER 12

THE SUBURBS NORTH OF PHILADELPHIA

IN THE HOURS following The Event, which is how it was now being referred to globally, massive tsunamis generated by all the seismic activity began crashing ashore on every coastline, everywhere in the world. There were no warnings since there was no power, no satellites to transmit tsunami buoy alerts through, and no scientists waiting for said warnings to arrive. Everyone and everything were already in a state of emergency. The devastation was horrific, the loss of life enormous, and the surprise complete. Most people only knew the ocean was coming when it hit them.

The entire eastern seaboard was devastated. Any low-lying coastal regions were completely wiped out, and some even remained flooded after the ocean receded. Some areas actually moved closer to sea level after the earthquakes. Manhattan Island was one of these areas, as were parts of Long Island, New York. Most of southern Florida was underwater, as was the city of New Orleans and dozens of other cities and towns. It was the same all over the globe—no one had fared any better or any worse. But it couldn't have been much worse.

Week one was a mass of confusion. A disorganized relief effort was launched with some success at first, until supplies ran out in the first three days. This was about the same time that people's own cupboards went empty. Supermarkets had been picked clean, and for the same reasons, the relief effort was down to a trickle in the first week. Because of the state of the roads, deliveries to stores or relief centers became nearly impossible. What was being delivered from warehouses was only to sites in very close proximity to the warehouses themselves. The military was hauling relief supplies, food, and water night and day via helicopters. The need was too great, however, and the relief centers were too few. By the end of the first week, refuge centers were overflowing with hungry, homeless, sick, and scared people.

Private citizens were working together as best they could in their own neighborhoods to offer comfort to those neighbors who were in need, but these efforts could only go so far. Looting and robbery were becoming more common, and the occasional gunshot could be heard in the nighttime hours. Andy and his family worked with their neighbors, splitting firewood and providing security. People shared knowledge and, at first, they felt like everything would be OK as long as they stuck together. There was even a huge neighborhood barbeque where everyone cooked up all the meat they had in their freezers before it spoiled. President Keller delivered another address to denounce the looting and further urge Americans to work together while FEMA got its arms around the problems at the local level.

Week two saw a rise in desperation as people began flooding relief centers for any sort of supplies and medications, as whatever prescriptions they were taking ran out. Pharmacies had been cleaned out in the first week by looters, thugs, and addicts. The government-run centers were now the only source of food and medications.

As the desperation grew, so, too, did the lines at relief centers. Those farther back in line saw the meager rations that were being provided and became concerned there would be nothing left when they finally got their turn. Their fears were inevitably realized when a man wearing a FEMA jacket stood on top of a National Guard five-ton truck with a bullhorn in hand and informed the crowd that supplies had run out for now but that more was coming soon. He said that everyone should go home and come back tomorrow, then apologized.

At first, the crowd groaned in disbelief, but then they began to get agitated. In moments, the crowd was crushing in on the relief center issue points, rampaging, stampeding, and assaulting the FEMA people, guardsmen, and law enforcement as they tore the center apart looking for any supplies at all.

This scene was repeated all over the country, especially in the cities where the population concentrations were the highest. Remotely located relief centers became too dangerous as crowds turned angry on a daily basis. Relief workers were losing their lives, and convoys with relief supplies were being hijacked. Food, water, and medical supplies were only being distributed from facilities deemed "FEMA camps," so, subsequently, a black market began to arise by the end of the second week.

Andy and his family found that the alliances and cooperativeness of week one were quickly eroding as neighbors began accusing other neighbors of hoarding food and other supplies. People began hunting the local deer population relentlessly, as well as any other game they could stir up. Andy traded some firewood and bottled water for some deer meat from two men he had never seen before who were butchering the deer in the parking lot at the end of his road. The local police department drove around the area broadcasting a stern warning about discharging firearms within city limits, but no one listened.

Those who felt they could fare better somewhere other than where they were took to the roads, headed to what they perceived as greener pastures. Some ran out of fuel attempting to navigate the confusing maze of broken roads and collapsed overpasses. Some were robbed by thugs and ended up in camps, or walked back to their homes if they were lucky. Others made it to their destination only to find out that they were no better off there than where they had started. A very small minority found themselves better off having left.

President Keller, with the backing of Congress, declared martial law. He also announced that due to FEMA's inability to provide relief, along with state, local, and federal law enforcement's inability to provide public safety, he was creating a new department called the Catastrophe Management Administration (CAT-MAN for short). This new department, the presidential statement read, "will be as well funded and as well armed as the military and answer to his office directly. It will begin taking over control of all relief and security efforts immediately." Free-thinking Americans, including Andy, raised an eyebrow at this but remained hopeful.

Week three saw the complete breakdown of society. Relief supplies were distributed only to residents of a FEMA camp. The FEMA camps quickly filled to overflowing. Gangs roamed neighborhoods that were quickly becoming deserted. Nothing traveled overland without having to pass CAT-MAN checkpoints or a gauntlet of criminals attempting to rob them. Some said that the CAT-MAN people were the criminals, extorting money or goods from people to get past their roadblocks. Others wondered how such a force could have been assembled so quickly.

It seemed that CAT-MAN was not playing by the same rules as any other federal entity, past or present. This became clear when, on several occasions, CAT-MAN officers opened fire on crowds during food riots inside FEMA camps. In more than one of these incidents, military personnel positioned nearby actually engaged and killed the CAT-MAN officers involved. This led to President Keller issuing orders for no military units to be positioned closer than one mile to any CAT-MAN operation.

In a move that further astonished observers, President Keller issued orders essentially releasing any military personnel from duty if they wished to return home to tend to their families in this time of crisis. A large portion of the active-duty force took him up on his offer. Having seen the hardship and deprivation of others, they were eager to return home and attempt to ease the suffering of their own loved ones, especially now that these CAT-MAN officers were obviously in charge. The black market was in full swing, and it was becoming obvious that CAT-MAN was somehow involved due to the open nature of the black-market operation.

In Andy's neighborhood, people's pets began disappearing from their yards. Andy recalled a program he had watched years ago about how people would act in a crisis. *People wouldn't eat their own pets, but they would have no problem eating other people's*, the expert had stated. Andy began escorting the dog in his backyard activities and, in fact, had to run off three individuals who actually threatened to take the dog regardless of what Andy said. They thought better of their threat when Andy produced a .45-caliber pistol and told them not to come around there again.

The talk radio announcer had been on every day for only two hours a day due to fuel shortages. He had been more and more outspoken about FEMA's inability to maintain supply chains and, more recently, about CAT-MAN's heavy-handed tactics. He reported on ham radio operator stories from around the area, talking about food and water supplies being hoarded in FEMA camps by CAT-MAN officials. He jokingly wondered how long he would be allowed to stay on the air if he kept bashing the government. With the onset of winter looming, Andy and Melissa talked seriously of making a run for her mom and dad's place in upstate Pennsylvania, about three hours away, before the roads went to complete hell.

Lying in bed, the fourth week of this new reality beginning, Andy slept fitfully. He had to choose. Would he try to stay here through the winter that was quickly approaching? Would he attempt to move his family to his in-laws' farm on roads fraught with danger? Or would he move them into a FEMA camp and subject them to the will of strangers? He could hear, in the distance, a low rumble. *Rrrrrgggggg.*

Was it a relief column on the highway? he wondered. *Not likely.*

He continued his thought process on whether to leave or not. *We would have to load the truck in secret and make several trades to acquire enough fuel to make the trip to the farm.*

Rrrrrrgggggg.

There it is again. What is that? Andy wondered but was preoccupied with his bug out/bug in dilemma. He continued his brainstorming. *If we encounter a roadblock, how will we get through? Are they letting people through? What if we encounter robbers? Larry down the street tried to leave, and he got robbed. They took everything, and they were lucky to make it back alive. They're in a camp now.*

Rrrrrggggggg! Andy didn't get a chance to wonder what that noise was again as Melissa was forcefully elbowing him in the ribs.

"Andrew, wake up! The dog is growling at something!"

Andy sat straight up, wide awake and acutely focused on the black mass of Gomer that he saw in the darkness. The jet-black dog was nearly invisible but for the growling. Gomer was staring at the bedroom door.

"I think someone is in the house!" Melissa said, sounding more pissed off than afraid.

Andy stood, grabbing the pistol from the nightstand, and moved toward the door. He had to confront whatever it was. His children's rooms were opposite his, so he needed to get to the top of the stairs and put himself between whoever or whatever was downstairs.

Andy moved as quietly as he could to the top of the stairs and then the landing. He had closed Gomer and Melissa into the bedroom and told his wife to get the .38 revolver he insisted she keep in her nightstand and cover the door until he returned. He reminded her not to shoot him when he returned, and that if there was any shooting from downstairs, to get to the kids as quickly as she could.

He could see three figures moving around in the darkness. They were in the living room.

Andy took a deep breath and said in an almost surreally calm but firm voice, "What are you doing here?"

The dark figures all jumped. One ran for the kitchen, presumably where they came in. The second put his hands up and yelled, "Shit!" The third turned toward the stairs with both arms out in front of his body.

Andy's first thought was, *Gun!* The sudden flash and *pop* confirmed his thought. Andy squeezed the trigger twice—*pop pop!*—as he had been trained, and the shadow dropped.

The man who had raised his hands and yelled was now yelling, "Don't shoot! Don't shoot!"

Melissa and Gomer appeared at the top of the stairs a moment later, the dog barking viciously, and Andy feared he would bite anyone that came near but saw that he was focused on the invaders.

A DAY LIKE ANY OTHER

The children appeared a moment later, yelling, "What's going on!" almost in unison.

"It's OK!" Andy yelled over the chaos. "It's OK, I got him!"

With that, David shined his flashlight first on the man with his hands up, who was repeating, "Don't shoot!" over and over. Then he shined the beam onto the dark mass on the living room floor.

"He's still movin', Dad!" David yelled nervously.

Andy recognized them both from his altercation over the dog. They had come for whatever they thought they could take and maybe sneak off with a fresh kill. *They thought they could come in the night and take me by surprise?* Andy thought. *Gomer Pyle Lemon had something to say about that. Good dog.*

"You there!" Andy gestured with his still-smoking pistol toward the "don't shoot" guy. "Get your buddy and get out of here. Don't ever come back."

"OK! OK!" the guy said as he came over to lift his friend.

"David! Keep the light on them!" Andy said, walking them toward the front door, wanting them out of the house by the most direct route possible.

As the two burglars exited the house, Andy said again, "Don't ever come back here!"

Andy was shocked when the man whom he had just shot said, "This ain't over. I'll get you."

"We'll see," Andy replied.

Andy closed and locked the door behind them, then went and cleared the kitchen where the only one of the three with enough sense to run had headed.

When he returned, Andy said, "We're leaving this week. We're going to your parents."

"Oh, thank God," replied Melissa.

"Grandma and Grandpa! Yaaay!" said Kathryn.

"You shot that guy!" David exclaimed. "They came to the wrong house!"

Came to the wrong house, Andy thought, looking up the stairs at his family. These guys were idiots. Would he be that lucky next time? Would the dog wake them up next time? Would they have to eat the dog? It was clear to Andy that his only choice was to try and get to his in-laws. In the short term, it was the most hazardous decision. But if they made it, they would be much better off in the long term, and there was no way he was taking his family to any camp. He would get them ready for the trip, and he would make sure they made it. No matter what.

"OK, everyone," Andy said, as calmly as he could manage, though he thought his heart would burst from his chest. "Excitement is over. Back to bed. We have a busy day tomorrow."

He knew if they had nearly as much adrenaline pumping through them as he did that no one was sleeping tonight. He needed them to go—he needed to think and plan their escape from their home. *The world has gone crazy,* Andy thought, heading upstairs to get dressed the rest of the way and grab the twelve-gauge shotgun from the closet. There would be no sleep for him tonight.

CHAPTER 13

THE SUBURBS NORTH OF PHILADELPHIA

THE SUN WAS rising. Andy had stayed up the rest of the night standing watch. Melissa had stayed with him and seemed to have slept a bit on the sofa beside where he sat, shotgun in hand. The kids had gone to their rooms, but he imagined they hadn't slept much either.

As the sunlight began to fill the room, he could see the evidence of last night's excitement. A small area of dried blood was visible on the rug where Andy's gunfight opponent had fallen. Andy thought, *Not much blood—maybe I only winged him.* That was good and bad. Andy hadn't wanted to shoot anyone and definitely didn't want to kill anyone, but the man had said he would be back. *Dead men don't come back,* Andy thought. Andy had had no choice. The man had pulled a gun and fired.

As the room got brighter and brighter, Andy could see more clearly the bullet hole in the wall behind the landing where he had stood just hours before. Examining the impact from his seat, Andy did not understand how he had not been struck. The hole was centered on the wall about four feet up, exactly where he had been when the man had fired. No matter how, he had missed and Andy's shots had hit. That was all that mattered right now. He was unharmed, and his family, food, and water were safe. The incident had forced him to make his decision about staying or going.

As the hours had passed, Andy's plan to bug out had taken shape. He would trade his stockpile of firewood for any gasoline he could find to augment what he already had in his truck and what he could siphon from Melissa's car. They would leave this populated area at night to avoid attracting any attention. They would carry what they could with winter's approach in mind, but they would have to leave most of their belongings behind. He hoped that they could make the normally three-hour trip in the overnight hours of darkness in approximately twelve hours, even with the roads being wrecked. If not, they had enough camping equipment to stay comfortable for a number of nights if need be.

He glanced over at the stack of bottled water in the corner of the room and thought, *Who knew stealing that water on day one would be the smartest thing I've ever done?* They had been able to acquire some extra food and water from the relief center in the first week, but after the crowds started becoming ugly, Andy had decided it was safer fending for themselves. There was no use fighting over supplies if he already had a good stockpile. He was very glad he was such a packrat all these years. Listening to other people's plights and dire situations, he knew he and his family were far better off than most.

They would, of course, bring all their food and water, keeping some set aside to trade with or, if needed, bribe with. Food and water were the new currency, it would seem.

Security would be another matter. He had trained his family in using firearms, but he had never trained them in how to use them tactically. *We'll have to work on that one,* he thought.

He could hear the kids beginning to move around upstairs. Gomer was starting to eye the back door for his morning business. *Well, I guess now is as good a time to get started as any other,* he thought, looking over at Melissa, who was awake and looking at him.

"Good morning, Mrs. Lemon," Andy said cheerfully.

"Good morning, Mr. Lemon. What's for breakfast?" Melissa replied.

"I was thinking maybe some pancakes," Andy said, smiling.

"That does sound good! We have any?"

"No, no pancakes today."

"Oh well, I guess we could just have the usual," Melissa said with a shrug.

"Beans and rice it is, my love!" Andy said, standing.

He kissed her on the forehead and headed for the back door to walk the dog, who was now standing by the door looking desperate.

"I'll be right back," Andy said as he exited with Gomer. "We have a lot to talk about."

"Can't wait," Melissa said, heading for the kitchen.

DAVID AND KATHRYN had joined Melissa in the kitchen by the time Andy returned with the dog. Andy had checked the perimeter of the property while Gomer was taking care of his business. The previous night's visitors had headed up the street in the direction of the nearest hospital, based on the trail of blood he had found on the front walk. Andy wondered how many gunshot victims the hospital was treating every night as of late and what kind of stories said victims were telling of how they got shot. He wondered if he would be getting a visit from the police. He felt he had been in the right and would do the same thing again if need be.

"Morning, guys!" Andy said as he entered.

He could tell they hadn't slept much either by the looks on their faces. Adrenaline takes time to wear off, and going to sleep right after witnessing something like that was not possible.

"Morning, Dad!" they answered in unison.

The looks on their faces didn't match the pep in their voices. They were excited about leaving and going to the farm. They had been real troopers considering how they had been living since the power had gone out and the water had stopped flowing. They had been eating a rotating diet of beans and rice, canned beef stew thinned out into a soup, and canned meat mixed with rice or pasta. The toilets had functioned for the first week—one just needed to flush by pouring a bucket of water into the tank before flushing. The rule was, "If it's not solid, don't flush it." Even this simple luxury had come to a stop once the toilet wouldn't flush anymore. They figured the treatment plant must have been full, and everything just started backing up upstream. Melissa wrapped the toilets in plastic wrap to keep the smell out. She then devised an ingenious portable toilet using one of the toilet seats and a five-gallon bucket that, which they deposited the contents of in a deep hole Andy had dug in the backyard. They had been using the water from the WaterBob David had filled in the tub for cooking and drank bottled water. They had managed to catch a good amount of water from a couple of rain showers using a large tarp and some storage tubs, the former contents of which were now strewn about in piles in the basement. They used this water for bathing.

It hadn't been all that terrible by some standards, and at least they still had a roof over their heads. Some people didn't even have that. The Lemons were in pretty good shape considering, but that was about to change. It wasn't safe anymore. They all knew it, and it seemed even the children were ready to move on.

"OK, everyone!" Andy started, sitting down at the table for his breakfast of beans and rice. "Exciting night, huh?"

"Man, Dad! You shot that dude like you were Wyatt Earp or somethin'!" David said, still caught up in the moment.

"Do you think he will be OK, Daddy?" asked Kathryn, always concerned for people. She had his father-in-law's love for healing in her.

"I don't know, sweetheart," Andy said, taking a mouthful of breakfast. "He seemed to be in pretty good shape when he left."

"Do you think he'll be back?" asked David. "He said he'd be back."

Melissa, not wanting the conversation to go there, interrupted before Andy could answer. "It doesn't matter, David. We're leaving anyway. Right, Andrew?"

She didn't like firefights going down in her house in front of her children. While she agreed that Andy had had no choice but to shoot that guy, she did not want it to happen again. She had already rolled up the blood-stained area rug and thrown it out into the yard.

"That's right. Mommy is right," Andy said. "As soon as we can, we're heading to the farm." The fact that his children were not more somber or distressed by his shooting a man in the living room was not lost on Andy. He noted it and chalked it up to the shock and trauma of the incident, but he imagined that once it all sank in, they might present symptoms of shock. He would have to be on the lookout as time passed.

He didn't relish the thought of nightly gunplay around his kids either and, like Melissa, didn't care to talk about it anymore. They were going to his in-laws' farm—at least, that's how everyone referred to it. About five years ago, Melissa's dad, Dr. Edward J. Taft, was head of thoracic surgery at a major Philadelphia hospital, until one day he decided he'd had enough. He packed up his wife, Christine, and moved to the mountains of Pennsylvania to live the life of a simple country doctor. That was exactly what he did, and he had never been happier. He ran a small practice in a small town, where he joked, "People pay me with chickens sometimes!" He wasn't kidding though, and he loved it. He grew corn and vegetables in his garden, and chickens and goats roamed free. He strived to become an off-the-grid homesteader. He made improvements every year, like turning an old-fashioned–looking windmill that pumped his water into a state-of-the-art solar array that harvested enough electricity to put power back into the grid. He would always giggle with delight whenever that check from the power company would arrive.

At first, Dr. Taft didn't take kindly to Andrew. A product of the 1960s college scene, Edward Taft was wary of servicemen and, as a doctor, abhorred violence. He had opened the bodies of too many young men in order to repair the results of violent encounters. He was shocked and disappointed that his only child would bring home such a man, one who was trained to be violent.

A DAY LIKE ANY OTHER

At first, Andy and Dr. Taft's relationship was strained but polite, with Andy always addressing his father-in-law as "sir." "Yes, sir" and "No, sir" were the norm for years until David was born. Dr. Taft finally accepted that Andy wasn't some evil menace sent to corrupt his daughter, but a human being and the father of his first grandchild.

Before Andy's first deployment to Iraq, he and Melissa visited her parents. Dr. Taft had taken Andy aside and told him, "You be careful, you hear me?" with a tear in his eye. "You're my only son, so you come back!"

Andy replied, "Yes, sir, I'm coming back—that's the plan."

Since then, they had been as close as a man and his son could be. Andy visited the farm as often as possible. He would invite his friends from the base to visit on long weekends and together, they had actually gotten Ed to fire a gun, something he said he would never do. Now that Andy was planning another visit, he hoped Ed was up for guests.

After breakfast, Andy sent the kids to start packing a bag.

"Only take necessities—warm clothes, socks, underwear, stuff for winter—and you only get one bag to pack it in. Then I want you to use your school backpacks to pack an overnight bag."

He would have them keep the smaller bags in the cab of the truck in case they had to abandon it in a hurry. He and Melissa would do the same. *Have to think of everything,* he thought.

While the kids were busy with that, he and Melissa consolidated all their food supplies into plastic tubs and cardboard boxes and carried them to the garage. They had started parking both vehicles in the garage after neighbors started reporting their gas tanks being punctured and drained. Normally there wasn't room to walk in the garage, but desperate times called for desperate measures. Andy joked that all it took to get the garage clean was the end of the world.

David was the first to appear with his bags packed and ready to go.

"Great! Good job, bud!" Andy said, glad to see his son appear in the garage. "How's your sister coming along?"

"Dad," David replied blank faced, wanting nothing to do with his sister's packing.

"Right," Andy said, getting the picture. "Let's leave the girls to pack on their own. I have a job for you anyway."

Andy then explained to David his plan to head out in the hours of darkness. In order to be as stealthy as possible, they would need to black out the brake lights on the truck. Andy handed David a large roll of duct tape and explained how he wanted the lights covered with as many layers as it took to block any light from getting through when the brake pedal was stepped on. David listened intently and began enthusiastically applying tape to the taillights. This was all still a big adventure to him.

As Andy left to go talk to the neighbors about acquiring some gas, David said, "We're goin' tactical!"

"You got it!" Andy replied.

BY THE TIME Andy returned, David had completed blacking out the taillights, and the girls had finished packing. A large pile of tubs, packs, and suitcases had grown in the garage beside the truck. Andy inspected David's project by having his son step on the brake pedal and activate the turn signals. Satisfied, Andy got David to start siphoning gas out of Melissa's car into gas cans, then turned his attention to the pile he would need to make fit in the bed of the truck.

He noticed a large blue tote he had not seen before. Pointing to it, he asked his wife, "What's in this one?"

"Blankets . . . and photo albums," she answered quietly.

He could tell it was starting to hit her that they were leaving and probably never coming back. Though the photo albums took up precious space, he wasn't about to leave them behind.

He went over and gave her a hug. "Can't forget those. I'm looking forward to seeing your folks."

"Me too," she said, putting her head on his chest.

"Let's get all this packed up so we can see where we are. I was able to get ten gallons—five from Henry and five from the Murdocks since they won't be needing it."

Henry and Rose Mills lived next door to the left. An older couple in their seventies, they were good neighbors with grown children spread out all over the country. Andy had told Henry about the intruders and that he was taking the family away as soon as possible. Henry told Andy that he thought he had heard something but wasn't really sure as he and Rose had both run out of hearing aid batteries. He also said it was good they were leaving,

"This is no place for children," Henry told him.

Andy asked if they would come with them.

A DAY LIKE ANY OTHER

Henry only said, "No, thank you, we've lived here a long time. We'll be OK. This is our home."

Andy left with the gas but not before giving the old man a hug and promising to send the kids over to say bye and to deliver some water and beans. Andy told him the wood stockpile was his now and not to spend it all in one place. They had both laughed and wished each other luck.

The Murdocks had been out of the country on vacation somewhere in Mexico. Andy couldn't remember where. He figured they wouldn't be back anytime soon, if ever, and there was no point leaving anything for the looters. He had grabbed a full, five-gallon gas can from their garage. He was actually surprised no one had broken in there yet. Once the truck's gas tank was topped off, he would return with whatever empty gas cans he had to top off from the Murdocks' car.

Once the truck was packed, Andy turned his attention to the safe in the far corner of the basement. While Melissa lit the way with a flashlight, David, Kathryn, and Andy started hauling weapons, ammunition, and all the important family legal documents they had locked away to the dining room. Andy was a strong believer in the Second Amendment and had been collecting firearms his entire adult life. He was also kind of a hoarder when it came to ammunition—he just couldn't pass up a good deal on bulk ammo. Melissa would ask, "Don't you have enough bullets already?" to which Andy would reply, "How much is enough?"

Now it was time to take stock. On the dining room table lay Andy's arsenal. He carefully checked and oiled each weapon. His collection consisted of one .38-caliber pistol that was his dad's; two 9-millimeter pistols; one .45-caliber M1911 pistol; two twelve-gauge pump-action shotguns with tactical barrels; one .30-06 caliber hunting rifle; and finally, his pride and joy, two AR-15, M4-style 5.56-caliber rifles. He also had many more firearms safely locked away at their cabin upstate on their in-laws' property. He was glad he had invested in the safe up there. It comforted him knowing he had backup firepower waiting there, and he was also glad he didn't have to move any more things into the truck tonight or, worse yet, destroy the extra guns so as not to let them fall into the wrong hands. Plus he had his latest addition, the .40-caliber pistol that had been dropped and left behind by the man Andy shot last night. Andy saw this as a good bartering item if need be.

He estimated that he had at least three hundred rounds of ammo for each caliber and at least four thousand rounds for the AR-15s. He hoped that would be enough.

David, Melissa, and him loaded all the magazines they had and stored them in whatever pouches and holders they could find. The balance of the ammo was split between their backpacks and the bed of the truck.

After dinner, Andy set up the dining room chairs to simulate the cab of the truck. He assigned each one of them two weapons, something that he never imagined in his wildest dreams he would ever have to do. In fact, in issuing weapons to his wife and his teenage children, he found himself nauseated. He assigned them specific seats in the truck where they would sit for the duration of the trip. He then posed several scenarios and assigned certain responsibilities to each one of them. They then ran through each scenario several times until Andy was sure everyone understood what they were to do, right down to who was responsible for getting the dog out of the truck in the event they had to leave it in a hurry.

What a sight this must be, he thought to himself. His family all sitting in the dining room like they were in a truck, armed to the teeth, then suddenly rearranging or getting up and running or pretending to shoot in this direction or that. The dog in the middle seat between the kids, wondering why it was OK to get on the furniture all of a sudden and what on Earth was wrong with the humans. Quite a sight it must have been.

Finally, as the last rays of daylight began to shine through the kitchen windows, Andy said, "OK, I think we're ready. We'll leave tomorrow night. We'll take watch tonight in shifts. Mommy will take the first shift. David, you take the second, and I'll take the last. We'll keep the dog down here tonight; nothing gets past his ears. If anyone hears something, just come get me. Don't try to be a hero."

"You don't have to worry about that," Melissa said sarcastically.

"OK, David, just come get me, alright?" Andy reiterated.

"Yeah, OK, Dad!" David replied with typical teenage attitude.

Andy wanted to be sure. He didn't want his son getting in over his head, nor did he want to be responsible for his son having blood on his hands.

Andy had taken the last shift since he wanted to be awake during the wee hours of the morning into sunrise. That was when he felt trouble would come.

"What about me, Dad?" asked Kathryn, not wanting to be left out.

A DAY LIKE ANY OTHER

"There are only three shifts in the night, sweetheart. You lucked out this time," Andy answered, hugging his daughter by the head.

There was no way he could ask his thirteen-year-old daughter to stand watch. It was bad enough having his sixteen-year-old son do it.

Andy stood on his front steps watching the sun set with Melissa by his side. He thought, *I've just loaded our belongings into the truck. I've issued weapons to my children and run quick-reaction drills for exiting a vehicle. I've assigned my wife and teenage son interior guard shift. We will be driving off into the darkness, probably never to return, and it all seems normal. What a messed-up situation.*

Andy looked at his wife and said, "Well, Mrs. Lemon, what would you say to heading upstairs and making sweet love in the old Lemon homestead one last time before you start your guard duty?"

Melissa looked up at him and said with a straight face, "I would say that's the best idea I've heard all day, Mr. Lemon."

As they turned and headed for the stairs, they heard David's voice from the darkness of the dining room saying, "I think I'm gonna puke."

Kathryn let out a giggle.

"Quiet, you two!" Andy replied as they headed upstairs.

"It's gonna be hard to leave," Kathryn said to her brother once their parents were gone.

"It will be OK. As long as we're together, right?" David replied, as any good big brother would. Then he punched his sister in the arm, like any good big brother would.

"Oww, I'm tellin' Mom," Kathryn said, rubbing the injured limb.

"She's up there. Go tell her," David replied, pointing up the stairs.

"Yeah, maybe later," Kathryn said, crinkling her nose.

They both laughed and nodded. They were heading off into the unknown, but at that moment, they both knew that what David had said was the truth. As long as they were together, everything would be OK.

CHAPTER 14

WASHINGTON, DC

"Any sign of Detweiler?" asked FBI Director Cummings.

"As you're the FBI director, I should be asking you that," replied President Keller.

"I don't remember being asked to look for him, Mr. President."

"He's obviously on the run."

"On the run from what?" Cummings said with a bit of disbelief in his voice.

"I don't know. You're the FBI. Why don't you find out? He's been missing three weeks, for Christ's sake. He's a scientist, an academic. Not a spy or someone who could stay hidden for so long!" the president said, becoming agitated.

"Maybe he doesn't want to end up like that guy. Or the vice president," Cummings said, gesturing toward the photos of NASA's Director Morris.

"What's that supposed to mean? Gregory Morris had a heart attack. And the VP died in a collapse caused by an earthquake," Keller replied, attempting to keep their conversation in low tones.

He looked around at the group that had assembled to memorialize Director Morris.

Dr. Morris had died two days earlier from a massive coronary infarction due to stress—at least, that was the story. There was a rumor that there was evidence his house had been broken into. Director Cummings had sent a team over to Dr. Morris's house at the time, but a team of CAT-MAN officials had already been there. Morris's wife had said that she thought she had heard her husband talking to someone downstairs, but when she had come down, her husband was on the floor unconscious and there hadn't been anyone else there, as far as she knew. He had died in her arms. That was all she had said before the CAT-MAN people shuffled her off into a waiting vehicle, presumably to accompany her husband's body to the morgue.

"What that means, Mr. President, is that a high-ranking government official with intimate knowledge of the greatest catastrophe in modern history is

A DAY LIKE ANY OTHER

suddenly dead, and the only people supposedly investigating is a group of mysterious individuals who suddenly appeared out of the shadows!" Cummings answered, now doing his best to keep his voice down. "And as for the VP, I've already submitted my report concerning explosive residue found in the rubble that was not consistent with any material found in the NORAD complex. That's what the FBI does. We investigate. We find the truth!"

The First Lady, seated next to her husband, turned toward Cummings, who was seated behind her husband, and said, "Can't the two of you have this conversation some other time? This is a solemn occasion, and they are about to start."

The irritation in her voice was genuine, yet her demeanor remained polite, and she was correct—the speakers seemed organized and ready to start the program soon.

"I'm very sorry, Mrs. Keller," Cummings began sincerely, "but your husband doesn't have time to see me, so I'm catching him when I can."

The First Lady turned around, giving her husband a squinted-eye look as she did. She was not pleased, and Keller knew it.

Cummings continued, "And now I hear you're talking about confiscating firearms. You know you don't have the authority to do that, right, Mr. President!?"

Keller became restless in his seat at this new accusation and said, "Too many CAT-MAN officers are getting shot, Bob. We have to do something. As for the authority, we are under martial law. I have all the authority I need."

Cummings paused, shocked by what he had just heard.

"I've heard the CAT-MAN people are getting shot because they deserve it. Extortion, illegal searches of private residences, brutalizing suspects, and then the food riot shootings. What does the attorney general have to say about this?"

Keller's face was beginning to show the anger he was feeling. He had heard enough, and it was clear Cummings wasn't going to give up. He turned to face Director Cummings.

"Look, Director Cummings, it's a done deal. I've already signed the order. The announcement is set for this afternoon. I don't care what the attorney general has to say. I have the authority, and I'm using it."

"Well, the bureau will have nothing to do with it!" Cummings said, his voice rising as the sentence ended.

"I imagine state and local police departments won't either, but I don't need them, and I don't need you. You need to be very careful, Cummings," President Keller said, looking Cummings straight in the eyes.

"You're right, Mr. President, I need to be careful, or I may end up like him," Cummings said, gesturing toward the photo of Director Morris again.

With that, FBI Director Cummings stood and walked out.

President Keller looked across the room at CAT-MAN Director Sykes, who was grinning at Keller. Sykes then mouthed the words, "I told you he was trouble."

Keller looked away, the blood now drained from his face. The First Lady gave Keller a glance; she looked worried as well. *If she only knew,* Keller thought to himself as the first speaker called for everyone's attention. Keller saw that Sykes was no longer in the room either. *Would she ever forgive me?*

DIRECTOR CUMMINGS WAS fuming the entire trip back to his office. His driver was well aware and refrained from the usual banter he and his boss would normally engage in. These were difficult times everywhere. In fact, that he was still reporting to work was the exception, but he would continue to do so as long as the FBI director kept saying, "I'll see you tomorrow." He had been detailed to drive the director and provide security for about three months now, and he had never seen Director Cummings so lost in thought or visibly upset. Whatever had happened at the White House must have been over the top to put this otherwise unflappable man in such a state.

As they pulled into the parking garage, the driver knew it was bad when Director Cummings leaned forward and said, "Special Agent Reed?"

"Yes, sir?" Reed replied.

"You go and be with your family. I'll get in touch with you when I need a detail again."

"Is everything OK, sir?"

To Special Agent Reed's surprise, Director Cummings said, "No. I'm afraid not. In fact, I'm getting the hell out of town as soon as I can collect my family. I just need to clean up something in my office."

As they pulled into the parking spot reserved for the FBI director, Cummings said, "I'll take the keys. You have a way to get home?"

"Yes, sir. I have a vehicle. Good luck, and thank you. It's been a privilege," Reed said, handing over the keys.

A DAY LIKE ANY OTHER

"The privilege has been all mine," Cummings said, taking the keys and shaking Reed's hand. "Good luck to you, son. It's dark times, so you watch your six. Always keep the faith."

"Yes, sir. You too," Reed replied as Cummings turned to walk away.

CUMMINGS ARRIVED AT his office door winded, having sprinted up several flights of stairs.

He knocked twice, then once, then twice again before unlocking the door and entering.

"Why are you back so soon?" Dr. Detweiler said in a concerned voice. "What happened?"

"We're leaving," Cummings said as he quickly shuffled papers and binders into a briefcase.

"What? Where are we going? What happened? Do they know I'm here?" Detweiler was looking more worried with each rapid-fire question.

"Keller has gone too far, and I'm not going to wait around and end up like Morris or Vice President Goodwin," Cummings said, opening a safe behind his desk.

"What did he do now?" Detweiler asked, calming down a bit.

"He's going to start confiscating firearms."

"Oh dear, that's not going to go over well."

"No. It's going to cause a lot of bloodshed. The CAT-MAN people are carrying out the order," Cummings said, looking up at Detweiler and waving a binder in front of him. "No one trusts CAT-MAN already. They're the tyranny citizens have been arming themselves against for two hundred-plus years in this country. All hell is about to break loose."

Detweiler stood back and took a deep breath.

"Why do we have to run because of that?"

"Because I told Keller that I wouldn't support him in executing this order and that I suspected foul play in Morris's and Goodwin's deaths," Cummings replied. "Norman, it's obvious to me now that President Keller is just a puppet and that this Sykes character is calling the shots."

"Where are you going to go? What about me?" Detweiler was becoming worried again.

"I'm going to collect my family, and we're going to Philadelphia. I have family there—we'll be safe with them," Cummings replied, handing Detweiler a semi-automatic pistol he had removed from the safe. "You and your laptop are coming with us, unless you like hiding in my office. Have the last three weeks been that pleasurable? You like hiding in my office?"

"Philly sounds good. But I'll pass on the gun," Detweiler said, attempting to hand the pistol back to Cummings.

"You know how to use that?"

"Yes, Bob, I know how to use it, but it's just not my thing," Detweiler replied, still holding the gun out toward Cummings.

"It just became your thing, Norman," Cummings said, closing the briefcase. "You have secrets that need protecting, and if you're coming with me, I'm going to expect you to protect my family as well."

Detweiler stood, looking at the pistol he had just been handed and contemplating what Cummings was saying. Being expected to use a weapon of any kind to protect anything or anyone had never entered into his thought process, ever. *I'm a scientist, a geek,* he thought.

Seeing that Detweiler was struggling with what he had just said, Cummings said,

"Consider yourself a special agent: Special Agent Detweiler. Can you use a gun now?"

Detweiler looked up and smiled. "Since you put it that way, I think so."

"Good, let's go before we get rounded up by some of Keller's thugs," Cummings said as he passed Detweiler, headed for the door.

"Special Agent Norman Detweiler. I like that," Detweiler said, following Cummings.

"Good, just don't point that thing at me, OK?" Cummings said with a smirk.

CUMMINGS AND DETWEILER made their way down the stairs with Cummings walking ahead, checking each landing, and Detweiler keeping an eye out for anyone coming down the stairs behind them. They didn't encounter anyone else, as the building was deserted for the most part, other than some security and a skeleton crew of agents. They arrived at the door that let out into the parking garage.

Cummings said, "You stay here. I'll go get the car."

Detweiler responded with a nod and grunt.

As Cummings was about to open the driver's door, an SUV that had been parked caddy-corner across from the director's spot suddenly started and pulled up quickly to block Director Cummings's vehicle into its spot, its tires screeching the whole way. Two men dressed as though they belonged in FBI headquarters jumped out as the vehicle stopped. Cummings thought, *Those aren't my guys!*

Director Cummings recognized what this was immediately and retreated to the front of his car, drawing his weapon as he ran. He wouldn't be taken without a fight. *They're not gonna make this guy disappear,* he thought.

Detweiler, who had been watching through the small window in the door, said, "Oh shit!" under his breath. He remembered the pistol Cummings had given him and attempted to draw it from the pocket of his jacket, fumbling with it and then getting it hung up on the jacket liner. *Some special agent!* he thought as he wrestled with his clothing for possession of the gun. He could hear someone demanding that Cummings drop his weapon.

"We don't want to hurt you. We just want to talk," the voice said.

"Yeah, like you talked to Director Morris!" Cummings yelled back. "How about you drop your weapons? I have some questions for you."

With that, both men began firing, one with a fully automatic submachine gun of some kind, the other with a handgun of some sort. Cummings ducked behind the front of his vehicle; with the first burst of machine gun fire, he knew he was completely outgunned. With the second burst—*brrr-raaaa!*—he knew that he would not come out of this one on top and hoped that Detweiler was already running in the opposite direction. As Cummings repositioned and steeled himself to return fire, he thought, *I'll buy you some time, Norman. Good luck, buddy.*

From the corner of his eye, Cummings caught a glimpse of another vehicle racing in his direction. *More of them!* The situation was dire, and Cummings knew these guys had no intention of talking.

Bang! Cummings cringed and braced himself as the sound of crunching metal surprised him. He peaked over the hood of his car to see the SUV his assailants had arrived in was now pushed up against his car. The vehicle he had seen racing toward them moments before had crashed into the SUV. Cummings got to his feet and raised his pistol, moving to see around the pileup. What he saw when he reached the other side relieved and surprised him at the same time.

It was Special Agent Reed, his driver. He was kneeling over one of the men, removing the submachine gun from his reach. Both were down. Reed had struck both of them with his car, which sat up against the SUV, steam coming from under the hood.

"Thank you!" Cummings said, lowering his pistol.

"No problem, sir," Reed said in a matter-of-fact tone.

"I'm sure glad you hung around," Cummings said, checking the man closest to him for any identification.

"I wanted to make sure you and your friend made it out of here OK," Reed replied, checking the man closer to him.

"What friend?" Cummings said, looking up.

Just then, Detweiler came running up, his pistol in hand finally recovered from his pocket.

"My God! Bob! Are you OK? Who's this?" he said, waving the pistol in Reed's direction.

"Sir," Reed began, "this is FBI headquarters. You don't have someone living in your office for three weeks and not have everyone know about it. Especially someone as noisy as this good doctor."

Cummings looked up at Detweiler and squinted.

"I tried to stay quiet, Bob," Detweiler said, his arms stretched out to his sides pleadingly. "Who are these guys? They're well-armed, whoever they are. Was that a machine gun I heard?"

"MP5 submachine gun, Doctor. We use them—SWAT teams and Special Forces, too," Reed said.

"But these guys are none of those," Cummings said, holding up the CAT-MAN ID card he had found in searching through the man's pockets.

"You better get out of here, Director Cummings. I'll delay things long enough for you two to get a good head start," Reed said, looking around. "You're gonna have to find another ride, I'm afraid. My car is smashed and yours looks like Swiss cheese."

"We'll find something," Cummings began. "Thank you again, Reed. You've done far more than just save me today."

"I'm just keepin' the faith, sir," Reed replied with a smile.

Cummings nodded and smiled at Reed as he and Detweiler trotted off toward the nearest exit to the street.

"Who was that, Bob?" Detweiler asked as they headed off.

"My driver," Cummings replied.

"Driver? Not a very good driver. He crashed right into those guys," Detweiler replied.

"Yeah, good thing, too. And where were you?" Cummings said with a smirk.

A DAY LIKE ANY OTHER

"I had you covered! You looked like you had things under control," Detweiler said, his voice raising an octave.

"Mmhph," grunted Cummings, giving Detweiler a wink as they made their way onto the street.

"No, really!" said Detweiler.

Cummings laughed and said, "What did I get myself into? Start looking for a car we can steal."

CHAPTER 15

THE SUBURBS NORTH OF PHILADELPHIA

THE NIGHT PASSED slowly. Andy took over night watch from David at 0200, and the night passed without incident. David reported that he had heard gunshots off in the distance around midnight, but there was nothing else to report from his shift.

Andy spent the rest of the night going over his plan. *Have we packed everything? Was everything where we could get to if we needed it in a hurry? Would we have enough gas?* He didn't want to overlook anything.

He went over his story in the event that he came to a checkpoint. If he encountered a military checkpoint, he felt he could talk his way through using the truth: "We're getting out of town and heading for my in-laws'." A CAT-MAN checkpoint might not buy that story, and he decided to avoid any checkpoints he wasn't sure were military or police. He went over the route he planned on taking as well. He laid out an old-school Rand-McNally map and thought, *Man, when was the last time I used one of these? Damn internet spoiled me.*

Based on what Larry from down the street had told him of his failed escape from suburbia, Andy figured they could get out of any built-up areas in two hours. They would head east and turn north when they came to the Delaware River. Larry said that some of the minor roads close to the river had flooded, but he could get around those by cutting through neighborhoods. From there, he could work his way northwest back toward Route 611, picking it up somewhere north of Doylestown. From there, they could follow any number of rural routes north and west to get them to their destination. Andy hoped to arrive there before daybreak but didn't have a clear picture of what lay farther north. Larry had only made it so far before getting robbed at gunpoint.

Andy was prepared to shoot it out with anyone they met on the road who might have nefarious intentions. He wasn't so sure if his family was prepared, though, nor should he be. Andy knew that if it came to fighting their way through trouble, it was going to fall to him to do the bulk of the damage. He couldn't expect his wife and children to do more than make noise in a firefight.

He hoped and prayed that he was up to it. The shootout in the living room was pure luck—Andy's shots hit, and the other guy's didn't. Fighting their way through a highway holdup would take quite a bit more skill. Andy had his Marine Corps training to fall back on but had never seen real combat. The incident two nights ago was the first time he had ever fired a shot in anger. He had taken David and Kathryn to play paintball on several occasions and had been impressed with both of them. They had seemed to grasp the basic concepts of fire and maneuver and had done well. But Kathryn had gotten bored, preferring to stay in the picnic area and text her friends. David had become overconfident and started getting shot early each round, causing him to become frustrated. Andy was glad he had exposed his kids to that but was now concerned that they —David especially—may take chances and get shot. It was no longer a game; this was for real, and he needed to get everyone through it in one piece. He would just hope for the best and rely on his brain to get them through any trouble.

As the sun rose, so did his family. The thing about having no lights meant that your day rose and set with the sun. Everyone seemed eager to get on the road, but Andy talked them down and handed out assignments to each of them over breakfast. David would drain whatever water was left in the tub into as many plastic bottles as he could. Kathryn would go through the basement again and make sure there was nothing left to eat or drink. Melissa would go through the attic and look for anything useful they may have forgotten. She would then decide what she wanted to bury in the yard of the things that they couldn't bring with them. Andy then asked his wife to please wake him when the radio programming was about to start if he wasn't up already. He also encouraged them all to get as much rest as possible.

"It could be a very long night," he said before heading upstairs for a nap.

ANDY EMERGED FROM the bedroom after a short but blissful sleep. He had dreamed of green fields with forests emerging majestically in the background, so he awoke feeling at peace and completely relaxed. *The calm before the storm?*

His instructions had been carried out to the letter. The children were resting in their rooms, and Melissa was dozing on the couch. He went down and kissed her on the forehead.

"How ya doin'?"

"I'm doin'," Melissa replied, "How you doin'?"

"I'm good," Andy said, looking out the back windows into the yard. "Ready to get this over with."

"I hear ya," Melissa started. "I just want to get there already."

"Yeah, I hope to be pulling up to your parents' road by this time tomorrow," Andy said, sounding hopeful. "What did you come up with to bury in the yard?"

Melissa sat up and looked around, then said, "I looked around everywhere, and, you know, I found not one thing. Everything that really matters to me is going with me, and they can put themselves in the truck all on their own."

Andy knew his wife. He thought he would give her the option just in case there was anything she wanted to stash in the event they were able to ever return.

"I figured that," he said with a smile. "Just thought I'd ask."

"All it takes is the end of the world to filter out what's really important from all the clutter," she said with a smile.

David and Kathryn emerged from their rooms, joining Andy and Melissa in the living room. They began getting the radio set up for the only remaining entertainment left in the world. Much to the children's dismay, that was talk radio. Even they, however, were eager every afternoon to hear what was going on in the world.

As the clock struck 1200, the radio came to life.

"Good morning, everyone. Tommy Rye the Talk Radio Guy here with you again. I hope all is well in your world today. With that, I'll get right to it. No time to waste—we're burnin' diesel, and there's no tellin' what our intrepid producers had to do to get it.

"CAT-MAN has instructed us not to do this, but who listens to them? So we're gonna start as usual with what's new from the ham radio world. I want to thank all our ham radio operators out there for using whatever power you have from batteries and such to keep us informed on what's going on out in the rest of the world. Really, amazing job guys. Keep it up. I'll keep reporting it as long as you keep sending it. Well, that is, until President Keller's Gestapo shuts us down. I'll probably end up in a gulag. Anyway, God bless the First Amendment.

"News from the ongoing situation from the Mexican border is in. Reports have it that Mexican troops are now engaging in firefights with our own troops

A DAY LIKE ANY OTHER

and local volunteers as they attempt to cross into Texas and Arizona. Someone needs to tell them that we're no better off than they are.

"Search and rescue operations continue into the areas of New York and New Jersey that have been flooded out. Refugee camps are full to bursting. Military officials running the operation say that the local population around the refuge centers are pitching in and doing their best to assist in operations, but there are just too many desperate people and not enough resources. We have reports from anonymous sources that CAT-MAN–imposed criteria are adding red tape to the process of getting supplies out to those centers. People are leaving the centers and heading out into the countryside to try and make their own way. God bless, and good luck to them."

"Dad, do you think Uncle Tony and Aunt Mary are OK?" Kathryn asked.

Andy's brother still lived on Long Island, and they had all been extremely concerned about the extended family since they heard about the earthquakes causing floods.

Andy just said, "I'm sure they are fine, Kathryn. They're Lemons, after all."

Andy wished he believed that. From what they had been hearing about the devastation in the New York metropolitan area, Andy was seriously concerned that his entire extended family had been wiped out.

"Let's see," the radio guy continued, papers shuffling in the background. "There are reports of CAT-MAN breaking up another food riot in Chicago, this time using water cannons. At least they didn't start shooting this time. How about feeding people, why don't you try that, jackasses? "The Keller administration has ordered all overseas bases closed and recalled all naval assets. This move has caused some to start settling old scores, i.e., one tribal group against another in several African nations, Christians being hunted down in Egypt, Sunni and Shia Muslims going at it, Russia invading Ukraine ... it goes on and on. I have a whole list here. It would take the rest of the show. Israel has been attacked on all sides—big surprise, right? They seem like they're holding their own, however. No surprise there either. US troops have come under sustained attack in all Afghan provinces. US Central Command says forces are consolidating and preparing to exit the country within the week.

"I see our friendly neighborhood FEMA official has just shown up in the control room, and look! He's brought some CAT-MAN friends. What's up, Jerry?" Tommy Rye asked his producer.

The producer's voice cut in.

"They have a statement from the president that they want us to read."

"Well, let's have it, Jerry. Let's see what our dear leader will have us do today," Tommy Rye said with a sneer in his voice.

The producer could be heard in the background saying, "You're not gonna like it" as he handed the printed statement to the host.

Tommy Rye began to read aloud.

"Blah, blah, blah, 'office of the president,' blah, blah, blah, 'do hereby abolish all personal gun ownership and instruct all gun-owning citizenry to turn in all firearms and ammunition to the nearest CAT-MAN facility immediately. Any failure to comply with this order will result in the forcible confiscation of said firearms and may result in criminal prosecution.'"

Tommy Rye couldn't read anymore.

"Well, there ya have it, folks! Dear leader Keller has just crossed the line into fascism! You've all heard the reports of law-abiding citizens defending themselves against hoodlums and sometimes CAT-MAN hoodlums! What's the matter? Too many of your henchmen getting knocked off by their intended victims?

"I've been sitting on this story because I didn't have enough proof, but it's time you folks out there hear it. I have it on good authority that these CAT-MAN folks have been recruited from all corners of Keller's political machine— the zealots of his party, you know, the dimwitted celebrity types swearing allegiance in internet videos. Except these zealots have no problem pulling a trigger. They're recruits from foreign entities of questionable backgrounds: criminals, anarchy groups, supposed anti-fascist groups (a.k.a. fascists) we've all become familiar with, and so on! And now they want your guns!"

"Dad, what's he talking about?" David asked, looking genuinely concerned.

"The government just took away our right to protect ourselves," Andy replied, putting both hands on his head. "We're leaving just in time."

"HEY! HEY!" the voice from the radio yelled. "Get out of here! Get your hands off me! CAT-MAN bastards!" There was the sound of a scuffle. "The Constitution is dead! Ya ever hear of free speech? I'm being arrested for what, sedition?" More scuffling, then a *thump!* The radio guy could be heard several feet away from the microphone yelling, "This is Tommy Rye the Talk Radio Guy, signing off and heading for the gulag! Good luck America!"

The radio went quiet. Andy and his family sat in stunned amazement.

Andy looked outside, wishing darkness would come quicker and wondering what his country had come to. *One day, there'll be a reckoning. Not today though.*

CHAPTER 16

WASHINGTON, DC

FEMA DIRECTOR WHITING stormed into the presidential offices demanding to see President Keller. He pushed past the president's secretary, then ignored the Secret Service agent posted at the door.

"Mr. President! You cannot do this!"

"Paul!" Keller said, startled by the sudden intrusion.

"Mr. President, you cannot start confiscating people's firearms!" said Whiting, genuinely angry. "You can't make my job any harder than it already is. If you start taking away people's stuff, especially their guns . . . Hell, they already don't trust us, thanks to his people," Whiting said, waving a finger at Sykes, who was seated on a sofa by the president's desk.

"Paul," Keller said, "please come in, have a seat."

"I don't want to sit, Will!"

Whiting had found his courage—finally. In the weeks since The Event, Whiting had seen a lot. He had done his best to bring relief to the people who needed it the most. Unfortunately for him, the need was equally urgent everywhere. He had seen the suffering firsthand. He had seen his requests for support ignored and supplies inexplicably disappear. He had seen the creation of a new agency, presumably to help him accomplish his mission. It had become apparent, however, that CAT-MAN had been created to replace FEMA and that its mysterious new director, this Mr. Sykes, never left the president's side.

"Fine, don't sit, but please calm down," Keller said. "You don't look so good, Paul. Are you losing weight?"

Whiting had lost weight. He had been working day and night to try and make things right.

"I'm sorry, Will. My people are fighting an uphill battle here, and it seems that at every turn, we are being met with resistance of one kind or another. This latest thing is just going to drive more people away. He put you up to this, Will, didn't he?" said Whiting, pointing at Sykes.

"I did what I had to do, Paul," Keller said, leaning forward in his seat. "I understand that this goes against one of our nation's fundamental beliefs, but there are just too many shootings going on. We have to do something." Keller paused for a moment, looking over at Sykes, who was calmly sitting with his legs crossed as if he were enjoying the show. "I am calling for a joint session of Congress tonight, Paul. We will handle this the old-fashioned way. We'll put it to a straight vote—yay or nay. I'll have the Supreme Court justices, the Joint Chiefs—hell, the whole government present. Does that put your mind at ease, Paul?"

"Well," Whiting began, somewhat stunned, "I see you've thought this through, Will."

Whiting was calming down; his face was starting to return to its usual color from the beet red it was when he arrived.

"I'm actually really glad to hear that," he said, with a bit of chuckle in his voice. "Texas and Arizona have already said they would secede with Alabama, Tennessee, New Hampshire, and a dozen other states promising the same if any agency attempted any confiscations."

"There," Keller said, coming to his feet. "You got yourself all worked up over nothing. We'll have this all cleared up this evening. We'll let the people's representatives decide."

"Oh, well, OK then," Whiting said, fixing his comb-over with his right hand. "I'm sorry for barging in like that, Will. I'll see you tonight then."

As he turned to leave, Whiting nodded toward Sykes. "Director Sykes."

Sykes only waved his hand as Whiting left, shutting the door behind him.

"I guess he's gonna be the next one to have a sudden heart attack, right, Mr. Sykes?" Keller said, slumping back down into his chair.

"I don't think so. He's a useful idiot. A great scapegoat," Sykes said, grinning. "This time tomorrow, he won't matter anyway."

"So what are we going to do about this joint session of Congress?" Keller asked, looking exhausted after his altercation with Whiting.

"You just get them all there, and we will do the rest," replied Sykes, smiling from ear to ear.

"You're really enjoying this, aren't you?" Keller said with disdain.

"I love the game, William," Sykes said, leaning back, extending his arms along the back of the couch.

"What game, Sykes?" Keller asked, genuinely confused.

"The game of king-making, William," Sykes replied, smiling again.

A DAY LIKE ANY OTHER

THE SUN HAD set, and Andrew, Melissa, David, Kathryn, and Gomer Pyle Lemon were on their way to what they hoped would be a new life in a safe place. They had spent the rest of the afternoon double-checking the house for anything they had missed, running Andy's quick-reaction drills again, and saying a sad goodbye to Henry and Rose next door. Andy had made good on his promise of water and food to pay for the gas Henry had given him.

The talk radio station had come back on briefly to inform listeners that Tommy Rye had suffered a mental breakdown from all the stress he was under and was taking a break from broadcasting. The anonymous voice on the radio also said that President Keller had called for an emergency joint session of Congress for the purpose of having a vote on the firearms confiscation order issued earlier today.

The voice read a statement from Congresswoman Eleanor Dreyfus from Delaware that stated in part, "I will wholeheartedly support President Keller's action in removing the hazard of privately owned firearms on the streets. This action is long overdue, and it's a shame that it took an act of nature of this magnitude to see it done, finally. Those of us who have worked so hard in the past for a nation safe from gun violence finally feel vindicated." Andy scoffed. The voice promised to come back on the air the minute a final vote tally was available.

They had been zigging and zagging now for three hours, avoiding downed trees, flooded intersections, and well-lit areas that Andy assumed were CAT-MAN occupied. At one point as they topped a hill, they were able to see their local mall-turned-refugee camp. Andy was appalled. They were all speechless. It looked more like a prison camp, surrounded with barbed wire and watchtowers—a tent city larger than anything Andy had ever seen, even in Iraq or Afghanistan.

"Don't ever let us end up someplace like that," Melissa had said as they looked over the monstrosity.

Once they had found the river, the drive seemed to become less nerve-wracking, other than the fact that Andy was driving without any headlights, making it necessary to drive excruciatingly slowly. They had cruised by several surprised pedestrians, whose purpose or intentions for being out in the dead of night Andy could not say, nor did he want to know.

In the distance, Andy could see a bridge silhouetted against the night sky, a dim light shining on this side of the Delaware. Andy figured it to be the New

Hope/Lambertville crossing from Pennsylvania to New Jersey. CAT-MAN was supposedly only dealing with the camps so far, and Andy figured that the military would guard something like a bridge. He stopped the truck and thought about it for a few minutes. *We're not actually crossing the bridge, so we might be able to sneak by unnoticed. They probably don't have the intersection blocked. What point would there be in that if it's the bridge they are protecting? Even if they stop us, I have my story straight: we're bugging out to the in-laws'. Can they blame us? Can't argue with reason.* Andy pressed on slowly, telling his family to stay alert but to keep their weapons hidden the way he had shown them. If this was a CAT-MAN checkpoint, he would hit the headlights and make a run for it. He hoped it wasn't CAT-MAN.

As Andy drove closer to the light, he could see what looked like giant rectangles sitting by the bridge. At first he thought they were shipping containers. He realized quickly that they were armored personnel carriers—Strykers, he recalled.

"They're PA guard," he said out loud, the relief clear in his voice.

As they crossed into the intersection leading past the bridge, Andy thought, *Almost there.*

"HEY!" said a figure standing directly in their path.

Andy, startled, crushed the brakes and stopped just short of hitting whoever was in their way.

"Everyone stay cool," Andy said, trying to take his own advice, despite the adrenaline rush he was now feeling. "Let's see who it is."

As the figure moved to approach the driver's window, the thought of just hitting the gas and taking off flashed through Andy's mind for a moment.

The moment was too long, and the figure was now standing at the driver's window. And they weren't happy.

"What the hell do you think you are doing driving around with no headlights?" said the figure, with a hint of a Hispanic accent.

Andy rolled the window down, thinking, *That's a fair question.* He didn't feel threatened by this man and decided it was safe to talk.

"Evening," Andy said, as though he had just been pulled over by a cop for running a stop sign.

"Evening, my ass! You almost hit me!" said the figure, who Andy could see was an Army lieutenant by the bars on his jacket.

"Yeah," Andy began, "sorry about that, Ell-Tee. We're tryin' to get out of Dodge without attracting any attention."

A DAY LIKE ANY OTHER

"Ell-Tee?" the figure replied, his tone changing at Andy's recognition of his rank. "You military?"

"I retired from the corps about a year ago. Gunnery Sergeant Andrew Lemon at your service, sir," Andy said, saluting. As a Marine, he would not normally salute uncovered and seated, but these were not normal times, and he knew this Army officer would appreciate it. "This is my family—Melissa, David, Kathryn, and Gomer." He pointed toward each of them with his thumb as he named them.

The lieutenant returned Andy's salute and said, "Lieutenant Rodrigo Ramirez, Pennsylvania National Guard, Fifty-Sixth Stryker Brigade Combat Team." He then nodded toward Melissa and the children, saying, "Ma'am" to Melissa and "Hey guys" to the kids in the back seat.

"How's it goin', Lieutenant?" Andy asked, feeling much more at ease with the situation.

"It was going good until some crazy jarhead tried running me over in the middle of the night," Ramirez said with a laugh. "We've been guarding this bridge for a week now, ever since Catastrophe Management took over the refugee camps. We'll be here until people stop trying to get out of Jersey. HQ thinks we'll spend the winter here."

"Are there a lot of displaced people still coming this way?" Andy asked, still holding out hope for his brother and his family.

"Every day, Gunny," Ramirez said, looking down. "They're more and more desperate as the days go by. New Yorkers and Jersey folks, all with the same story. If you were on the second floor or higher in a sturdy building, you were OK. If not, you got washed away. Whole areas totally destroyed, gone. Survivors getting rescued from rooftops. Manhattan is under six feet of water—only way in or out is by boat. They're coming here thinking our camps might be better than the ones closer to the coast. We gather them up here, and CAT-MAN comes and gets them. Poor bastards could have saved themselves a long trip. Our camps are no better than any other."

At that moment, the radio came to life.

"Good evening. Breaking news from Washington!" the same anonymous voice as earlier said, now very excited. "President Keller's executive order banning private gun ownership has passed both houses of Congress and been deemed constitutional by the Supreme Court! Imagine! All in one evening's work! Democracy at its best in these hard times. Americans can sleep easier in their beds knowing they will soon be safe from the roving bands of gun-toting hooligans that have plagued us since The Event."

Andy looked up from the radio and said, "Does that sound right to you, Lieutenant?"

"Not even a little bit, Gunny," Ramirez replied, nodding his head.

"It's a world gone mad," Andy said, looking Lieutenant Ramirez in the eyes.

"Yes, it is," Ramirez replied. He looked down into the cab of the truck at the shotgun that Melissa was not doing a good job keeping concealed. "You better get moving before someone sees you. You want to go unnoticed when traveling around here these days."

"Yeah," Andy began, knowing they had lingered too long, "we have a ways to go. What do you know about the roads north of here?"

Ramirez removed his cover, exposing a close-cropped patch of dark hair that he stroked as he pointed with the other hand toward the north.

"Everything north of here toward the river is clear to Easton. Make your way to Route 611, but stay away from the turnpike—CAT-MAN controls it."

"Thank you, sir," Andy said as he put the truck in gear.

As Lieutenant Ramirez and Andy shook hands through the window, Ramirez said, "One more thing. There have been reports of people getting robbed and even murdered on those rural roads. Be careful."

"Thanks again, Ell-Tee. We'll be alright," Andy said as he started to pull away. "I have fire team Lemon backing me up."

As Andy's truck quickly became invisible in the darkness, Lieutenant Ramirez laughed to himself and thought, *Crazy jarhead. Hope you make it.*

ANDY HAD FOLLOWED Lieutenant Ramirez's suggestions, working his way back to Route 611, but now he was forced to start moving along rural roads through the countryside. Morning was still hours away, and Andy was starting to wonder if he had made a bad decision dragging his family out into the unknown. The danger was increasing with every mile they drove.

"Holy shit!" Andy shouted, braking hard and cutting the wheel to avoid something large blocking the road.

The truck halted, and three sets of headlights turned on, flooding the darkness with blinding light. Andy was blinded. Voices were shouting, "Turn off the vehicle and get out with your hands up."

A DAY LIKE ANY OTHER

Andy's eyes were starting to adjust now, and he saw the object he had avoided was a Jersey barrier. There was another to his front right and another farther away to the left. It was a CAT-MAN checkpoint. The Jersey barriers were set up to force approaching vehicles to slow down to drive through the S-curve they created.

The voices were getting louder and more urgent now.

"Get out of the vehicle, or we will fire!"

Andy saw bullet-riddled cars to his left and right along the roadside. Kathryn was screaming from the back seat, Gomer was barking wildly, and David was shouting "Fuck! Fuck! Fuck!" over and over.

Melissa screamed, then turned to Andy, shouting, "Back up!"

Andy heard her and somehow turned the headlights on and put the truck in reverse simultaneously. The headlights coming on blinded the CAT-MAN officers at the roadblock, much the same way Andy had been at first, and they didn't fire. Andy had the gas pedal to the floor, and the distance from the roadblock was quickly increasing. The CAT-MAN officers' vision was returning, and they began firing. Andy could not see the muzzle flashes since he was turned around looking out the back window, but he could hear the rifles firing and rounds striking the truck. He heard the driver's side mirror explode and saw two bullet holes appear in the back window. At this point, everyone but Andy was screaming.

Andy once again crushed the brakes, fishtailing the truck around so he was looking out the now bullet-riddled windshield. The maneuver was far from movie-stuntman quality, and Andy wasn't sure exactly how he pulled it off, but he had, and they were now speeding off away from the checkpoint. Andy's adrenaline was really pumping. His family had stopped screaming, and Gomer was growling out the back window at the CAT-MAN officer who had stopped firing.

"Is anyone hurt?" Andy shouted.

They all answered pretty much in unison that they were OK.

"Man, I bet we really scared the shit out of those guys," Andy said.

With that, what had been pure terror moments before turned to laughter.

Melissa commented through her laughs, "Oh, yeah, I bet they were crapping their pants. I know I was."

This caused the laughter to increase into hysterics.

"Let's not do that again," Andy said, trying to stifle his own laughs while also trying to get his nerves under control. *I have to be more careful,* he thought, looking at the bullet holes in the windshield. *Any of those could have killed us.*

CHAPTER 17

A RURAL ROAD SOMEWHERE IN UPSTATE PENNSYLVANIA

THE SUN WAS rising. They were making better time as the sun rose higher in the sky. Andy figured they could make it to the farm in less than two hours, barring any more detours or delays. Melissa, who was managing the map, agreed with his assessment. *We're gonna make it,* Andy thought to himself.

"Dad, I have to pee," came Kathryn's voice from the back seat.

"Yeah, I need to go too," David added from directly behind Andy.

"It has been a long time. We could all use a stretch," Melissa agreed, looking at Andy.

Andy grumbled. They were finally making good time. He guessed it wouldn't hurt to stop for a stretch. Up ahead, Andy saw a partially collapsed overpass. Past it, the highway continued on for about half a mile then turned right and went behind a thickly forested area. *That looks pretty safe, I'll stop there,* he thought.

"OK, but be on alert. Everyone check the area before they drop their drawers," Andy said, looking over his shoulder.

"Dad," said Kathryn, as teenage girls do when their dad says something embarrassing.

Melissa laughed and nodded.

David smirked at his sister and laughed under his breath.

"I'm gonna pull up under this overpass. Stay on this side of it!" Andy said, dead serious. "Got it?"

"Got it!" was the reply from his three traveling companions in unison.

Andy brought the truck to a stop under the overpass. The left lane was partially blocked with rubble from the overpass. *Earthquake damage,* Andy thought. The right lane was clear. It appeared that whatever rubble was there had been pushed to the side. Andy threw open the driver's door and stepped out, his AR-15 in hand. He swung the rifle up as he moved to the front of the truck to check the other side of the overpass. Melissa got out and went over into the bushes adjacent to the overpass. David went to the back of the truck, and Kathryn went behind the pile of rubble in the left lane, none of them having any regard for security as Andy had instructed. Fortunately for them, Andy was focused on the bushes to his right, and he thought he saw movement on the backside of the overpass.

"You see something?" David asked, zipping his fly. He had noticed that his dad was focused on something.

"I don't know. Get your rifle and come over here," Andy said, not moving his gaze.

David's face turned serious as he grabbed his AR from the back seat and trotted over to join Andy at the front of the truck.

Upon David's arrival at his side, Andy said, "I need you to watch those bushes, right there up against the overpass. OK?"

"OK," David replied.

"I'm going up and over to have a look from up top," Andy said as he moved to run around the backside of the truck.

As he ran past and headed up the overpass berm, Melissa said, "What's going on?"

"I thought I saw something! Get your shotgun and get over there next to David," Andy replied in a half whisper as he ran.

Andy topped the overpass and crossed the roadway to the other side in seconds. He raised his weapon and leaned out to look down the opposite side into the suspicious bushes.

"DON'T SHOOT!" came a panicked voice from below.

Andy could see that behind the bushes was a depression of some sort, maybe a drainage catch basin. He couldn't tell. Within the depression were a dozen dirty faces looking up at him, the fear in their eyes shocking to Andy. He lowered the weapon.

"DON'T SHOOT! We don't want any trouble!" came the voice again. It was a tall, slender man with a white beard. His hands were up over his head, and the look on his face was desperate.

"All of you get up on the road! Right now!" Andy said forcefully. He had to make sure there was no threat.

As the group began to move out of the bushes, it became obvious to Andy that these people had been sheltering here. An old, beat-up brown tarp was all they had to protect themselves. He felt the chill of the coming winter already in the air, and he felt bad for these people, some of them children. Andy assessed each of them as they made their way up onto the road surface in front of the truck. There were three adult men, one of whom was obviously injured and had to be supported by the other two to walk. There were two adult women and an assortment of children ranging in age from fourteen to an infant in the arms of one of the women.

By the time they were all on the road, Andy was sure they were not a threat. He moved down the berm into their "camp." They had nothing but the tarp. Andy wondered how they had come to this.

"David! Get a case of water out of the back for these people," Andy said as he emerged from the bushes and headed to join the assembled refugees.

"Who are you people?" Andy asked as he approached. "Did you spend the night here?"

"Oh, thank you!" said the bearded man. "My name is Hank Johnson. This is my wife, Frances. This is our family, and these folks are the Taylors—Mike and Lois and their kids."

"What are you doing out here in the middle of nowhere?" Andy asked, shaking Hank's hand.

"We were heading north yesterday afternoon. We got around that corner"—he pointed toward where the highway turned right, about a half mile ahead—"when all of a sudden, a big box truck pulled out and blocked the road. These four guys came from all sides and stuck guns in our faces. They robbed us. Took everything we had. Same thing happened to the Taylors. They drove right by us, but we couldn't stop them."

"We didn't see them in the bushes. We don't blame them for hiding," said Mike Taylor. "They shot through the door and hit Uncle Charlie when he couldn't get the door open fast enough," he continued, referring to the injured man whom Melissa and Kathryn were now kneeling over, examining his wounded leg. "They took everything. Even the baby food. These people are ruthless."

Andy looked up toward the bend in the road and thought, *So close. We're almost there.* Still looking down the road, Andy asked, "Do you think they're still there?"

"Probably. From what I saw, they were camped there," said Hank.

"Well," Andy started, "if I were them, I'd be watching us right now. Let's get everyone off the road and to the other side of the overpass. Melissa, kids, let's get these people some food and blankets while we figure out what we're going to do."

As the Lemons' new friends settled down with the case of MREs that Andy felt they needed more than he did, he and Melissa got out the map as David watched the road in the direction of the robbers, binoculars in hand.

"What do you think?" Andy said in a low tone to Melissa.

"It's a long way around to get past this intersection and back to the farm," Melissa said, tracing the route they would have to take to get past the danger ahead.

"And we don't know what's on those roads," Andy said.

After the close call with the CAT-MAN roadblock, he wanted to get this trip done as soon as possible. They might not get so lucky next time. Andy remembered the bullet-riddled cars. The CAT-MAN roadblocks were death traps. Andy believed the only reason they hadn't started firing immediately was because Andy had surprised them—having no headlights on had given them no warning. He wasn't going to chance it. He felt he had better odds dealing with these bandits.

"What are you thinking?" Melissa said, looking up from the map. "I don't like that look."

"It's a long, uncertain way around this," Andy said, looking at his son, who was now obviously listening to their conversation. "These people are stuck out here with nothing and all these kids." Andy gestured toward the group huddled together under the Lemons' blankets.

"Andrew. I don't like the sound of that," Melissa said, keeping her voice down but her intensity elevated.

"There's only one option," Andy said, looking away as he turned to address the Taylors and the Johnsons.

"Hey folks," Andy started, "you guys wanna get your stuff back?"

"How we gonna do that?" Lois said, bouncing her baby as she fed it MRE applesauce.

Andy turned and looked toward his family, which was now assembled by the truck, watching and listening.

"We're gonna take it back. It's still early. If we're lucky, they're still sleeping, but if not, we still have the element of surprise."

Hank looked over at Mike. Andy felt Hank was game but wanted to see Mike's reaction.

Satisfied by a nod from Mike, Hank said, "We're in, but there's four of them and only three of us."

"Hey!" David said from his post by the truck. "There's four of us."

A DAY LIKE ANY OTHER

Melissa's face went pale, but she didn't react, not wanting to cause a scene.

Andy was counting on David being part of the plan, but he also knew he would have to sell Melissa on the idea.

"OK then, let's get you guys armed up," Andy said.

Andy retrieved the shotguns from the truck and handed them, along with two pouches full of shotgun shells, to Hank and Mike.

"You guys know how to use these?" Andy asked, making sure Melissa couldn't hear.

They both answered that they did. Andy then proceeded to the back of the truck and pulled the hunting rifle from its case. He turned to hand it to Melissa, who was standing there staring at him. It was more like she was staring *through* him.

Before Andy could speak, Melissa was in his face, talking slowly and firmly.

"What exactly do you think you're doing?"

"We need to get through, and these people are desperate. There's no other way," Andy said, softer than his wife but just as convincing. She wasn't convinced.

"What about David? He's just a boy!"

"He grew up the minute the lights went out. It's a whole new world now," Andy replied, stone-faced. "I need someone I can count on to watch my back, Melissa. I don't like it either, but this is where we are. I need your help too."

He handed her the hunting rifle.

ANDY HAD POSITIONED Melissa on the overpass against the guardrail so as not to be observed. She would watch over the road and woods in the distance from there. Her chances of hitting anything at that range were unlikely, but she could watch and warn Andy via handheld radio if any of the bad guys came into her view. It would also fall to her to stop anyone trying to come toward the overpass if they escaped Andy and his group. She wasn't happy with any of this, but Andy was right. She had given Andy a kiss and then David, telling him, "Be careful and do what Dad tells you." She now watched through the rifle scope for anything moving down the highway and said a silent prayer that those people were gone.

Andy, David, Mike, and Hank had circled around through the woods, taking a route that no one watching from the north could see. They now found themselves on the reverse slope of a small hill opposite where the men who robbed Hank and Mike should have their camp. Andy crawled up the bank and the others followed—David to his left, Mike to his right, and Hank to the right of Mike. As they came to the top, they could see the box truck positioned to pull out onto the highway quickly, just as Hank had described. There was a campfire going and what looked like some kind of pot set over it on a grate. Two tents were nearby, as well as three vehicles. Andy assumed Hank's and Mike's vehicles were among them.

A moment later, Andy saw a man emerge from one of the tents and begin talking to another man. Andy couldn't see him but assumed he was in front of the box truck. He thought he heard the man by the tent ask, "Are they still just sitting there?" They had been watching them, but it didn't seem for very long, as they were still waking up. Andy was convinced now that he had done the right thing.

He looked at David and then at Mike and Hank and whispered, "OK, David, when we go down there, you cover the other side of that truck so no one gets behind us. Hank and Mike, stay with me just like you are. Don't get ahead of or behind me. If I stop, you stop. If I run, you run. If I start shooting, you start shooting. That being said, no one fires unless they absolutely have to. Everyone ready?"

David whispered, "Ready."

Mike and Hank both muttered, "Ready."

Andy took a deep breath and said, "Let's go." He stood and rushed toward the little camp that lay only twenty-five yards away.

The man who had been emerging from the tent was now standing by the fire. Two other men were standing by the other tent—one was putting on a jacket, and the other appeared to still be waking up by the way he was stretching. Andy assumed the fourth man was still in front of the truck. The man by the fire began to look in their direction, so he must have seen them as they emerged from the forest.

Andy yelled, "GET ON THE GROUND! GET ON THE GROUND! GET ON THE GROUND!"

Closing the distance as quickly as he could, he held his rifle in front of him and trained it on the man by the fire. Andy could feel each footstep as he ran. He felt as though his heart would burst, but everything around him was more vivid than he had ever experienced before in his life—the smell of the forest, the dampness of the air, the sound of his own voice. Yet it seemed like an eternity, like time was standing still in the moment it took to run a few yards.

A DAY LIKE ANY OTHER

The man by the fire was startled and staggered backward, and the two men by the tent, equally startled, jumped in place as if the ground had suddenly thrown them into the air. The man who had been putting his coat on suddenly drew a pistol from his coat pocket and pointed it at Andy and the others as they charged toward him. Andy saw and fired as he ran, hitting the man several times in the torso. The man clutched his arms in front of himself and spun around to the right. The second man by the tent was no longer sleepily stretching and had picked up some kind of rifle from just inside the tent. Andy fired and hit him as well, and he fell backward, landing inside the tent, his feet sticking out of the opening. Andy heard gunshots to his right and then more gunshots to his left.

The entire scene had taken less than ten seconds, the time it takes to run twenty-five yards on a full adrenaline rush. Andy stopped running when he got to the fire and took a knee to collect his thoughts.

Andy quickly assessed the situation. Hank and Mike were right there beside him, and David was standing by the back of the truck, exactly where Andy had instructed him to go. They all seemed OK. The man who had fallen into the tent was not moving, and the rifle he had picked up lay across him diagonally. The other man Andy shot had spun around and landed on the hood of one of the cars behind the tent; he, too, was motionless. The man who was by the fire had been shot by Hank and Mike simultaneously and was very obviously dead by the amount of damage sustained by his chest and abdomen. *Two shotgun blasts at close range will do a lot of damage,* Andy thought.

Finally, satisfied the threat had been neutralized, Andy said, "Is everyone alright?"

Hank said, "OK," still pointing his shotgun at the dead man in front of him.

Mike said, "Yeah, yeah, I'm OK." He had lowered his shotgun and was staring at the man he had just shot, looking like he might vomit.

"David! You OK?" he asked, turning his attention toward his son, who was still standing by the back of the truck.

Andy felt a brief moment of panic as he came to his feet and ran to his son's side. Arriving at the back of the box truck, Andy saw that David was staring at a motionless body lying in the tall grass beside the truck's front tire.

"Are you alright?" Andy said, somewhat irritated, more from fear that his son was injured than from his not responding.

"I shot him," David said, still staring at the body.

Seeing that David was OK but visibly shaken, Andy softened his tone. "You did what you had to do. You did what I told you to do."

"He was gonna shoot you. He was leaning over the hood of the truck. He was gonna shoot you. So I shot him," David said, his voice almost robotic.

"That's why I needed you to come. To watch my back," Andy said, slapping his son on the back.

"Is everything OK? We heard shooting! Are you guys OK?" It was Melissa on the hand-held radio.

Andy took the radio from his jacket pocket, keyed the mic, and said, "Yeah, we're all OK. Gather everyone and everything and drive on up."

"Oh, thank God," came Melissa's voice from the radio.

Andy had led his first bona fide assault. It was on four unsuspecting hoodlums who had meant to rob them if they had gotten the chance and who were preparing to do just that. Had Kathryn not requested to make a bathroom stop, they would have driven right into an ambush, and Andy and his family could quite possibly have ended up sharing that tarp with the Taylors and the Johnsons. Or worse, they could have been shot like Uncle Charlie or dead like these poor bastards. Andy had been lucky again, saved this time by his daughter's full bladder. They had overcome in the end, and that wasn't luck; he had led these amateurs and won. His son had stepped up and most likely saved his dad's life.

Andy would have to watch David over the next few days since he didn't know how his son would deal with taking a life. For that matter, Andy didn't know how he would deal with taking a life either.

ANDY AND HIS family said their goodbyes to their new friends, who were eternally grateful. Uncle Charlie said, shaking Andy's hand, "I'll repay you somehow. One day, you'll see." They had swept the camp and, once the Taylors and the Johnsons had reclaimed their stuff, found a large stash of what they presumed was stolen property, which was split three ways. They all took their share, promising to use it to help anyone they might find along the rest of their journeys. They felt funny taking something that was previously stolen. Hank and Mike said they would deal with the bodies since Andy and his family had done enough already and sent them on their way.

As Andy drove away, he remembered the scene of his decision to attack those men. The way his family had stood watching him. It was the scene from his dream. He hadn't realized it until now. That was the second time that had happened, and he felt a little freaked out. At the same time, he was comforted, thinking, *Maybe there's someone watchin' out for us after all, a higher plan.* He was also struck by the realization that if they had arrived at that place half an hour earlier, while it was still dark, they would have driven right by, unnoticed. The robbers would have been asleep in their tents, and the Taylors and the Johnsons would have been huddled under their tarp. He wondered how many similar scenes he had driven past in the preceding hours of traversing backroads under the cover of darkness. It's like they were meant to stop right there, at that exact moment. They had helped some good people in need and had ended some bad people. He felt remorseful for killing those men and was concerned for David, who hadn't said much since the firefight. Andy felt in his heart, though, that what they had done was justified and put it out of his mind for now. As he drove, he felt like things were going to be OK in the end. He hadn't felt that way for a long time. He looked in the rear-view mirror at his children and thought, *There's the future. Keep it safe.*

CHAPTER 18

UPSTATE PENNSYLVANIA, THE TAFTS' FARM

ANDY AND HIS family had arrived at Melissa's parents' place without any further incidents. Ed and Christine were shocked and surprised by the sudden arrival in their front yard of their only child and her family, yet thankful. They had been getting news from the outside via Ed's ham radio and stories from passing strangers headed north and west. The stories they told were horrific and disturbing to the Tafts, and to know that Melissa, Andy, and the grandkids were living through it was maddening. To have them arrive as they did was the best surprise they could have ever wished for; their babies were all back and safe. Dr. Taft hugged Andy like he had never hugged another man before in his life and, with tears in his eyes, thanked him for bringing his baby girl back to him.

Andy chose not to tell his in-laws about the firefight on the highway. As Andy thought about it more, he realized it was more like a massacre; those guys had no chance and never even got a shot off. He feared the doctor, being somewhat of a pacifist, wouldn't fully understand why they did what they did. Nor did he want to tell them their sixteen-year-old grandson had killed a man. There would be time for all that later, but right now, Andy just wanted everyone to enjoy this most joyous reunion. He did, however, have no choice but to tell him about their escape from the CAT-MAN roadblock. The truck had sustained multiple bullet holes. Dr. Taft couldn't help but notice the exploded mirror, and the holes in the windshield were hard to overlook.

Despite Andy explaining the scene and describing the condition of the cars around the roadblock, Dr. Taft, always the optimist, suggested the CAT-MAN officers must have been startled half to death the way Andy had just suddenly appeared there. Why else would they just start shooting the way they had? Andy felt himself getting frustrated and almost shouted, "Look! You weren't there!" He, instead, took a deep breath and changed the subject. Dr.

A DAY LIKE ANY OTHER

Taft hadn't experienced the world outside yet and couldn't completely comprehend its brutality, so Andy would let it go for now. He wasn't going to get into an argument with his father-in-law right now, and he absolutely didn't need anyone second-guessing his decisions. He was doing enough of that all on his own.

Over the next few days, the story of their lives in the weeks past was shared. Though the Tafts had been safe and fed thanks to Ed's obsession with preparedness, they had been worried sick and wondered if they would ever see their family again. In the coming weeks, it would become clear that Dr. Taft's decision to leave his comfortable life behind for this new, simpler life would save them all. His ham radio was proving quite useful as well, keeping them informed on the crumbling world outside the little safe haven they had created. Stories were circulating about CAT-MAN atrocities, about ham radio operators who were caught passing on such stories having their equipment smashed, and about anyone else who spoke out against Catastrophe Management or President Keller suddenly disappearing. There were stories about gun owners getting into shootouts with government officials who came to their doors wanting their firearms, presumably turned in by their neighbors for the price of some extra rations. Most people were just hiding their firearms in the hopes no one would turn them in. Andy told his father-in-law about the shootout in the house the night he had decided to leave and head north. Dr. Taft only said, "Hmmm, it's a lucky thing you weren't killed."

Andy and his family had settled into their house, the house Dr. Taft had built for them on his property about five hundred yards from his home. He loved having his family around him, and he proved it when he had had the little three-bedroom cottage built for his daughter's family. There was a good stock of food and several sources of water. What they all appreciated the most was having electricity. The initial power surge from The Event had knocked Ed's solar array offline, but he had installed several layers of protection in his circuit and was able to get the power back on quickly. When Andy had asked him why he had installed such expensive and sophisticated fail-safes, Dr. Taft had scratched his head and said, "I don't know really, just seemed like the thing to do."

On the day before Thanksgiving, an SUV came driving up the private road that was more or less a very long driveway to the Tafts' farm. Andy was in the bedroom and became aware of the vehicle by the sound of the gravel crunching under its wheels. Not knowing what to expect and being on high alert since the world had gone to shit, Andy opened the window enough to allow him to track the vehicle through the scope of his hunting rifle, which he kept next to the window. As the vehicle approached, Dr. and Mrs. Taft emerged from their front door, something Andy had already told them several times since he'd been here was a bad idea. Christine had said, "It's just rude not to greet guests when they arrive," to which Ed nodded and said, "We have no enemies here. It's OK, Andrew." Andy thought now, *Hope you guys are right.*

As the SUV came to a stop, Andy clicked the rifle's safety off and focused in on the driver's-side door, which was exactly where his father-in-law was headed. Andy thought, *This guy has no idea.* As the driver's door opened, Andy saw a giant of a man step out and knew exactly who had arrived, which was confirmed as Dr. Taft rushed toward the giant and took him in an embrace that more resembled a child hugging an adult than two grown men embracing.

As Andy raced down the stairs and headed for the door, he called to his family, "Come on, everyone! Uncle Sasquatch is here!"

FRANCISCO EDUARDO VASQUEZ (Gunnery Sergeant, United States Marine Corps, retired) was a mountain of a man. Standing over six foot seven inches, he was an impressive sight. Tall and large framed but not overly muscular, with a thick layer of black hair atop his giant head, thick eyebrows, and the obvious lack of a neck, his first staff non-commissioned officer had dubbed him "Sasquatch," referring to the mythical hairy ape man of the Pacific Northwest. Thus, Sasquatch, Squatch for short, was his name henceforth and forever more. He and Andy had met as young men starting their lives in the corps and had become fast friends. Over the many years of their respective careers, they had remained the closest of friends and were more like family.

Gunny Vasquez had retired eight months after Andy did and was just beginning his new life in the civilian world when The Event occurred. He and his wife María, daughters Donna (age fifteen) and Susanna (age eleven), and son Miguel (age nine) had settled in the suburbs outside of Fort Dix, New Jersey, his last duty station. Like Andy, he had done multiple trips to Iraq and Afghanistan as a member of the Marine Aircraft Wing. He was glad to be done with that and at the same time wished he could go back.

At the time of The Event, Sasquatch had just started a new job as a contractor on the base. After The Event, he had pitched in with refugee relief, doing what he could to help the masses of people flooding in from coastal areas that had been destroyed by the tsunami and earthquakes. He told Andy and Dr. Taft how every day, people had come by the hundreds and then the thousands. He told them how FEMA had quickly become overwhelmed and Catastrophe Management people had started showing up, treating people like livestock rather than human beings. He spoke of altercations between FEMA, the military, and CAT-MAN over the distribution of food that resulted in CAT-MAN basically pulling rank and shutting down all distribution until the opposition relented. One such altercation had resulted in his temper getting the better of him, and Sasquatch had actually picked up a CAT-MAN officer and thrown him into a dumpster.

It was soon after that incident that he had decided that he and his family could no longer stay there. Too many refugees had been showing up, there had already been two food riots, and desperate people had "escaped" from the camps and scavenged through the surrounding neighborhoods for anything they could find, sometimes using force to take what they needed. CAT-MAN had put up barbed wire fences and guard towers, and they had shot people trying to leave if they hadn't stopped when challenged. Even so, they had been getting out and creating a difficult situation for the entire area. Sasquatch wasn't confident in his family's safety there anymore. Like Andy, he had to make a choice, so he had decided to take his chances on the road. He knew that he would be welcomed at the farm, as he and his family had spent many weekends there with the Lemons and Tafts. He had become very close with the Tafts, sometimes visiting even if Andy and his family couldn't make it. He would refer to the Tafts as his "new age, silver-haired, hippie mom and dad." Dr. and Mrs. Taft loved the Vasquezes as well, and they loved most of all having all of them together: the Lemons and Vasquezes and all their children. They relished the idea that their already beautiful family had grown.

The Vasquez family, much like Andy's crew, had tried to travel at night. Sasquatch had not thought to blackout the taillights with tape. (He told Andy, "Man! That's sick! Why didn't I think of that?") They too had encountered military personnel on the road and had had no problem getting past them using the same tactics Andy had. They were all members of the same club, after all. The National Guardsmen had also directed them around any CAT-MAN roadblocks and checkpoints, just as Lieutenant Ramirez had directed Andy. They had not encountered any highway robbers or CAT-MAN checkpoints as Andy had.

It was only when they were alone that Andy told his friend of the shooting on the road and of David's shooting one of the bad guys as he was about to shoot Andy.

Sasquatch responded, "Damn! That's one hard little dude."

Andy asked his friend not to say anything to the Tafts and if he would keep an eye on David, as he wasn't sure how he was dealing with it.

"You got it, bro," Sasquatch replied with a nod of his head.

Sasquatch asked if Andy had heard from Wally, who made up the final piece of their "trio of trouble," as Mrs. Taft referred to them. Andrew Lemon, Francisco Vasquez, and Walter (Wally) Childs had earned that reputation from many an exploit in the various adventures they had shared. Though Wally was younger than Andy and Sasquatch, he was accepted into the family, first as a younger sibling needing to be looked after, then growing into a full-fledged member of the group.

Andy had not heard from Wally since receiving the call that Wally's fiancée, Amanda, who had also been a Marine, had been killed in Afghanistan by a rocket attack on Bagram airfield six months ago. At the time, Wally had been stationed at Quantico, Virginia, as a member of HMX-1, the presidential helicopter squadron, as an air crewman. Andy had known that Wally was a mess and said he was coming down immediately. Wally had just said, "Thanks Andy, I got it, I'm OK. The chaplain is here, and the command is sending over a psychiatrist. It's all good, man. She went out with her boots on. We should all be proud of her."

Andy, out of concern for his friend, had gotten in contact with Wally's bosses and asked what the real deal was. They had said it was bad and that Wally was going to spend some time at Walter Reed Army Medical Center for a few days. Andy regretted not going to see his friend, but the command had said not to on recommendation from the psychiatrist. Andy wondered where his friend was and if he was alright, and he once again felt that regret. Sasquatch, seeing Andy's face change, said, "Man! I'm sure he's fine! Probably livin' it up on government-provided psychedelic meds, man. Wish I had some right now! The world's lost its mind!" They both laughed and agreed that they would see their friend again one day.

It was decided that Sasquatch and María would bunk with Tafts, as they had an extra bedroom, Donna and Susanna would share Kathryn's room, and Miguel would bunk with David at the Lemons' cottage. As they all sat down to Thanksgiving dinner, Andy looked around the Tafts' dining room table at

A DAY LIKE ANY OTHER

the faces of his most beloved, and he almost forgot about the world gone mad. Winter was coming, but they were safe. His family was safe. His friends were safe. They had plenty of food thanks to Dr. Taft's new lifestyle. They were far away from the masses of hungry, desperate people, from CAT-MAN, from the uncertainty and danger. He thought to himself, *I have been blessed. We will start over, right here. A new beginning with those whom I love.*

CHAPTER 19

UPSTATE PENNSYLVANIA, THE TAFTS' FARM

As the days grew colder and the first snow of winter began to fall, the Lemon, Taft, and Vasquez families settled into their new arrangements. Dr. Taft assigned everyone an area of responsibility.

"Just because it's winter doesn't mean there isn't work to do," he said when all the children groaned at his announcing the work assignments.

He also knew it was important to keep everyone busy. Cabin fever was a sickness he had a cure for: hard work. He also had one of the adults assigned to monitor the ham radio. There was information coming in every day, and he didn't want to miss any of it. This was another way to keep morale up. It turned into a great source of entertainment as well, with the children giving nightly news reports of the day's incoming radio traffic. All that was suitable for general consumption, that is.

There was a lot of chatter about the hardships of the FEMA camps and CAT-MAN strong-arm tactics. There were more reports of ham radio operators being tracked down, then shut down if the government didn't like what they were saying—specifically, if they contradicted the news and information reports being put out over the conventional radio channels, all of which were now under the direct control of Catastrophe Management. Andy remembered how Tommy Rye had been removed while on the air, and he wondered what became of him.

The ham radio operators started referring to the government broadcasts as "Keller's daily propaganda reports." Every day, the government-provided host—most assumed they were CAT-MAN cronies—would come on and tell of the wonderful conditions in the camps. Of how many tons of relief supplies were delivered to this camp or that camp, or of power being restored to certain areas, and that everyone should be patient because repair crews would be coming to their area soon. Before the government broadcasts were even finished, the ham radio set would start going crazy with people contradicting the government's claims.

"I live within a thousand yards of that camp, and they haven't had a delivery in three weeks! I know because my street is the only one the trucks can use to get through!" one excited operator said following a report.

Others would say, "If power is restored to this area, they must have skipped my house. Sure wish it was. I'm almost out of gas, and I don't know how much longer I'll be able to keep broadcasting."

The government was reporting that Congress had voted to stay in Washington through the winter to make sure the peoples' voices would continue to be heard. Sequestering themselves into the Capitol Building and sending their staff home, claiming this would streamline the process, they would use CAT-MAN assets to assist in the daily workings of government.

Civilian reports, supposedly gained from leaks within the government, said that Congress, along with the Joint Chiefs, the president's cabinet, and all the Supreme Court justices, were actually being held in the Capitol Building under CAT-MAN guard. They said that President Keller had appointed himself king and was holding the rest of the government hostage, their presumed compliance giving his orders legitimacy. This claim caused quite an argument, even among the ham radio crowd. For some, it was too outlandish to believe that a president, even one as far left as William Keller, would so blatantly disregard the Constitution and take power so completely from the people. The argument went on for days and would reignite every time another order came out of Washington.

Andy and Dr. Taft had a heated argument after an order came out instructing citizens to report their neighbors for violating any presidential order and offering a reward for turning in anyone still possessing a firearm. Dr. Taft was insisting that there were too many guns out there, to which Andy disagreed vehemently. After an hour of back and forth, the conversation became heated.

Andy blurted out, "If it wasn't for private gun ownership, we never would have made it here!"

Dr. Taft became quiet and asked, "What do you mean by that? What happened?"

Andy then recounted the events on the highway and the previous home invasion that had prompted Andy to risk the road in the first place. Andy left out the part about David saving him and arming Melissa with a sniper rifle to cover their backs. He could see by the look on his father-in-law's face that, though they had heard many horror stories, this one hit too close to home.

The conversation ended, but not before Andy told Ed, "The day may come that you need to pick up a gun to protect your family. You should think very carefully about that."

Sometime in mid-February, amid government claims of CAT-MAN successes in all areas and the continued expansion of the agency, the call went out for more volunteers. The ham radio network went ballistic again, claiming that several states had officially separated from the United States, jailing CAT-MAN officers and swearing to defend their borders from any more coming in.

Stories of disease and sickness running rampant through the camps were common. In some states, urban areas were firmly under government control, while rural areas just a few miles away were a toss-up between safe areas controlled by locals or no-go zones controlled by criminals. Some on the radio net theorized that CAT-MAN's call for more manpower and promise of reward to turn in neighbors was a call to the criminal element to move on its more peaceful neighbors.

It was also during this period that Andy started having recurring disturbing dreams again. This time, the dream began with him trying to make his way through a blinding blizzard, and in the distance, he could hear muffled moans and cries. His first thought was, *It's the wind*. As the blizzard subsided, he found himself standing on a hillside looking out over a valley, and on the valley floor was what looked like a city, but he couldn't tell for sure because of the snow still swirling around. Something didn't look right, though. He glanced down and was startled by a man sitting at his feet. The man was wretched looking, covered in filth. His face was thin and drawn, his eyes were sunken, and his body was frail. Andy looked up from this poor, pathetic human being to see that the snowstorm had cleared from the valley, revealing that what he thought was a city was really a refugee camp, much like the one they had seen as they had made their escape all those months ago. But this camp went on as far as the eye could see. The wails and lamentations he had been hearing were coming from this camp.

Andy looked back at the man to find him standing in his face, startling Andy again. The man looked directly into Andy's eyes and said, "Free them!" The force in his voice did not match the frail face it came from. Andy attempted to speak but could not; he attempted to back away but could not move. The man put his face closer to Andy's and said, "Free them! Help will come!" Andy

A DAY LIKE ANY OTHER

felt a panic coming over him, and he wanted to run, looking around for a way to escape this walking skeleton. Andy looked back at the man who seemingly had him captive in his own dream. "GO!" the man yelled in Andy's face. Andy, finally free, stumbled backward to the ground. Upon hitting the ground, Andy woke up and thought, *Here we go again.*

CHAPTER 20

UPSTATE PENNSYLVANIA, THE TAFTS' FARM

As the winter snow began to melt and the first signs of spring began to show themselves, everyone at the Tafts' farm started to feel more spring fever than cabin fever. Dr. Taft was excited to see seedlings sprouting in the greenhouse from the seeds he and the children had planted. He said, "Look everyone! We will eat next winter too!" He was right, of course. That was the life they were all to live now. Things had changed, and Andy thought it was for the better in some ways.

Andy was still troubled by his latest recurrent dream. He had been awakened every night for weeks now. He had discussed it with Melissa at length, and they both agreed that based on his previous dream, this new nightly torment meant something. Andy felt that he was being directed to go back south toward Philadelphia and that maybe if he did, more pieces to this latest riddle might fall into place. Melissa tried to argue that he should stay put here because the man in the dream said help would come. Of course, she also didn't want Andy to leave, especially not to go back into that mess of a world outside their little farmstead.

The ham radio chatter was increasing as quickly as the temperature was. Talk of scientists disappearing and military officers (the few who still remained on duty) being required to report for retraining in refugee operations if they wanted to remain on active duty fueled the conspiracy theories. Talk of CAT-MAN officers with heavy foreign accents led some to speculate that President Keller was selling the country out to foreign interests while his countrymen were starving. Those who hadn't gone to seek refuge in a camp and somehow survived the winter were now being subjected to searches of their premises by CAT-MAN officers without warrants, under the pretense they were searching for illegal firearms and other contraband. The definition of other contraband basically meant anything the CAT-MAN officers felt like taking. Enraged

A DAY LIKE ANY OTHER

homeowners had no recourse but to endure the searches since any local police who still remained on duty were trumped by the CAT-MAN authority. Residents began hiding their few remaining valuables along with their guns and food.

The horror stories coming out of the camps were too disturbing to believe. There were no official reports from the government, and the daily news reports kept painting a merry picture that contradicted private accounts. Those who did escape the camps told of starvation and sickness. Diseases that America hadn't seen in generations were now running rampant. Cholera, the plague, tuberculosis, and typhus were some of the torments. Other more common illnesses like tetanus, influenza, and botulism were claiming lives due to inadequate medication supplies and poor sanitation conditions. If the stories were to be believed, people were dying by the thousands inside the camps alone. There was no way to count what kind of death toll there was outside the camps, where it was more or less the Wild West with a sprinkling of CAT-MAN harassment.

As Andy, Sasquatch, and David set out one morning on their first hunting expedition of the spring, Andy told Sasquatch about the dream and his feeling that he should head south to see what he could discover. As they walked, Andy spoke quietly to his giant friend, as he hadn't told David yet and didn't want him to know, since he might influence Andy's decision.

"If you head south, then I'm going with you," Sasquatch said, looking off into the distance, searching for game. "You're my bro! Someone's gotta watch your back."

"Thanks, I was hopin' you'd say that," Andy said, glancing over his shoulder at David, who was looking off to the left.

"What do you think it means?" asked Sasquatch. "Creepy shit," he added with a shiver.

"I'm not sure," Andy began as he stopped to look through the scope of his hunting rifle, "but if it's another premonition of the damn future, then we're in for another wild ride."

"Regardless, if you go, I go," Sasquatch said, raising his AR to look in the same direction as Andy. "If it weren't for you guys, we'd probably be in a camp somewhere, or worse."

"It means a lot, brother," Andy said, facing his friend. "I'm glad you're here."

"Yeah, man," Sasquatch replied.

Andy stopped, turning to David, and said, "You guys stay here. I'm gonna go up the trail a bit and take a look."

David and Sasquatch nodded and sat down on a fallen tree trunk, watching as Andy proceeded up the trail. David had his shotgun across his lap.

After a time, Sasquatch said, "Your dad told me about what you did at the overpass."

"Yeah," David said, looking up at his Uncle Sasquatch. "What did he tell you?"

He loved the giant man like family and had only ever known him as "uncle." David liked that Uncle Sasquatch had always treated him like a man and talked to him as an equal.

"He said you did exactly what you were told. You went right where your dad told you to, you held your corner, and you shot that dude," Sasquatch said with pride in his voice. "You don't have no regrets about it, neither. If you hadn't killed that guy, your dad would be dead. Then we'd all be up shit's creek."

"Yeah," David said, looking down. "He told you that?"

"He's proud of you, little dude," Sasquatch said, looking down at David.

"Yeah?" David said, returning his gaze to his uncle.

"Yeah," Sasquatch replied.

David looked away and said, "If you guys head back down south, I'm going with you."

"And you have incredible hearing too," Sasquatch said, smiling. "That's up to your dad. And your mom! She's gonna have a cow at that one!"

"Yeah, probably," David said with a smile. "She still thinks I'm a kid."

"She's a mom. That's what they do." Sasquatch was still grinning.

"Can I ask you a question?" David said, seemingly wanting to change the subject.

"Yeah man, ask away."

"Does Donna have a boyfriend back home?" David asked, his voice cracking.

"Dude," Sasquatch began, whipping his head around to look down at David. His tone had suddenly changed to that of an angry Dad. "It's the end of the damn world, and now I got to worry about your hormones being around my oldest daughter?"

"Um! I-I mean—" David said, flustered and embarrassed.

"Calm down, dude. Calm down," Sasquatch said, laughing. "I'm just messin' with you. No, she don't have a boyfriend."

"Oh! You scared me for a second there," David said, holding one hand to his chest.

A DAY LIKE ANY OTHER

"I'm a dad. That's what I do," Sasquatch said, smiling wide. "She's just like her mother. You may want to rethink this; María is scary, bro."

They were both laughing at Sasquatch's ding on his wife as Andy walked back up the trail toward them and said, "You guys havin' a party up here? You're gonna scare all the game away."

Their attention turned back toward the house as they heard a gunshot off in the distance, then another and another. Sasquatch stood and turned, as did David.

Andy said, "What would they be shooting at?"

Not another word was said as all three took off in a full sprint back toward the farm.

As they ran the one hundred yards or so back to the edge of the woods, several more shots rang out. Andy thought, *The first two were from a shotgun, the third was a pistol, and the rest were a mix of several different weapons all firing at the same time. My God, it's a firefight!* The thought of his girls in a firefight caused him to run even faster, passing Sasquatch and David.

Andy arrived at the wood's edge first and stopped, raising his rifle to look through the scope. David and Sasquatch dashed past him, headed for the house, both still in a full sprint. He could see an SUV of some kind parked in front of his cottage, the front facing him. He'd never seen it before. He saw one man lying by the passenger side, clutching his stomach, and a second man was lying face down by the front steps not moving. A third man, who appeared injured as well, was staggering around the front of the vehicle, headed for the driver's side. As Andy's attention turned to the fourth man, who was firing an AR at the house, he could tell that gunfire was erupting out of his front door and striking the SUV. *What the hell?*

There were only moments between the time Andy arrived at the wood's edge, clicked the rifle's safety off, and squeezed the trigger. The heavy .30-06-caliber round covered the two hundred yards to the fourth man in another moment, striking him solidly between the shoulder blades. The man staggered and turned the rifle up, not sure where the shot had come from. Andy racked the bolt, chambering another round, but it wasn't necessary. The man fell to his knees, then to his side, and lay on the ground in the fetal position, his open eyes looking directly at Andy.

As David and Sasquatch reached the house, weapons up and at the ready, Sasquatch began yelling, "Hold your fire! Hold your fire in the house! They're all down!"

The firing stopped. The dead quiet that followed was surreal. David covered Squatch as he went from man to man, checking them for life by nudging them with his foot. It seemed he moved in slow motion; there was no sound, no smell.

David was startled back to reality by Andy running past him into the house yelling, "Is everyone OK? Is everyone OK? Melissa! Kathryn!" David's senses were now hyper alert, and the silence was gone. The dog was barking wildly, and his dad was in the house, yelling, "My God! What happened!? Who are these guys?" Kathryn was weeping, and his mom was speaking so fast he couldn't understand one word of it. Sasquatch was standing over one man, his rifle pointed directly at his face, yelling, "This one is still alive!" The SUV was still running. In the distance, he could hear his grandfather yelling as he ran closer, "Oh my God! Oh my God!" The smell of spring was intermingled with the smell of gunpowder. The sun was brighter than it had ever been. He felt very different from the sickness he had felt at the overpass. Instead, he felt very alive.

Over the next ten minutes, Andy was able to get Melissa to calm down enough to tell them what had happened without the hysterics. Soon after Andy, David, and Sasquatch had left, María had gotten her children and returned to the Tafts' so they could all work in the greenhouse. Kathryn and Melissa were boiling water to do laundry when Melissa saw an SUV by her dad's house. She didn't think anything of it. Her dad was a doctor, and sometimes people would visit him for advice or treatment. She watched as the SUV left her dad's and headed her way. She remembered that they were all in the greenhouse, so she went outside to speak to whoever was approaching and let them know the doctor was around. As she went outside, Kathryn followed, watching from the open front door.

As the SUV pulled up, Melissa could see four men in the vehicle who were dressed pretty much the same. Thinking that was odd, she told Kathryn to stay put. The men got out of the truck, and Melissa realized they were Catastrophe Management officers. She began to worry that they were here to ask questions about the shooting on the highway or the one back at the house.

"Hey there! What can we do for you?" she said, trying to sound calm.

"That depends," said the man getting out of the front passenger seat. "Catastrophe Management! We're canvassing this area looking for contraband."

"Contraband?" Melissa said with a bit of a chuckle. "No contraband here."

"No? We'll see," said the apparent leader. "Do you have any guns or explosives?"

"No, those are illegal," Melissa said, trying to sound serious.

A DAY LIKE ANY OTHER

"What about excessive food stores?" the man asked. By now, the other three men were out of the vehicle. One was leaning with his back against the rear passenger door. Another was leaning, his arm outstretched, on the hood by the passenger side front fender. The driver was standing by the driver's door, watching across the hood. They were all armed with rifles and with pistols on their hips.

"What's excessive?" Melissa answered, thinking the question ridiculous.

"Are you the only ones here?" the man asked.

"No, there's a bunch of people who live here." Melissa didn't like the question, nor the way he looked around when he asked it. "They'll be back any minute."

Turning toward Kathryn, Melissa said, "Kathryn, honey, can you go check the oven please?"

"The oven?" Kathryn said, confused.

"Yes, honey, go check it please," Melissa said again, this time giving her daughter a firm look.

"I'm gonna need to search the premises," the man said. "I'm gonna need to search you too, I think. What do ya think boys?! Strip search this one?" he said with a laugh.

His companions laughingly said, "Yeah! Strip search!"

Melissa, beginning to back away, tried to stay calm and said, "Ha ha guys, very funny," forcing a smile.

"No! Not funny!" the leader said, lunging forward to grab Melissa. "You're all alone here. You ladies need some company, and here we are."

Melissa broke free from the man's grasp and fell backward onto the porch stairs. As he moved toward her, the other two men on that side of the SUV moved toward her as well.

From the open front door came a deafening blast. Melissa felt a wave of heat rush past the top of her head. The leader's abdomen exploded, and Melissa was sprayed with something wet. The man who had been by the rear door stopped and tried to raise his rifle toward the open door. He was hit in the stomach with the next blast and staggered backward. Melissa reached behind her and drew the .38-caliber pistol from the holster on her belt in the small of her back. Andy insisted she carry it at all times; she thought he was paranoid, but she did it anyway. She raised the pistol and began firing at the third man, who was backpedaling toward the front of the SUV where he had come from. She wasn't sure if she was hitting him, but she kept shooting until the pistol was empty, then scrambled into the house. Kathryn kept firing the shotgun, now at the man returning fire over the hood. Melissa retrieved an AR from the rack next to the oven—that's where they kept it and the shotgun that Kathryn was still firing—and began firing out the front door at the SUV without really aiming. There was a distant gunshot, and then she heard Francisco yelling. She had dropped the weapon and embraced her daughter, both of them slumping to the floor and shaking.

Dr. Taft tried to save the man Melissa had shot with the .38, a skinny guy with thick black hair. He applied pressure to the worst looking of the holes. All the while, Sasquatch held the man by the collar, lifting his head and yelling in his face, "Why did you come here? What do you want from us? Who are you?"

The man was quickly going into shock and could only manage fragmented sentences. "We're . . . CAT-MAN . . . sent to look for contraband . . . was in the camp . . . volunteered . . . extra food . . . swore the oath . . . I'm sorry . . ." Those were the last words the CAT-MAN officer said before expiring, going limp in Squatch's grip.

"Put him down!" Dr. Taft yelled at Sasquatch, grabbing his arm. "He's gone!"

Standing up, angrier than anyone had ever seen him, Dr. Taft screamed at Sasquatch, "What have you done?"

Squatch looked at Dr. Taft in the eyes, the adrenaline still pumping but the anger subsiding, seeing that the doctor was extremely upset. As gently as he could, he said, "Ed, it wasn't me. It was the girls." He pointed toward the house.

Dr. Taft looked toward the house where Kathryn and Melissa, who were covered in blood spatter, were now emerging with Andy. He rushed over and grabbed both of them in his arms. "Are you hurt? Are either of you hurt?"

Squeezing him tightly, they both said, "No. We're OK." They began to cry again.

Andy went over to Sasquatch, who was now going through the man's pockets. Andy knelt down beside his friend and said, "What were these guys doing way out here?"

"I don't know. Looking for trouble," Sasquatch said. "Looks like they found it." His usual smartass tone was back after having been reserved with Dr. Taft.

"Yeah. Looks like it," Andy said, with a deep breath, the excitement starting to wear off.

Looking up toward his in-laws' house, Andy saw María, Mrs. Taft, and the children running up toward them. Andy started their way, not wanting the little ones to see all these dead bodies. As he approached them, he saw another SUV emerge from the woods, headed up the road toward the Tafts' house. Andy's first thought was, *Oh no! There's more of them!* Instead of trying to stop them, Andy now hurried them toward his house and called for everyone to get inside. As the SUV got closer, it became obvious to the driver that something was wrong, and he began to slow down. Andy took a firing position at the back of the CAT-MAN SUV, and Sasquatch did the same at the front. David opened the dining room window and aimed with the AR his mother had just used to shoot the CAT-MAN vehicle, having replaced the magazine with a full one.

The vehicle came to a stop about twenty yards away, and the front passenger-side door opened slowly. A man began to get out, his hands high above his head so everyone could see he wasn't armed. As he came around the opened door he said, "Andy! Squatch! It's me, Wally! Don't shoot! What the hell is goin' on here?"

Andy stood and looked at Sasquatch, who was giving him a toothy grin.

"Wally's here!" Andy said, relieved and joyful all at once. "Wally's here," he said quietly to himself with a smile.

CHAPTER 21

UPSTATE PENNSYLVANIA, THE TAFTS' FARM

WALLY'S ARRIVAL AT that moment was the best possible thing that could have happened. With Wally back, the team was complete. Andy felt a huge sense of relief knowing Wally was OK and having him here to help him through whatever lay ahead.

Wally had brought company with him as well. Along the road, Wally had met Uncle Charlie from the overpass incident and told him where he was going and who he was looking for. Uncle Charlie's eyebrows had risen, and he had said, "Is that right? Well, I'll help you find him." Not only did Uncle Charlie come along, but he had also brought backup: Charlie's nephew, Ryan Taylor, and John Redstone, Ryan's brother-in-law and a Lenape Indian, the native people of that part of Pennsylvania. They had been all stunned by the sight they had driven up on but recovered quickly once they realized it was CAT-MAN officers who were down.

Uncle Charlie waved his hand to Andy and said, "I told you I would pay ya back, and here I am. We know just what to do with this trash, if you'll let us help ya."

Andy almost didn't recognize Uncle Charlie. The last time he'd seen him, he had been shot and was suffering from blood loss; he had looked like death. Uncle Charlie had recovered fully from his injury. A wiry man with bowlegs, his white hair and beard framing dark, piercing eyes—in another time, he'd pass for a cowboy.

They loaded up the CAT-MAN bodies and all their gear into the CAT-MAN SUV, and as Uncle Charlie, Ryan, and John Redstone drove off to dispose of the trash, Andy and Sasquatch turned their attention to their long-lost friend.

"It's goddamn good to see you, Walter Childs!" Andy said, shaking his friend's hand.

A DAY LIKE ANY OTHER

Walter Childs was the picture of a midwestern boy: tall and lanky, square-jawed, with thick blond hair and striking blue eyes. Andy and Squatch would tease Wally, saying that he was the poster Marine of their little group. "You make us all look good, Wally. Come stand by me, bro, so people will like me better!" Squatch would tell him, to which Wally would reply, "Ah, man."

Ever modest and humble, he was a good man and a better Marine. He graduated from recruit training with a meritorious promotion, and at every other school he attended, he graduated at the top of his class. He was the only one of the trio to become qualified as an air crewman and was also the only one of the three to actually fire a shot in combat. As a UH-1N Huey aerial gunner/observer, Wally earned his combat aircrew wings in Iraq, participating in several aerial engagements of enemy ground targets.

Wally was the youngest of the three and had still been on active duty when Andy and Squatch were retiring. Following his last tour to Afghanistan, he had received orders to HMX-1, the presidential helicopter squadron—a prestigious assignment, especially for an air crewman.

Andy and Sasquatch were both incredibly happy to see Wally. To have him show up immediately following the shootout with the CAT-MAN thugs was impeccable timing, another of Wally's many gifts. Wally seemed OK, mentally and physically, to his friends, but Andy and Squatch both thought, *We're gonna have to keep an eye on him.*

Wally's arrival at the farm was the end of a long journey that began at the Marine Corps base in Quantico, Virginia. He had spent the winter there, having been released from Walter Reed Hospital and deemed stable enough to return to limited duty. In reality, everyone who wasn't bleeding was released once The Event occurred since there were too many injured. Unfortunately, there were no beds for anyone but the most precarious mental illness cases. Wally was fine with that. He felt he was OK, and the counseling he had received in his time there had seemed to help enough. He knew he was not OK in the classic sense, but he needed to carry on, especially now that the world had gone to shit. Amanda had died in the combat zone—she was a Marine and knew the risks. He had to get on with life, even though he knew he would never be the same.

He returned to HMX and assisted in operations through the winter. As spring began, headquarters issued orders, presumably prompted by the White House, allowing another round of voluntary end-of-service requests. Wally felt he needed a change and took his leave of the Corps, setting out to find his friends, who were now his only family. He had traveled through Washington,

DC, happy to have chosen his Harley Davidson to make the trip as he navigated his way through miles of empty cars and around multiple roadblocks set up to keep travelers away from the city center and all the government buildings. He was forced to take backroads exclusively to get around Baltimore and Philadelphia, taking him miles out of his way and adding two days to a trip that should have taken four hours.

Wally couldn't imagine Andy staying put in the suburbs when the farm was the logical place to go given the present state of the world, so he decided to go straight there and forgo the more hazardous road through Philadelphia. Finally, north of Philly, he found himself on some random backroad, pretty sure he was headed in the right direction, his final destination being the Tafts' farm. It was there that Wally encountered Uncle Charlie, who was more than happy to help any friend of Andrew Lemon. None too soon as it turned out, as Wally had picked up a nail in his rear tire and would be on foot before too long. Uncle Charlie sadly had to inform Wally that he had no way to repair the tire but would be happy to look after the bike for him. Wally had spent the night with Uncle Charlie, the Taylors, and the Johnsons. They had all found refuge not far from the scene of the highway shootout, and there they had spent the winter with Charlie's nephew, Ryan, and his family and extended family.

Uncle Charlie, Ryan, and John returned about two hours later. When Andy asked what they had done with the CAT-MAN vehicle and bodies, Uncle Charlie said, "We put them somewhere special. Nothing to worry about. They'll never trace them back up here."

Andy took Uncle Charlie at his word and invited them in to get caught up. Melissa still seemed in shock, as did Kathryn. They were both upstairs in the master bedroom. María and Mrs. Taft were upstairs with them.

Andy wasn't sure how to deal with his wife and daughter having just killed people. He wanted to tell them that they did what they had to do to keep from getting raped—or worse. He wasn't all that good at gentle counseling and thought it best to let the females of the family handle this delicate time. He would talk with them later. They had done what needed to be done. He knew it, and he knew they knew it too. In time, they would be fine, he hoped. He had other issues to deal with. He turned his attention to Wally, Uncle Charlie, Ryan, and John Redstone.

"I bet you boys didn't think you'd be driving up here to help me dispose of bodies, did you?" Andy said once they were all seated around the dining room table.

"Honestly," Uncle Charlie began, "nothing surprises me anymore. I'm glad we were able to help."

Andy spent the next twenty minutes telling his new guests about the months since the overpass incident in the fall, ending with his latest dream and his thoughts about going back south. He attempted to lower his voice so David couldn't hear, to which Sasquatch said loud enough to startle Andy, "Bro! He heard us in the woods. He says he's going with."

Andy sat back from his attempted whisper and cast a look at David, who was across the room on the sofa.

Seeing his father's dirty look, David said, "It's not my fault you don't know how to talk quietly."

"Well, I can't speak for my nephew or John," Uncle Charlie said, leaning forward, "but I'll make that trip with you."

"I'll go," said Ryan, stroking his long red beard. "You helped my uncle, so I'm willing to help you."

"I'll go too," John said, sitting straight up in his chair, his long, dark hair shining in the sunlight spilling in from the open window. "I promised my sister I'd keep an eye on Ryan."

"There may be some shooting," Andy said, dead serious, mindful of the fact that every member of his family, minus the dog, had blood on their hands. "It has a way of following me around these days. I can't guarantee anyone's safety."

"We know the risks, Andy," Uncle Charlie said, looking first at Ryan then at John. "We're with you. It just seems like the right thing to do. This isn't our first rodeo; I was with air-cav in Nam. Ryan and John were in the first Gulf War—that's how they met one another."

"Thanks, guys. It'll be good to have you along," Andy said. "I didn't know you were air-cav, Charlie."

"Well, the last time we met, Andy, I was busy bleedin' out. Touting my war record wasn't really on my mind," Uncle Charlie said with a laugh.

"Alright, then," Sasquatch said, standing. "When do we leave?" He went to look out the window.

"I was thinking three days from today," Andy began, looking around the table. "That gives us time to get things situated here and for you guys to get ready," he added, nodding toward Uncle Charlie. "We can meet you on the road somewhere, maybe where Wally found you."

"Sounds like a plan," Uncle Charlie said, looking toward Ryan and John, who were nodding in the affirmative. "How much firepower we bringin'?"

"Whatever you think we'll need," Andy replied. "Squatch and I are gonna have to figure that out here at the farm as well. Make sure the girls are set up, just in case."

"Hey, man," Sasquatch began, peering out the window, "I think your father-in-law is gonna have a stroke. That's the third time he's walked out to look up the driveway. I think maybe he's waiting for the cops to come."

"Yeah," Andy said, getting up to join his friend by the window. "You know how he is. He doesn't like guns to begin with, and now his daughter and granddaughter have shot up some dudes on his property. I'll go down and talk to him."

"I'll go talk to him, bro," Squatch said, staring out the window at Dr. Taft, who was now pacing. "You need to go talk to your girls."

"Yeah, thanks." Andy looked upstairs, where he knew his girls were hurting. Then he turned his attention to Uncle Charlie, Ryan, and John. "So, in three days at high noon, right?"

"Three days, high noon," Uncle Charlie confirmed, shaking Andy's hand as he headed for the door.

"We'll be there," Ryan said, shaking Andy's hand, looking him straight in the eyes.

"Glad to be on board," John said as he passed, slapping Andy on the back.

Wally also rose and headed out with his new friends. "Off on another adventure, and I just got here."

Sasquatch and Wally saw Uncle Charlie's crew to their vehicle, shaking hands and exchanging small talk.

Uncle Charlie, once he settled behind the steering wheel, said, "I don't know why it seems like such the right thing to do. It's pretty crazy when you think about it, but I'm goin'."

"That's how it always is with Andy," Sasquatch said, standing by the driver's window.

"He has a way of getting people to do what he wants," Wally added, "but he does it by getting *you* to want to do it."

"It's a talent he has," Sasquatch added. "He doesn't even know he's doing it."

"Oh, great! We just got mind tricked into going into who knows what!" Uncle Charlie said with a laugh.

"Don't worry, Army, we Marines will keep you safe. As usual," Wally said with a smile.

"Ooooohhhhh!" was the response from Ryan and John.

A DAY LIKE ANY OTHER

Uncle Charlie just sat shaking his head side to side. "Well, I hope so. I'm getting too old for this shit." With that, he put the SUV in drive and headed off. As he pulled away, he said, "Three days! Where we found ya—if you jarheads can find it again!"

Sasquatch and Wally just smiled and waved as the SUV drove toward the driveway. They headed toward Dr. Taft, who was now standing on his porch waving to Uncle Charlie but still looking down his long driveway.

Sasquatch turned his head toward Wally and said, "You can find it again, right? The place we have to meet them?"

To which Wally replied, "Yeah! Well, I think so."

Sasquatch laughed and said, "I hope you're messing with me." Then he added, "Come help me talk Ed down from his paranoia."

Wally just smiled. "Sure thing. I think that was south of here. Or was it east?"

"Don't make me hurt you, little man," Sasquatch said as they walked.

ANDY SENT DAVID to make sure all the empty brass shell casings were picked up from the front of the house, then headed upstairs to talk to Melissa and Kathryn.

Before heading outside, David said, "I'm going with you guys."

Andy replied, "We'll talk about that later."

Andy arrived at the landing to hear María's voice saying, "You know you did what you had to." Her voice was firm and unwavering, her accent adding fire to her words. She was tough. She had to be. Born in the Mexican barrio of Tijuana, her parents had immigrated to the US when she was twelve. She was a good match for Francisco, who often used his massive size to intimidate and bully. Although the top of her head only came up to his chest, she didn't put up with any of it. "I keep him in line," she would say.

Andy listened from just outside the open door as she went on.

"Those bastards had no business coming here. Putting his hands on you, threatening you? I would have done the same thing. Kathryn! Girl, you saved your mom! Don't forget that. Family looks after family. It's all we got anymore. Don't feel bad, either one of you! They got what they deserved! They won't be attacking any more women."

Thank you, María, Andy thought as he entered the room.

"Hey, ladies. How we doin'?"

Melissa was seated on the bed, her legs out in front of her, as was Kathryn. María sat facing Melissa with her feet on the floor, and Donna sat with her legs folded, holding Kathryn's hands. Mrs. Taft was standing by her daughter, arms folded, looking traumatized.

"I'm trying to tell these two that they shouldn't feel bad. They're feeling all guilty," María replied. "Where's my husband?" she added, looking out the open bedroom door.

"He went to go talk to Ed," Andy replied.

"Oh my God. My dad." Melissa said, putting her head in her hands. "How is he dealing with this?"

"He's having a bit of an issue. I seriously think he thinks the cops are on their way," Andy replied.

"And my husband is going to talk to him?" María said as she stood. "Then I better get down there—the man has no tact. Come on, Donna, we need to go spare poor Ed. He's been through enough today."

Mrs. Taft left as well, kissing her daughter and granddaughter on the head before exiting. "Honestly, girls, you weren't given much of choice in my opinion. Try not to dwell on it too much," she said as she walked out.

As María and Donna left the room, María added, "Look, ladies. It's a different world now. I would expect my girl Donna to protect me in the same situation, and if it were me, Melissa, I would have shot them all in the balls."

As María and Donna headed downstairs, Andy heard David on his way up.

"Miss María. H-hi Donna," he said with a stutter.

Andy couldn't help but think, *Through all this, the kid is still shy talking to girls.* His next thought came out of his mouth as David entered the room. "Didn't I tell to pick up all that brass?"

"I looked three times! Dad, we picked it all up!" David replied with a scoff.

"Well, go look again! We need to make sure we got it all!" Andy said, perturbed.

"You just don't want me here when you tell them!" David shot back.

"Tell us what?" Melissa asked, looking at Andy.

Damn it, boy! Andy thought.

"Tell us what, Andy?" Melissa said again.

"That him, Uncle Squatch, Uncle Wally, and those guys are going south in three days!" David said, answering for his father, who was staring a hole straight through his son's head.

"Is that true?" Melissa said, looking again at Andy.

A DAY LIKE ANY OTHER

"Yeah. It's true," he replied, still staring at David, who was looking anywhere but at his dad.

"It's the only way I'm going to get any peace," Andy said gently, "given what happened after I had that other dream. I haven't had that one since. I don't know what else to do."

"That's just great," Melissa began, not quite angry but getting there. "So all of you are going off into a world gone crazy and leaving us here alone. How many times have we done this, Andy? How many times?" Her voice was starting to rise.

"A lot," Andy said, looking down. "This time it's not some far-off foreign land. It's our country—it's our people. You didn't see what I saw in that dream. If places like that exist here in this country, and someone or something wants me to go do something about it, Melissa, how can I ignore it?"

Melissa had her face in her hands again. After several long moments of silence that seemed like an eternity to Andy, she raised her head and said, "You're right Andrew." Melissa stood and walked over to her husband. "I've stood by you through all those deployments, all those months away, all the not knowing if you're alive. This is the same thing. Except this time, it's right here. If you feel something, if you think it will bring you some peace, if some higher power is compelling you to go do this, then who am I to stand in the way?"

Andy stood, looking at his wife. He knew she would agree that he should go. He was not prepared for the strength and conviction in her voice. In fact, at first, he thought she was messing with him. He was waiting for the sarcastic, "Oh, we'll be OK here all by ourselves?" but she was serious. All he could do was nod once as he looked into her eyes.

"I'm the wife of a warrior. This is what we do. Right?" Melissa said, a tear in her eye. The deployments had hardened her. Andy felt bad about all she had been through supporting him through his career. He was also very proud.

"I'm going, too!" David blurted, not wanting to be forgotten.

Andy removed his rapt attention from Melissa.

"No! You are not!" Andy snapped at his son.

"Why not?" David snapped back.

"Because you need to stay here and protect your mom and sister!" Andy replied, saying the first thing that popped into his head, pointing at Melissa.

"That's bullshit!" David shot back.

"Watch your mouth, boy!" Andy said. He was getting angry.

"That's bullshit and you know it!" David was unfazed. "Mom and Kathryn just wasted three guys! They don't need protecting!"

The boy was right. Andy stood there, once again, in stunned amazement, staring at his son.

Melissa ended the silent staring match between father and son.

"No, Andy, he's right. We'll be fine." She knew her son just as well as she knew Andy. "You know as well as I do that as soon as you clear the driveway, he'd be on his way over the mountain to head you off at the highway on-ramp. He knows the way better than both of us. You need someone watching your back anyway, right? Didn't you say that?"

Now Andy and David were both staring at Melissa. Kathryn came over from across the bed and took her mom and dad in a hug, then gestured for David to join them. Not another word was said. The Lemons stood and embraced as a family. Father and son would head off into the unknown in three days. The girls would be left to tend the farm and fend off whatever dangers came about while the men were away, like some kind of throwback to the Dark Ages. This was the new world María was speaking of. She was right—for better or worse, this is how it was now.

CHAPTER 22

DAY 1
UPSTATE PENNSYLVANIA, THE TAFTS' FARM

THREE DAYS PASSED in what seemed like the blink of an eye. Melissa didn't talk much. This was normal pre-deployment behavior for her. She had to steel herself for the imminent departure of her husband. This time, of course, was different. Not only was she saying goodbye to her husband, but her son was going as well. She had never imagined the day she would send her son off into the unknown like this. With Andy, she knew what she was getting into when she married him—well, at least she thought she knew.

Kathryn paid special attention to Andy's instructions on how to keep all their firearms clean and where to hide them if need be, as well as how to get out of the house with no one seeing and all the best places to hide in the forest if that became necessary. She gave her dad hugs every chance she could. She too was a trooper; she was a full member of the warrior clan the Lemons had become.

For David, time seemed to stand still. He packed his backpack, checked it, then checked it again. He couldn't wait to get on the road. Andy, Walter, and Francisco all agreed that David had the same restless spirit as they did when they were young. This worried Andy to a degree while at the same time filled him with pride. Wally and Squatch agreed with Andy that David would need supervision to keep him from being reckless, and they promised Andy they would keep him from doing anything stupid.

Dr. Taft never really acknowledged that they were leaving, but he took every opportunity to give helpful first aid hints and packed a small medical kit for them to take with them. Mrs. Taft, ever the optimist, passed the time planning projects for them for after they returned.

María, like Melissa, had been through this many times before and prepared herself in her own way. The usual hard edge she put forth was on hold, and she let her softer side come through publicly, with her husband especially. She was tough, no doubt, but anyone who really knew her knew that it was, for the most part, just a show.

As dawn broke on the day that the boys would be leaving, David had been up for over an hour already. His gear was by the front door, ready to go. He was dressed and sat anxiously on the front steps. Andy hadn't had the nightmare since his decision to make the trip south and felt refreshed; he felt good and ready to get on with it.

The Lemons had a quiet breakfast as a family. No one said much; they had all been here before. They all knew this was the hardest part—that time before the actual leaving, that period of time where saying goodbye is so close but has not yet happened. Once the farewells were said and the travelers departed, all there was to do for those staying behind was get back to life as best you could. For those departing, the mission at hand became their priority. For all concerned, life went on, just in a new reality.

As planned, Andy loaded the pickup, its taillights still blacked out from their escape from suburbia, and headed, family in tow, down to the Tafts' to pick up Squatch and Wally. Squatch's kids had spent the night with their parents at the Tafts' to have as much time with their dad as possible. Everyone was already outside, and Squatch's and Wally's gear was piled, ready for loading. Squatch's little ones, normally rambunctious, were quiet and somber. Wally began loading the truck while Andy and Squatch said their farewells. He knew the deal—best to be ready to roll once all that needed saying was said.

Andy went to his mother-in-law first. He hugged her and said, "Take care of my girls."

"I will," she said, drying a tear. "You be careful."

Andy smiled and said, "I will."

Next Andy went to Dr. Taft, hugging him as well, and said, "Thank you for everything you've done for us. We wouldn't have made it this far without you."

"Andrew," Dr. Taft began, "I'm very proud of you."

Andy felt a tear in his eye but fought it back. "Thank you, sir, that means a lot."

"You be careful," Dr. Taft said, releasing his hug and shaking Andy's hand. "We need you back in one piece. Good luck, son."

Dr. Taft had seldom called him "son," and Andy was a little bit surprised by it but deeply touched. For a moment, he thought, *Why am I leaving again?* Instead, he said, "I'll be back as soon as possible."

A DAY LIKE ANY OTHER

Andy turned to his family. To his right, Sasquatch was surrounded by his family, little people all attached to his giant frame. It looked more like a dogpile than a group hug.

Melissa was holding David's face and speaking quietly, her eyes locked on his. David nodded each time she paused. As Andy approached, David turned to give Kathryn a long hug, and Melissa turned her attention to him.

"You watch your ass," Melissa said, her voice strong and forceful. She was the gunny's wife; she would send him off with all her love and confidence. He would know she was OK, and he would do his job with a clear mind and return to her. This had been her part to play, and she was very good at it. It was said that the hardest job in the Corps was a Marine's wife.

"Yes, ma'am," Andy replied, embracing his wife. "You watch your ass too, and remember everything I told you."

"Don't worry about us. We'll be fine. We always are," Melissa said, squeezing him tight.

They kissed, and Andy turned to hug Kathryn. "Take care of your mother, sweetheart. We'll be back as soon as possible."

"I will, Daddy," Kathryn said, squeezing her dad tightly around the neck. "Look after David."

Sasquatch came over to hug Melissa and Kathryn as Andy and David went to say farewell to the Vasquez family. Andy, with David right behind him, hugged each one of them. Not a word was said, nor was one needed. He noticed David giving Donna an awkward hug and stuttering, "I'll see you when I get back." Andy smiled to himself and gave María a wink. She had noticed their awkward teenage exchange as well and smiled.

Wally made the rounds quickly, and they all piled in, no one talking. They all waved, one group to the other, as they pulled away. The die was cast. Those who stayed went about their morning business, and those who left began thinking of the road ahead.

AFTER TWO HOURS of driving down backroads, most in terrible condition after winter had had its way with them, the boys found Uncle Charlie, Ryan, and John just where they said they'd be.

As Andy pulled up beside Uncle Charlie's pickup, he rolled the window down and said, "I see you boys haven't changed your minds."

Uncle Charlie replied, "I see you boys managed to find your way back."

Andy liked Uncle Charlie. He had a way about him that somehow made Andy feel safe and confident—maybe he reminded him of his dad, Andy couldn't be sure—but he was glad he was along for the ride.

After some discussion about which route to take based on what Uncle Charlie knew of the local roads and Wally's trip up from Virginia, a route was agreed on and traced out on two maps, one for each vehicle. They took stock of their gear and supplies. Everyone had prepared pretty well. They had all brought sleeping bags and some kind of shelter, as well as backpacks in the event they had to abandon the vehicles. They had packed what food they could, opting for lightweight versus heavy canned goods. Andy thought, *Well, we'll all be the same kind of hungry.*

They had a mix of firearms. Andy armed himself only with his .45-caliber M1911, and he gave his AR to Wally. He figured he'd rather have that firepower available rather than have it sitting in his lap while he drives. David had an AR and a 9-millimeter pistol as a backup. Andy thought about taking his third AR but then reconsidered. The CAT-MAN vehicle was shot up pretty badly with what was obviously a 5.56-millimeter weapon. He, at first, thought it best to leave the girls only with shotguns and the hunting rifle. Those would be more easily explained in the country setting of the farm, and they could hide the remaining pistols easily enough. He also didn't want the girls getting into any firefights that would warrant the firepower of the ARs. He had told them to retreat into the forest as their first recourse. With that being said, the third AR was sighted in for Melissa already, and if she needed it and didn't have it, it could end up catastrophic. Andy still had mixed feelings on the subject, but he had to put them aside as there was nothing he could do about it now.

Sasquatch was armed with his own AR, which he had actually bought from Andy when Andy decided he wanted a different model. Uncle Charlie had with him an M1 Garand, a vintage World War II/Korean War .30-06 caliber monster. Andy was glad to have the heavy caliber rifle and commented that "Uncle Charlie brought the heavy artillery." Ryan and John had armed themselves with twelve-gauge shotguns and 9-millimeter pistols that they had exchanged one Christmas coincidentally. "Great minds think alike," they had laughingly said, brandishing their new sidearms.

They took some time and practiced covering one another should the lead vehicle stop to clear a roadblock or should they encounter robbers. If an obvious hostile roadblock was encountered, they would attempt to avoid it if they discovered it in time. If not, they would fight their way through it, so they

A DAY LIKE ANY OTHER

practiced countering an ambush. If it appeared that the road was blocked by locals trying to keep trouble at arm's length, they agreed that Andy would talk to them while everyone else would stay with the vehicles looking friendly but remaining prepared should negotiations go badly. Satisfied with their coordination and communication, they divided up the extra fuel and water between the vehicles and set off south.

Along the way, they encountered one group of townsfolk who had been guarding the roads into town. They had been menaced by some thugs who were invading people's homes and stealing their supplies. The local police chief had deputized two dozen volunteers and set up checkpoints. Andy exchanged safe passage through town for five hundred rounds of 5.56 ammunition, which the chief was glad to get.

The chief told Andy what he knew of the road ahead on the other side of town. He told them that several CAT-MAN vehicles had come through, headed in all directions. The officers had tried to confiscate the weapons from his deputies until he arrived and ran them off. The CAT-MAN officers were becoming bolder, and the chief had thought there may actually be a shootout, but the CAT-MAN officers finally backed down once they realized they were outgunned.

Andy thanked them and, without telling them about the incident with Melissa and Kathryn, told the chief not to trust the CAT-MAN officers and that it was good that he had run them off. The chief wished them well and told them they were welcome back anytime.

Andy didn't like the idea of CAT-MAN being so active on the roads. As he drove on, he thought they would have to fight them if they tried to stop them or take their stuff.

At another point in the trip, as they rounded a curve in the highway, Andy had to crush the brakes to keep from hitting a beat-up car that was straddling the road. Squatch saw someone crouching behind it and immediately said, "Ambush!" As they had practiced, they all piled out of the vehicle and lined up in front of Andy's pickup. Uncle Charlie, seeing what they were doing, executed his part of the plan and pulled up next to Andy's truck, his vehicle emptying. As it turned out, there were three men hiding behind the beat-up car. At the sight of all these guns coming at them, one of them wielded by some kind of hairy giant, they thought better of their current endeavor and ran for the forest, stumbling and tripping over one another as they scrambled to get away. As they swept past the car, Sqautch could see the men disappear into some pines and yelled after them, "You boys best not try that shit again! We'll be back, and we're not letting you run away next time!" As scared as they were already, Andy was sure that after hearing Sasquatch's booming voice echoing after them, they wouldn't try to rob anyone again anytime soon.

After pushing the car into a ditch and deflating the tires so no one could move it into the road again, the boys pressed on to within a few miles of the Willow Grove Air Station. Andy knew it was being used as a FEMA camp and thought it the best place to start trying to figure out what his dream was about. He didn't want to spend the night too close to the camp for fear of being discovered during the night. They found a dirt road that led off the highway and followed it to a small clearing that looked like the edge of a farm field. Satisfied it was safe here, the group set up camp and settled in for the night, assigning guard watches and relief intervals.

Though they had no fire, they had some good camaraderie in the waning daylight. Andy explained how Sasquatch got his name, to which Ryan and John nodded and Uncle Charlie said, "Yeah, I can see that." Wally and Squatch assigned Ryan the title of "Ryan the Red Viking Axe Man" due to his thick red beard and ruddy complexion. John Redstone became "Big John," to which he said, "I can live with that."

A good deal of time was spent giving David a hard time about his apparent crush on Donna and his total lack of skill in talking to girls. Even in the coming darkness, one could see David blushing, which only brought more razzing.

Finally, as the sun set, Ryan the Red, usually very quiet and stoic, spoke up and said, "Oh, man! The kids would end up looking like Andy!"

Laughter erupted from the camp. Somewhere in the darkness, Sasquatch could be heard growling. This brought more laughter. Andy thought to himself, *I've really missed this.*

DAY 2
THE WILDERNESS SOMEWHERE NORTH OF PHILADELPHIA

THE NIGHT PASSED without incident, and as the sun began to rise, so did their little camp. They agreed a small fire would be OK, and they boiled water for some instant coffee that Ryan had brought along. Not much was said as they packed up the camp and loaded up for the last leg of their trip. This was why they had set out. In the next few hours, they would look upon what the world had become.

Andy was particularly quiet. He was haunted by the face of the man from his dream. Though he hadn't had the dream in days, the face was right there in the forefront of his mind. He was troubled by what lay ahead. What if the terrible scene in his dream was accurate? What would he do? What *could* he do? *Maybe it's not that bad. I guess we'll see,* he thought as he slid into the driver's seat.

"Let's go see what's up the road," Andy said finally, putting the truck in gear.

THE FARTHER SOUTH they drove down Route 611, the more familiar things seemed to become—yet nothing was as it had been. Andy had been down this road countless times before, but what lay before him was nothing like he remembered. The street signs told him he was heading in the correct direction, and he knew exactly where he was. However, the devastation of The Event and the earthquakes, combined with the harsh effects of the long winter, had turned the suburban paradise he had left into what looked like a warzone. Abandoned and burnt-out vehicles lined both sides of the road. The road itself told a sad tale of nature at its worst—cratered and cracked, covered in leaves and debris. Another winter might render this unrecognizable as a road. The houses that lined the road were a mix of burnt-out, abandoned, and collapsed, with the occasional inhabited house only noticeable by the curtain quickly being shut as they passed, the occupants presumably wishing to remain invisible. There was no one on the streets. It was a suburban ghost town that put everyone on edge.

As Andy approached a large intersection, he recognized it before he saw the street sign. Street Road was the last major intersection before reaching the naval air station. *Here we go,* he thought.

From the middle of the intersection, Andy saw something by the side of the road, sitting on the curb. Small and dirty, he thought it was a trash bag at first. He realized all at once that it was a person, lying on their side, facing away from him.

As Andy brought the truck to a stop, Squatch said, "Why are we stopping?"

"There's someone over there," Andy said, pointing toward the figure on the curb.

Leaning up in the seat to see over Andy out the driver's window, Squatch said, "That dude looks dead, bro."

"I'm gonna check it out. Cover me," Andy said, opening the door.

"Check it out?" Squatch said, surprised, then added, "Why?" as he opened the passenger-side door to get out.

Wally had followed Andy's lead and was walking with him toward the pathetic figure.

As Andy reached down to touch the motionless figure, he hesitated when David said, "Dad! Be careful."

Andy touched the shoulder of the figure, causing it to jump and quickly sit up. Everyone took a step back with a start. Andy could now see that the figure was a male as he began to crawl away from Andy on one elbow, the other arm clenched tightly to his side, wet with blood.

The man was saying, "I don't want no trouble! Just let me go! Just let me go!" His voice was desperate and pathetic, a broken voice from a broken man. Suddenly, Andy realized, he recognized this man.

"Larry!?" he said, moving back toward him as he crawled.

"You know him?" Wally said, still following Andy.

"This is my neighbor!" Andy said, getting into a crouch, closer to eye level with Larry, who still didn't realize he was safe. "His name is Larry. He lived down the street."

"My God! Andy!" Larry had recognized Andy, finally. "Thank God! Thank God!"

Andy could see now that Larry was indeed bleeding. "Larry, man, you're hurt! What happened?"

"Andy! Andy!" Larry was delirious.

"It's me, buddy," Andy said calmly, gently taking Larry's arm to try and see where his injury was. "What happened to you?"

"We tried to leave," Larry said, seeming to get it together a bit.

"I remember, but you came back," Andy replied, looking Larry in the eyes.

"Yeah, we came back," Larry said, looking like he was going to drift off again.

"Did you go to the camp, Larry?" asked Andy, bringing Larry back around.

"Yeah, we went to the mall first, by the house," Larry said, looking up at Andy. Andy nodded that he understood where he meant. "But . . . but it got too full, so they moved us up here. They herded us up and packed us into trucks like animals. It was awful. They brought us up here to the old base. But that was overcrowded too. The CAT-MAN guys, they're not good people, Andy. The terrible things we saw . . ."

Andy could see Larry was starting to drift off again. *Is it blood loss? Is he going into shock?* Thoughts were starting to flood his mind, then it dawned on him.

"Larry! Where's your family?" Andy asked, once again gaining his friend's attention.

"My family?!" Larry replied, grabbing Andy by the shoulder of his jacket. "They're down there, in the camp!" His voice was becoming desperate. "They're in the camp! Andy, you have to free them!"

Andy rocked back and said, "What did you say? Larry, what?"

"Free them!" Larry said, his face right up to Andy's, practically touching.

Everyone had heard what Larry had said. Sasquatch was the one to say what they were all thinking. "I think you found your guy, bro."

Andy sat staring into Larry's face in disbelief. He had once again had a dream come to reality. As Larry bent his head to Andy's chest and began to weep, Andy's mind began spinning. *Free them.* There it was, plain as day. *Now what?*

"Someone's coming," Ryan said from the bed of Uncle Charlie's truck, where he had climbed to act as lookout.

The drone of engines could be heard coming toward them from the east.

In between sobs, Larry said, "They found me."

Andy looked up in the direction of the noise and said, "Not good."

It was too late to try and run. They would have to deal with whoever it was face to face.

"Get ready!" Andy yelled to his traveling companions.

As he stood, leaving Larry to curl back up into the fetal position, Andy felt an anger building up inside him he hadn't ever felt before in his life. *Whoever did this to this good man is going to pay, and let it start now.*

The noise was almost upon them, and they could see the top of something big approaching. At that moment, they all knew they were in over their heads. But they all stood their ground. What would be would be.

"This should work out well!" Squatch yelled sarcastically over to Andy, who was standing in the middle of the road.

The monstrous machine stopped just feet from Andy, and a voice from inside yelled, "Get the hell out of the road, moron!"

CHAPTER 23

THE SUBURBS OF PHILADELPHIA, APPROXIMATELY ONE MILE NORTH OF THE WILLOW GROVE NAVAL AIR STATION

ANDY STOOD FACE to face with the giant vehicle, unwavering. The voice he had heard was coming from the top of the vehicle. Andy saw the top of a helmeted head.

The person was now speaking into a microphone attached to the helmet. "There are seven individuals, all armed, and two pickup trucks blocking the intersection."

There was a pause. Andy presumed whoever was on the other end was speaking.

"I did, sir. They're not moving."

Andy realized he was standing in front of a Stryker armored personnel carrier. He felt his anger starting to lessen—these were not CAT-MAN officers. Andy became suddenly aware of the vehicle's massive size. At just over ten feet tall and weighing over twenty tons, it could have driven right over him and the trucks without even noticing they were there. *This is stupid,* Andy thought of his decision to stand in the road blocking their passage. *I let my anger get the better of me. Can't let that happen again.*

"Why am I not surprised to find you blocking my convoy?" came a voice from Andy's right.

Andy looked over, snapping out of his thoughts to see a familiar face. Andy smiled with relief and genuine happiness. "Lieutenant Ramirez!"

It was the National Guard officer Andy had almost run over in the fall, when he was making his escape to the farm. The lieutenant was smiling as well, shaking his head.

"The last time I saw you, you were headed north in the middle of the night. What are you doing here blocking my intersection?" Lieutenant Ramirez said, shaking Andy's hand.

A DAY LIKE ANY OTHER

"If I told you, you wouldn't believe me!" Andy said, smiling. "Look, El-Tee, my friend is hurt. He's bleeding, and I think he may be going into shock." Andy gestured toward Larry, who was still lying where Andy had left him. Wally and David were now kneeling by him. David was saying something to Larry, but Andy couldn't hear.

Ramirez shouted up to the commander of the vehicle Andy had stared down. "Hey, tell the MEV to come up. We have a casualty."

As Andy and Lieutenant Ramirez walked over toward Larry, Andy could see that the convoy he had stopped was several vehicles deep. "Wow! I didn't realize I was blocking a whole convoy. We thought you guys were CAT-MAN. Sorry about that, El-Tee."

"Look, if we are going to keep meeting like this, you can just call me Rod," replied Ramirez.

"That just wouldn't feel right El-Tee," Andy said as they walked. "You almost ran me over this time."

"I guess we're even. If we were CAT-MAN, you would have been run over," Ramirez said with a smile. "I'm leading eight M1126 infantry carriers and an M1133 medical eval vehicle to Fort Indiantown Gap. We got a few HUMVEEs along too. They finally decided to pull us off those bridges."

Uncle Charlie and Sasquatch were moving the pickups out of the intersection as the MEV was pulling up to where Larry lay.

Ramirez said, "So who is this guy?"

"He's my neighbor. His name is Larry. He said he came from the camp up ahead. He's in pretty bad shape," Andy replied.

"What's he doing way over here?" Ramirez said, looking on as the medic began to assess Larry. "The reason we even came this way is because it keeps us from coming within one mile of any camps."

"Yeah, well, he says it's pretty bad down there. He was delirious," Andy said, helping Larry into the back of the MEV. "His family is there; I don't know why he would leave them to come way over here."

"I can answer that!" said a nearby onlooker.

A crowd had begun to gather off to one side of the intersection. Apparently, they hadn't seen anything but CAT-MAN traffic until now and couldn't help but come out to see what was going on. A short man in baggy clothes was emerging from the crowd of twenty or so raggedy people.

"Who are you?" Andy asked.

"My name is Kevin. I'm the pastor of that little church over there," Kevin said, pointing southwest. "Larry and some others have been coming to me looking for supplies all winter. I heard shooting coming from the camp last night and got worried that they had shot more people, so I came looking to see if I could find any survivors."

"Who shot more people?" Ramirez asked.

"The CAT-MAN guards at the camp," Kevin replied, shocked that anyone would even ask that question. "They have them on starvation rations up there. We're able to buy food from the black market, which somehow seems to have plenty of supplies, and we give it to whoever gets here to bring it back."

"Are you sayin' that the CAT-MAN guys are starving people while at the same time supplying the black market?" Wally asked.

"It sure looks that way," Kevin said with disgust. "The boxes say 'relief supplies' right on them. Rumor has it that the CAT-MAN officers actually put the guys robbing the convoys on the payroll and are now working a racket with the relief supplies."

"How are they getting away with that?" Ramirez said, incredulous. "Where's the oversight?"

"There is no oversight," Kevin replied somberly. "They do what they want, and apparently they have the power to do it."

At that, the medic came over and got Lieutenant Ramirez's attention.

"Sir," the medic began, "this man's been shot through the forearm. It went right through but missed the artery. He's lucky in that regard, but he's severely malnourished and dehydrated. I started him on IV fluids, and his blood pressure seems to be coming up. Sir, I haven't seen anything like this before. Even the people we processed at the bridge were in better shape than this guy."

"Thank you," Ramirez replied to his medic, who returned to his patient.

"He's lucky he survived the cholera epidemic," Kevin said, chiming in. "It's terrible down there. It's an unsanitary cesspit. You should go see for yourselves. Try not to get shot, though."

Andy was feeling that sick, angry feeling again. This was why he had come back, but what could he do? Then it came to him. In the dream, he had heard the words, "Help will come." Andy looked up at the long line of armored vehicles. A wave of excitement washed over him.

He turned to Lieutenant Ramirez and said, "We should go down there and do just that."

A DAY LIKE ANY OTHER

"Do what?" Ramirez said, knowing what Andy was going to say already. "Go down there? It's against my orders."

"I know it is." Andy was smiling, but his voice was dead serious. "You're going to disobey that order, lieutenant. It's unlawful, and it's your duty to disobey it."

Ramirez was shaking his head from side to side. "No, don't gimme that unlawful order crap."

"Lieutenant, look at him," Andy said, pointing to Larry, who was actually starting to get some color back in his face. "And he's the one who was well enough to sneak out and get food! You heard what Kevin said. A racket with the relief supplies! Criminals on the payroll!"

Ramirez was looking down at the ground, hands on his hips. "There's no proof of any of that."

"There's enough proof!" Andy said, once again pointing to Larry. "It's our duty to protect the people, El-Tee, against all enemies, foreign and domestic!" He was on a roll. "So if we go down there and everything is hunky-dory, you can arrest me, apologize to the CAT-MAN guys, and be on your way."

Andy could tell Ramirez was thinking about it. "But what if we go down there and it's like Kevin says? And we put a stop to it? We would be saving lives!"

Ramirez looked up at Andy, expressionless.

"It's just the right thing to do," Andy said, looking into Ramirez's eyes.

Ramirez thought for a minute. Then he looked down the road toward the base. He turned and looked down his convoy. Without looking at Andy again, he climbed into the MEV, put on a headset, keyed the microphone, and said, "All units, listen up. I have it on good authority that the FEMA camp just south of here is mistreating its refugees. I intend to conduct an inspection of that facility and the conditions of its inhabitants. I am willfully disobeying orders to do so. I will not order any of you to follow me in this endeavor. If you wish to accompany me, then fall into column behind my HUMVEE. Anyone who does not wish to go will remain here and await my return. No one will be judged disloyal if they choose to remain behind. Again, if you come with me, you will be disobeying a standing order."

With that, Ramirez signaled for his HUMVEE to come up.

Seeing this, Sasquatch pulled the pickup next to Andy and said, "Man, you should have been a salesman. Get in."

"No, you're riding with me. I go down, you're coming with me," Ramirez said, walking toward his HUMVEE but looking at Andy. "I'm driving, Rogers," Ramirez said to his driver.

"No, sir!" Rogers replied. "I'm your driver. That just wouldn't be right."

With that, Ramirez had his first volunteer.

Andy nodded to Rogers as he climbed into the back seat of the HUMVEE. Rogers nodded back, smiling from ear to ear.

As Andy, Ramirez, and Rogers pulled away, Sasquatch, Wally, and David followed right behind. Pastor Kevin jumped in with them at the last minute, with Uncle Charlie, Ryan, and Big John behind them. As they watched in the rearview mirrors, Ramirez and Andy saw as, one by one, Lieutenant Ramirez's vehicles pulled into the intersection and fell into column behind him.

Andy leaned forward and said, "They love you, man! I think every one of them followed."

Ramirez just nodded back to Andy. His attention was on the road ahead and what his fate may look like if they found the camp to be safe and sanitary. He also wondered what he would do if the camp was as bad as Kevin had described. *What did I get myself into?* he thought.

It was only a short drive to the camp. Before it even came into view, a horrible stench began to permeate the air, a mix of rotting trash and human feces. Andy truly began to feel that he was doing the right thing; he was committed now regardless. As the perimeter of the base came into view, the first thing that got his attention was a guard tower, complete with a machine gun. The two CAT-MAN officers in the tower turned around, shocked at the sight before them, one of them frantically talking into a handheld radio.

Andy leaned forward once again and said, "Why does a refugee camp need guard towers and machine guns?"

Ramirez didn't react. He just stared ahead, his jaw clenching.

After passing another guard tower, the HUMVEE arrived at the front gate of the old air station. CAT-MAN officers were scrambling in every direction. Rogers brought the HUMVEE to a stop at the guard shack adjacent to the gate. To their front was a sandbag bunker containing several CAT-MAN officers, all armed with M16s, along with one machine gun that was pointed straight at them. A CAT-MAN officer approached the driver's side window, where Rogers sat, still smiling.

A DAY LIKE ANY OTHER

"You can't be here!" the CAT-MAN officer yelled, waving his hand at the HUMVEE. "Turn around and go back! You're in violation of the one-mile military exclusion order!"

Andy said, "He looks pissed."

Ramirez only glanced at Andy as he opened the door and got out.

Seeing this, the CAT-MAN officer appeared to become more nervous. "Get back in your vehicle and exit the exclusion zone, immediately!"

Ramirez ignored the order and said, "We have reason to believe that your camp has become unsanitary. We are going to conduct an inspection of your facility."

"You have no authority to do that!" The CAT-MAN officer was backing up toward the guard shack. "You can't come in here!"

"I'm not asking your permission," Ramirez said, reaching into the HUMVEE for his radio handset.

Ramirez put the handset to his ear and said, "Lead Stryker, come up here and prepare to engage the guard shack with your .50-cal."

The lead Stryker pulled out of line and roared up to where his lieutenant was standing. The vehicle stopped and the turret mounted. A fifty-caliber machine gun came to life and adjusted to point directly at the guard shack. One CAT-MAN guard inside took off running, sure he was about to be destroyed by this metal monster.

"First squad," Ramirez was speaking into the handset again. "Disarm all these CAT-MAN people and take charge of this position. Lead Stryker, stay here. Everyone else, follow me." Ed got back in and pointed forward.

With that, they were moving again. Ramirez's troopers were disarming every CAT-MAN officer they saw. The convoy followed, and as Ramirez's HUMVEE came to a stop in front of the base headquarters building, directly across from the gate on the backside of a small traffic circle, he spoke into the handset again. "I want the MEV and the HUMVEEs here. Strykers, form a perimeter around this building. No shooting unless you are fired upon."

As he exited the vehicle, Ramirez turned to Andy and said, "This is why we came here! Let's go, Gunny!"

Andy replied, "Aye aye, sir." He was already moving in that direction.

As the convoy drove past them, Andy was joined by the rest of his traveling companions, all of whom were grinning like they had broken into their parent's liquor cabinet. The air hung over the whole camp like a brown haze, and a distant din could be heard. The group entered the building and began spreading out. Andy and Ramirez headed upstairs to where they thought the base commander's office would be. They found a large door at the end of the hallway that said "CAMP COMMISSIONER." They entered without knocking and found a startled man attempting to start a fire in his trash can.

"Whoa!" Andy yelled. "I don't think so!" He slapped the match out of the man's hand.

"Get out of here!" the camp commissioner said angrily. "You're in violation of—"

"Shut up!" Andy cut him off. "We've heard that line already."

"Andy," Ramirez said, standing by the window. "Come look at this."

Andy went over and was taken aback by what he saw. What lay before him was something out of a horror movie. He saw row upon row of tents, shanties, and otherwise third-world-looking dwellings. People milled about in groups, each one looking more miserable than the next. The smell was even worse once associated with the sight that produced it. Larry wasn't exaggerating; it was horrible. From where Andy was, he could see some of the closer groups, and they looked every bit as bad as Larry, covered in filth and looking extremely weak.

"You!" Andy turned his attention back to the commissioner. "How many people are in this camp?" Andy was getting angry again.

"I-I'm not sure anymore . . ." The commissioner was stuttering. As Andy moved angrily toward him, he blurted out, "Seventy-five thousand, maybe."

"How could you not know?" Ramirez was angry now. "You are responsible for these people. Why aren't they getting enough food?"

"We feed them, but there's too many. The supplies aren't coming . . . it's not my fault!" The commissioner was genuinely scared.

"I've heard that you're selling the supplies to the black market!" Andy said, slapping the man out of his chair.

"No, that's not true—" the commissioner said, trembling on the floor.

"Shut up!" Ramirez cut him off this time. "I'm going to search this base, and I'm going to look at your papers, starting with these." Ramirez grabbed a fistful of paper from the trash can. "And if I see you did anything illegal, I'm going to let those poor people out there have a word with you!"

"No!" said the commissioner, panic in his eyes.

"Yes!" Andy said, getting right in the man's face. "Where's the food stockpiled?"

"The hangers," the commissioner said, bowing his head.

A DAY LIKE ANY OTHER

Ed opened the window and called down to two of his Strykers that had taken up position on the backside of the building. "Sergeant Phillips!"

"Sir!" Phillips replied.

"Take two Strykers over to those aircraft hangers and have your infantry check them for supplies."

"Check the hangers! Hooah!" Phillips replied, dropping down into the commander's hatch as the vehicle began to move.

Sasquatch appeared in the doorway, entering the room and ducking his head through so as not to hit his head on the top of the frame. This caused the commissioner to recoil even further back behind his desk. "Hey, you two need to go down and talk to some very interesting people we just met. I'll keep your friend company," he said, eyeing the commissioner.

"Don't damage him," Andy said as he left the room. "We're not done with him."

"We're gonna be great friends by the time you get back, bro," Squatch said, pulling up a chair and having a seat across from the commissioner.

ANDY AND RAMIREZ reached the bottom of the stairs to find Wally, David, and three people who were obvious camp residents. Their appearance was much the same as Larry's: dirty clothes and faces, grimy hands, tired eyes, and very thin. Wally was chatting with one of them when he saw Andy at the bottom of the stairs.

"What a mess, huh," Wally said, turning to Andy and Ramirez.

"Yeah, and we haven't even had a good look yet," Andy replied.

"Who are these guys?" Ramirez asked quietly, referring to the three men Wally was with.

"When we rolled up," Wally began, "these guys came running up to the fence line. They were waving their arms like crazy, trying to get us to come over. So me and David went to see what's up. Turns out these guys are FEMA reps."

"FEMA?" Ramirez said, surprised. "Why are they locked up with everyone else?"

"They said they were managing a camp south of here, at a mall not far from your house, Andy," Wally said, his hands folded as though he was giving a presentation. "So things started getting crazy, and they started arguing with the CAT-MAN guys, stuff like cutting rations and medical care. Well next thing ya know, these guys got orders to transfer down here.

The CAT-MAN guys were waiting for them. They got out of their vehicle, and these CAT-MAN guys grabbed 'em and roughed 'em up, then threw them into the general population. The FEMA guys who were here got transferred out about the same time. They don't know what happened to them. CAT-MAN wanted total control, no room for arguments."

"Damn," Ramirez said in disbelief.

"Yeah, damn," Wally continued. "There were eight of them when they got here. The other five died in the cholera epidemic that hit this camp a couple of months back."

Andy, Ramirez, and Wally stood staring at the FEMA guys. *What these poor bastards have been through,* they thought.

"Lieutenant." It was Rogers. He was holding a handset that was connected to a field radio he carried on his back to his ear. He continued, now having his lieutenant's attention. "Sergeant Phillips says the hangars have shipping containers stacked three high, full of food and supplies. He says there's quite a bit of ammunition as well—5.56-, 7.62-, and .50-cal."

"Thank you, Rogers." Lieutenant Ramirez began issuing orders. "Rogers, take the HUMVEEs and get as much ammo as you can carry. Get it distributed to the company as quickly as you can. .50-cal is priority. Send Sergeant Marshall in on your way out."

"Yes, sir," Rogers said as he left, handing the field radio to Ramirez.

"If I didn't know any better, I'd say you have a shortage of ammo," Wally said, watching Rogers leave.

"You would be correct," Ramirez said, slinging the radio set over his shoulder.

"So you bluffed your way through the gate," Andy said, smiling.

"That is correct," Ramirez replied, also smiling. "We have no .50-cal ammo and only thirty rounds of 5.56 per man. This was a humanitarian operation—why would we bring ammo?"

Andy and Wally were still grinning when Sergeant Marshall walked up.

"Rogers said you needed me, sir," Sergeant Marshall said, addressing his officer.

"Yes," Ramirez began, "go get that big mouth that tried to stop us from coming through the gate and explain to him that he's going to help you, or else bad things will happen. Take him, two Strykers, and a squad of infantry. Use whatever of the CAT-MAN vehicles you need and go round up all the CAT-MAN people and all their arms and bring them back here."

"If they resist?" Sergeant Marshall asked.

A DAY LIKE ANY OTHER

"Deadly force is authorized," Ramirez replied. "Go by the hangars first and get ammo from Rogers."

"Hooah!" Sergeant Marshall said as he left.

As he exited the building, he passed Pastor Kevin, who was on his way in with Uncle Charlie, both men looking sick.

"We have to do something!" Kevin was upset. "These people haven't eaten since last week. Some of them are extremely sick."

Andy looked at Ramirez, who said, "This is your show, my friend. I came here to help you. I'll do whatever you need me to do."

Andy thought for a moment, looking from face to face. They were all looking at him. David was wide-eyed, and Kevin and Uncle Charlie were still out of breath, Kevin anxiously waiting for an answer. Then Andy's eyes came to the FEMA guys, who were now drinking water and eating MRE crackers.

"FEMA guys!" Andy called to them, waving them over. "You guys think you're well enough to help us?"

The FEMA guys nodded that they were, looking at one another as they did.

"Kevin, do you think you could round up some people to come in here and help out?" Andy asked, taking Kevin by the shoulder.

"I could, for sure," Kevin replied.

"OK, then." Andy had a plan. "Uncle Charlie, take Kevin and round up as many volunteers as you can find. FEMA guys, get cleaned up and get down to the hangers and start getting those supplies ready for distribution. Wally, there must be a public address system somewhere in this building. Find it and make an announcement. Tell them the camp is under new management, that we're getting supplies ready for distribution, and that we need anyone with any law enforcement, military, or medical experience to please come to the headquarters building."

The mood in the room, which had been somber and desperate, changed in that moment. There was a new plan, and they were hopeful it would work. Andy looked around at the faces again, and they had changed. He saw hope in their eyes.

"Let's get it done," Andy said with force.

With that, the group dispersed to execute their part of the plan. Sasquatch appeared at the bottom of the stairs. He held the camp commissioner by the collar and pushed him out in front of him.

"Hey, bro," Squatch began, "my new buddy says it's not his fault. He says he had orders to cut rations and that the people really didn't matter. It was about keeping them under control at all costs. His boss is from the United Nations, and he's at city hall in Philly. Maybe we should go pay him a visit next. Whaddya say?"

"The UN?" Andy said. "What the hell are they doing here?"

"Answer my friend's question!" Sasquatch said, shaking the commissioner like a ragdoll.

"I don't know!" The commissioner was even more skittish than before—Sasquatch had a way with people. "I mean, I was told to come to Philadelphia, so I did what I was told. I flew into Philadelphia."

"Wait a minute." Ramirez had been listening to the radio chatter between his different squads, but he was struck by something the commissioner had said. "You flew in? When did you fly in?"

The commissioner was silently staring at the floor. Squatch gave him a shake, and the commissioner answered quietly, "The week before The Event."

Andy, Ramirez, and Sasquatch were stunned. They stared at the commissioner in disbelief. He had said he was summoned *before* The Event. The government had known at least a week before and had kept it a secret. The United Nations was operating on American soil for the first time in history. This was way bigger than corruption within CAT-MAN; they were only a tool.

"Maybe we should go downtown and have a chat with this UN guy?" Andy said, finally.

"If we are, we need to go soon," Ramirez said. "My commanding officer will be wondering where I am in six hours. After that, there's no telling what will happen."

"Attention in the camp! Attention in the camp!" Wally had found the public address system. "This camp is now under new management! Food and medical supplies are being prepared for distribution at this moment! Any camp occupants with law enforcement, military, or medical experience, please report to the headquarters building!"

It started with the din becoming louder, then there was some yelling that quickly became raucous cheers. Seventy-five thousand voices raised up as one, and the building shook. Andy thought he saw a tear in Squatch's eye. It was a once-in-a-lifetime moment. They had given these people a chance to survive. They had uncovered a conspiracy, and he felt there was more to uncover. *Where did this road end?* Andy wondered. He looked over at David, who was in awe of the thunderous celebration, mouth agape.

"Let's do it!" Andy said. "Let's go downtown!"

A DAY LIKE ANY OTHER

"Yes!" Sasquatch said, shaking the commissioner again. "You have a message you want me to give your boss?"

They were here. They needed to follow this to its root. Wherever the road led, they were on it now, and there was no going back.

CHAPTER 24

BROAD STREET, HEADED SOUTH INTO PHILADELPHIA

Once again, Andy, Squatch, Wally, and David were on the move. Andy had elected to drive. Squatch sat beside him in the passenger seat, cradling the MK-240G machine gun he had claimed from the pile of CAT-MAN weapons that Sergeant Marshall had returned with. It was a large, .30-caliber machine gun. Upon picking it up, Squatch had said, "Finally, a weapon worthy of a Bigfoot! Belt fed, baby!" They were approaching city hall, and Andy could feel the nervous excitement building.

They had liberated the massive camp located at the former air station without firing a shot, and they had found a massive hoard of supplies of all sorts and evidence of an international conspiracy that began before The Event actually struck. They left two Stryker vehicles and two squads of infantry to help get the relief effort off to a good start with its new team of managers. Pastor Kevin had returned with two dozen volunteers and the promise of many more once the word got around. The CAT-MAN officers were rounded up and locked away in one of the now-empty shipping containers, its former contents distributed to the starving masses in the camp. The FEMA reps who had come forward went to work with such energy that one could forget they were just a short time ago part of the starving masses they now served.

On the way downtown, the convoy had made a short detour to another camp—the mall located near Andy's house. They had arrived to find that all the CAT-MAN officers had left. The convoy entered the perimeter of the camp, a barbed wire wall that surrounded the entire mall parking lot-turned-tent city. It was the same horrible scene they had found at the air station. Starving people, brutality and cruelty, and rampant disease were the tale the survivors told.

As they had done at the air station, several FEMA employees came forward and told the same story of being suddenly transferred and immediately interred upon arrival at their new camp. They told of the CAT-MAN guards becoming extremely animated, then gathering at the entrance of the camp and beginning what looked like a disorganized attempt to build barricades. When they heard the sound of the approaching Strykers, they panicked, piled into their vehicles, and sped off to the south. Once again, a massive stockpile of supplies was located, along with evidence of illegal activity based on the way some supplies had been separated out, as if preparing a customer's order.

The FEMA officials were put in charge, and a call went out to the camp for law enforcement, military, and medical professionals. Lieutenant Ramirez left two Strykers and two squads of infantry, as he had at the air station. Uncle Charlie, Ryan, and John also stayed behind and began scouring the local neighborhood looking for volunteers. Not nearly as sprawling as the air station, the mall was still an impressive and awful sight. As they had pulled away, Andy had felt like this was what he had been sent back for, but he wasn't nearly done.

They had passed several hospitals, all of which appeared to be long inactive. The few people they saw on the street weren't much better in appearance than the camp inhabitants. They stood and watched in amazement as the convoy drove past. The commander of the lead Stryker waved as he passed. Some people waved back, but most just stared blankly. City hall came into view up ahead, the convoy quickly closing in on their final destination. Andy looked ahead and saw that the road in front of the Masonic Temple had been blocked with police cars.

Lieutenant Ramirez's voice came over the radio. Andy had grabbed a spare so he could stay in communication with Ramirez. "Stop fifty yards short of them."

The convoy stopped. Andy saw Ramirez get out, walk to the head of the column, and call to the men crouching behind the police vehicles, "You guys Philly PD?"

A voice from behind the barricade called back, "Catastrophe Management! You need to turn around and go back!"

"We've just come from two camps where the refugees have been mistreated. We are here to speak with whoever is in charge of this district," Ramirez replied.

"You need to turn around and go back! Or we will fire!" said the voice again.

"We're coming through. You need to move," Ramirez said calmly.

"Turn around and go back the way you came!" was the response from the barricade.

Ramirez turned and walked back to his vehicle. His voice soon came over the radio again. "Lead vehicle, on my command, put a burst of .50-cal through that barricade, then push through and take up position at the foot of the city hall. We're going to take up positions north, south, east, and west. Double envelopment—no one gets out of the circle."

After a few long moments of intense stillness, the only sound being that of the vehicle engines, neither side moving, Ramirez spoke over the radio again. "Lead vehicle, open fire."

The sound of the .50-caliber machine gun firing a long burst was deafening. It caused Andy to jump even though he knew it was coming. The barricade looked like a line of giant sparklers, white sparks flying in all directions as the heavy half-inch diameter projectiles impacted the sides of the police cars. CAT-MAN officers on the opposite side were cut down with chunks of flying metal. Those who could still move crawled or staggered back toward city hall as the lead vehicle pushed through the center of the barricade. As the convoy rolled past, Andy saw that the machine gun burst had killed or injured every CAT-MAN officer who had been behind the police cars, and many lay there in pieces.

"Glad that Stryker's on our side," Andy said.

The lead vehicle came to a stop at the foot of city hall. Lieutenant Ramirez went to the left, and Andy followed, along with the Stryker directly behind him. The rest of the convoy turned right—a double envelopment. These guys knew their business. In seconds, the building was surrounded. Andy, Squatch, Wally, David, and Lieutenant Ramirez, along with two squads of infantry, were headed up the steps into city hall.

Sasquatch had the camp commissioner from the air station by the collar, pushing him ahead. Upon entering the building, Squatch said, "Take us to your boss! And don't screw around. You saw what happened to those boys at the roadblock!"

The commissioner said, "OK! OK!"

He didn't like being pushed around. It was obvious he wasn't used to it, nor did he appreciate being handcuffed to his seat on the drive down from the air station. Ramirez had placed him in a HUMVEE with three of the biggest men in his unit with instructions to make sure their passenger arrived in one piece, to which they growled, eyeing down the commissioner. After being around him for a little while, they started to pick up a European accent of some kind. They ascertained that the man had flown in from Geneva, Switzerland, a full week before The Event, and his specialty with the UN was political negotiations. This raised the question of why someone so unqualified for disaster relief would be brought in before a catastrophe. Perhaps his boss would have some answers.

A DAY LIKE ANY OTHER

It became obvious that he was taking them to the mayor's office, but upon arriving, the placard identifying it as such was covered with a piece of cardboard that said "District Governor." Not knowing what to expect, Andy had everyone stand back as he opened the door. As the door swung open, they peered in to see a man with white hair and a potbelly stuffing hundred-dollar bills into a briefcase.

Andy, disgusted, said, "Are you kiddin' me?"

The district governor was startled and threw his hands up in the air. "Don't shoot!" he said as money fluttered down around him.

There was a handheld radio on the desk that was going crazy with chatter, one voice exclaiming, "They're in the building!" Another was calling for a doctor, and a third was frantically crying out, "We can't get out; they're behind us!"

Andy picked up the radio and handed it to the governor. As he did, he said, "Tell them we won't hurt them if they lay down their arms. Tell them to proceed to the main entrance and wait there for further instructions."

The governor took the radio and followed Andy's instructions. Simultaneously, Ramirez got on his radio and instructed his troopers to expect prisoners at the main entrance. The governor handed the radio back to Andy, then turned and, in an angry tone, said something to the commissioner in some foreign language that no one present understood. The commissioner sheepishly replied in the same language. The exchange caused Andy to rush forward, grabbing the governor by the throat, pushing him back against a filing cabinet.

At the same time, Squatch grabbed the commissioner by the nape of his neck, much the way an animal would grab its young, flinging him around toward the door. "That's enough of that filthy pig Latin!" He ushered him out of the office.

Across the room, Andy was saying, "Don't talk to him! Talk to me! There's gonna be a time for talking real soon, and you and I are gonna have a lot to talk about!"

The governor responded in the same language he had spoken to the commissioner; this time, his tone was insolent.

"I don't think he likes you," Wally said with a smirk.

"We're gonna speak English now, understand?" Andy said, squeezing the governor's throat tighter.

"I understand," said the governor, struggling for breath as his airway was being crushed.

"What are you doing here?" Andy began his interrogation.

He released the man, then sat in the big chair behind the governor's desk, causing the governor to smirk in disdain. Seeing the governor's displeasure with him sitting in his seat, Andy put one dirty boot up on the desk, causing the governor to look away in disgust. This made Andy even happier.

"Answer the question," Andy said calmly. He didn't offer the governor a seat. It had to be clear that he no longer was in charge.

"I was asked to come here by your president in order to manage relief efforts following this great catastrophe," the governor replied, looking straight ahead. His accent was much more noticeable than the commissioner's—heavier but still European.

Lieutenant Ramirez, seeing the situation here was well in hand, turned his attention to the security of the building. He left the room and gathered the troopers who had accompanied them into the building. He instructed them to search the building and report back ASAP.

Andy was short on patience, still angry about this man speaking another language to the commissioner.

"When did you receive this request?" Andy asked, his impatience evident.

The governor didn't answer and instead stared straight ahead. Andy thought maybe this man had had some military training by the way he locked his head and eyes straight to the front without wavering.

After a few moments, Andy finally said, "Look, your buddy out there in the hallway already told us he got the orders before The Event, so you're not helping yourself by trying to keep secrets. It's only going to hurt you by not talking to me."

The governor stood staring, not moving.

"Not to mention, when we found you, you were trying to make off with what looks like hundreds of thousands of dollars based on what's strewn about on the floor here. We've found evidence of CAT-MAN people selling relief supplies on the black market. Looks to me like you may be getting kickbacks from that activity. I'm just sayin', it doesn't look good."

"Yes. Before," the governor said, finally.

"Now we're getting somewhere," Andy said with a smile. "See, we can have a conversation. You carry yourself like you were in the military."

The governor took that as a compliment and stood a little straighter.

"I was in the military too. So when did you start working for the United Nations?" Andy asked.

"I do not work for the United Nations," the governor replied.

A DAY LIKE ANY OTHER

Andy was surprised but was careful not to show it when he asked, "Oh, well, who do you work for?"

The governor visibly began to sweat. He knew already he had said too much—his erect posture was wilting a bit—but his stare fixed on the wall across from him. Andy knew he was on to something. There were too many questions being added to a list of already too many unanswered questions. Andy wasn't an interrogator; he was out of his element and, quite frankly, didn't have the patience for the games this guy was obviously ready to play.

"Sasquatch! Can you come back in here please?" Andy called out the office door from his seat. A moment later, Sasquatch was looming in the doorway.

Andy turned his attention back to the governor and said, "This is my friend. We call him Sasquatch. He's not a nice person like me, and right now, he's not very happy. Do you know why he's not happy, Mr. District Governor?"

"I do not know why," the governor said, trying not to sound nervous.

"He's not happy because I wouldn't let him beat the shit out of your friend, Mr. Camp Commissioner," Andy continued. "Are you wondering why I haven't asked your name? I didn't ask your friend his name either. Do you know why?"

"Why?" the governor replied, starting to wilt a little further.

Andy stood up and walked calmly over to the governor so as to be in his line of sight and said, "Because I don't care. Because when I dump your miserable carcass into one of those mass graves, filled with tens of thousands of people you were supposed to look after, the mass graves you helped create, I'll go on with my life knowing justice was served to a no-good, no-name nobody."

It was obvious the governor was trying to think of something to say by the way his mouth moved with no words coming out.

"I don't know who you think you're protecting or why you think you should. Hell, given the state of the world, I would say all bets are off. You carry yourself as someone who may have had some training, in the military or something, to maybe resist torture—that was probably a long time ago though." Andy could see that the governor was thinking. "Now we're not gonna torture you; that's not our thing." The governor closed his eyes in relief, just for a moment.

"Hey, Andy. You need to come see this." It was Ed Ramirez. His men had found something.

"Sure thing," he replied. Then, turning back to the governor, he said, "What are we going to do? This is what my giant friend is going to do: bounce you off of everything in this office just because it amuses him, and what amuses him amuses me."

The governor looked worried again.

As Andy passed Squatch on his way out, he whispered, "No closed fist."

Squatch growled deeply, never taking his eyes off the governor.

Andy left, closing the door behind him, giving David a wink as he did. The first crash of a body hitting what sounded like a filing cabinet made them all cringe. Ramirez was waiting in the hallway with two half-starved-looking men in baggy, dirty clothes.

"Hey, Andy, you sure you weren't an interrogator?" Ramirez asked.

"I've watched a lot of cop shows in my day," Andy said, smiling.

"Promise me you won't ever sick your man-ape on me." As if on cue, there was another crash and a muffled yell, which had to be the governor.

Ramirez continued, "We found these two locked up in a basement office. One says he's the mayor, and the other says he's some radio talk show host."

"Is that right?" Andy asked. The sound of breaking glass could be heard in the background.

Andy looked closer and recognized the tall Black man as Martin Travis, the mayor of Philadelphia. "Mr. Mayor, we're in the process of removing some trash from your office," Andy said, shaking the mayor's hand.

"Thank you." The mayor had Andy's hand in a firm grasp with both of his hands. "They locked me up down there months ago when I wouldn't order the police to start shooting the looters. There was other stuff too, but that was the last straw. They wanted things done that I just refused to do. Thank you! Thank you!"

Andy saw the mayor was sincere in his gratitude. Andy had never trusted politicians very much, but he could see this man was no longer a politician—he was a survivor. "We're just here trying to make things right, Mr. Mayor. Your city needs you, sir. You should get cleaned up and get some food and clean clothes. The hard work begins right now."

"I'm ready to do what needs doing, son," the mayor replied as one of the troopers gestured for him to follow, presumably to take him down to the MEV to get checked out.

"What's your story?" Andy said to the short, balding white man standing before him, shaking his hand as well.

"Hi," the man started, "I'm Tommy Rye the Talk Radio Guy."

"Dad!" David said, excited, recognizing the name.

A DAY LIKE ANY OTHER

"We were wondering what had become of you," Andy said, smiling, as more crashing and a shouted "No!" came from the mayor's office. "We were listening the night they pulled the plug on you."

"Yeah," Tommy Rye began, "not a good night. They dragged me out of there, and I've been here locked up in the basement ever since. They didn't like what I was saying, I guess, which was the truth. Go figure."

"We need to find you a microphone. There's a lot that needs saying. We've discovered so much just today," Andy said, excited that he had found a voice that people would recognize and respect. The wall behind him shook and vibrated for a moment. Sasquatch was having a good time. *I'll need to call him off soon,* Andy thought.

"Dad," David said, getting Andy's attention, "they've been transmitting the daily news program from city hall. There's a microphone here somewhere."

"Why didn't I know that?" Andy asked, impressed at his son's attention to detail.

"Go get cleaned up a bit, Mr. Radio Guy. I'm goin' to find you that microphone. Daily broadcast starts in forty minutes—you up for it?"

"I'm ready," Tommy said, his face brightening.

"David, can you take him down to the MEV please?" Andy said as the wall behind them shook again. "I need to rein in Uncle Squatch and talk to our new buddy."

ANDY ENTERED THE mayor's office to find Sasquatch holding the governor upside down by his ankles, the governor flailing his arms and trying to anticipate which direction he was about to be thrown. His hair was a mess, and sweat was pouring from his face. His clothes were torn and soaked with sweat as well. He looked as though he had been thrown around the room by a giant—because he had. He had no broken bones or broken skin. He was bruised and exhausted but perfectly fine. In the corps, they called this wall-to-wall counseling, used for making minor adjustments in the attitude of subordinates. Though it was against the rules, it still happened, and Sasquatch was extremely good at it.

Andy asked Squatch, "How's it goin'?"

"I was just admiring Mr. Governor's nice shoes; he has good taste," Squatch replied, not the slightest bit out of breath.

"Hey, Mr. Governor!" Andy began. "Where's the radio equipment?"

The governor was busy trying to push up against the floor with his arms and didn't answer, prompting Squatch to shake him and say, "Answer the question!"

The governor raised one arm and pointed as he said, breathlessly, "End of the hall . . . then right . . . sign says 'Communications Director.'"

"Thank you," Andy replied. "See, he's very helpful. Let's give him a break. Have him clean up the mess he's made of the mayor's office, then lock him up in the basement. Just keep him and that commissioner guy separated."

With that, Squatch dropped the governor, who landed in a heap on the floor like a sack of potatoes. "You got it," Sasquatch said with a smile, then turned his attention to the governor again. "You heard the man! Clean up the mess you've made here!"

THE COMMUNICATIONS OFFICE was exactly where the governor had said, and Andy now sat behind a microphone, headphones on. He looked the part of radio talk show host. The mayor and Tommy Rye sat next to him with their own mics and headphones. Tommy Rye was instantly energized upon seeing the room full of radio equipment and got right to work getting set up for the scheduled daily radio broadcast. Except today, it wouldn't be a CAT-MAN broadcaster—it would be Tommy Rye the Talk Radio Guy, back from exile.

Andy had been unsure about running all this equipment, but Tommy assured him that it was no problem and that he could do the duties of engineer and host. At first, Andy had had no intent to get on the radio, but Tommy had insisted that Andy say something. As the clock ticked toward noon, Andy thought about what a crazy day it had been. They had rolled out just after dawn, liberated two death camps, and captured the city hall of a major city, all before noon. His mind then turned to what exactly he would say.

Tommy Rye began counting down from three and pushed a button on his engineer board. An "On Air" sign was illuminated on the wall behind him, and he began to speak.

"Hello out there, America. This is Tommy Rye the Talk Radio Guy, recently liberated from a CAT-MAN dungeon here in Philadelphia City Hall, along with the mayor and about two dozen others who refused to drink President Keller's fascist Kool-Aid at the hands of his Catastrophe Management henchmen. I want to take this moment and let my family know, wherever you are, that I am well—a few pounds lighter and beaten up, but not broken and ready to fight this fight. I love you guys and miss you!

A DAY LIKE ANY OTHER

"As I said, I have the mayor here, and I will be turning the mic over to him shortly, but first I want to put on the man who liberated me from my imprisonment. For obvious reasons I will not use his name, so that being said, you're on," Tommy said, pointing to Andy.

Andy sat up closer to the microphone, cleared his throat, and began to speak. "Earlier today, on good authority, a group of private citizens attempted to enter two Catastrophe Management-controlled camps. The purpose was to investigate allegations of refugee maltreatment, poor conditions, violence, starvation, rampant disease, misallocation of relief supplies, corruption, and other accusations. We were denied access and forcibly entered these camps. The conditions found there were far worse than we had anticipated.

"The camps were liberated from government control and are now under the supervision of other more responsible parties. It was then decided to take up our grievances with the district governor, located in Philadelphia City Hall. Once again, armed Catastrophe Management officers denied us access, and once again, we gained access forcibly. We are now in control of city hall. The mayor was freed from captivity and is prepared to resume his duties for the people of Philadelphia.

"I come to you today as a private citizen of the United States to tell you what you may already know. The republic has crumbled into a fascist state run by President Keller and his CAT-MAN enforcers. What we uncovered today has made it clear that the time has come for the people of the United States to once again come together in order to throw off an abusive government. It is our right and our duty as free people to declare the Keller government and all his minions and all their powers null and void, effective immediately.

"We ask that no one needlessly throw their life away in futile engagements with superior forces but that they take the action available to them according to their own means and situation. Those who have ever sworn an oath to uphold and defend the Constitution of the United States, today is the day that you fulfill that oath. To those who have never sworn an oath, swear one now and defend your freedom. Your nation needs you and her people need you—hundreds of thousands who now languish in camps, held there like prisoners, deprived of basic needs while great stockpiles of supplies go hoarded for the profit of corrupt managers and foreign directors. This a general call to arms to any able and willing to take up the fight.

"We now occupy Philadelphia City Hall. Any of you who would stand up for liberty are welcome to join us here. We will remain here as long as we can. The government will seek to remove us and restore their absolute rule, free from the inconvenient will of the people. It is time for good people to once again stand up for what is right. Thank you all. God bless you all, and God bless this great nation."

Andy stopped speaking and leaned back in his chair with a sigh. He had just called for revolution. He looked around the room, and everyone was still watching him, their faces strong and somber. Everyone stood tall, and Andy could see the determination on their faces. He knew in that moment that every one of them would follow him to whatever end.

Tommy Rye took over the microphone, and, with a somber voice, he said, "There ya go, folks. Right here in Philadelphia, the cradle of liberty, the second American Revolution begins. God bless you, sir." Tommy nodded across at Andy.

Tommy turned the mic over to the mayor, who began issuing a series of orders, basically calling all Philadelphia police, fire, and city government employees back to work immediately. He authorized them to remove all Catastrophe Management officials from their duties, by force if necessary. But Andy's impassioned speech was still ringing in everyone's ears. This was the moment people would remember as the turning point.

SOMEWHERE IN UPSTATE Pennsylvania, Melissa was thinking, *My god, Andy. What have you gotten yourself into?* She had been listening along with Kathryn and the rest of their little community. Andy's voice was unmistakable—they had all known it was him as soon as he had uttered the first syllable of his speech. Immense pride had filled her as an American, but immense fear had filled her as a wife and mother.

"Stay safe, my love," she prayed as the last beams of sunlight left for the day.

MRS. KELLER SAT looking at her two daughters playing happily. Her husband, the president, sat across the room, avoiding eye contact with her. They too had listened to the broadcast, but neither had said a word. *The world is at a crossroads*, she thought. *Which road will it take?*

CHAPTER 25

DAY 3
PHILADELPHIA CITY HALL

As dawn rose on the first day of the second American Revolution, Andy wondered if it would also be the last. He had made an impassioned plea for good people everywhere to stand up for themselves, but he wondered if anyone would have the will to join them. He hoped for the best, but at the same time, he doubted the resolve of modern man. Had the American spirit been so dampened and watered down by the luxury and convenience of life made easy? Had the will to exercise one's personal freedom been replaced by the desire to stay safe? Was the United States of America to become just another monarchy or oligarchy, a modern feudal system, the dawn of a new Dark Age? Would the American people succumb to tragedy and forever relinquish their birthright and freedom, becoming peasants who live and die at their master's will? Andy couldn't know, and though he dared to hope, in his mind he began to plan the trip back to the farm just in case.

His fears were soon quieted as he exited city hall on his way to find a place to relieve his bladder. It seemed, through his grogginess, that there were a lot of people milling around. Lieutenant Ramirez found Andy urinating in some shrubs, and his excitement could not be contained, nor could it wait for Andy to finish his morning business.

"There you are!" Ramirez said excitedly.

"Yes. Here I am," Andy said dryly, still barely awake.

"Look," Ramirez began, oblivious to Andy's condition. "Last night, we got all the prisoners sorted—about three dozen, most of them pretty low ranking, but there were a couple of big fish too. It's gonna be fun talking to them. But afterward, people started showing up, people who heard your broadcast last night! Andy! They've been showing up all night! They're still showing up! You did it!"

Andy's mind was still foggy. What was Ramirez saying? He did what? Finally, Andy asked, "What are you talking about?"

Ramirez smiled and said, "Look!" pointing toward Dilworth Park off to Andy's right.

The park adjacent to city hall, which was empty the night before, was now an encampment. Hundreds of people were now camped there: a hodgepodge of old and young, light and dark, all shapes and sizes, all together. Andy felt a little weak-kneed. He had never imagined such a response. He had called, and here they were.

"That's not the best part!" Ramirez was almost giddy. "Wait until you see who showed up this morning! You're not gonna believe it! Hurry up playing with your pecker and let's go. I can't wait for you to meet these guys!"

Andy buttoned up his camouflage trousers and said, "I really can't imagine what could possibly be so exciting this early in the morning."

"You'll see," Ramirez said as he led Andy back into the building.

Andy was intrigued and still in shock at what his words had manifested. *Maybe we aren't headed home just yet,* he thought.

ANDY FOLLOWED RAMIREZ back into the building. As they were walking past the group of CAT-MAN prisoners, Andy stopped and stared at one of them. He recognized the man's face. Though he hadn't seen him for some time, his face was etched into Andy's memory. Andy forgot about following Ramirez and went toward the group. They were seated, leaning against a wall, about ten CAT-MAN officers under guard by one of Ramirez's troopers.

Andy addressed the soldier guarding the group. "Have we interviewed any of these people?"

"Not yet," replied the soldier.

"When we do, he's first, and I want to talk to him," Andy said, pointing to the man who hadn't noticed he was the subject of the conversation and just continued to sit and stare at nothing.

Ramirez had noticed Andy wasn't following him and came back to see what had happened.

"What's up?" he asked, meeting Andy, who was coming in his direction again.

"One of those prisoners is the guy I shot in my living room before we bugged out," Andy said without looking at Ramirez.

A DAY LIKE ANY OTHER

"Damn! They really found people of the highest quality to hire, didn't they?" Ramirez said, looking back at the group of prisoners as they walked.

"Yeah," Andy began. "That's what I was afraid of, but it could work to our advantage, too."

"Maybe," Ramirez agreed, but he had something much bigger to tell Andy. They approached two men, one a tall, slender Black man, the other a short, thin white man who had the stereotypical look of a scientist or computer guy.

"Andy, I'd like to introduce you to FBI Director Robert Cummings and the chief science advisor to the president of the United States, Dr. Norman Detweiler."

Andy was wide awake now and paying complete attention to everything Ramirez was saying, but he was still a little confused—no, skeptical.

"How do we know who they really are?" Andy asked, shaking each man's hand in turn.

Ramirez smiled and said, "There's an FBI office in this building. We found this on the wall."

Ramirez reached around him and produced a framed photograph. It was a picture of the Black man, and the caption at the bottom of the photo said, "FBI Director Robert Cummings." He handed the photo to Andy.

"Well, that's good enough for me," Andy began with a laugh. "I suppose you vouched for the scientist."

"He needs vouching for, usually," Cummings said with a laugh.

"Robert keeps me out of trouble," Detweiler said, smiling.

"What the hell are you two doing here?" Andy asked, nodding his head.

Over the next few minutes, Cummings and Detweiler told their tale of escaping FBI headquarters, President Keller's usurping the Constitution, the mysterious Mr. Sykes, and the unsettling demise of the NASA director. They spoke of the decision to keep The Event a secret of the highest order and spoke of their regret for going along with it, though it was too late for that now. They had escaped Washington, DC, collected Cummings's family, and made their way to Philadelphia. They had spent the winter there with Cummings's parents, hiding out like the fugitives they were. They agreed after hearing Andy's speech the night before that this was their only chance to get the truth out and to further investigate exactly what was going on.

Andy had listened intently; these men had been in the room with President Keller when all these decisions were made. He didn't know whether to be angry that they had had the power to do something before, that they maybe could have prevented at least some of the turmoil, or grateful that they had come to him seeking help. Andy decided there would be time for anger later—if that was warranted. Time would tell. Right now, he had two of the most important people in the country at his disposal. "Well," Andy said finally, "I don't know how I can help you guys. But you can sure help us right now. Will you help us?"

Cummings and Detweiler both eagerly agreed that they would help.

Detweiler asked, "Do you have somewhere I could charge my laptop?"

Andy chuckled, glancing at Ramirez. "Sure, but we don't have internet."

"Very funny," Detweiler said with a smile. "I haven't charged this in months, and we really can't afford to lose the data I have saved on it."

"What data?" Andy asked.

"All of the NASA data from the months leading up to the solar event that destroyed life as we know it," Detweiler replied, looking over his glasses at Andy.

"Wait a minute!" Ramirez interrupted. "Are you saying NASA knew something was coming and didn't say anything about it?"

Detweiler's face turned serious. He was about to blow their minds, and he knew it.

"In a nutshell, yes. My team was denied access to this data. We were asked to verify that The Event was coming, but we were only permitted to look back seven days. We asked ourselves why anyone would do that. President Keller's insistence that we keep The Event a complete secret was another red flag. Things didn't add up, so I had my people hack into the NASA mainframe in the hours before The Event. All that data is now stored here on this laptop. I need somewhere to charge it up and somewhere to spend some quality time with it. I was able to start going through all the NASA files while I was hiding in Robert's office, but I haven't gotten very far since we left DC."

"I think we can set you up, Doctor," Andy said. "It seems they have plenty of fuel stockpiled and more than enough functioning generators. You go figure it all out. Meanwhile, I have a few people I'd like the FBI director to talk to and a few thousand documents to review—executive orders, martial law decrees, relocation orders, stuff like that—all with congressional endorsements that just don't seem right. That is, if you don't mind, sir?"

"I don't mind at all. That's why I'm here," Cummings said, grasping Andy's shoulder. "I think I may need some help though. If I give you a list of names and addresses here in Philly, do you think you could track them down?"

"Who are we tracking down?" Andy asked.

"The Philadelphia FBI field office agents," Cummings replied.

A DAY LIKE ANY OTHER

"Well," Andy began, taking a moment to think, "we have to get all these people who are showing up organized. It may take us time to get that done, but make your list, and we'll make it happen."

"I understand," Cummings said with a smile. "Why don't we start interviewing your new friends to kill some time?"

"Sounds like a plan," Andy said.

ANDY COULDN'T BELIEVE their good fortune. To have the FBI Director and the presidential science advisor show up was beyond his wildest dreams. The fact that they had brought evidence of some kind of conspiracy was disconcerting. The stakes had been upped far beyond corrupt refugee camp administrators and Catastrophe Management officers abusing power. This was a conspiracy that potentially went all the way to the highest levels of power. He was starting to feel like he was in way over his head.

Andy left Ramirez, Squatch, and Wally to figure out who exactly had shown up during the night and get them organized based on their skill sets, while he and Director Cummings set to interrogating the CAT-MAN prisoners. Andy sent Detweiler with David to get set up in Tommy Rye's newly claimed radio studio. The studio was running on surge-protected power, and Andy figured that would be the safest place for Detweiler's computer.

Andy sat behind a large desk in the office of the deputy mayor, and Cummings sat on a sofa off to Andy's left. As requested, the first prisoner brought to them was the man Andy had shot. It had been dark that night in the living room, but David had shined the light directly on the man's face, and Andy was sure it was him.

Just to be sure, when the man entered, his hands zip-tied behind his back, Andy asked, "Do you remember me?"

The man stood, staring at Andy's face for a few seconds and then his face suddenly changed from the tired, angry I-can't-believe-this-is-happening face, to the I'm-in-deep-shit face.

"I remember you," the man said, trying to sound calm. "You're the guy who shot me."

"You shot him?" Cummings asked, raising his eyebrows.

Cummings already knew the story. He was very good at what he did, and one of those things was questioning suspects. They had something on this guy, and they were going to use it to play him.

"That's right," Andy began. "Tell him why I shot you."

The man stood staring at the wall behind Andy.

"Was it because you broke into my house?" Andy wasn't waiting for the man to answer. "Was it because you pulled a gun on me?"

"Yes," the man answered quietly, looking at the floor.

"Look," Andy changed to a gentler tone, "shit hit the fan, and we're all just trying to survive. Right?"

"Yeah," the man replied, still looking at the floor.

"What's your name?" Andy asked.

"Norm Turner," the man answered, looking up at Andy, his face still somber but more relaxed.

"Norm, I'm Andy. This is Robert." Andy had him and he knew it.

Norm nodded to Robert and said, "Hello."

Andy continued, "You did something bad, and you paid a price for it. I'm willing to move past that."

Norm stood a little taller with that statement.

"There are much bigger things going on here than home invasions during the end of civilization as we know it. I need you to tell me how you came to work for Catastrophe Management and everything you know about it. Can you do that for me?"

"I'll tell you whatever you want to know," Norm replied with a shrug.

Over the next twenty minutes or so, Norm told Andy and Robert about his life from the moment Andy shot him to the present. While Norm had been in the hospital receiving aid for his gunshot wounds, the medical supplies ran out, and most of the hospital staff were either dead or gone. Things were desperate.

During those days of chaos, a man who said he was from Catastrophe Management paid Norm a visit. The CAT-MAN official said that he knew Norm was there for a gunshot wound and said that he admired his resilience in bouncing back from such a terrible thing. The man told Norm that he was looking for strong people to come join Catastrophe Management and wondered if Norm would be interested. When Norm hesitated, the man told him that if he joined CAT-MAN, he would get him moved out of this hospital to a CAT-MAN–run hospital, one that had a full staff and full stock of supplies. Norm said the man never asked how he got shot or anything else about his background. Norm had only needed to swear an oath to President Keller and sign a contract stating that he agreed to follow the orders of the Catastrophe Management administration. It was here that Cummings stopped Norm.

"They made you swear an oath to President Keller?" Cummings asked in disbelief.

"That's right," Norm replied. "'I, Norm Turner, do solemnly swear to obey the orders of President William Keller, as handed down by the Catastrophe Management administration, and bear allegiance to no other under pain of death.'"

Cummings looked over at Andy as he sat back in his seat with a sigh. "Go on," he said, the disbelief evident in his voice.

"Well," Norm continued, "they had moved me out of there the next day, and sure enough, the CAT-MAN hospital was way better. Before you know it, I was up and about. They had given me this uniform and sent me to guard the FEMA camp at the mall—the one you guys passed on the way here."

Andy felt his blood pressure rising. *I should have finished him off that night,* he thought. Andy remembered the sight they found when they liberated that camp, and here before him stood one of the people responsible. Andy controlled himself. Norm was happily telling them everything they needed to know, and Andy wasn't about to stop him. Justice would be done, just not right now.

Andy thought carefully before he spoke, then finally said, "What do you know about relief supplies being diverted to the black market?"

The color left Norm's face, and Andy had his answer, but he let Norm speak.

"I don't know a whole lot, but from what I saw, some of the guards were taking stuff and running it to the black market. But I wasn't involved in that."

"Of course not, that wouldn't be right," Andy said as sincerely as possible. Then he added, "Do you know if these crooked guards were kicking any payments up to the camp leaders, the CAT-MAN higher-ups?"

Norm got quiet and was looking at the floor again. "I don't know if I should say any more. I mean, I have rights. Right?"

Andy couldn't take it anymore. Without raising his voice but changing his tone, Andy said, "Norm. We stopped at that camp on our way here."

Norm looked as though he was going to vomit and actually glanced at the window as if he might use it to escape.

Andy continued, "What rights did those people have? We saw how you left them when you ran off. We have the camp commissioner from the air station and the district governor in custody. Do you think they are going to show any loyalty to you? You need to tell us what you know, or maybe we'll just take you back to that camp and see what kind of treatment you get from the refugees you were guarding."

Andy had Norm's attention, and he looked at Andy and said, "OK! So we all took stuff and kicked a cut up to the camp leadership, but the reality that everyone knew but no one talked about was that the camps needed to empty, one way or another. Those were the orders from Washington. All these people were a major burden, and they needed to go, but you didn't hear that from me."

Andy glanced at Cummings, whose jaw was hanging open at Norm's revelation.

Andy repeated what he had just heard, wanting to believe he had heard wrong. "The camps needed to empty?"

"That's right," Norm replied. "There were all kinds of CAT-MAN higher-ups who kept coming through the camp. They were always wanting to know why the camp was still so full of refugees. They never outwardly said to get rid of them, nor did they say what to do with them. They just wanted the camp empty."

"If they wanted the camps emptied, why didn't they just have you run them all out? Then the camps would be empty," Cummings asked.

"That would have been the logical thing, but the very first rule we learned was that nobody leaves the camp for any reason," Norm replied, looking over at Cummings.

Andy was feeling very sick and very angry when he asked, "So basically, if the refugees couldn't leave and you had orders for the camp to empty, then in reality you guys were running an extermination camp?"

Norm was quiet again. He had said too much, and now he felt cornered.

Cummings saw that Norm was terribly frightened by what Andy had said. Cummings saw that the words had resonated with Norm and saw the opportunity to bring this interrogation home.

"Norm, why didn't you put a stop to it? Why did they have so much power over you?" Cummings said.

Norm looked up and sheepishly began to speak. "There were some guards who raised protests early on. The camp leadership would say that their concerns were noted and a special team was being sent to investigate the allegations. Then the investigation team would arrive, usually three or four vehicles loaded with dudes, all of whom weren't Americans. Russians and Chinese, for sure—we could tell by their accents. There were other foreigners too. Europeans maybe; we weren't sure. But these guys would show up and ask to speak with those individuals raising their concerns. The concerned guards would go meet with these CAT-MAN investigators, and a little while later, the investigators would leave, and we would never see the guards who spoke up ever again. So it didn't take long for the rest of us to figure out that if we wanted to keep our comfortable lives and our own personal safety intact, then we were to keep our mouths shut. So we went along to get along and didn't really think too much about right and wrong anymore. I know it's not right, but we did what we had to do to survive. At least, I did."

Andy sat staring at Norm, who was now staring blankly at nothing. Andy's anger and disgust were now replaced with a feeling of emptiness. He felt like going back to the farm and forgetting everything he just heard.

Cummings stood and went to the office door, where he summoned the soldier who had brought Norm up to them.

"Soldier," Cummings said quietly, "we're done with this one. Can you please bring up the next prisoner? Keep any who we interview separated from those who we haven't."

"Yes, sir, no problem. We have a couple of places to keep them corralled," the soldier replied before leading Norm away.

Over the next three hours, Andy and Cummings heard the same exact story from twenty-two different CAT-MAN officers. The disturbing conclusion they both came to was that a foreign organization, with the blessing of the White House, was systematically exterminating large portions of the US population. They were recruiting American citizens with nefarious backgrounds to carry out their plan, and anyone who stood up to them disappeared, thus sending a clear message to anyone else who had a problem carrying out their orders.

The burning question that remained was *Why?* Perhaps after interviewing the camp commissioner and the district governor, they might know more, but that was going to have to wait. Andy and Cummings were both exhausted and agreed that they should not interrogate them without first bringing what they had learned already to rest of the group. They wanted to have everyone's input before they took on the CAT-MAN higher-ups.

"Let's go see how Detweiler and your boys are making out," Cummings suggested.

"Yeah, maybe they have something cheerful to tell us. Lord knows we don't have anything good to tell them," Andy replied, getting up from the desk.

CHAPTER 26

THE WHITE HOUSE, WASHINGTON, DC

P RESIDENT KELLER SAT behind his desk with one arm folded up and supporting his chin. His other arm was extended and resting on the desktop, his fingers drumming on the surface. Moments ago, Catastrophe Management officers assigned to the Capitol Building had arrived at the White House with the First Lady in tow. For the fourth time this week, she had attempted to enter the Capitol Building, and for the fourth time this week, she had been denied entry and escorted back to the White House. President Keller wasn't sure how to handle the situation. She was a stubborn woman and was used to getting what she wanted once she put her mind to it.

After a long silence and what amounted to a staring match between them, President Keller said, "Why, Joyce?"

"You know why." The First Lady's tone was more combative than her husband's. "I've told you why."

"Why don't you tell me again, because it still doesn't seem to make any sense to me? Nor does it make sense to the people who keep bringing you home every day," Keller replied calmly.

"I have friends in Congress, William. I haven't seen or talked to any of them all winter." She was getting more and more curt with every word she spoke. "If you expect me to believe that they have voluntarily sequestered themselves into the Capitol Building, to the point where even I, the First Lady, cannot have access to them, well then I tell you that's bullshit, Mr. President."

"Joyce," Keller began quietly, "you're getting yourself all worked up—"

"Don't say it's over nothing, William," she said, cutting him off. "It is over something, and after that radio broadcast out of Philadelphia last night, my fears have been confirmed. There are evil forces at work here, Mr. President, and I am starting to believe that you are on the wrong side."

Simultaneously a knock came on the door and the satellite phone in his pocket began to vibrate. Keller began to sweat and said, "Come in." He knew it was Sykes—his phone was probably buzzing as well. Sykes entered and stood just inside the door.

The First Lady laughed sarcastically and stood. "Well, that's my cue, Mr. President. Your puppet master is here to bail you out, or maybe the person on the other end of that phone buzzing in your pocket is the master and you're both puppets."

Keller sat motionless, like a stunned mouse waiting for the cat to finish him. Sykes hadn't moved, but his expression revealed that he too was shocked by the First Lady's comment about the phone.

"Did the two of you really think you were getting away with something? The only two functioning phones in the entire building, and you think people won't notice them when they start buzzing like crazy? Pathetic."

With that, she exited the office, laughing and smiling as if leaving a comedy skit.

As the door shut. Sykes came over and took the seat previously occupied by the First Lady. President Keller had his forehead resting on the desk surface, the satellite phone buzzing away in his right hand. After several cycles of buzzing, Keller finally lifted his head and pushed the answer button.

"What?" he said, his voice dripping with distaste.

"What?" Mr. X replied. "I should be asking you that. What are you going to do about your wife, Mr. Keller? I'm sure you'll figure something out. Put me on speaker; I need Sykes in this conversation."

Keller pushed the speaker button on the phone and tossed it on the desk, leaning back in his chair with a sigh.

"OK, we're all here now," Keller said with more than a little attitude.

Mr. X ignored Keller's obvious disrespect and got right to the point. "Listen up, both of you. This business in Philadelphia could really screw things up. The last thing we need is some kind of revolt. Whoever these people are, they are beyond Catastrophe Management's ability to control. We want to know what's being done about it."

Keller acted as though he wasn't paying attention and said nothing, knowing that Mr. X wasn't really talking to him anyway.

Sykes leaned toward the phone and said, "Well, there are units from the Tenth Mountain Division operating out of Dover Air Force Base in Delaware. I've sent for the Army chief of staff, and he should be here soon. When he arrives, we'll have him issue orders to Tenth Mountain to deal with the problem in Philadelphia."

Keller snorted at Sykes's response.

"Do you have a problem, Keller?" Mr. X asked.

Keller leaned forward toward the phone and said, "My only problem is why you two even include me in these conversations."

"We include you, Mr. President, because you are the one issuing the orders. Don't you want to know what it is you're telling people to go do?" Mr. X replied with a laugh, at which Sykes smiled.

"But I'm not really issuing the orders, now, am I? You guys are," Keller said, stating the obvious. After the altercation with his wife, he was in no mood for playing this game with Sykes and Mr. X.

"As far as the world knows, you *are* the one issuing these orders, so just keep on doing what you're told and everything will be just fine. Is that understood, Mr. President?" Mr. X had no patience today either.

"Oh! I understand perfectly!" Keller replied, raising his voice. "If things go to shit, you people have someone to blame and get off scot-free while I get drawn and quartered."

"I'm glad you finally understand your role, Mr. President," Mr. X replied dryly. "Now, when your general gets there, you'll tell him to send those soldiers Mr. Sykes was talking about to Philadelphia and get control of things again. Got it? Another thing you need to think about is that if something like this can happen in Philadelphia, then it can happen anywhere. So you need to get some kind of protection around the Capitol Building. If these hooligans get inside there, your goose is cooked, Mr. Keller."

"Just the Capitol Building? What, you don't care about me anymore?" Keller said sarcastically.

"Very funny," Mr. X began. "The White House has an eight-foot fence around it and is surrounded by open fields. You live in a fortress. The Capitol Building is wide open, and if anyone gets in there and figures out that you've been holding the legislative and judicial branches of the government prisoner there, as well as the Joint Chiefs of the military . . . well, my friend, you'll wish you'd listened to me. Get some tanks to put around it—that will scare anyone away."

A knock on the door signaled the end of their conversation. The voice of Keller's secretary from the other side announced the arrival of the Army chief of staff.

"Get it done, gentlemen!" Mr. X commanded.

The phone went dead.

A DAY LIKE ANY OTHER

GENERAL MARTIN OWENS—the picture of an Army officer, tall and lean with close-cropped hair—entered the room, strode over to face the president, and saluted. "You sent for me, Mr. President?"

"Yes, General, please have a seat. How have you been?" President Keller said, returning General Owens's salute, then shaking his hand as he led him to take a seat by Mr. Sykes.

"I'm good, sir, thank you for asking," replied Owens.

President Keller got right to the point. "General, I suppose you've heard what's happened in Philadelphia."

"Yes, sir, I've heard. Sounds like some kind of uprising. I'm sure Catastrophe Management has things under control," General Owens said, looking over at Mr. Sykes, who was pretending to take notes on a pad of yellow legal paper.

"Well, actually, General, CAT-MAN is in a little over their heads on this one," Keller replied, also looking at Sykes.

General Owens wasn't going to let Sykes ignore him and addressed him directly. "Mr. Sykes, you're the Catastrophe Management director. What seems to be the problem? I would think you folks would have something like this well in hand."

There was no love lost between Sykes and Owens. Sykes would have made Owens disappear like so many others, but Owens's family was well connected, and thus General Owens was off-limits. Sykes had to play ball with this one even though he didn't like it.

"Well, General, it would seem that it's some of your folks going rogue who are the issue. Some PA National Guard troops are at the heart of this. So, out of respect to the Army, we thought it best if you guys handled it."

"What did you have in mind?" Owens directed his question to President Keller, purposefully turning to face the president. He didn't want Sykes to think he was asking him.

"Well, General, it's my understanding that we have some troops who could deal with this situation stationed at Dover Air Force Base in Delaware."

"There are some units of the Tenth Mountain Division in Dover providing security for the air base and that portion of the Interstate 95 corridor. They could be in Philadelphia tomorrow afternoon if the order was given today."

General Owens's reply was measured. He didn't like the notion of US combat troops deploying into a US city to face down other US combat troops.

"OK, then!" Keller said cheerfully. "Consider the order given. I'll have it drafted and send a signed copy over to the Pentagon within the hour. You get those boys rolling, General. Deadly force is authorized, as you know, under Executive Order 33, 'Declaration of Martial Law.'"

"Yes, sir. We'll get to the bottom of this," General Owens said as he stood. He had heard enough and was ready to leave, but he had one question. "Mr. President, it's been months since we've heard from General Mattlin or any of the other Joint Chiefs. How are they, sir?"

Sykes shifted in his seat, turning his attention back to his legal pad now, which was now covered in doodles. Keller slowly rose to his feet and cautiously began to speak.

"That's nice of you to ask, General. They are all doing just fine. I saw them all just the other day. They are all just as steadfastly committed to seeing this through as they were in the fall. I'm still in awe of the legislative branch's decision to sequester themselves the way they have, and I'm even more in awe of the Supreme Court's and the Joint Chiefs' show of solidarity by joining them in their self-imposed seclusion. The people's representatives wanted no distractions through this crisis. Most of my senior staff joined them as well. It really is a shining moment of selflessness on display, isn't it? A model for us all."

"Yes, sir. It certainly is," General Owens said with a somewhat forced smile. "I'm glad they are doing well. Please give them my regards the next time you see them."

"Thank you, General. I'm sure that will be appreciated," Keller said, leaning on his desk with both arms, his fists clenched. "General, there's one more thing I need you to do, if you would."

"What's that, sir?" General Owens asked, turning his attention from Keller's clenched fists back to the president's face. "I'll do what I can."

"In light of the recent events in Philadelphia"—Keller relaxed his hands and spoke in a more relaxed tone than before—"and with the potential for similar events to take place in the future, I believe it prudent that we take certain precautions, particularly at the Capitol Building. We wouldn't want all of the good work they've done over there being jeopardized."

"What did you have in mind, Mr. President?" General Owens asked, cocking his head to one side. He was intrigued by what Keller's next stroke of genius would be.

"Well," Keller began, clearing his throat. Sykes looked up from his doodles—he too was intrigued. "I was thinking a few tanks would deter any kind of trouble like we've seen in Philadelphia. Just a handful, a show of force, that kind of thing."

General Owens blinked hard at President Keller's response. He glanced down at Sykes, who was looking up at Owens like a child waiting to hear if he could have ice cream. General Owens thought for a moment, then said, "I think I could find you some tanks, Mr. President. I just don't have any officers to put in command. Whatever unit I sent up would be led by a non-commissioned officer. Almost all the officers below the rank of lieutenant colonel have either resigned their commissions or reported for retraining, and the very few who haven't intend to leave the service as soon as possible."

Keller smiled widely and said, "That would be fine, General. I know I would feel much better knowing that the people's representatives had some real firepower protecting them."

General Owens thought to himself, *That's the craziest thing anyone's ever asked me to do.* Aloud, he said, "Yes, sir. Is there anything else I can do for you, sir?"

"No, General, that about does it. I'll have that order done and sent right over, as well as one requesting the tanks."

Keller extended his hand, and General Owens shook it, then saluted smartly. President Keller returned the salute. General Owens turned and exited the office, being sure to completely ignore Sykes.

As the door clicked shut, Keller sat back in his chair and said, "I don't think he likes you, Mr. Sykes. But all in all, I think it went well."

"Yeah," Sykes began, "the feeling is mutual. I'm surprised you brought up putting tanks around the Capitol Building."

"Seeing how your CAT-MAN people have managed to piss everyone off, I figured Mr. X had a good point," Keller replied. "Let's hope whoever he gets to go to Philadelphia is up to the task."

Sykes grunted in agreement, then said, "You're getting better at that 'Congress-voluntarily-sequestered-themselves' story. I almost believed you."

"Yeah, well, I'm a good liar, don't ya know? That's not a problem," Keller replied. "What to do about my wife? That's a problem."

Sykes raised his eyebrows and went back to doodling, grateful he didn't have to deal with the First Lady.

GENERAL OWENS WAS still fuming as he entered the Pentagon. He had once considered going into politics after his time in the Army was up, but after seeing how politicians have behaved since The Event had soured him to the idea. Nothing President Keller had done since The Event had made any sense. It seemed those in leadership had done everything wrong—the opposite of common sense. Then the whole notion of the entire government, minus the president, locking themselves away in the Capitol Building so as not to be distracted was ludicrous. No one believed that story. Now they wanted him to order his units to go to Philadelphia and squash an uprising that CAT-MAN had brought on themselves and weren't able to contain on their own? *I'll be damned if I order my troopers to fire on American citizens,* he thought as he entered his staff's suite of offices.

"Listen up, people!" Owens shouted to get everyone's attention. "We're going to redeploy the Tenth Mountain detachment from Dover to Philly. We need to get in contact with Colonel Reynolds up there and make it clear that he is to proceed to Philadelphia and assess the situation and proceed with caution to achieve the best outcome. OK, people, let's make it happen."

General Owens had left his orders as vague as possible; he would leave it to the commander on scene to make the final decision on how to proceed. Keller and Sykes wouldn't like that. They wanted him to roll in there and crush any and all opposition. *Screw them,* Owens thought with a grin.

"Oh, listen up, I almost forgot!" Owens grabbed everyone's attention back for another announcement. "The geniuses at the White House want some tanks posted at the Capitol Building, so let's find some M1s to park up there so the politicians can feel nice and safe from the boogeyman. Thank you all! Carry on!"

Owens smiled as he headed for his office. He had heard the stifled chuckles and seen the raised eyebrows from his staff as they listened to his orders, even as they went to carry them out. *I love these people, my troopers. They get it. They get it,* he thought as he shut his office door.

"Tomorrow should be a very interesting day," he said to himself as he took a seat behind his desk. He prepared to write a private letter with the official orders to be delivered to Colonel Reynolds.

CHAPTER 27

PHILADELPHIA CITY HALL

ANDY AND DIRECTOR Cummings left their interrogations and found that in the hours they had spent becoming more and more infuriated with each prisoner they spoke with, Ramirez, Squatch, and Wally had been successfully sorting out the mass of people who had answered Andy's call. To start out, they had called for everyone to sort themselves into one of the following groups: law enforcement, military, health care/emergency services, and none of the above, who ranged from construction workers to computer technicians. They all had heard Andy's speech and just wanted to be part of whatever was to come. Then, they formed lines according to their grouping to get registered. They took the first person in each line and had them begin making a list of each person's name, area of expertise, age, sex, and whether or not they were armed. If armed, they noted what with and how much ammunition they had.

The first group to get tasked was the growing number of Philadelphia police officers. They were given the list of FBI agents Cummings had provided and were sent out into the city to start tracking them down. They had already returned with seven agents, who were immediately led to the mayor's office to begin sorting through the file cabinets full of documents recently captured from the district governor, as well as the piles of documents liberated from the two camps captured the day prior. They all happily got to work, eager to help in any way, especially once they learned of Director Cummings's presence and of his harrowing escape from Washington. It hadn't taken them long to begin uncovering the dirty details of Catastrophe Management's relief supplies and refugee-handling procedures. There was definitive evidence of undue influence from unknown entities outside of the federal government, as well as blatant disregard for human lives and a mandate for absolute control.

Within each group, a hierarchy was established based on longevity and general rank structure. Military and law enforcement were easy, already having established rank structures, but the other groups had a messier time sorting out who was senior. After some deliberation, it hashed itself out. With new people arriving with each passing hour, it became a full-time occupation to sort and register people, and the process continued on throughout the night. By morning, the process had become matter of fact. Working in shifts, registrars had newcomers sorted as quickly as they arrived, and just as quickly, their group leaders had them assigned to tasks or duties. In a matter of hours, it was running like a well-oiled machine.

Philadelphia police and firefighters were reporting for duty in large numbers, and Mayor Travis had them turning around and heading back out into the city to round up any supplies CAT-MAN had hidden around the city. Captured documents had stated that supplies should be stockpiled apart from obvious relief centers and Catastrophe Management facilities in the event of unrest. Mayor Travis also instructed his police officers to arrest any CAT-MAN officers they came across. They were also to put out the word that Catastrophe Management was no longer in control and that all critical emergency services personnel and all essential city employees were to return to their place of work and begin operations immediately. The city was beginning to buzz again by the morning of the second day.

The first responders with military experience who didn't fall into one of the other critical professions or identified more with their military background were separated by service and then by whether or not they had ground combat arms occupational specialties, i.e., "grunts." From the grunts, platoon commanders were chosen, and around them, forty-man platoons were formed, folding in those persons other than grunts equally among the platoons.

The resulting units were hodgepodges of Army- and Marine-led platoons made up of members of all services, with members ranging in age from nineteen to seventy years old. Those with special forces training—SEALs, Marine Force Reconnaissance, Army Rangers, etc.—were separated into their own group. This group would be used as scouts and was immediately sent out in all directions to assess any threats, as well as see what was in the general area that could be useful. Snipers and medics formed their own units as well and set about getting properly outfitted.

Altogether, they had about five hundred trigger pullers, with that number growing by the hour, and some were more qualified than others. Most were armed to some degree, and the rest soon would be as the platoon leaders sorted through the hundreds of guns CAT-MAN had confiscated in their contraband sweeps and stockpiled in city hall. Sasquatch had reluctantly relinquished his M240 machine gun to an actual trained Army machine gunner. It was a scruffy-looking motley crew of misfits, but they were still a force under a unified command, which was more than they had been a few hours earlier.

For the time being, everyone assembled at city hall (with the exception of Philadelphia police and fire, who fell under the mayor's office) would report to Sasquatch, Wally, or Lieutenant Ramirez, and ultimately to Andy. This caused immediate protest from Andy, who said, "Why should they answer to me?"

Sasquatch laughed and replied, "Because you're in charge whether you like it or not." Wally, Ramirez, and Cummings all nodded and smiled in agreement.

Tommy Rye, after getting Detweiler situated in one corner of the studio, had made his second broadcast from what he now referred to as "the recently liberated, free-radio Philly." In his broadcast, he continued to explain the justification for the obvious revolution underway, passing on horror stories from camp survivors or actually putting them on the radio in person. A good deal of time was devoted to Mayor Travis, who made an impassioned plea for Philadelphians to work together to bring the city out of the mess CAT-MAN had created on top of the natural disaster. He thanked all those who had come forward already and reiterated the need for everyone to do their part in turning things around.

Detweiler had pored over his computer data from the time he got set up in Tommy Rye's studio until late into the night. He was shocked and amazed to discover that NASA had been tracking solar activity patterns that could be interpreted as warning signs of a major coronal mass ejection event for at least four months. In fact, the federal government's own computer models had said that a historic solar event was imminent and, in the weeks leading up to the actual event, the probable date had been narrowed down to within ten days plus or minus. Furthermore, he discovered internal NASA memos reiterating the need to keep this matter of the utmost secrecy and keep the matter compartmentalized to only the highest level of NASA management. It was still not clear to him as to why such strict secrecy had been imposed.

Andy and Cummings had briefed Squatch, Wally, Ramirez, and Mayor Travis on what they had learned from the CAT-MAN prisoners, and they had all agreed that interviewing the district governor and the camp director would need to be handled delicately. Neither of them was a US citizen, and both of them obviously had much more to lose in telling the truth. It was agreed that neither of them would be interrogated until the next day. Until then, they would be sleep- and food-deprived.

At first, the mayor, a good liberal, protested, saying that such treatment was torture. He relented and agreed after Andy explained, again, what they had found in the camps and asked how the mayor had been treated in his time living in the basement of his own city hall. Andy thanked the mayor and said, "I know two wrongs don't make a right, but we need answers here. This thing seems to go all the way to the top, and we just don't have time to play nice."

The mayor agreed and suggested he go talk to both of their prisoners. He had worked with both of them in the early days of the relief effort until his protests had landed him in hot water. He would appeal to their own self-preservation instincts and tell them that Andy and company were nothing more than an angry mob bent on revenge. He would tell them that they weren't even interrogating the lower-ranking CAT-MAN prisoners and that they were just hanging them as they found them—that they would probably hang him if they knew he was talking to them like he was right now. Of course, none of that was true, but he thought if they had a restless night to think, it may cause them to slip up and actually tell the truth. He would tell them that his captors already knew a great deal about CAT-MAN operations and of the foreign influences at work within the relief efforts. He would implore them to tell the truth because some within the revolt's leadership were just waiting for an excuse to terminate them, and telling a lie that they already knew the answer to would be enough reason to convince the rest to kill both of them. He would tell them that the time for protecting whoever they worked for was over and that they needed to look out for themselves. They were sure to be cut loose by whoever sent them here in the first place. Why should they sacrifice themselves for someone who doesn't care about them?

Cummings liked the idea and thought that such a plea from the mayor, combined with deprivation tactics, would work well. Neither the district governor nor the camp director were young, fit men, and neither seemed resistant to harsh treatment. They were both visibly shaken by being taken prisoner and were probably ready to break as it was. The group unanimously agreed and set 1100 hours the following morning to begin the interviews. This way, if anything profound was learned, they would have time to get it broadcast on Tommy Rye's daily program.

It had been a busy day. The city hall they had found the day before had been transformed into a bustling hub of activity and excitement. As the boys turned in for the night, they were comforted by the sight of "their" troops manning barricades on the street below.

A DAY LIKE ANY OTHER

"What should we call them?" asked Sasquatch, looking down from city hall to the ragtag mob positioned below them.

"I don't know, man," Wally began. "They look like a bunch of nasty civilians to me."

"No way!" Sasquatch replied. "They are hard chargers disguised as nasty civilians, with a few bearded mountain men thrown in for character."

They all laughed, and Andy chimed in with, "Well, we're gonna need to call them something."

"Just for the record, you jokers look just as nasty as they do," Ramirez said, pointing generally toward Andy, Squatch, and Wally and bringing another round of laughter.

"They look like pictures of the Continental Militia from my history books—you know, from the revolution," said David, totally serious.

Tommy Rye, who had been sitting nearby enjoying the banter, stood up and shouted, "From the mouths of babes! Continental Militia it is! That's going out in tomorrow's broadcast!" Then with a dramatic wave of his arm, Tommy said, "Behold the New Continentals, ready to fight the new revolution."

Everyone fell silent. They all looked around at each other, expressionless. Finally, Wally spoke.

"The New Continental Militia. I can live with that."

Andy raised an imaginary glass as if giving a toast and said, "The New Continental Militia."

In response, all present also raised an imaginary glass and repeated, "The New Continental Militia."

The Continental Army of 1775 had been resurrected. But would this new band of patriots measure up to their namesake's legacy?

DAY 4

DAY FOUR BEGAN for Andy with a man sporting a giant gray beard apologizing for waking him up. He identified himself as a military policeman guarding the CAT-MAN prisoners. Apparently, the district governor had had enough of being harassed every ten minutes all night and had desperately requested that Mayor Travis come see him. The mayor's reasoning with him and painting Andy's band as nothing more than bloodthirsty murderers had worked. It was

0530 when Andy arrived in the basement. Mayor Travis was in with the district governor, and the man was singing like a bird. One of the guards, a less hairy but equally gray man, was listening from the open door, writing down every word the two were speaking. Andy was careful to stay out of sight so as not to upset the stage the mayor had so masterfully set the day before. By 0630, the mayor was emerging from the room looking exuberant, smiling from ear to ear.

"Nicely done, Mr. Mayor," Andy said, tipping an imaginary hat to Mayor Travis.

"Politics is nothing more than theater, young man. That poor fellow never had a chance against me," replied the mayor.

About then, another guard appeared and stated that the camp commissioner was requesting to see him. It seemed he was ready to sing as well.

Mayor Travis took Andy's shoulder, stood tall, and swung his other arm out dramatically, saying, "You see, Act Two is about to begin."

Andy smiled and asked, "Did Act One tell you anything useful?"

"Oh yes! Just wait until you read those notes," Mayor Travis replied, turning serious, then walking off toward his next victim down the hall.

Things were coming together nicely, and Andy wondered how long their good fortune would last.

Over the next four hours, Andy, Sasquatch, Wally, Cummings, Detweiler, Mayor Travis, and Ramirez went over the information they had accumulated thus far. Tommy Rye was purposely left out for now to ensure only information not deemed "classified" be put out over the airwaves. Tommy Rye agreed, saying, "Yeah, I have kind of a big mouth anyway. We don't want the bad guys knowing everythin' we've learned."

The mayor's chat with the CAT-MAN senior leaders had brought answers to a great many questions, and it was time to bring things together. In short, the following charges were passed on for Tommy to read on air at noon:

1) Based on hacked NASA files, NASA had had information months ahead of The Event that was kept secret not only by order of the White House but also by some outside entity that, based on email traffic, the NASA brass seemed even more afraid of than their own chain of command.

2) Based on interviews with CAT-MAN prisoners as well as captured documents, Catastrophe Management Administration was purposely recruiting criminals, convicts, organized crime members, gang members, fascist/anarchist/communist organization members, and other dubious characters and degenerates under the pretense that they would be easily controlled with payoffs and sweet deals. In return, they were expected to carry out illegal acts.

3) Based on interviews with CAT-MAN prisoners, captured documents, eyewitness accounts, and the testimonies of high-ranking CAT-MAN officials, Catastrophe Management Administration's upper and middle management was manned by foreign operatives who reported not to the US government but to the same outside entity that had muzzled NASA.

4) Based on interviews with CAT-MAN prisoners, captured documents, eyewitness accounts, and the testimony of high-ranking CAT-MAN officials, Catastrophe Management Administration had purposely deprived refugees of relief supplies in order to thin out the US population, thus creating a smaller, more docile, easier-to-control citizenry.

5) Based on interviews with CAT-MAN prisoners, captured documents, eyewitness accounts, and the testimony of high-ranking CAT-MAN officials, the Keller administration, with congressional approval, had usurped several articles of the Constitution in order to establish a dictatorship over the population at large.

6) Without actually capturing and interrogating this outside entity, the true intent of the aforementioned charges remained unknown for sure. However, one could surmise the ultimate goal could only be the complete overthrow of the US Constitution—the complete subjugation of the US population and the replacement of a government of the people, by the people, and for the people, with some kind of foreign-controlled oligarchy that was more akin to the feudal Europe of the Dark ages than to the United States envisioned by the Founding Fathers.

No sooner had Tommy Rye begun his noon broadcast than one of the scouts appeared looking for Wally, who was overseeing the scout platoons. The scout, a young man no older than twenty-five, spoke quickly and urgently with Wally in low tones, glanced over at Andy, and left as quickly as he had arrived. Wally gestured to Andy to come out of the broadcast studio, and Andy signaled to Tommy to keep on with his broadcast.

"Hey, man!" Wally began. "The scouts we sent south say that there's a large column of HUMVEEs headed this way."

"HUMVEEs?" Andy replied.

"Yeah," Wally continued. "They say that about a dozen are headed this way, and the rest are all stopped this side of the Walt Whitman Bridge where they crossed over from Jersey, with a bunch of five-ton trucks still on the Jersey side."

"Who the hell are they?" asked Andy.

"From the markings on the vehicles, they look like regular Army, not National Guard," replied Wally.

By now, Sasquatch, Ramirez, and Mayor Travis had joined the conversation.

"What's regular Army doing here?" asked Sasquatch.

"It's probably Tenth Mountain. They were operating out of Dover, Delaware," Ramirez chimed in.

"Maybe it's a coincidence. Maybe they're just passing through," Mayor Travis said hopefully.

"Not likely," Ramirez began, waving one hand in front of him. "If they left the bulk of their force at the bridge, then that means the group headed this way is a recon element. They're coming to see what we're up to here."

Well, that was one short-lived revolution, Andy thought to himself, regretting his earlier pondering of how long their luck would hold out. Then he said, "Let's get everyone ready to meet them then. They'll be here soon."

With that, Ramirez, Wally, and Sasquatch ran for the stairs, headed for ground level. They needed to get everyone to the barricades as quickly as possible. The stronger the show of force, the more chance they had of averting any more bloodshed. Andy turned to Mayor Travis and quietly told him to keep Tommy's broadcast going regardless of what they heard going on outside and to keep Director Cummings and Dr. Detweiler from being harmed no matter what, to which Mayor Travis agreed with a nod. Andy ran for the stairs. David ran up beside him, keeping pace.

"What's going on, Dad?" David asked as they descended.

"Trouble," Andy replied. "Go back and stay in the radio studio!"

"No way!" David replied as they both exited the building.

"I'm not going to argue with you!" Andy said, the volume of his voice increasing.

"I'm not going to argue with *you*!" David replied, matching Andy's increase in volume.

Andy stopped and turned to face David, just as Wally came running up, shouting, "They're about three minutes out, Andy! Coming straight up Route 611 from the south."

A DAY LIKE ANY OTHER

Andy didn't have time to deal with his son and instead ran for the south barricades, shouting to David as they ran, "Stay right by my side!"

David replied, "OK, Dad!"

Andy arrived at the southern barricades to find Sasquatch directing a group of Militia to a position behind a Stryker that Ramirez was clambering to the top of. Wally, who had arrived with Andy, handed him a radio handset. Andy couldn't help but notice that the handset came complete with a radio set strapped to the back of a radio operator and thought, *The boys have really done a great job getting all this organized.* There wasn't time for his admiration. He could see the tops of the HUMVEEs coming into view, weaving around wrecked and stalled vehicles.

Andy spoke into the handset, "Nobody fires unless we're fired upon. Let's see what they want." Then he handed the handset to the radio operator.

After a few seconds, the radio operator said, "All units acknowledge—no firing unless fired upon."

The lead HUMVEE stopped about one hundred yards away, and a man got out and started walking toward the barricade. Andy could clearly see that the man was dressed in full Army battle dress, complete with an armored vest and a Kevlar helmet. The soldier carried only a pistol worn in a shoulder harness, and Andy assumed he was an officer. Andy took a deep breath and thought, *Well, at least it's not CAT-MAN.* There would have been a fight for sure had it been.

The soldier stopped about one hundred feet from the barricade, removed his helmet, and shouted, "Who's in charge here?"

Andy could see that the soldier wore a silver oak leaf on his flak vest. *A lieutenant colonel,* Andy thought. *A battalion commander—they sent an infantry battalion after us.*

After a few long moments, the soldier repeated, "Who's in charge here? I need to speak with whoever is in charge!"

Andy's radio operator, with the handset still to his ear, said, "Lieutenant Ramirez wants to know if you want him to talk to this guy, and Sasquatch is asking if you want him to shoot him."

Andy looked first at the Stryker Ramirez had crawled into and saw a head popping out of the commander's hatch, looking at him. Andy assumed it was Ramirez wanting to know what to do. Andy then glanced toward Sasquatch, who had his rifle sighted in on the soldier in the road, but, like Ramirez, was looking at Andy.

Wally, who was a few feet away, finally said, "You need to go see what he wants, Andy. We'll cover you."

Andy knew Wally was right. It was up to him. He had led them down here, he had gotten them into this, and he was in charge of the whole mess. Andy nodded to Wally with a half-smile, then stood, handed his rifle to his radio operator, and started to walk around the barricade. As he approached the soldier, Andy could read the man's name tag, which read "Reynolds," and thought, *Well, Lieutenant Colonel Reynolds, let's see what you have to say.*

Andy came to a halt about six feet in front of Lieutenant Colonel Reynolds and said, "I'm in charge." It was hard for Andy to get the words out. He didn't feel like he was solely in charge. Without his friends, they wouldn't have come this far.

"Lieutenant Colonel Mathew J. Reynolds, Second Battalion, Twenty-Second Infantry Regiment, Tenth Mountain Division," replied Reynolds.

His tone was even and direct. He was serious but not harsh, and his body language was relaxed in spite of over a hundred guns pointing at him. Not tall or overly burly, his appearance, like Andy's, was that of a regular guy. White hair, piercing blue eyes, and a ruddy complexion gave you the feeling of being in the presence of a wise grandparent. He had a steely-eyed gaze that looked right through you and gave the impression that he was not to be messed with. Andy immediately thought, *I like this man. I hope we don't have to kill him.*

"My name is Andy. We'll leave it at that for now." Andy didn't want to give too much away. "What brings you to Philadelphia, Colonel?"

"I wish I could say it's a pleasure to meet you, Andy." Reynolds wasn't going to kiss anyone's ass. He was sent here for a reason, and he was going to get right to it. "But it would seem that you and your people have upset some folks in DC. They sent me here to find out what exactly is going on." After a long pause where Reynolds had expected Andy to explain himself, he continued, "What the hell is going on here, son?"

Andy thought for a moment about Reynolds's question. What the hell *is* going on here? After a few breaths, Andy looked at the ground and took a few steps closer to Reynolds. The man wanted to know what was going on, and Andy was going to tell him, but he didn't want to feel like he was yelling.

"Colonel, I'm going to tell you a story that you are going to have a hard time believing."

With that, Andy began to recap the last few days, beginning with finding Larry on the side of the road, then how the Strykers had come into their company. He told of the conditions they found at both camps and how they liberated both, along with thousands of documents. He described how they had captured city hall and found the mayor locked in the basement and how Catastrophe Management had taken over a city. Andy told of the interviews they had conducted with the CAT-MAN prisoners and of the foreign influence on the government since The Event.

Lieutenant Colonel Reynolds listened to Andy's tale. When Andy was done, he said, "I've heard all of this already on your radio program, but what proof of all this do you have? That's a tall tale, and you are going to have to do more to convince me. This is the big time, son."

Even before Tommy Rye came on the radio, he had heard rumors about all the things Andy had just told him, but he would need proof of what Andy said they had uncovered. He couldn't proceed just on hearsay.

Andy thought for a moment. He had figured this man wouldn't be easily convinced.

"OK, fair enough. I told you it would be hard to swallow. How about you come take a look? Have one of your vehicles come pick us up, and I will show you the two camps we liberated. When we get back, you can look at whatever documents you want. It's not very interesting reading until you figure out what it all means. Then it becomes riveting and nauseating at the same time."

Reynolds looked at Andy as if he had said something ridiculous. "You're gonna show me? In one of my vehicles? What's to stop me from circling the block and taking you into custody?"

"You won't do that, Colonel," Andy said calmly.

"Why won't I?" Reynolds asked.

"Because you want to see for yourself," Andy said, without hesitation. "You've heard the rumors just like the rest of us, and now you have a chance to see for yourself. Your orders were to come here and run us out, and if you meant to do that, we would be in a firefight right now, and you wouldn't have left the bulk of your force at the river. So let's go have a look."

Reynolds stood and stared at Andy for a few long moments, and Andy knew he had hit the nail on the head.

"Fine," Reynolds began, "let's go have a look."

ANDY AND LIEUTENANT Colonel Reynolds had driven north to both of the camps Andy and company had liberated. Reynolds was appalled at what he had seen and the stories he had heard from the near skeletons in the makeshift infirmaries. Even after liberation, many survivors were in bad shape. The medical staff had to carefully ration food portions, as too much food too quickly could kill those too near starvation. Things were looking up, though. Many people who were well enough to move were now living with families or at churches or schools in the local area, and volunteers were showing up every day looking to help out in some way.

Lieutenant Colonel Reynolds did not speak the whole ride back while Andy told him of the siphoning of supplies to the black market, CAT-MAN hit squads removing FEMA people or CAT-MAN guards who raised protests, and of CAT-MAN higher-ups flying in from Europe weeks before The Event. Andy showed Reynolds some of the documents they had seized and shared the written transcripts from the interviews with the CAT-MAN prisoners. Reynolds read them but only nodded occasionally as he read.

Upon arriving back at the barricades after their road trip into the hell of CAT-MAN atrocities, Andy exited the vehicle and said through the open window of Reynolds's HUMVEE, "Well, Colonel, you've seen for yourself. If you want to see more of those documents, you know where we'll be. If you decide to shoot it out, you know where we'll be. It's up to you. It was a pleasure meeting you, sir."

With that, Andy stood back from the vehicle and gave Reynolds a nod, not waiting for a response. The HUMVEE drove up the street to rejoin the rest of Reynolds's reconnaissance column.

As the HUMVEE came to a stop, Reynolds got out and was immediately surrounded by his soldiers. They were asking, "What did you see, sir? Are the camps as bad as they say?" "What's our next move?" They had heard the rumors and horror stories. Many of them had families that may or may not be in one of those camps somewhere in the country, and they wanted to know what their commanding officer had seen. They were gathered around him, eagerly waiting for some kind of information. They trusted him, and they would carry out his orders—whatever they were—but right now, they needed to know what he had seen.

Lieutenant Colonel Reynolds stood silently. He had seen the evidence and the camps for himself firsthand. In his mind, he was carefully considering what to do next. Would he surround city hall and destroy the obvious rebellion that was burgeoning there? That's what Washington wanted him to do. Would he turn his column around, head back to Dover, and report that under the

A DAY LIKE ANY OTHER

Constitution, he did not have the authority to become involved in a law enforcement matter? That would be within his rights to do, but it would be nothing more than a cop-out, the let-someone-else-handle-this option.

Or would he join them? He felt in his heart that this was what he must do, but twenty-four years of service to the United States, of following orders that he didn't always agree with and trusting the judgment of superiors above him, was in conflict with what his heart told him. He thought of General Owens's letter that had come with his orders to move to Philadelphia. It had pretty much given him the authority to use his own judgment. His orders were simple: "Move command to Philadelphia, assess the situation, and, using your best judgment for optimal outcome, proceed as necessary." General Owens had followed his orders from the White House and sent a force to Philadelphia, but Owens had left it to him to decide what to do. The moment Lieutenant Colonel Reynolds decided—whatever his decision was—he felt the fate of the country lay in the outcome. Lieutenant Colonel Reynolds's entire life, his entire career as a professional soldier, the fate of his troops, his family, and the course of his nation's future came down to this one moment in time.

Reynolds looked each man in the eye individually, lingering only a moment, just long enough to acknowledge that he had heard them. He then reached inside the HUMVEE and picked up his radio handset. Putting it to his ear, he spoke.

"Sergeant Major, this is Reynolds. How do you copy?"

Sergeant Major Webb was with the convoy at the bridge with the rest of the Second Battalion.

"Loud and clear, sir! What did you find out?"

"I found out a lot, Sergeant Major." Reynolds paused only for a moment, looking up the street toward Andy and the barricades. "I need you to do me a favor."

CHAPTER 28

UPSTATE PENNSYLVANIA

IT WAS DEFINITELY a police vehicle. Melissa thought she had seen a lightbar atop the SUV parked at her parents' house, and she now confirmed her suspicion using the binoculars she kept by the front door. *Now what do they want?* she thought to herself, glancing at the coat of fresh paint on the doorframe that now covered the freshly repaired bullet holes from her and Kathryn's shootout with the CAT-MAN lowlifes. She could see her dad talking to two men—one she was sure was one of the local sheriffs based on his uniform, but she couldn't get a good look at the other man. After watching for a few minutes, she saw them gesturing in her direction, and before she knew it, they were climbing into the SUV and were headed her way.

"Shit," she said out loud as she ducked back inside the front door.

"Language, mother!" said Kathryn, emerging from the living room at her mother's profanity.

"Kathryn!" Melissa was visibly concerned. "Get your gun and get upstairs, but don't shoot unless I tell you to!"

"What?" Kathryn was confused and quickly concerned. "Shoot at what? What's going on?"

"The police are on their way, and you can probably guess why! Go quick!" Melissa said, knowing it didn't take long for a vehicle to travel the distance from her parents' house to the cabin.

"Shit!" said Kathryn as she ran up the stairs, grabbing the AR-15 from the hallway on her way.

"That's what I said," said Melissa, composing herself as she heard the SUV pulling up out front.

"THIS IS MY daughter, Melissa," said Dr. Taft, climbing out of the back seat. Melissa had waited a few moments before emerging from the house so as to give the impression that she had been busy with something besides watching them through binoculars.

"Hello," said Melissa, stopping at the top of the front stairs. She wanted the ability to duck back inside if things went as badly as the last time they had had visitors.

"Hello, Melissa," said the man in the police uniform. "I'm Sheriff Dunlop, and this is Mr. Myers from Catastrophe Management."

Mr. Myers, tall and blond, looked like something out of a safari movie, dressed all in khaki with a pistol hanging under his arm in a shoulder rig. He nodded but did not speak. Melissa could see that he was looking at the house and the ground in front of him like he was looking for something. She felt her heart rate increasing and didn't dare look at her dad, who she could see from the corner of her eye was two shades paler than his usual old-white-man complexion.

Sheriff Dunlop, in contrast to Mr. Myers, was a stereotypical small-town sheriff, complete with a potbelly and a shiny revolver hanging from his hip in a drop holster like he was some kind of Old Western cowboy. He spoke as he walked toward the steps.

"Melissa, like I was tellin' Dr. Taft, Mr. Myers here is conducting an investigation into the murders of some of his people."

"Oh my God!" Melissa was genuinely shocked, but not for the reason Sheriff Dunlop thought.

"I know, it's horrible," Sheriff Dunlop said, putting one foot up on the stairs, "The way we found them was even more horrible."

Mr. Myers looked up from his seeming scrutiny of every blade of grass in front of the stairs, squinting as if mentally noting Melissa's reaction to the news of the murdered CAT-MAN officers.

"The way they found them?" Melissa asked. She remembered that Uncle Charlie, Ryan, and John had disposed of the bodies but never said what they did with them. She hadn't wanted to know at the time, but now she regretted not asking.

"Yeah!" Sheriff Dunlop was eager to tell her the story; it seemed the most exciting thing he'd ever experienced. He continued, "They were all shot up. One fella had fifteen holes in him."

"My God!" Melissa said, trying to sound shocked. She was well aware of the degree of damage she and Kathryn had inflicted upon the CAT-MAN officers who had attacked her.

"Yup!" Sheriff Dunlop wasn't done. "They were all piled up in the back of their vehicle like trash. Found them down at the highway interchange. Then to boot, whoever killed them spray-painted on their vehicle: 'Found guilty of assault, attempted rape, and attempted murder. Sentenced to death.' Pretty sick scene."

Melissa was speechless and just stood there staring at Sheriff Dunlop.

Mr. Myers crouched down and picked up something shiny, looked closely at it, then tucked it in his pocket. He said, "Sheriff Dunlop, it's time for you to stop talking. You talk too much. We're done here. Let's go."

His accent wasn't American or European. *South African, maybe*? thought Dr. Taft.

"Well, OK," Sheriff Dunlop replied with a chuckle. "Your wish is my command."

As Mr. Myers and Sheriff Dunlop climbed back into the SUV, Sheriff Dunlop looked straight into Melissa's eyes. His face was much more serious, giving her the impression he wasn't the hillbilly sheriff she thought he was. Not knowing if she should take that as a good thing or a bad thing, she raised her arm and waved. Sheriff Dunlop was smiling and talking Mr. Myers's ear off as they pulled away.

"Did you see what he picked up?" asked Dr. Taft urgently as he bounded up the stairs.

"It was an empty shell casing, Dad," replied Melissa, slinking down onto the top step, exhausted from her performance and feeling nauseated.

"The boys picked them all up! I saw them pick them all up!"

Dr. Taft was frantic. All the blood that had drained from his head while their visitors were present was back, and then some. His head was beet red and looked as if it would explode.

"Well, apparently they missed one," Melissa replied matter of factly.

"And what was Charlie thinking, leaving them on the highway like that?" Dr. Taft asked, slumping down beside his daughter.

"He was sending a message, I guess," Melissa replied.

"What was all that about?" María asked as she and Donna approached from the Tafts' house.

"Yeah, Mom, that didn't sound very good," Kathryn added, emerging from the front door, rifle still in hand.

"It wasn't good," began Melissa. "They'll be back. With more CAT-MAN people, I'm sure."

A DAY LIKE ANY OTHER

"Oh, shit! What are we gonna do?" asked María, putting one hand to her forehead.

"We're gonna get ready," replied Melissa. "If they come back, we'll be ready for them."

CHAPTER 29

PHILADELPHIA CITY HALL

WELL, AT LEAST they aren't shooting at us," Ramirez said to Andy, who stood next to him at the barricades.

"He was pretty upset by what he saw at those camps. He didn't say as much, but I could see it on his face," Andy replied.

"Who do you think he's talking to?" asked Uncle Charlie.

Andy had taken Uncle Charlie aside at the newly liberated mall camp, apprised him of the situation, and instructed him to round up Ryan, John, and all of Lieutenant Ramirez's men and have them head to city hall. If there was going to be a fight, Andy wanted all of his heavy firepower present, including most of all the armored Strykers. Uncle Charlie quickly carried out Andy's request and arrived at city hall a few minutes after Andy had returned with Reynolds. Reynolds had dropped Andy off and returned to his small convoy at the other end of the block. He was now talking into a radio handset.

"He's probably calling in an airstrike on us," said Wally, causing everyone within earshot to laugh except David, who instead looked worriedly at the sky.

"Wait!" said Sasquatch. "Here he comes."

Lieutenant Colonel Reynolds was striding down the street toward them with a trooper carrying a radio on his back in tow.

"Well, it's not an airstrike," joked Wally dryly, much to David's relief.

"So are we going to duke it out, Colonel?" Andy called out as Reynolds grew closer.

"Not right this minute. Maybe a little later on. I have someone checking on something for me right now," Reynolds replied as he reached the barricades. He noticed Uncle Charlie and the sudden arrival of more armored vehicles. "I see you brought up reinforcements from those camps—smart move. You're Uncle Charlie, right?"

"That's right," Uncle Charlie replied. His tone was tense. Everyone was tense—this could get very violent very quickly.

A DAY LIKE ANY OTHER

Reynolds turned his attention to the young officer standing beside Andy. "Lieutenant Ramirez."

"Yes, sir," Ramirez replied, standing a little taller.

"Andy here told me how you came to be part of his merry band," Reynolds said, waving his hand in Andy's direction. "What I'm curious about is why you chose to resign your commission instead of going to retraining. Almost all of my officers chose to stay in the service, and the ones who didn't had very specific reasons for getting out. I'd like to hear yours, if you don't mind telling me."

Ramirez, a little surprised at the question, didn't answer at first, looking at Andy for a moment, then at Reynolds, and then at the ground for a moment more. When he looked up, there was a tear in his eye, and he spoke.

"Sir, my family is from Cuba originally. My grandfather was an officer in the Cuban army when the communists took over. Batista escaped with most of his loyal officers, but my grandfather did not escape. He thought they would kill him right away when he was captured because they knew he was loyal to Batista. He was surprised when they said to him, 'We will not hurt you, but you need to go through re-education.' So he agreed to go to a re-education camp. What choice did he have? He could go to the camp or get a bullet in the head. After he went to the camp, he started thinking the bullet would have been better. The 'instructors' at this camp beat him and starved him and mistreated him, and it was the same for all the officers there for re-education. Some of them died right away; others got sick and then died.

"My grandfather was very strong, so he made a plan to escape. He waited until the right time, when the guards were distracted, and he crawled out through a sewer pipe. When he got to the river where the pipe emptied, he swam all night. After two days, he made it back to my grandmother and my father and uncle, who were just small boys. He told them to take food and water and go with him. So they ran. He took them to a boat, and they all sailed to Florida.

"When I heard that the government wanted me to go for retraining, I thought of my grandfather and said, 'I will not go.' That's why I will resign my commission once I return to our base at Fort Indiantown Gap."

"That's an interesting story, lieutenant," Reynolds said, leaning with one arm on his side of the barricade. "You know, when the order came down for the junior officers to report for retraining or resign, it didn't sit well with me. I couldn't help but think that it sounded a lot like Stalin's purge of the Red Army. The communists gained total control of the military by getting rid of its officer corps."

"I tried to explain that to my friends, the other officers in my unit, but they didn't get it. They said, 'But this is America, that could never happen here,'" Ramirez replied.

Reynolds stood up straight again, looked up at city hall, and said, "That's what I said when my boys were heading off for retraining: 'That could never happen in America.' Those camps I saw today were something I always thought could never happen in America, either."

"What are you going to do about it, Colonel?" Andy asked calmly.

Lieutenant Colonel Reynolds did not answer, but instead turned and looked back south down Broad Street toward his troopers, who were all out of their vehicles looking north toward him. Lieutenant Colonel Reynolds then looked up at the sky, put his hands on his hips, and turned back toward Andy.

"I've never been to Philly."

"Welcome to Philadelphia, sir," Andy replied.

He gave Ramirez a look and a shrug, to which Ramirez responded with a nod and a raised eyebrow.

Reynolds's radio operator shattered the awkward silence.

"Sir, Sergeant Major Webb," he said, handing the radio handset to Reynolds.

Reynolds took the handset and, putting it to his ear, said, "What did you find, Sergeant Major?" Reynolds listened and nodded, occasionally glancing at Andy and Ramirez. After a short time, Reynolds said, "Thank you, Sergeant Major. It's good you weren't spotted. Head back to the bridge and wait there for me. Gather the troops together and let them know what you saw. I'll be back shortly."

With that, Reynolds handed the handset back to his radio operator. Then, putting his hand on his shoulder, he said, "Son, do me a big favor and go tell those boys over there that it's OK and to go ahead and drive over here so I can talk to them."

Reynolds spoke more like a loving father than a tough combat leader. At that moment, Andy knew Reynolds would not fight them. He truly wished Reynolds would join them.

A few moments later, Reynolds's small recon convoy pulled up to the barricades. Troopers started getting out and gathering around him. He stood with his back to Andy and company while his order was being carried out. Andy felt a smile starting to creep across his face but quickly restrained himself. He felt that Reynolds was about to join them but still didn't want to get his hopes up.

A DAY LIKE ANY OTHER

Reynolds began to speak, satisfied that all his men were present. "Troopers, I've seen some terrible things today." He stopped and looked down at the ground, then turned slightly and glanced back at Andy. "Those camps are worse than the rumors."

Reynolds's troopers listened intently, their faces serious and stern. Some looked worried, and others looked angry.

"I know all of you stayed when the option to leave the service came around with the thought in mind that those you cared about were safe back wherever you call home. I believed that too. Now I can't say that I believe it at all, and I'm sorry if anything I said convinced any of you to stay."

Reynolds's men were dumbfounded. As a group, they weren't sure what to do or what to say, until finally, one man spoke up.

"What are you going to do, sir?"

Andy was eager to hear the answer to that question as well.

Reynolds, without hesitation, said, "I'm going to resign my commission and join these good people."

Andy's heart soared, but he was still able to control his urge to smile and kept a straight face.

Reynolds continued, "I sent Sergeant Major Webb on a recon run to the stadium complex south of the city. He told me there's a massive camp there. He said it's worse than anything he's ever seen, and that's pretty bad considering the sergeant major has been to places like Somalia and Ethiopia.

"I can't order any of you to stay, I know you all have families, people you care about, who could be in a camp too, and you'll want to go make sure they're OK. I can, however, ask you to stay, at least a little while, and maybe together we can ease some suffering. If anyone wants to leave, I won't stop them. We'll join back up with the rest of the battalion at the bridge. I'll give them the same speech, and we'll figure things out from there. So let's load back up and head on down there."

With that, Reynolds's troopers trotted back their vehicles and, one by one, started turning around for the trip back to the bridge.

Reynolds turned to face Andy and said, "That is, of course, if I'm welcome."

Finally, Andy was free to smile and did so from ear to ear. "Colonel Reynolds, sir, you are most welcome."

Reynolds smiled as well. "Great. I know I'm not in charge anymore, but I'd like to suggest we liberate that camp today."

Andy looked at Ramirez, then at Sasquatch, both of whom had broad smiles on their faces.

"What'd you have in mind, Colonel?" Andy asked, already knowing Reynolds had a plan.

"Well," Reynolds began, "I'm going to go see how many of my men will stay. If there are enough, I'll deploy them around that camp to the east and the south. You folks come rolling down Broad Street from the north and seal off the whole complex, joining up with my people in the southwest. Can you be ready to roll out in one hour?"

Andy was thinking, *For someone who isn't in charge, it sure sounds a lot like he just gave a bunch of orders.* Reynolds was correct, though. They should liberate the camp at the sports complex. It was a large complex with stadiums where all the Philadelphia sports teams played. With enormous parking lots and huge stadiums, Andy could only imagine how many refugees were penned up there.

Andy looked around and said, "Colonel, if you can muster a force to help us, then we'll be ready to move in an hour."

"Alright, then," Reynolds began. "I'll deploy my battalion in one hour as a blocking force. You guys are the assault force, so you push the bad guys out, and we'll gather them up. If you get into trouble, we'll move to support you. Sound good?"

"Simple enough," Andy replied.

"The CAT-MAN guards down there have to be on high alert after what we've been doing up here," Wally interjected.

"They won't expect the colonel's force coming in from the east, so it may be enough of a surprise to make them panic and run again," said Ramirez.

"Still, though, Wally has a point. These guys are going to be ready for a fight, so we'd better be ready too," Sasquatch added.

"Maybe," Andy said, stroking his chin, "we'll roll in fast with the Strykers in the lead and divide the force. The rest will deploy east to west and sweep south, but the Strykers and Ramirez are the main effort. Are you OK with that, Lieutenant?"

"I'm OK with that," Ramirez replied.

"I'll have my communications people find the CAT-MAN frequencies and try to walk on them if they try to get a defense coordinated or get word out about what's happening. Getting walked on is when two users on the same frequency try to talk at the same time, resulting in garbled static for anyone listening, essentially jamming transmissions," Reynolds explained.

A DAY LIKE ANY OTHER

At that, Andy said, "I'll have the scouts who have been watching your people at the bridge reposition to get eyes on the sports complex, and I'll have a couple of them escort you back to your convoy. When you are ready to roll, send them back here with any last-minute changes. When I receive the message, I'll call you on the radio with the code word 'Asphalt.' When you're ready, reply back 'Spare Tire.'" Andy had looked around and just used the first things he saw as code words. "We'll both then execute the plan."

"I'll see you at the ballpark then," Reynolds said, reaching out to shake Andy's hand.

"At the ballpark," Andy replied, grasping Reynolds's hand in a firm handshake.

As Reynolds drove off to the south to rejoin his battalion, Andy called for all platoon leaders to meet him in front of city hall. They needed to get organized for an assault, and they only had an hour to do it.

It was quickly becoming obvious that liberating the sports complex wasn't going to be an easy thing. The moment the lead Stryker had crossed West Oregon into Marconi Plaza, the neighborhood to the east erupted with gunfire, forcing the entire convoy to halt. The Stryker's armor was thick enough to prevent the small arms fire from causing any damage, and the up-armored HUMVEEs had a level of protection. However, the rest of the convoy was made up of civilian vehicles, which would be ripped apart by the heavy fire. Andy ordered the convoy to halt and moved to the corner to assess the situation. He was quickly forced back the moment he peeked his head around the building by an explosion of fire impacting directly to his front and to the side of the lead Stryker behind him, which was sticking out halfway into the intersection.

"They were waiting for us this time!" Ramirez yelled over the banging of the Stryker's .50-caliber machine gun, engaging muzzle flashes from the group of houses that were now obviously occupied by CAT-MAN officers.

"We're gonna have to sweep that neighborhood," Andy replied, pulling out his Philadelphia tourist map.

There were cases of tourist maps at city hall. While they were not up to military standards, they were very detailed in that every street in the city was on them. Andy had given his orders and assigned objectives to his platoon leaders using these maps, and every platoon leader had one. Andy had to change the entire plan now on the fly.

"We have to move, bro!" Sasquatch said, running up from further back in the convoy. "We're stacked up for ten blocks!"

Andy nodded and directed Ramirez and Sasquatch to look at the map.

"Ramirez, you take the Strykers and the HUMVEEs through this fire and take up positions to the west as planned. Squatch, you take the northern force and move down West Shunk Street. Deploy your force and sweep south to the sports complex."

Andy wasn't happy about doing this. West Shunk Street was one block farther north than he had wanted to deploy the northern force.

"To support you both, I'll deploy the rest of the western group into these buildings to put fire on those houses shooting at us. When the fire lessens, we'll move south and join up with Ramirez. I'll call Reynolds and tell him the plan has changed and that, if possible, they should move into the camp. We are now supporting them instead of the other way around, OK?"

Andy looked up from the map, expecting input from Ramirez or Sasquatch. Instead, Sasquatch shouted, "Got it!" as he turned to run back down the street to carry out his part of the plan. Ramirez slapped Andy on the back and yelled "Roger!" He turned to organize his vehicles to make the run through Marconi Plaza.

Quickly, Andy stood and shouted to Wally, who was a few feet away, "Get people in these houses and put fire on those houses."

Wally only gave a thumbs-up and quickly started shouting for the platoon leaders to start getting their troops into firing positions.

Looking north, Andy could see vehicles making the left turn down West Shunk Street. Simultaneously, Andy heard the volume of fire increasing from the CAT-MAN positions and turned to see Stryker vehicles moving across the plaza. Andy reached his arm out toward his radio operator, who instinctively slapped the radio handset into Andy's outstretched hand.

Andy spoke into the handset. "Spare Tire, this is Asphalt!"

"Go ahead, Asphalt!" replied Reynolds.

"What's the situation over there?" Andy asked, increasing the volume of his voice as machine guns began firing from the buildings beside him. It was Wally's group getting in the fight.

"We are in position to the east and south. We've taken forty-two prisoners. All the resistance is to the north. You boys OK up there?"

"We've got a pretty good fight on our hands here. You are the main effort now. Move into the camp and eliminate any resistance!" Andy replied as another burst of machine-gun fire thundered behind him.

A DAY LIKE ANY OTHER

"Roger that, Asphalt," Reynolds replied calmly, wondering how Andy had come up these call signs but glad he was moving into the camp.

Reynolds then quickly started getting his men into action. As any good commander would, Reynolds had a plan if it fell to him to liberate the camp and began issuing orders to make that happen. *It's going to be a good day,* he thought.

Satisfied that securing the camp was in good hands, Andy turned his attention to the building volume of fire he could hear coming from the neighborhood Sasquatch was assaulting. Andy called for Squatch on the radio.

"Man-Ape, this is Asphalt. What's your situation?"

"The situation is shitty!" Sasquatch yelled in reply. "All of these streets lead straight into the CAT-MAN fire. It's like walking into a bullet funnel! We have a bunch of casualties, including Uncle Charlie and Ryan!"

Andy's first impulse was to go help his friends.

"I'll be right there!" he called back urgently.

"Why?" Sasquatch replied. "So you can get pinned down with us?"

Andy knew Squatch was right. Just then, Andy heard fire coming from the direction Ramirez had just headed. Andy needed to do something, and he needed to do it now. He thought for a moment, then peeked around the corner toward the row of houses across the plaza they had taken fire from originally. He turned to David, who had been beside him the entire time.

"David!" Andy said, taking his son by the shoulder and pointing toward the MEV. The MEV was part of the command element and thus had stayed behind when the rest of the Strykers had moved south along Broad Street. "Go tell the commander of that vehicle to move it over to help with the casualties. Go with them and tell Uncle Squatch we're maneuvering to help him!"

"Maneuvering to help him," David muttered to himself as he rose to carry out his father's instructions. His eyes were wide, and his face was white as a sheet; he had never been in a battle before, and it showed. Neither had Andy, for that matter, and he wondered if he looked much like his son did right now. Andy didn't need David to tell Sasquatch anything—he was about to call him on the radio and tell him what he was up to—but Andy knew what he had to do, and he didn't want David with him when he did it.

"Hang on, Man-Ape! We're gonna take some pressure off you. Don't shoot us," Andy yelled into his handset.

"Roger!" replied Sasquatch.

"What are we doing?" Wally asked as he ran toward Andy, who was signaling for the platoon positioned along the buildings behind Wally to come to him. Wally had been listening to Andy and Sasquatch's exchange and imagined whatever Andy had in mind would include him.

"I'm moving to those buildings with the reserve platoon. You cover us, and when we get there, join us and we'll sweep the block from west to east!" Andy replied, pointing toward the east.

Wally nodded and returned to inform his platoon leaders of the new plan.

Andy gave Wally a few seconds to get positioned, then called over the radio, "COVERING FIRE!" With that, what was previously the steady firing of units engaged in the firefight erupted into one continuous roar of gunfire as Wally's group and Sasquatch's group both acknowledged Andy's order and began pouring fire onto the CAT-MAN positions.

Andy took a deep breath and yelled, "Follow me!" to the platoon stacked up behind him. He took off running toward the closest house on the offending block.

As Andy ran, he could see the houses he was running toward raining chunks of wood and concrete. Anyone inside would think the building was going to collapse. Though Andy felt very exposed out in the street, he was glad he wasn't in those houses. Covering the hundred yards or so in a full sprint, Andy arrived winded but relieved to have crossed unscathed. There had been only a couple of bullet impacts near his feet, and as the rest of the platoon finished crossing, Andy could see that rounds were indeed striking around them as well. The entire group had managed to cross without casualties and was already getting to work providing covering fire for Wally's platoons to cross. *Good,* Andy thought, reaching his arm out toward his radio operator.

Suddenly, the sidewalk around Andy began erupting with chunks of concrete. Andy's radioman fell backward, struck several times in the chest, spraying Andy's face with blood. Momentarily stunned, Andy watched as the radioman fell and as two men behind him started shooting up at the roof above them.

"Holy shit! That was close! Are you OK?" Wally yelled directly into Andy's face. He had been running across and had seen the whole thing.

Regaining his composure, Andy replied, "Yeah, I'm OK," and began wiping his dead radioman's blood from his face. "Get people up on these rooftops and start sweeping down West Oregon Street. I'll have the reserve platoon sweep south toward the complex along the edge of the plaza."

A DAY LIKE ANY OTHER

Wally nodded and ran off toward the first of his platoons to come across, directing them down the street. He couldn't help looking at the body of Andy's radioman as he left.

Andy knelt beside his radioman, a young man with freckles and blonde hair, whom Andy had not had the opportunity to ask his name. Andy picked up the handset he had been reaching for when the man was shot and called Sasquatch.

"We're across. Hold your fire. Get your casualties taken care of and reassemble on West Oregon ASAP."

"Copy," replied Sasquatch.

Andy could see already that the CAT-MAN resistance was breaking. They were flanked, and with Andy's troops kicking in doors while their comrades covered from nearby rooftops, the situation was untenable for the CAT-MAN troops. They began to fall back.

"Asphalt, this is Keystone." It was Ramirez.

"Go ahead, Keystone," Andy replied, while he and another man gently removed the radio from his deceased radioman's back.

"Good call getting us down here quick." Ramirez was calm, but Andy could hear the adrenaline in his voice. "We engaged a large force of CAT-MAN vehicles that were headed your way from the Navy Yard. My boys are mopping up what's left of them in FDR Park." Franklin Delano Roosevelt Park was adjacent to both the sports complex and the Philadelphia Navy Yard.

"Roger, good job," Andy replied, hoisting the blood-soaked radio onto his back.

"Asphalt, Spare Tire." Reynolds was calling now.

"Go ahead, Spare Tire," Andy replied as he walked south along the edge of the plaza. The sound of gunfire was becoming less often and farther away with every step he took.

"We've moved into the camp—all the resistance has run or been dealt with. I'm sending a company over to the Navy Yard; all the prisoners say that's the headquarters for this operation. This camp is enormous. They had it well defended, and they were waiting for us. Good job getting it done, Asphalt."

"Roger, let's get ready for a counterattack. They had a lot of people here, and they're not going to be happy about losing it," Andy replied. *Good job*, he thought, trying to convince himself to feel proud of their victory, but instead he just felt guilty. They had won, but his nameless radioman was lying dead back there with countless others.

Just then, Andy reached the end of the street. The sports stadiums were very prominent in the skyline now. Andy stopped in his tracks as he topped the highway that ran east to west along the northern edge of the complex. What had once been vast parking lots was now the home to the largest FEMA camp Andy had seen yet. Even after liberating two other camps, Andy was still awestruck and horrified at what he saw. As the firing died down, Andy could hear a combination of wailing, cheering, and general celebrating from the camp occupants. They were beginning to line the fence in front of him, and they looked just as pathetic as the people in the other camps.

As Andy drew closer, he could see that many of them were in tears, some were being supported by their companions, and all were dirty and malnourished, sick and starving. Reaching the fence, he put his hand against it, and a young woman with blonde hair and freckles put her hand against his, looking into his eyes with tears in hers. Andy thought again, *Good job*. His radioman being killed just two feet away from him had shaken Andy, but he carried on in the moment as hundreds of lives were in his hands. The farther away he got from the place where his radioman lies, and as the sound of gunfire lessened, the heavier the weight became. As he approached the sports complex, he knew they had won, but instead of feeling victorious, he felt ashamed. He had left the farm, his family, and come here to put all these good people at risk and had now gotten some killed. The sight of that young woman brought him back to reality. He had given orders and led people to their deaths. But if he hadn't, all these thousands of innocent people would still be in bondage. He said it to himself again, this time out loud, "Good job."

CHAPTER 30

PHILADELPHIA, PENNSYLVANIA

Once again, good afternoon, ladies and gentlemen. It's Tommy Rye coming to you from the cradle of liberty, beautiful Philadelphia, Pennsylvania. Some of you are hearing my voice today in real time for the first time. Thanks to another hard-fought victory by the New Continental Army over the tyrannical Catastrophe Management thugs, today's broadcast is being transmitted via the massive media equipment liberated from the Philadelphia sports complex. Also liberated were approximately 150,000 of our countrymen who had been illegally imprisoned there..."

It had been a victory. Andy was listening to Tommy Rye's program from his new digs at the Navy Yard and had chosen solitude, except for David of course. David had been quite angry with his dad at first for sending him away with the MEV. After seeing him covered in blood with a look on his face he had never seen before, he chose not to press the issue.

They had liberated the massive camp and the Navy Yard, where they found container ships loaded with supplies. They had taken 423 prisoners and killed thirty-eight. These CAT-MAN troops had been waiting for them. They had put up a fight until they were surrounded and began to panic. Andy was sure his force would have sustained substantially more casualties if not for Lieutenant Colonel Reynolds coming in from the east. The enemy had not expected that and did not react well to the flanking attack. As it was, Andy was not happy about taking casualties. As few as they were, five were killed, including Andy's radioman, one of Ramirez's infantrymen, and three from Sasquatch's force, including Uncle Charlie.

Andy's heart had sunk upon seeing Uncle Charlie's lifeless body. Ryan had been shot in the abdomen, and the medics here had patched him up as best they could, but it was very likely he would need surgery in the near future. John would be taking him and Uncle Charlie's body back home at first light. Andy had asked John to look in on his family if possible and had let them know that he and David were OK. John had said he would and that he would return with more troops as soon as he could.

Reynolds had not waited for sunrise to depart. He had informed Andy that he would be taking one company of infantry and most of the trucks and heading to Fort Dix, New Jersey. Most of Reynolds's officers had been assigned to Fort Dix for retraining, and he felt obligated to go there and, if necessary, rescue them. Andy had understood and wished Reynolds good luck. Reynolds had promised to return with more weapons and more troops. Reynolds had felt he needed to leave immediately before Army headquarters figured out that he had changed sides. He also couldn't bear the thought of his young officers in some kind of prison camp for another minute longer. Reynolds had sent a courier to report to General Owens and deliver his resignation, along with a letter for General Owens's eyes only.

Sadly, FDR Park was the site of at least twelve mass graves, a testament to the conditions in the camp. Ramirez had taken charge of securing the perimeter, which was no easy task, as the perimeter was now all of South Philadelphia. He had also had to consider reports that a large CAT-MAN force may still have been stationed at the Philadelphia International Airport just across the Schuylkill River to the south, so he had positioned troops on all the bridges in and out of South Philly.

Andy felt very low. They had won a great victory, but Andy had given orders and people had been killed as a result. He was going to have to come to grips with that and at the same time figure out what to do next. He lay quietly listening to Tommy Rye, but he was thinking about Melissa and Kathryn.

UPSTATE PENNSYLVANIA

MELISSA SAT LISTENING to the radio. The more she heard, the sicker she felt.

They had worked all morning erecting a swinging gate on the road leading up to the property. Dr. Taft had had it delivered last summer but never felt the need to install it until today. Melissa had noticed through the trees that a black SUV had passed by on the main road at least twice while they worked. They had also rigged a canned bullhorn to blast if the gate was opened to warn them if someone was coming up the driveway.

A DAY LIKE ANY OTHER

Whatever you're doing, Andrew, hurry up and get it done and get your ass back here, Melissa thought as Tommy Rye continued to speak about the goings-on in Philadelphia.

THE WHITE HOUSE

PRESIDENT KELLER WAS beyond angry. It was bad enough that Sykes was standing in front of him telling him that Philadelphia was lost, but now his satellite phone was buzzing. Keller took it from his pocket and threw it against the wall. Almost immediately, Sykes's phone began to buzz.

Sykes hit the answer button and said, "Yes, sir." Then he put the phone on speaker.

"Mr. President." It was Mr. X, of course. "Don't you know it's very childish to throw things when you're upset?"

"What do you want!?" Keller asked impatiently.

"I want history to see you as a successful president," Mr. X began calmly. "This business in Philadelphia is beginning to spark insurrections all over the country. Whoever you sent up there to deal with it obviously wasn't up to the task."

"We haven't heard anything from General Owens yet, so we have no idea what happened in Philadelphia today!" Keller shot back.

"We don't need General Owens to report back to tell us that these terrorists have captured Philadelphia in its entirety," Mr. X replied calmly.

President Keller chose not to respond, as he knew Mr. X was correct. To argue the point with him further was futile.

"Now, here's what you are going to do," Mr. X began. "Mr. President, you will send a SEAL team to Philadelphia with orders to eliminate the leadership of these terrorists. Mr. Sykes will assemble his team and get to Philadelphia so we can get some reliable intelligence. Mr. Sykes, you should be prepared to end this should the Navy fail where the Army already has. How long until you're ready?"

"My team is ready and standing by, sir," Sykes answered immediately.

Keller was confused. "Wait, Sykes has a team?" he asked.

Sykes did not answer. After an awkward pause, Mr. X began to speak.

"Do you know what Mr. Sykes did before he came to work for me and my group?"

"I have no idea," Keller replied, staring at Sykes. "The subject never came up."

"He was British special forces," Mr. X said, matter of fact.

"So now you're a mercenary?" Keller asked, still looking Sykes in the eyes. Sykes did not answer.

Instead, Mr. X said, "'Mercenary' does not accurately describe Mr. Sykes's profession. It's more of a security job—I would say that describes it better. Wouldn't you say so, Mr. Sykes?"

"Yes, sir. That's what I do, security," Sykes replied.

But his face had changed, Keller could see, right before his eyes. His usual distant, expressionless indifference shifted to something dark and dangerous, as if he no longer needed to put on the act of simple bureaucratic minion. He was now free to be who he really was, and it was a great relief to him.

Keller was taken aback by the instantaneous shift in Sykes's demeanor and looked away quickly.

"Who the hell are you people?" Keller asked calmly but cautiously. "Some kind of secret society? Have all those conspiracy nuts been right?" Keller added sarcastically and at the same time seriously.

Mr. X laughed, and Sykes smiled an evil smile.

"Mr. President, the people in those groups only wish they were one of us," Mr. X said. "They have their secret meetings, and the conspiracy theorists theorize, and all the while they are still only second string. The members of our organization are the descendants of the monarchies of old, descendants of giants from before the recording of time. We were the ones recording the history, my dear boy. We have always run the world, and this present disaster gives us the opportunity to regain the total control over the planet that we haven't had in hundreds of years."

President Keller was stupefied. The nightmare he was living just kept getting more and more bizarre. Finally, he spoke.

"So why do you need me, and what difference does it make if Philadelphia is in the hands of these people?"

"Mr. President," Mr. X said, his voice dripping with the growing impatience he felt with Keller. "I thought I had been clear as to why we need you, but I can see now that you are not as savvy as we thought you were, or maybe the end of the world has you rattled. No matter; I will explain it for you in the simplest of terms possible. You, Mr. Keller, are the duly elected representative of the people; the people see your face and believe someone is looking out for them. Now at this point, we all know that is just not true; you work for me and my people. We need you as the front man for our endeavors—every organization needs a good front man. Oh yes, we could eliminate you easily enough and just take over or replace you with the Speaker of the House. I imagine he is pretty pliable at this point, having been locked up in the Capitol Building all winter. Or we could have an election; those always turn out as we desire regardless of which party wins or who happens to be running. All of that would be very messy and take a lot of time, so for now, you are our man. That being said, you are in this now, on our side. If we lose, you lose, and history will remember you as such. We win and we write the history. Remember that: the winners always write the history.

"As for the terrorists in Philadelphia, they are making people doubt that you have their best interests in mind, and that's bad for all of us. You see, Mr. President, America has always been the problem. When the British monarchy lost control of the colonies, it created a place where people could actually be free—free to think, free to make their own decisions, free to move around as they please. Freedom is an obstacle to our attaining what we have always wanted and always had until the founding of America: total control. Over the past two centuries, we have whittled away more and more of those freedoms, but Americans have something in their DNA that makes finishing the job impossible. People all over the rest of the world will succumb easily enough. You see, they have always had the peasant mentality, and that's why they embrace socialism so readily. Americans are different. That's why this disaster is such a blessing—it gives us the opening we needed to inject government control directly into the pumping hearts of the American people. Desperate for relief, they will do whatever and believe whatever they are told."

Keller just stood speechless and deflated. He had known what he was a part of—he didn't need Mr. X to explain it—but he had just never wanted to believe it.

"I know, Mr. President, it's difficult to digest. Let's get on with the business of fixing this mess and we can talk again later. Mr. Sykes will get you a new phone as soon as possible. I hear that there are tanks being unloaded at the Capitol Building. Well done, Mr. President. There's a bit of good news."

Mr. X sounded almost fatherly, like he was relishing Keller's pain and eager to see the end of the rebellion in Philadelphia. *He really did get off on all of this,* Keller thought, still unable to speak.

"One other thing." Mr. X had remembered something. "There were some CAT-MAN officers murdered in upstate Pennsylvania and left at a highway intersection as a message. Perhaps that's where this rebellion began; you should check it out."

"I'll send a team over from New Jersey, sir," Sykes replied, with Keller still mute.

"Alright then, let's get to work, gentlemen," Mr. X said before hanging up abruptly.

Keller didn't move. Sykes tucked his phone into his jacket pocket and turned around to exit. The entire conversation had taken place just inside the door to the Oval Office. Sykes was startled upon opening the door to find the First Lady standing there with the girls.

Sykes snapped, "How long have you been standing there?"

"Don't ever take that tone with me, Sykes. Unlike my husband, I still have a pair, and you don't scare me," replied the First Lady as she pushed past Sykes, never breaking the death stare she had locked upon his eyes.

Sykes chuckled slightly and went on his way.

"What are you doing here?" Keller asked his wife, still sounding deflated.

"Your children wanted to spend time with their father, if that's not too much of an inconvenience," Joyce replied, still irritated by her encounter with Sykes.

Keller squatted down and embraced his girls as they came through the door with their mother.

"How long were you standing there, Joyce?" Keller asked calmly.

"Long enough for your babysitter, Sykes, to burst out and startle all of us," Joyce replied.

"Did you hear any of our conversation?" Keller asked, still remaining calm for the sake of his daughters, who were hanging on him like two monkeys.

"Why would I hear anything? Who's stupid enough to have a conversation just inside a doorway?" Joyce replied as she crouched down to kiss her daughters. "Have fun with Daddy." Without another word, she stood and left the room.

As she left, Keller thought, *I hope you are telling the truth, Joyce. I really do.*

CHAPTER 31

THE US CAPITOL BUILDING, WASHINGTON, DC

SERGEANT FIRST CLASS Anthony Maddox was not happy. He and his soldiers had been grateful to be moving out finally, but this was not what they had hoped for. They had been aboard Marine Corps Base Camp Lejeune in North Carolina for joint training with their Marine counterparts when the shit hit the fan. They had been stuck there all winter. They had assisted in catastrophe relief wherever they could, but their minds had been elsewhere.

When word came that they were moving out, their spirits soared. They were all eager to get back to Fort Bliss, Texas. They had had no word from family and friends, and their officers who had accompanied them to the training had left for retraining. Sergeant Maddox and his men were starting to feel like they had been abandoned. Their hopes of heading home were soon dashed when they were informed that orders, directly from the Army chief of staff, were sending them north to Washington, DC.

Upon arriving at the city limits, they were met by a CAT-MAN officer who led them through the city to the Capitol Building. The CAT-MAN officer instructed them to set up a perimeter around the building and to await further instructions. Sergeant Maddox didn't quite understand why one would need to surround the United States Capitol Building with six M1A2 Abrams main battle tanks, but he didn't bother to ask. At least they had a change of scenery. Perhaps after this, they would be sent home. He also took solace in the fact that receiving orders to move meant that they had not been forgotten about. That was what he had told his soldiers as they began unloading their tanks and equipment off the flatbed trailers that had carried them from North Carolina, and their morale had seemed to improve a bit.

It was going to be dark soon, and everyone was hustling. They had been traveling all day, and all were looking forward to a rest. One by one, the Abrams tanks were started and rolled off their trailers. At sixty-two and a half tons and almost twenty-six feet long, it required great care and precision to unload these metal monsters. Sergeant Maddox's crews were top-notch, which explained why they had been chosen for the joint services training. Each tank was then driven to a point around the building that Maddox himself had picked, one on each corner and one each centered on the building's front and back entrances. Maintenance teams were unloading crates and erecting tents. Even with all this activity, Maddox knew there were still a couple of more hours until his people could rest.

In the waning light, Maddox saw two black SUVs pull up not far from where he stood, yet far enough away so as not to get crushed by any of the heavy machinery moving about. A slender woman got out of the second SUV and started walking toward him. *What now?* Maddox thought as he began walking toward her. As she got closer, something seemed strangely familiar about the woman.

FIRST LADY JOYCE Keller walked quickly. She knew she would have to talk fast since it wouldn't take long for the CAT-MAN officers to spot her. An enormous Black man dressed in Army camouflage was striding toward her. She hoped he was someone in charge.

"Ma'am, it's not safe for you here right now," Maddox said as he moved within earshot of the woman.

"I know, soldier. I won't take much of your time," Joyce replied, extending her hand to shake Maddox's.

Taking her hand, Maddox said, "That's good, because the CAT-MAN folks are all shaken up about something that went down in Philadelphia today. They want us all set up immediately."

"I understand. Do you know who I am, soldier?" Joyce asked. She could see that he had stripes, but she wasn't very good at remembering what rank they actually represented.

"Yes, ma'am, you're First Lady Joyce Keller," Maddox answered without hesitation.

"I'm flattered. And what's your name?" Joyce replied. She was genuinely flattered that he recognized her.

"Sergeant First Class Anthony Maddox, First Armored Division, ma'am," Maddox replied.

A DAY LIKE ANY OTHER

"Sergeant." Joyce took a deep breath before continuing as if to give herself one more chance to change her mind. "I have been trying to get into that building all winter, and no one will let me. Do you find that odd?"

Maddox turned to look toward the Capitol Building behind him. "Yes, ma'am, that does seem odd."

Joyce came and stood next to Maddox, her tiny frame dwarfed by the giant tanker beside her. "Sergeant, I come here every day, and every day they turn me away. Things are not right here."

"You want me to keep an eye out for something, ma'am?" Maddox wasn't stupid—he knew she hadn't come here to chat.

Just then, several CAT-MAN vehicles pulled up, boxing in the SUVs by the curb. Secret Service agents piled out of the SUVs and confronted the CAT-MAN officers as they attempted to move toward the First Lady. A shouting match ensued, with the Secret Service agents insisting that the CAT-MAN officers could not approach the First Lady and the CAT-MAN officers insisting that they would.

"My time is up, sergeant," Joyce began. She took Maddox by the elbow and walked him farther away from the road and the heightening tension there. "I need you to get inside that building and find out what's going on, who's in there, and if they're OK. Can you do that for me, sergeant?"

"Do you think they would just let me in if I asked?" Maddox asked sarcastically.

"Not likely, but they do have some very lovely shower facilities, or so I've heard," Joyce replied, patting Maddox on his giant arm, causing a small cloud of dust to kick up.

Maddox nodded as a broad smile crept across his face. "I'll see what I can do, ma'am," he said, grinning.

Suddenly, the ruckus that had been curbside was beside them. A CAT-MAN officer was shouting and pointing his finger at Joyce. "What are you doing here?"

Maddox stepped between Joyce and the CAT-MAN officer, who quickly became less aggressive in the presence of the camouflaged giant.

"I wanted to see what all the activity was. The sergeant was just telling me that it isn't safe to go any closer," Joyce replied in a voice as sweet as honey.

"You're not supposed to be here," the CAT-MAN officer replied, speaking now more respectfully.

CAT-MAN officers guarded the president now. Special Agent Billings, along with the rest of the presidential security detail, had been removed and assigned to the First Lady. He now arrived between Maddox and the CAT-MAN officer.

"We should head back now, Mrs. Keller," he said, looking the CAT-MAN officer in the face.

"You're probably right, Ryan. The sergeant still has a lot of work to do tonight," Joyce replied with a smile. Taking Maddox by the hand, she said, "Thank you, sergeant. I'm sorry to have interrupted you and brought all of this chaos into your evening."

"No problem, ma'am. It was a pleasure to meet you," Maddox replied, shaking the First Lady's hand.

The First Lady was escorted back to her SUV. It pulled away with the CAT-MAN vehicles close behind to make sure she didn't come right back, Maddox presumed.

One of Maddox's tank commanders walked up and asked, "What the hell was all that about?"

Maddox looked at him and said, "We've arrived in crazy town is what that was all about."

CHAPTER 32

DAY 5

PHILADELPHIA, PENNSYLVANIA

THEY HAD RECEIVED a radio call from Reynolds the night before, but it was garbled and barely readable. What they had deciphered definitively was that he had made it to Fort Dix and liberated a retraining center, but beyond that, they couldn't understand much. They had no idea when or if he would return or knew any details of what else he had found there.

Sentries posted on all the bridges to the south had been engaged in sporadic firefights with, presumably, CAT-MAN forces all night, resulting in casualties on both sides. Their defensive perimeter was sound and strong since the Delaware and Schuylkill rivers were formidable obstacles. A reconnaissance element had been put across the river to scout the airport and had reported back that a large CAT-MAN force was indeed gathering there. There were no armored vehicles there yet, so the Strykers were still king of this battlefield. By first light, all was quiet again.

Andy bid farewell to John and Ryan. He also took a moment to bid a silent farewell to Uncle Charlie, whose remains were zipped up into a military body bag.

John could see Andy's grief and said, "He went out with his boots on, and that's how he would have wanted it. Don't beat yourself up, not now; there's still a lot of work to do. More people will die—it's just a fact. We started something, and we need to finish it."

Andy nodded in agreement, and, with that, John drove off, headed north. Andy hoped he would return, but he wouldn't blame him if he didn't. Right now, it felt like they were taking on the world, and the world hadn't yet awakened fully.

David had been eager to return to the home they had left in the fall, and Andy figured it was a good excuse to get away from his new responsibilities as revolution instigator, at least for a little while. So he and David and two HUMVEEs full of heavily armed soldiers—Sasquatch and Wally had insisted they not go alone—headed back up Broad Street toward their old neighborhood. After a quick stop at the mall FEMA camp to check on how things were going, the group headed off to the east.

After only two blocks, Andy's heart began to sink. The entire area was burned down. All the houses were gutted, some burned to the foundations. Andy assumed a fire had started, and with basic emergency services no longer available, the fires had spread and burned until they went out on their own. David said nothing as they drove, maneuvering around piles of charred wreckage and burned vehicles.

Arriving in front of their old house, Andy and David both let out a gasp. Their house was nothing but a shell. David jumped out of the HUMVEE and ran up to the black mass that was the front door. It was somehow still closed and probably locked just as they had left it, a cruel irony to the fact that most of the walls were pretty much gone. Andy joined his son at the front door and could see that David had tears in his eyes. All Andy could think to say was, "At least we weren't here when all this went down." Of course it was true, but it wasn't what David was in any mood to hear right now. He gave Andy an angry look before going to sit in the HUMVEE to await the ride back to the city.

Andy looked around in disgust. His neighbors' houses were as destroyed as his, and he hoped they had been able to somehow escape the firestorm that had claimed their piece of suburbia. *They probably ended up in a camp somewhere,* he thought.

Andy could see a car winding its way through the rubble-littered street and heading in their direction. The soldiers who had accompanied them saw it too.

"You want us to turn them around?" asked the soldier manning the machine gun atop the HUMVEE closest to the approaching car.

Andy thought for a moment, then said, "No, let's see if they have any idea what happened here." Andy knew what had happened here, and he wasn't quite sure why he said that. He just felt the need to see who they were.

The car—a large, older, luxury type—came to a stop about ten feet in front of the lead HUMVEE. A large man with an AK-47 rifle got out of the passenger-side door. Likewise, equally large men got out of the driver's and back seat doors, all armed with AK-47s. The man from the passenger-side started walking toward Andy with his hands up. The driver stood watching and smiling. The two men from the back seat were seemingly helping another person get out, but Andy could not see who it was.

"Hello," the passenger-side man said as he walked. "You are the man who lived here, yes?" His accent was Eastern European but didn't quite sound Russian.

"Who are you, and what are you doing here?" Andy asked, not prepared to divulge anything to a stranger.

"Yes, of course," began the large stranger standing before Andy. "My name is Dmitry Koval. Zat is my grandmother, Anna, and zos men are my brozers."

Andy looked past Dmitry at the three men helping a tiny woman, bent over and walking with a cane. Anna was wrinkled and obviously very old, yet she still did not appear frail. One man was holding her by the upper arm to steady her, and the other two walked ahead, clearing debris from her path.

"Why are you looking for who lived here?" asked Andy, still looking at the entourage that approached him from the street.

"My grandmother, zince she vas a small child, sees zings ven she sleeps, and zen zey come true. So ven she says vee must all leave Republic of Georgia and go to America, vee go. She says vee must all move from za city into za countryside, vee move. Ven she says zat za hard times are coming, vee say, but vat hard times? Everyzing is wonderful, and zen *poof!* All zis happens."

"Your grandmother is a psychic, but that doesn't tell me why you're here," Andy said politely. He liked this man and was looking forward to meeting his grandmother, but Dmitry still hadn't answered the question.

About then, David appeared by Andy's side, curious as to what was going on. He nodded to Dmitry, who nodded back. Dmitry's brothers and Anna also arrived, and Andy could see Anna, with eyes squinted, looking at his face. After a few short moments, she took hold of Dmitry's arm and said something in what Andy assumed was Georgian, to which Dmitry replied in kind, bending slightly at the waist toward Anna's face.

Looking up from Anna, Dmitry said, "She zays you are za one she has seen in her dreams. Ven she heard your voice on za radio, she knew she must come here to find you and tell you."

Andy was confused and stood staring at the duo who were again chatting in Georgian.

Looking up from Anna again, Dmitry said, "She zays you have dreams too, and they come true. She vants to know if you know who za men are who speak to you."

Andy was dumbfounded. He glanced at David, who was staring wide-eyed. "I don't know what you are talking about," Andy said after a few moments.

Dmitry looked down at Anna and said something, shrugging toward Andy. Anna looked up at Andy, squinting her eyes, then looked over at David and smiled, pointing as she spoke. Dmitry nodded as he listened, then as before, translated. "She is sure that you are za one and zat zis is your son and zat he is very brave. She says you must finish vat you have started. You must go to za white marble building and free all who are there."

Andy was amazed. He looked from Dmitry to Anna and back to Dmitry again. *How could she know that? She's referring to the Capitol Building,* he thought to himself.

"I know zis is hard to believe. Vee have all come to accept vatever she tells us because she is always right in her predictions. She also zays zat I must go vis you to keep you safe." Dmitry said with a smile as he translated for Anna, seeing that Andy was at a loss for words.

Andy stood staring at Anna. *Well, things just got a little stranger, if that was possible,* he thought. Anna stared back at him, a smile cutting through her wrinkled face.

After a few long moments, Andy said, "My father was in one of the dreams, and one of my neighbors was in the second one."

Anna's face lit up as Dmitry translated what Andy had said. Anna replied excitedly, pointing toward Andy. As she finished, she gestured for Dmitry to tell Andy what she had said. Apparently, he was not doing so fast enough. "She zays zat man zat is your neighbor—you saved his life—and your father has passed away many years ago now."

"That's right," Andy replied, which Dmitry translated, prompting another flurry of chatter from Anna.

Dmitry nodded to Anna and once again turned to translate for Andy. "She zays zat zere are two angels who valk behind you and who are always vith you. Zey vill help you when you need zem za most."

Andy felt a chill go up his spine and saw David turn to look behind where they stood.

Anna put her hands on Dmitry's neck and pulled his head down so she could kiss him on both cheeks. She then shuffled over to Andy and kissed him on both cheeks as well. She then turned and patted David on his cheek with her hand, looking into his eyes with love as she would her own children. With that, Anna began to head back toward the car. Dmitry's brothers, one by one, shook his hand and embraced him in a strong hug with their other arm, doing the same to Andy and David, then each of them turned to help Anna back to the car.

Andy watched as Anna and her grandsons loaded up and drove away, still not quite sure what had just happened. Turning to Dmitry, Andy said, "That's quite a woman. Does she always get her way?"

Smiling, Dmitry replied, "Yes, always."

"Well, I guess that means you're stuck with us," Andy said, looking up at his new bodyguard.

"Yes, zat vould seem so," Dmitry said, smiling down at Andy.

"Well, Dmitry, I guess we better head on back and figure out exactly how we're going to give Miss Anna what she wants."

With that and a wave of his arm, Andy said, "Let's head back, boys. Dmitry, you ride with us. I want to know everything you've seen on your way here."

ON THE WAY back to the city, a runner on a dirt bike found Andy and delivered a message stating that Reynolds had made contact and to meet Sasquatch and Wally at city hall. When Andy arrived back at city hall around noon, his friends were there waiting for him.

Upon seeing Dmitry, Sasquatch said, "I thought I was the mass of manliness in your life. Who's this guy?"

"This is Dmitry. He's joining us—it's a long story. You heard from Reynolds?" Andy said as he walked toward his friends.

"That's right," began Wally. "He sent a messenger that arrived about an hour after you left." Wally stopped talking and glanced up at Dmitry.

"He's OK, Wally, please go on," Andy said, appreciating Wally's desire for operational security in the presence of a stranger.

"OK, if you say so," Wally continued. "Reynolds is on his way back with a convoy full of goodies—81-millimeter mortars, ammo, medical supplies, rifles, equipment of all sorts—and more volunteers. He liberated a retraining center, and it was just as bad as we feared. It was nothing more than a detention center. Reynolds called it a gulag. He left a contingent of troops to secure the area and provide care for the folks they liberated. As was the case with every other camp they liberated, local citizens started coming out of hiding, offering their assistance however they could."

The messenger said he had personally recognized some of the people they liberated as being officers from his own unit. He said Reynolds had been in tears at the pitiful sight of his young officers, sickly and emaciated, none of whom would be anywhere close to ready for duty for a very long time. The messenger also said that Reynolds wanted to propose a plan when he got back that would involve moving out to the east across the Delaware River. He would deliver the details once he arrived. Squatch, Wally, and Ramirez had already ordered the company commanders to start preparing a plan of action should a large-scale movement to the east be required.

Satisfied that there was nothing more to do until Reynolds arrived, the group headed into city hall to listen in on Tommy Rye's broadcast and get a debrief from Andy about his trip back to his old neighborhood. Most of all, they wanted to know who Andy's new friend was.

AS TOMMY RYE started his broadcast, Sasquatch and Dmitry had to be shushed. Already, they had begun to argue about which was better: the AK-47—Dmitry's preferred weapon—or the M16, which Squatch felt was overall the better firearm. Observing the two giants arguing like old friends, Andy knew Dmitry was going to fit right in.

THE SUN WAS directly overhead, and Sykes was feeling frustrated that he still had several hours to wait before making his final approach to Philadelphia City Hall under the cover of darkness. He and his team of ten men had driven all night from Washington, and the going had been slow and tedious even with their night vision goggles. The roads were unkept and damaged from The Event, and damage compounded by winter erosion had caused more than a few close calls when large potholes (more akin to craters) suddenly appeared ahead of them. They had hidden the vehicles as far north as they could, then set out to swim across the Delaware River. None of his team had made such a swim in many years, but they all made it across together just before dawn and found shelter in an abandoned apartment just outside the security perimeter set around city hall.

Mr. X had sent him to take out as much of the rebel leadership as he could and to destroy the radio transmitters. Mr. X had told Keller to send a SEAL team, but he was an impatient man, and since Sykes was heading there any-

A DAY LIKE ANY OTHER

way, he figured he'd give his man the first crack at the insurgents and leave the SEAL team as a backup. Sykes wasn't sure if the rebel leaders would be at city hall, but he did know the transmitter was.

"Maybe we'll get lucky and get them all with the transmitter," Sykes told his team when he gave his mission brief.

AT JUST ABOUT sunset, a convoy of six HUMVEES came roaring past Sykes's hiding place. Sykes thought, *Now that looks like a juicy target.*

"Everyone get ready. We move as soon as it's dark, and it may take us some time to find a place to get inside," he said quietly to his team. *It's gonna be a good night*, he thought.

REYNOLDS WAS EXHAUSTED, but there was no time for sleep. He had raced from Fort Dix with his six-HUMVEE convoy, leaving the rest of his now reinforced battalion to move at their best possible speed. He saw an opportunity, but they would need to move quickly if it had any chance of working.

He walked briskly up the stairs into city hall, calling to the guard commander as he passed, "Is everyone here?"

"Yes sir, since about noon," replied the watch commander.

Good, Reynolds thought, quickening his pace.

CHAPTER 33

PHILADELPHIA CITY HALL

SYKES HAD THOUGHT it would be more difficult to get past the posted sentries. Apparently, he and his men looked just like everyone else in the rebel camp. They moved casually once inside the perimeter; they had nothing to fear as long as they didn't look suspicious.

Before long, they were standing beside city hall. There were guards at all the doors, so they would have to find another way in. These sentries were asking questions of anyone entering. Around the south side, they found a pile of wrecked cars pushed up against one corner of the building. One by one, they quietly scaled the wrecks and crawled through a broken second-floor window. Once they were in, they needed only to make their way to the radio equipment and perhaps encounter some of the rebel leadership along the way. Sykes knew that once they started destroying things, the leadership was sure to turn up, and then they would have their chance.

COLONEL REYNOLDS STORMED in, a man on a mission. He had seen too much today and was near exhaustion, but he wasn't about to rest until his plan had been heard. Andy, Sasquatch, Wally, Ramirez, Cummings, Detweiler, Tommy Rye, and all the company and battalion commanders were assembled in the courtyard of city hall.

Andy thought Reynolds looked like shit, but he wasn't about to tell him that. He had had a rough day, and seeing his officers in such miserable condition had pushed him to the edge.

Andy was eager to hear what Reynolds had in mind. He didn't waste any time in asking, "So what are you thinking, Colonel?"

All eyes turned to Reynolds, and all banter stopped immediately. Reynolds looked around at each man, and removing his cover, he began to speak.

A DAY LIKE ANY OTHER

"I've seen things today that I could have never imagined happening in the US. I'd seen it overseas and in documentaries, but nothing prepares you to see your own men like that. It's clear to me now what's happening here. It's Soviet-style reeducation camps—gulags. The communists purged the czar's army of all loyal officers, and those they didn't kill, they broke down into obedient servants. That's what CAT-MAN is doing here. We captured a number of the CAT-MAN leaders at the Fort Dix camp. They are all foreign mercenaries working for the UN but getting paid by some mysterious organization. Even among themselves, the CAT-MAN people talked about it as if it were just a rumor."

"That's a lot of information, Colonel. How'd you get so much out of them?" asked Cummings.

"Mr. FBI Director," Reynolds began, "it's best you don't know."

Cummings nodded in the affirmative.

Reynolds continued, "CAT-MAN is moving all their forces in this direction, and as more and more camps are liberated or abandoned, more and more CAT-MAN personnel become available to attack us here. Eventually, they will have a large enough force to fix us here, surround us, and finish us off—either by force or by starving us out. Either way, we can't stay here."

Reynolds had paused to let that sink in, and Andy admired Reynolds's professionalism and his bearing. *This man is the real deal,* Andy thought.

Reynolds began again, pointing at a large map he had drawn on the concrete with a piece of charred wood. "What I'm proposing is the movement en masse of the entire force to the east across the Delaware River and south toward Annapolis, where there is another large reeducation camp. We liberate that camp and march on Washington itself. The bottom line is that we have to keep moving or we'll die. We'll have to scrub our personnel rosters and figure out who we leave behind to guard the city and who goes with. I believe the bulk of the CAT-MAN forces will follow us as we move toward Washington—they won't have a choice. Whoever we leave behind, as long as they stubbornly defend the bridges to the east, west, and south and properly barricade and defend to the north, should be able to hold out."

The assembled commanders all stood, studying the map and commenting quietly to one another. Andy's head was spinning. Things had become very real suddenly. He had started this inadvertently, and now he was going to be responsible for the movement of an army to march on Washington.

"Colonel, could I have a word with you in private, please?" Andy said, a little more forcefully than intended.

Andy led Reynolds off to the side, out of earshot of any of the others, who were all watching the two walk away.

"What's up, Andy?" Reynolds asked. "I know it's risky, but we don't really have much of a choice."

"Colonel," Andy began, putting his hands up in front of him, "it's not that. I agree with you—we can't stay here and survive."

Reynolds looked at Andy with a quizzical look. "Then what's up?"

"Colonel, I am in way over my head here," Andy said, trying to keep his voice down.

"Go on," Reynolds said, seeing that Andy needed to get this out.

"Me, Sasquatch, Wally—we're air wingers, mechanics. Before this, the only one of us to fire a shot in combat was Wally, and that was from a helicopter. We're not grunts. Sure, we believe every Marine is a rifleman and what little bit of that training we've had has brought us this far, but what you're proposing is way beyond anything I'm prepared to lead. I'm not telling you because I don't want to do it—I'm telling you because it's too important for a combat novice to lead. You need to take over command."

Andy finished his rant and felt immediately better. He was ready to make the march on Washington; he just wasn't going to lead it.

Reynolds stood staring at Andy for a long moment, then, with a smile spreading across his face, he spoke. "And that's exactly why you are the leader of this army, son."

Andy was stunned and just stared back at Reynolds as the colonel began speaking again.

"I haven't known you for very long, but I know all about you. The dreams; shooting up the bandits on the highway; what you did at the camps; making the call to change the main effort to my force at the stadium after your radio operator got killed right in front of you; sending Ramirez through the kill zone in the Strykers to cut off reinforcements—you've done everything right. If you want, I can have one of my men drive back up to Fort Dix and pick up some combat-action ribbons for you and your friends if that will make you feel better. Because let me tell you, this is way worse than any combat I've ever seen in twenty-five years of service. I understand how you feel, but the bottom line is that all these people are here because of what *you've* done. They heard your voice on the radio and were compelled to come join *you*. You convinced me, and now I serve at the pleasure of Andrew Lemon. I'm in this to end just like everyone else here."

A DAY LIKE ANY OTHER

Andy felt very silly. Reynolds was correct of course, but Andy had just needed someone to remind him. The world was out of control, and Andy had somehow ended up somewhere he had never imagined himself.

"Thank you, Colonel," Andy said, finally. "I needed to hear that. It doesn't mean that I don't feel a little bit sick to my stomach right now."

Reynolds nodded in the affirmative and took Andy by the shoulder. "We all need a shot of reality sometimes. I'm always here if you need to vent. Now, what do you say we get this army on the road? For the record, I feel pretty nauseous too, so don't feel bad."

Andy took a deep breath and said, "Let's get moving, Colonel. The boys already have everyone gearing up to move to the east."

Reynolds leaned in to talk quietly to Andy. "You are the heart and soul of this army. There is plenty of experience in this force to make this happen. Let them handle the details, and we can win—I know it—but you need to lead us. There are forces at work here beyond our control."

Andy looked Reynolds in the eyes and nodded. He understood and was prepared to do whatever it took.

The meeting quickly turned chaotic as battalion and company commanders began hashing out the details of the plan. Andy thought, *Here we go. God help us.*

CHAPTER 34

DAY 6

PHILADELPHIA, PENNSYLVANIA

IT WAS JUST after midnight before the plan was sufficiently underway, and Reynolds took his leave to head back to his column waiting on Interstate 295 in New Jersey. Word had come that the troopers he had left at Fort Dix had come across two Bradley Fighting Vehicles complete with crews and flatbed trucks to transport them, and he was eager to get back and inspect them and meet the crews. Andy walked Reynolds out to the HUMVEEs parked on the south side of city hall.

"Thanks again, Colonel," Andy said, shaking Reynolds's hand.

"Thank you, Andy," Reynolds replied, taking Andy by the shoulder.

"Why are you thanking me?" Andy chuckled.

"For making all this possible." Reynolds looked Andy in the eyes. "I'll see you on the road. Don't take too long—history is watching."

With that, Reynolds closed the door and gave Andy a wink as the column began pulling away.

There was still a lot left to do, but things were falling into place, and Andy hoped they could be moving out before dawn. Andy watched as Reynolds's HUMVEEs pulled off, then turned and headed back into city hall. Andy hadn't taken ten steps when his thoughts were shattered by what he thought was gunfire coming from inside. *Who the hell is firing their weapon inside the building?* he thought angrily. When the firing became more rapid and sustained anger turned to concern, his pace hastened. *What the hell is going on now?* he thought and began to run as another burst of automatic fire rang out.

A DAY LIKE ANY OTHER

THE ACTIVITY ON the street had been increasing all night. Sykes had expected things to quiet down the later it became, but just the opposite was true.

"We need to make a move for that radio or get the hell out here!" one of his men had whispered in the darkness, crouched by the window they had used to access the building and looking down at the activity on the street below.

Sykes knew his man was right. The situation was deteriorating quickly. Finally, he decided they would go for the radio transmitter and then escape in the chaos that would ensue afterward.

"OK," Sykes began quietly, "four of you will come with me and destroy the transmitter. The rest of you will stay here and be ready to come back us up if there's trouble. We'll all move back to the river from here when we return." Sykes pointed to each of the men who would come with him, then stood and turned for the door. "You hear any shooting, you get out here and start shooting anything that's not one of us," Sykes said to the men he was leaving behind.

With that, he opened the door and stepped out into the hallway. *Let's get this done and get out of here*, he thought to himself, nervous excitement building in his gut.

DETWEILER WAS GIDDY with excitement. Even though he and Cummings wouldn't be going with Andy on the march south, all the activity and the prospect of marching on Washington had him feeling energized like never before in his life. It had been decided that he and Cummings, being the only two members of Keller's cabinet known to remain alive, were to be protected with the precious radio transmitter. In the event the city fell, they could melt back into hiding just as they had done over the winter.

He was returning to the quarters on the second floor of city hall that he shared with Cummings, Tommy Rye, and Mayor Travis to retrieve a few books he had promised to share with David. As he stepped into the hallway that led to his room to the right, he recognized a familiar face walking toward him from the left. *My God, it can't be!* he thought, panic building quickly as he quickened his pace. The door to his room was just a few steps away. *Oh my God, oh my God, oh my God*, he thought, trying not to break into a run. *Maybe he didn't see me!* He ducked into the room, quickly closing the door behind him.

WELL, WELL, WELL, what have we here? Sykes thought at the sight of Detweiler.

He turned to the men behind him and whispered, "We're going to grab that little pip-squeak; I know some people who want to talk to him."

His team members nodded in unison and then followed Sykes down the hallway. *What a bonus this is,* Sykes thought, approaching the door Detweiler had just entered.

"HE'S HERE!" DETWEILER half-shouted as he entered the room.

"Who's here?" Cummings replied, startled at Detweiller's abrupt arrival.

"Sykes!" Detweiler replied, looking for a way to lock the door.

"Did he see you?" Cummings replied. Detweiler had his full attention now.

"I don't know! It was only for a second, but he looked right at me!" Detweiler was desperate to lock the door.

"Get away from the door!" Cummings said forcefully.

Detweiler stumbled away from the door toward Cummings, who was chambering a round in an M16 rifle he had picked up from the desk in front of him. He handed it to a stunned Detweiler. Picking up and chambering a round in a second M16, Cummings crouched behind the desk, pointing the rifle toward the door.

"Get down here beside me!" Cummings said, shaking his head for Detweiler to move next to him behind the desk.

The two men crouched behind the desk, ready for the door to open.

"If I shoot, you shoot!" Cummings said, moving the rifle's selector lever with his thumb from the safety to three-round burst.

"I don't know how to do this!" Detweiler said in frantic tones.

Cummings looked over to see Detweiler trembling. He calmly reached over and moved the selector lever on Detweiler's rifle to burst as well.

"Point it at the door, and if I shoot, you shoot. Just squeeze the trigger and keep squeezing until there's nothing left to shoot at, OK?" Cummings said calmly.

The two M16s had recently been liberated from the CAT-MAN armory in city hall. Cummings signed out twice, once for himself and once for Detweiler. He had hoped to train Detweiler, but now he found himself giving a crash course in the worst possible situation.

A DAY LIKE ANY OTHER

"OK! I'm OK!" Detweiler replied, but Cummings didn't believe him.

As Cummings settled in behind the rifle, the door swung open, and he was looking straight at Sykes's grinning face. The grin instantly disappeared a moment later when Sykes realized that he had not only found Detweiler, but he had also found FBI Director Cummings, who was pointing an M16 rifle at him.

Cummings squeezed the trigger, letting three rounds fly, all of which struck Sykes squarely in the chest, causing him to stumble backward out of the doorway. Detweiler fired also, all of his rounds impacting the doorframe. Cummings's second burst struck the man who had followed behind Sykes. The first round hit his chest, the next penetrated his neck, and the third struck his skull just above his left eye. Detweiler's second burst impacted the wall where the man Cummings had just shot was now slumped against, obviously dead, blood gushing from his head. Sykes's third man at the door leaned out and fired a wild full-auto burst from his MP5 submachine gun into the office toward Cummings and Detweiler, but they were ducked down behind the heavy desk, which stopped most of the 9-millimeter rounds, and the rest just flew over their heads. Cummings returned fire, but the man was barely visible, protected by the door frame, and his rounds missed the mark, hitting the doorframe and the wall. Detweiler's third squeeze of the trigger, having a better angle than Cummings, found its mark, striking the man in the side, shoulder, and neck. He, too, slumped to the floor.

Cummings and Detweiler crouched behind the desk, the barrels of their rifles smoking, ready for any other targets to present themselves in the open doorway. After a long moment, an object flew through the doorway, bouncing off the front of the desk and coming to rest halfway between the door and the desk. Cummings knew what had flown into the room, so he spun and threw himself at Detweiler, tackling him to the floor.

The grenade went off with a thud, filling the room with smoke and hot shrapnel.

ANDY WAS IN a full sprint by the time he reached the center of city hall's courtyard. Sasquatch and Dmitry met him there. Moments ago, they had been arguing again as to which weapon was better: the M16 or the AK-47. They could hear there was a full-blown firefight underway on the north side of city hall, but it was now clearly moving outside the building.

"What the hell is going on?" Andy shouted as he ran, swinging his rifle up to the ready.

"Nothing good!" Sasquatch shouted back, running alongside him.

As the trio exited onto the street, they saw the shooting had moved off to the east, but the aftermath of the firefight remained. Several smoke grenades were still burning on the street. Medics were tending to three wounded men that Andy could see. As Andy walked through the smoke to the east, he came across three of his men pinning a wounded man to the ground.

"Who is he?!" Andy barked at the trooper kneeling on the man's head.

"I don't know!" the Militiaman barked back. "We were on guard at the north entrance. We heard shooting from inside, then this guy and probably seven or eight of his buddies started shooting and popping smoke all over the place out here. It looked like they had come out of city hall based on where all the fire was coming from. The rest of them moved off to the east."

"Get him a medic," Andy said. "I want him interrogated before he dies."

Andy was pissed and wanted answers. Andy continued on down the street to the east, and the chaos was only building. Wounded men were staggering out of the smoke, and medics and Militiamen were rushing into the smoke. Andy arrived at the eastern roadblock to find several of his men down and a group of Militiamen standing over three dead men, who he assumed by their similar dress to be part of the force that had done this.

One of the soldiers, whom Andy assumed was in charge of the roadblock, saw him approaching and started giving him a report.

"They came from that pile of wrecked cars. We were on guard here at the roadblock, and they just started shooting. Two of my men are dead, and two others are wounded. We got these three, and the rest moved on down the street to the east. We're pretty sure we hit a couple more, but they all disappeared into the smoke."

"OK," Andy said, nodding his head. "Let's get this mess cleaned up and get a patrol together to go after them."

Wally came running up out of the smoke to the west with Cummings and Detweiler trying to keep up.

"Andy, dude!" Wally began. "You gotta hear this!" He pointed toward Cummings and Detweiler.

"It was Sykes!" Cummings said, breathless.

Andy could see that both Cummings and Detweiler were bleeding from dozens of cuts all over their bodies. , in the case of Detweiler, concerned him.

A DAY LIKE ANY OTHER

"Sykes? The CAT-MAN director?" Andy replied in disbelief.

"Yes!" Cummings shot back. "Only he's not only the CAT-MAN director. He's some kind of goddamn commando, and he brought a hit squad with him. I shot him square in the chest, and another guy too. Detweiler here dropped a third, but we only found two bodies when we came out of the office."

"Well, shit!" Andy began, looking at Detweiler, who was still trembling. "Good job, professor," he said, truly impressed. "You know the two of you have to come with us now, right? You'll be safer. If Sykes made it out, this place is way more valuable with you two and the radio transmitter here."

Detweiler stopped trembling for a moment and said, "Ya hear that, Director Cummings? We're going back to Washington!"

"Is that a good thing or a bad thing?" Cummings asked sarcastically.

"I'm not sure. Seems like an out-of-the-frying-pan-into-the-fire situation, doesn't it?" Detweiler replied, still stammering a bit.

IT HAD BEEN a hard sprint from city hall to the Delaware River. The shooting had stopped almost immediately after the first couple of blocks, but Sykes's team wasn't taking any chances. More than half the team had gone down. Sykes had taken three rounds to the chest and had been saved by the ceramic plate in the front of his vest and the pistol he had had holstered on his chest. He would later find a bullet lodged in the slide. They had all been running on sheer adrenaline, but now that was starting to wear off, and they all needed a moment to regroup. They had to find a way back across the river before they were tracked down. Sykes was winded from the run and from being shot in the chest at nearly point-blank range. Dropping to his knees, he let out a deep-throated howl that caused his men to stop and turn their attention toward him. One of them asked, "You OK, boss?"

Sykes looked over with a scowl and snapped, "No, I'm not OK. I was just shot in the chest and ran halfway across Philadelphia. How the hell are you?"

Everyone looked around at each other, and all at once, they began to laugh. They were alive.

"Yeah, we're fucked," quipped back another man.

"Alright, let's get across the river. We need to get out of here and report what the hell is going on and that we found some old friends," Sykes said, breathing deeply and looking back in the direction they had come from. *The things you find when you're not looking for them,* he thought.

CHAPTER 35

DAY 7

PHILADELPHIA, PENNSYLVANIA

THE REMAINDER OF the night had passed without incident. Several patrols had been sent out looking for Sykes and what was left of his team but had come back empty handed. There were too many places they could be hiding, or they could have slipped back across the river. Andy hoped they tried and failed and that their lifeless bodies were at this moment washing out to sea. He knew in his heart, though, that that would have been too easy. They hadn't seen the last of Sykes.

Andy and company quickly agreed to implement a daily password system to prevent any unwelcome visitors from entering the perimeter in the future. Anyone wanting to join them would have to prove who they were and where they were from. Last night was a close call and could have turned out much worse had Director Cummings and Detweiler not stood their ground and fought off Sykes and his team.

Preparations to roll out had continued, and by first light, the entire force was lined up, prepared to move out in a convoy once the word was given. Philadelphia police and fire department personnel were to stay behind to defend their city, along with anyone who volunteered to stay behind and wasn't considered essential to operations. Also left behind were those who, though eager to make the march, were too sick or injured to make the journey. They were assured a spot defending one of the many bridges across the Delaware or Schuylkill Rivers into Philadelphia from the west, south, or east or manning one of the barricades to the north.

The immediate danger was the CAT-MAN force massing at Philadelphia International Airport just across the river to the south. Recon teams had confirmed their presence and estimated their numbers to be around two thousand.

A DAY LIKE ANY OTHER

It was decided that a small force consisting of former Army Rangers and Marine Force Reconnaissance were to approach the airport from the west, having crossed the Schuylkill River by means of the Passyunk Avenue Bridge, which wasn't yet guarded by any CAT-MAN forces. They were to infiltrate, locate, and destroy as much of the CAT-MAN supplies and vehicles as possible, then disengage before sunrise and make their way back to the perimeter by whatever means possible. The purpose was to disorient the CAT-MAN forces in the hopes they wouldn't be a threat to the convoy as they left and to diminish their ability to attack the city once Andy's forces were gone.

Andy was grinning from ear to ear as he gave the order for the convoy to head out. The explosions from the direction of the airport had been going off for two full hours now, and reports from the teams that had returned were pretty much the same—whatever they had found, they had destroyed. There had been eleven wounded, but they had all made it back. One twelve-man team was still unaccounted for, but the most recent set of explosions gave Andy a pretty good idea of where they were.

"Hope those boys have a solid plan for getting out of there now. The sun is rising, and they'll be hard-pressed to get back if they're caught in the daylight," Andy said, looking to the southwest. The morning's first light revealed plumes of smoke rising from across the river, a testament to how effective the night's raid had been.

"From what we've heard, the CAT-MAN dudes are like chickens with their heads cut off over there," replied Squatch. "They'll find their way home." He was crunching on an MRE cracker smothered in peanut butter.

Noticing what his friend was eating, Andy frowned and said, "You're not gonna shit for a week eating that much MRE peanut butter. You're never gonna learn."

"I have a cast-iron digestive tract," replied Sasquatch with a smile as he took another massive bite of the cracker.

"I don't wanna hear you bitching when your guts are all bound up," Andy said, backing away and holding his hands up in front of him.

"The breakfast of champions, bro," replied Squatch with a smile, savoring the last bite.

"I wanted to see you boys off," said Mayor Travis, walking up and interrupting Andy and Squatch's back and forth. "And thank you—you gave me my city back."

"Mr. Mayor, we were only doing what was right." Andy shook the mayor's hand.

"Yeah, bro, liberating cities is what we do," quipped Squatch with a thumbs-up.

Vehicles had been rolling past them, and it would soon be time for them to go as well. Lieutenant Ramirez had led the convoy through Philadelphia from city hall to the Ben Franklin Bridge and had crossed the Delaware into New Jersey. Andy, Squatch, David, and Dmitry would be the last to leave. Andy had wanted to wait until all the teams from the attacks on the airport had checked in and also to make sure everyone else got going OK. He had also wanted to see if any more volunteers showed up. They had been arriving all night, some coming from as far away as upstate New York, Ohio, West Virginia, Virginia, and even North Carolina. All had a tale to tell of the road they had traveled and how they had heard Andy's voice on the radio and knew that this was where they needed to be.

"Good luck, boys!" yelled Tommy Rye from the top of the stairs.

It was time to go. The end of the convoy was approaching—two armored HUMVEEs, each complete with .50-caliber machine guns in the turret on top.

Andy gave Tommy a salute then turned to get in the passenger-side door of the HUMVEE Colonel Reynolds had sent over for him. "Compliments of the Fort Dix motor pool," Reynolds had told Andy in a note that was delivered with the vehicle. As Andy got in, he noticed David and Dmitry were both still sleeping in the back seat.

Squatch, getting into the driver's seat, also noticed. "I guess it's all just too much excitement for them."

"Wake up!" yelled Andy. "You two gonna sleep all day? We're leaving now."

"Oh, Andy!" protested Squatch, "Why'd you wake him up? Now I'm gonna have to listen to how great the AK-47 is all day!"

"Just drive," Andy replied, rolling his eyes then speaking into his radio handset. "Cobra, Cobra, Cobra."

That was the code word that the convoy had departed Philadelphia and, more specifically, that he was on the road now as well. He felt that sick feeling coming on again, but it was soon replaced by exhaustion. This was the first time he had sat down in hours. He knew he wouldn't sleep for several more hours, but he was just happy to be seated. *I'm getting too old for this shit,* he thought.

"Yes, just drive," came Dmitry's groggy voice from the back seat.

"How long till we get there, Dad?" asked David.

A DAY LIKE ANY OTHER

"Not sure, buddy," replied Andy.

Andy wasn't sure of much of anything at this point, other than the fact that the danger grew with every mile they drove.

NEW JERSEY, SOMEWHERE SOUTHEAST OF PHILADELPHIA

SYKES COULD SEE through his binoculars that a long line of military vehicles stretched out to the north was being joined by another line of vehicles coming from the west. *Now what are you up to?* he thought. His team had swum through the river and arrived back at their vehicles as the sun was rising. They were all exhausted, but as they got to the top of a small hill, something caught the corner of Sykes's eye. He told the driver to stop.

"What's up, boss?" the driver asked.

"I'm not sure, but it doesn't look good," replied Sykes, sounding concerned. "We need to get back. I don't like the looks of this at all."

CHAPTER 36

INTERSTATE 295, WESTVILLE, NEW JERSEY

THE ROUTE TO the rendezvous point with Colonel Reynolds's main force had taken Andy through Philly and across the Ben Franklin Bridge into New Jersey. But instead of turning south onto Route 676 in North Camden, they had continued onto Route 30, since parts of 676 were either collapsed, unstable, or jammed with inoperable cars. They turned south onto Route 130 and followed it to Interstate 295 in Westville, New Jersey. As they drove up on the ramp, Andy could see military vehicles stretched out in columns to the east and west. He could not see where the columns ended.

The convoy from Philly, made up mostly of private vehicles with a few buses and military trucks thrown in, was stacking up on the shoulder next to Colonel Reynolds's convoy. Andy called out to the first soldier he saw and asked where the colonel was.

"Up the line about half a mile with the Bradley crews," the soldier replied, pointing west. Andy found Reynolds just as described, standing beside two massive, armored vehicles that, at the moment, were chained down on two flatbed tractor trailers.

The Bradley Fighting Vehicle, like most military equipment, had several variants, but these were M2s. At twenty-seven tons and nine feet eight inches, they were impressive. The Bradleys' main mission was to provide protected transport for up to six troops of infantry. The main weapon was the M242 Bushmaster chain gun, which fired belted 25-millimeter rounds. They also had a coaxial 7.62mm machine gun to the right of the main gun. They also could carry TOW anti-tank missiles, which these vehicles obviously didn't have, as Andy could see into the mounts. *Too bad. Those would have been nice to have*, he thought as they pulled up.

Reynolds had been speaking with the Bradley crews, but, seeing that Andy had arrived, he excused himself, as it was time to get the convoy moving.

"Hey, Colonel, looks like you found yourself some new toys," Andy proclaimed.

"They're a nice addition to our little insurrection," replied Reynolds. "I only wish we had more ammo for the main gun. There're only seventy high-explosive incendiary rounds a piece. We do have a couple of thousand practice rounds though, which is fine. They're still 25-millimeter projectiles, so I'll take 'em. We should transport them on these flatbeds to save the tracks. We only have the parts to replace pieces, not the whole tracks, so we'll deploy them if we need them."

"Yeah, getting shot is never a good thing, especially by something that big," Andy replied. "I agree we should save wear-and-tear on the tracks, just as long as these boys can get them into the fight quick. I don't suppose they have any TOW missiles stashed anywhere?"

"That was the first thing I asked," replied Reynolds, raising his eyebrows. "Unfortunately, no anti-tank missiles. What we do have is a pretty formidable fighting force." Reynolds began bringing Andy up to speed on what the final organization they had assembled looked like. Reynolds's staff, along with the newly formed operations staff from the volunteer force, had tallied up the numbers and reorganized personnel to optimize each unit. Any Army personnel who had been on active duty at the time of The Event had basically been reinstated at their previous rank and folded into Colonel Reynolds's command. A good number of volunteers had joined them from Fort Dix and from Dover, having arrived with the rest of Reynolds's command. Within hours, his understrength battalion had grown to three fully manned battalions—approximately 3,200 soldiers.

The rest of the volunteers had been organized by branch of service and military specialty and totaled around three thousand. Marines had been kept with Marines and Army with Army, as it became clear there was a language barrier when it came to both tactical and non-tactical lingo. Not to mention the "that's not how we did it in the Corps/Army" arguments, which the operations team had encountered among themselves in getting things organized. US Navy, US Air Force, and US Coast Guard volunteers had been distributed among Army and Marine units based on their experience and given jobs therein.

Those who were the furthest from combat ready due to age, health conditions, or poor conditioning had been assigned other jobs like driving trucks and so forth. It was agreed that everyone was at least rusty when it came to fighting in a war, so training was to be conducted whenever possible, and those not coming from combat arms specialties were to be brought up to speed as best as possible.

The volunteer force had been organized into three battalions as well. Getting it all organized, from battalion commanders (all three had been off active duty for many years but eagerly accepted command, knowing they still had what it takes) down to squad leaders, had been nothing more than an organizational miracle. This force henceforth would be referred to as the Militia. The Militia consisted of two Army battalions and one Marine battalion, broken up into three companies each and then three platoons each. There were also the reconnaissance groups, the last of which had finally checked in after Andy had rolled out just after daybreak. They had all made it out but ended up swimming in the river and had started taking fire about halfway across. Philly police had seen their predicament and had provided cover fire until they were safely across.

For now, Reynolds's troopers would take the lead and send out patrols ahead of the main force, but the Militia would be expected to leapfrog over those patrols starting this evening. Reynolds already had troops guarding the Commodore Barry Bridge to prevent any hostile forces from crossing the Delaware River into New Jersey and possibly blocking the march from moving south. Reynolds also had a force protecting the Delaware Memorial Bridge, where the entire force would cross before turning south on Interstate 95 toward Baltimore.

"We're ready to get the whole show on the road now that the Militia is here. We'll go as soon as you give us the word," Reynolds said, having finished briefing Andy and making sure to end it by reminding everyone that Andy was in charge.

"Thanks, Colonel. You and your people have done an amazing job," Andy started. He then noticed something odd over Reynolds's shoulder off in the distance. "What's that?" he asked, pointing past Reynolds.

Reynolds turned and saw immediately what Andy was looking at. "Shit, that looks like a body hanging from a tree," Reynolds replied, sounding disgusted. He looked through his binoculars. "Looks like more than one, actually."

Andy had recovered his binoculars from the front seat and saw that there were at least ten bodies hanging by the neck from several trees a short distance away. "They're CAT-MAN." Andy could see that they were all wearing the CAT-MAN standard-issue gray urban camouflage.

A DAY LIKE ANY OTHER

"We had no idea they were there, Andy," Reynolds said sincerely, looking up from his binoculars.

"There's no way you would have, Colonel. It's pitch black at night these days," Andy replied. "I don't think it's a good idea to leave them like that either. It sends the wrong message, and we don't want to lose the higher moral ground."

"I'll send a squad to cut them down," Reynolds said.

"And I'll get Tommy Rye to put out a statement condemning this sort of thing. I get that people are pissed—I'm pretty pissed too—but history is watching, so we need to do this right," Andy said, feeling torn between what he knew was right and reveling in the fact that ten bad people had met their end in a way they deserved.

That afternoon, Tommy Rye delivered the message on the air.

"A message from the Militia leadership. Be it as it may that CAT-MAN officers have committed countless unspeakable acts upon the American people and the desire for retribution against any and all CAT-MAN officials is strong, it is requested that any CAT-MAN personnel taken prisoner be turned over to reliable law enforcement authorities for due process under the Constitution.

"This may seem counterintuitive given what CAT-MAN the organization has done to our countrymen, but the eye of history is upon us, and retribution by the mob is always looked upon harshly. One must always remember that we are the good guys and must behave as such. CAT-MAN officials who surrender should be taken into custody and turned over for due process, as stated previously. However, in the event CAT-MAN officials choose to stand and fight, then feel free to send them to hell by whatever means necessary."

IT WAS LATER reported by the squad sent to remove the CAT-MAN bodies that a group of locals met them as they were cutting the bodies down. Apparently, the CAT-MAN officers had been the local enforcers and were apprehended by a group of armed civilians after a brief firefight. The locals said that after a summary "trial" of sorts, all the CAT-MAN officers were found guilty of various crimes and hanged immediately. The group of locals never said they personally carried out the punishment, and the squad leader never asked. That's how it was left.

CHAPTER 37

THE US CAPITOL BUILDING, WASHINGTON, DC

SERGEANT MADDOX COULD see something was going on. The usual lackadaisical CAT-MAN officers manning the Capitol Building were in high gear all morning, filling sandbags then stacking them around the entire building using the existing marble rail as their guide. It was clear they were fortifying the entire building and doing it quickly. It was chaos. They had even doubled the crew they had sent to dig trenches next to his tanks, which were already in revetments his troopers had dug using a bulldozer they found nearby. Maddox asked several CAT-MAN officers what was going on, but every one of them just said that they couldn't talk about it. The one thing Maddox was sure of was that they were scared. *Things just might get interesting around here,* he thought, a grin forming on his face.

"SO LET ME get this straight," Keller said, his face buried in his hands, "the people who took over Philadelphia have joined forces with at least one US Army unit and are now on their way south along Interstate 95, basically headed straight toward us."

"That's—" Sykes started to answer, but Keller wasn't done.

"Plus, Cummings and Detweiler are with them?" Keller looked as though he might have a stroke at any moment.

"We don't—" Sykes tried again, but Keller still wasn't finished.

"So the only two people who aren't locked up in the Capitol Building and know what's really going on and can expose all of us are on their way here with an army that has already proven it doesn't give a crap about what the legitimate government of this country has to say. Does that about sum it up, Mr. Sykes?"

Keller finished his rant, slapped both hands on his desk, and flopped back in his chair, exhaling forcefully.

A DAY LIKE ANY OTHER

Sykes understood Keller's frustration but was in no mood for temper tantrums. He had arrived back in the capital and had immediately begun getting things in motion to further fortify the city. He was exhausted. Half his team was dead, he had failed to destroy the radio equipment or kill any of the rebel leadership, and his ribs were sore, making breathing painful. The ceramic plate in his armor vest had saved his life, but the impacts had still left their mark. The plate was cracked and useless now, but it had done its job. He would have to find a new one soon; he knew this fight was far from over.

"Mr. President, I understand this is a lot to absorb"—Sykes was absolutely patronizing Keller—"but you have it pretty straight. We don't know for sure that Cummings and Detweiler are alive. One of my guys threw a frag grenade in where they were, so it is possible they're dead. Everything else you said was spot on, though."

"Spot on, he says!" Keller replied, disgusted. "Well, I guess we better let Mr. X know what's going on."

"No need. I already told him. That's why there's so much happening right now."

"You already told him?" Keller shot back.

"Yes. I called him from the highway about two hours ago." Sykes's patience was wearing thin.

Keller was livid. "Well, if you two have things all under control, then why are you even bothering to tell me?"

"Excellent question, Mr. President," Sykes said as he stood to leave. "I'm telling you because I can't order a SEAL team to go kill the bastards who are headed this way right now to hang you. Where is that SEAL team, anyway? We had this conversation a couple of days ago, didn't we?"

Keller's face went red with anger. He shot back, "We're trying to find enough SEALs to make up a team since you geniuses disbanded most of the military!"

"No matter. Get Special Operations Command on the ball, or we really won't have a use for you," Sykes said as he walked toward the door, leaving Keller to stew.

"I'll get Special Operations Command on the ball when I'm damn good and ready!" shouted Keller at the closing door.

I really hate that guy, Keller thought, slumping back in his chair again.

TOM OLIVA

SPECIAL OPERATIONS COMMAND, THE PENTAGON

SIX HOURS LATER, the third request from President Keller for a SEAL team arrived on the desk of Rear Admiral Kane. Under normal circumstances, such requests would go across several other desks before ever arriving on his, but things were anything but normal. As the commanding officer of Special Operations Command, he wouldn't be involved in such matters until they were much further along in the planning process. Nowadays, his desk was the first stop. Like every other unit in the US military, his was on a skeleton crew. This request was straight from the top, and although he had already ignored it or made excuses due to staffing issues, he knew he would have to deal with it at some point, regardless of if he felt it was more CAT-MAN bullshit.

"Master Chief, can you come in here please?" the admiral said, calling out into the outer offices. They had moved his headquarters up from Florida to DC a few weeks after The Event due to communication issues, and they were now working out of the Pentagon.

"You needed me, sir?"

Master Chief Theodore Norwood looked like the SEAL team poster boy, with close-cropped blond hair above a chiseled face. He had spent his career with the teams or on Coronado Island training SEALs. He had no family besides the Navy, so when everyone else had headed home after The Event, it had been easy for him to stay on active duty. Now he, the admiral, and a handful of other personnel were left to keep the lights on at Special Operations.

"Yeah, chief, I need you to go over to the White House with me so we can figure out what exactly it is that they need from us," Admiral Kane said, gesturing for the master chief to take a seat.

"What could they possibly want from us? There's like a dozen of us total," Master Chief Norwood replied, amused.

"Well, I can't put them off anymore, hoping they'll forget about us. The president's personal secretary brought this request over in person, so they're not going to stop," the Admiral said, tossing the request letter onto his desk.

Master Chief Norwood picked it up and began to read to himself. *Locate and destroy insurgent cell leadership.* He said aloud, "They want us to go do CAT-MAN's dirty work because they started something they can't finish."

"It sure looks that way, doesn't it?" the Admiral replied. "How many operators can we put in the field?"

A DAY LIKE ANY OTHER

"Six, including me, sir," replied Norwood.

"Well, tell them to get ready for an operation. You and I are taking a ride over to the White House tomorrow afternoon," Kane said, taking the request back from Norwood.

"Aye aye, sir," replied Norwood, who then turned to go get the boys moving. *This is gonna suck,* he thought as he left the office.

US CAPITOL BUILDING

SERGEANT FIRST CLASS Maddox had taken the First Lady's advice and sweet-talked his CAT-MAN handlers into letting him and his soldiers use the showers in the basement of the Capitol Building, mostly because the First Lady had made such a point of it. He was seriously curious as to why. She was correct—the shower facilities were top-notch, and they were all enjoying them, especially the hot water. They were in heaven. Too many months of cold water to wash with had made something as simple as hot water a luxury.

Sergeant Maddox had finished dressing and was standing in the entryway to wait for his men to finish and for their CAT-MAN escort to return and walk them out of the building when he heard something coming from the air conditioning duct above him. Then the noise spoke in a whisper. "Are you alone? Where's the guard who walked you in?"

It was a woman's voice. She sounded desperate.

Sergeant Maddox was a little shocked but calmly looked around and responded, "I'm the only one here. The CAT-MAN dude said he'd be back in thirty minutes, and that was about twenty minutes ago, so he'll probably be back soon. Why are you in the ducting of this building?"

"My name is Eleanor Dreyfus. I'm a congresswoman from Delaware," the voice said through the duct grate. "We overheard the guards saying that the First Lady comes here every day. Is that true?"

"Yeah, it's true. In fact, I just talked to her. She's the one who told us about these showers," Maddox replied. "Why do you keep calling the CAT-MAN guys the guards?"

"Because they're keeping us prisoner here—all of Congress, the Joint Chiefs, the Supreme Court, and who knows who else," Dreyfus replied.

Maddox felt a sick feeling creeping into his gut. "Prisoners? How can that be?" he replied.

"It can be because Keller and those CAT-MAN bastards would never get away with what they were doing if the government was functioning," Dreyfus replied. "Look, we don't have much time. Tell the First Lady that we're all prisoners here, and she has to get me out somehow so I can tell the world what's going on."

Maddox was still feeling sick and a little stunned but had questions for the duct woman. "How did you know I'd be here if you're prisoners, and why are you the one who has to get out?"

"We knew because the guards have big mouths, and we overheard them talking about bringing you and your men in for showers," she began, speaking faster. She knew time was running out, and the guard could return any second. "It has to be me because I'm the only one who will fit into this duct—I'm five foot two and weigh ninety pounds. Will you tell her?"

"I'll make sure she gets the message," Maddox replied. "But you should go now. I think I hear the CAT-MAN guys coming back."

"Thank you. I'll come back here every day about this time," she replied.

"Ma'am," Maddox began, "you stay safe."

"Thank you. You be safe as well," Dreyfus replied as she slid away from the grate.

I guess I know what side I'm on now, Maddox thought, taking in what had just happened.

THE WHITE HOUSE

"Excuse me, ma'am." It was Special Agent Ryan Billings, the head of Joyce Keller's Secret Service detail. "May I have a word with you in private?"

"Of course," she replied, leaving her daughters to continue coloring on their own.

They both put their hands over their mouths and spoke in whispers, something they started doing as Billings became increasingly convinced the entire White House was bugged and under video surveillance. Joyce had even begun wearing a robe into the shower and only disrobing once the shower doors were shut.

"I'm sorry to bother you, but the agent we have watching that place says your new friends went inside this afternoon," Billings said in a mumble.

A DAY LIKE ANY OTHER

"Is that right?" Mrs. Keller said in a low tone. "Well, I'll head over first thing tomorrow morning. I think I'd like to talk to Sergeant Maddox again. Don't tell anyone else, not even on your detail. We'll head over even before the girls are awake, OK?"

"Yes, ma'am. Sounds like a plan," he replied.

CHAPTER 38

DAY 8

0445 HOURS,
THE CAPITOL BUILDING, WASHINGTON, DC

THE SUN WAS just starting to create a glow on the horizon when Sergeant Maddox was awakened by the voice of his corporal of the guard.

"Sergeant Maddox. You awake? There's someone here to see you."

"Yes. I'm up. I'll be right there," he said groggily, quite evidently not up. *These CAT-MAN dudes are really starting to piss me off. Now they're waking me up before the damn sun,* he thought as he headed for the tent flap.

"This couldn't wait until the sun rose?" he asked as he exited the tent, intentionally sounding more than a little perturbed.

"I'm very sorry to wake you, Sergeant Maddox, but no, it really couldn't wait," Joyce Keller said sincerely.

"Oh. It's you. I'm sorry, I didn't know," Maddox replied, giving a dirty look to the soldier who had awakened him.

"Don't be sorry. I'd be irritated if it was the other way around," she said with a smile.

"What can I do for you at this early hour, ma'am?" Maddox replied.

"I understand you've been inside," she said, gesturing toward the Capitol Building.

"You coming here saved me the trouble of trying to get you a message, actually," he said with a grin.

"Tell me everything quickly. I don't have much time," she replied, moving closer to him and speaking in a lower tone.

A DAY LIKE ANY OTHER

0712, INTERSTATE I-95/I-695 INTERCHANGE

ANDY AND COMPANY had spent the previous day leapfrogging south on Interstate 95, and they had camped for the night under the I-95/I-695 interchange just to the northeast of the Baltimore city limits. They had traveled all day, and not one shot had been fired by either side. Within two hours of setting off, just after sunrise, they had encountered a CAT-MAN roadblock, the occupants of which had quickly fled upon seeing the size of the force approaching them. Subsequently, any additional roadblocks they encountered were abandoned. CAT-MAN had destroyed several overpasses along the route, but these were of no account; the lead elements of the column would find a route around before the main column arrived.

The leapfrogging of units at the front of the column was working flawlessly. The lead unit would move out approximately a mile, hold its position, and then fall in at the back of the column once it had passed. Additional platoon-sized units were pushed out ahead as many as five miles at times. The entire route was reconned, and anyone trying to get eyes on the main force would be hard-pressed to do so. They had also found two more incidents of mob justice—one group of CAT-MAN officers was found blindfolded and shot and another group was found hanged. There wasn't much that could be done; people were angry and hungry for justice.

The more pressing issue was that the scouts sent ahead to Baltimore had reported that both the Fort McHenry and Baltimore Harbor Tunnels were completely flooded, and all three bridges were damaged and unpassable. The plan had been to skirt around the heart of the city to the south, liberate the retraining camp at Annapolis, then proceed into Washington, DC, via I-95. Now their options were either to go straight through downtown, which was sure to be a bloodbath, or take I-695 around the city to the north, putting them far out of their way if they were to push on to Annapolis.

Andy had been poring over the map for hours now. The sun was just starting to rise, but since being awakened with the news of the tunnels and bridges, he could not rest. A meeting of the command staff had been called, and it was agreed to send scouts out to the southeast to try and find another way across. Andy, Colonel Reynolds, Lieutenant Ramirez, and Squatch had all been lingering by the communications tent waiting for any word from the scouting parties. They needed to get the army moving soon, and they didn't know in what direction to send them. Finally, around 0700 hours, reports started coming in, not only from the scouts to the southeast but also from the scouts that had been sent into the city and northwest to check the I-695 route should they be forced to go that way.

"So here's what we've got so far," Reynolds began, then paused as Wally walked in.

Andy noticed that Wally had walked up in the company of a young woman, clearly one of the medics due to the oversized medical pack she carried. She quickly walked off in another direction as Wally entered the tent. Andy gave Wally the evil eye, at which Wally looked away sheepishly.

Reynolds continued, "From what we can tell, all of the CAT-MAN folks are coalescing in downtown Baltimore. Interstate 695 to the north is under their control, but there don't appear to be any fortifications yet, which tells us that they're not sure what we're going to do other than continue on to DC somehow. The teams we sent south haven't found anything other than Team Three, whose leader is on his way back here to report in person and then return south with personnel possessing the appropriate skill sets."

"Appropriate skill sets? What the hell does that mean?" asked Squatch.

"That's a great question. Andy, where was Team Three headed?" asked Reynolds.

"They were supposed to check the Sparrows Point Shipyard for any seaworthy craft that could take a force across the Patapsco River at worst, or all the way to Annapolis at best. They must have found something," Andy replied, checking his map and notes.

Wally, seeing his chance to exit before finding out what Andy's stink eye was all about, jumped up. "I'll go scrub the rosters for Navy or Coast Guard folks who might have the expertise we need." Then he disappeared out of the tent flap.

Andy grumbled under his breath then asked, "Is there anything else, Colonel?"

"Yeah, Team Seven says there's at least one drone watching us. They saw it when it crossed the horizon in front of the rising sun," Reynolds replied.

"OK, well I guess that was inevitable," Andy said as he stood. "When Team Three's leader gets back, we'll have more to go on. Squatch, let's go see how Wally's doing until then."

It was Squatch's turn to grumble. He had seen the same thing Andy had and knew that Andy wasn't going to let Wally think he didn't.

A DAY LIKE ANY OTHER

"Sure, boss, let's go see Wally," Squatch replied with a little too much enthusiasm.

0745 HOURS, UPSTATE PENNSYLVANIA

THE SUN WAS already up, and Melissa could hear the usual sounds of morning around the farm. The children were up and about, and she could hear María getting breakfast together for them. Melissa knew she needed to get up and help. María hadn't slept much either since they had heard Andy's voice on the radio that first day. Both of them were putting on a happy face for the children, but they were both deeply concerned that they would never see their husbands again.

In the past when their husbands were away, they had taken solace in the fact that the full weight and power of the US government was on their husbands' sides. This was very different. In fact, it was the opposite. Their husbands were fighting against the government, and from what she could surmise from the radio show out of Philadelphia, they were on their way to Washington, DC, at this very moment.

A dozen different horrible scenarios were flashing through her head when she heard a car door slam from the direction of her parents' house. Her first thought was, *Are my boys back?* But that thought was fleeting since it was impossible. Her next thought was, *My God, is it the CAT-MAN people?* They had been watching the farm since the day the sheriff was there asking questions with that awful CAT-MAN person. María snapped her out of her thoughts, startling her.

"Hey, Melissa! Your dad just called over on the radio. He said he needs your help right now," María said, calling up the stairs to her.

"OK, I'm on my way," she called back, jumping out of bed. *What could be so urgent?* she thought as the tension built in her gut.

As she exited the house, she saw an SUV parked at her parents' house and recognized it as Uncle Charlie's. What she saw next caused her to break into a full run. Her parents and John Redstone were carrying what could only be a body wrapped in a blanket toward their front door.

She covered the distance between her house and her parents' house in what felt like moments and caught them just as they were entering the front door.

"Who is this? What happened?"

"It's Ryan—he's shot," answered John as they all heaved Ryan onto the dining room table. "I've been trying to get him over here, but that CAT-MAN car is always parked out on the highway. This morning was the first time it wasn't there. I'm sorry to bring him here; it's putting you all in danger, but after we got back and buried Uncle Charlie, Ryan started taking a turn for the worst. They patched him up right away, but the medic said he would probably need surgery. I'm really sorry."

"Don't be sorry. You did the right thing bringing him here," replied Dr. Taft as he rolled Ryan onto his side to examine the bullet's exit wound.

"Uncle Charlie is dead?" asked Melissa, the panic having subsided. Her fear had been that it was Andy or David in the blanket, and seeing now that it wasn't, she was able to focus.

John looked down at the floor and said, "Yes, in Philly right at the start."

"Are Andy and David OK?" she asked, then added, "And Squatch and Wally?"

"They're all OK. Well, at least they were," replied John.

"Melissa, we have to get ready for surgery. Ryan is bleeding internally. We can grill John later," said Dr. Taft, cutting in calmly, always in control. He was in his element regardless of how long he had been out of it. He then turned to his wife and said, "Christine, dear, can you please go tell María not to let any of the children come down here? Then get right back. I'll need you to assist as well."

Without saying a word, Mrs. Taft headed out the door and headed for Melissa and Andy's house. As she crossed the driveway, she glanced toward the highway and saw through the trees two CAT-MAN vehicles sitting side by side and facing opposite directions. Her heart sank and she thought, *Well, they weren't gone for long.*

1017 HOURS, INTERSTATE I-95/I-695 INTERCHANGE

IT WAS PAINSTAKING, the waiting. Scout Team Three's leader had returned and reported that they had found a dredging barge and tugboat at the Sparrows Point Shipyard that appeared seaworthy. A team of former Navy and Coast Guard boatswains, mates, and enginemen were sent back with him to assess the vessel. That had been two hours ago, and they had heard nothing.

A DAY LIKE ANY OTHER

Since then, Andy's time had been spent going over possible contingencies if the vessel was deemed seaworthy, like approximately how many troops it could carry. He had also gone over reports from the scout teams in the city, who were now taking fire from CAT-MAN positions if they got too close. His frustration was building, as was Colonel Reynolds's. The waiting was maddening.

He had also confronted Wally about his new "friend." Her name was Jessica Adams, a US Army medic with two tours to Iraq who was now serving with the Militia. Wally had assured Andy that there was nothing going on and that they had become friendly while getting things organized in Philadelphia. Andy had accepted that explanation but had made it clear to Wally that he was now one of the top leaders of this force, and he needed to maintain a high standard of moral judgment. Squatch added that it hadn't been that long since Amy had been killed, and they didn't want to see him get hurt like that again.

"We're playing a dangerous game here, bro. Chances are pretty high we all catch some lead in the next few days."

Andy had agreed and said, "We don't want to see you get hurt like that again."

Wally had understood and reassured them both that he was well aware that they were in the most danger they had ever been in and not to worry. That's where that had been left, and they had all moved on to carry out the tasks at hand.

At last, a rider arrived from the shipyard with news of their progress. Word went out for the command staff to assemble at the headquarters tent. Once they were all there, the briefing began.

"OK, whadda we got?" said Andy, trying not to sound perturbed at having to wait for what had seemed like an eternity to get an answer on the barge and tug.

It was the same scout team leader who had brought them the news from the shipyard initially. He spoke quickly as he could sense the collective mood and needed to get back to his team. "Well, the crew we brought over has been at it since they got there. The engines on the tug wouldn't start at first, but after a few adjustments, they got them started and running well. They scoured the shipyard for fuel but could only get the fuel tanks filled halfway. They feel the vessel is seaworthy enough for the trip to Annapolis. The barge is in rough shape—it appears to have been used for a dredging operation—but is also seaworthy. They recommend no more than three hundred bodies, though, due entirely to available space."

"Thank you. You and your boys have done amazing work. Please chime in if you have something to add while we plan this out," Andy said, speaking to the visibly exhausted scout team leader.

Andy then turned his attention to the command staff, which consisted of Reynolds, Ramirez, Sasquatch, Wally, Andy, Reynolds, headquarters staff, and all six battalion commanders (three from Tenth Mountain and three from the Militia). He had also asked Director Cummings and Dr. Detweiler to attend since they would be entering Washington, DC, at some point in the very near future, and it was thought they might have something to offer having lived there recently. It was a full house of all seasoned warriors and leaders in their own right. Andy felt enormous pressure and extreme calm simultaneously. They had looked at several options for liberating Annapolis then getting to DC, all of which had risks, but he knew that this team could get it done.

"In my opinion," Andy began, "we have to go with plan A."

Plan A was simple: The main force would move out to the northwest along I-695, circling Baltimore to the I-195 interchange and ending up at the Baltimore/Washington International Airport. From there, the Militia would continue south along I-97 and relieve a force that had been sent by sea to secure and hold Annapolis. There was a fear that the prisoners would be moved or executed if it became obvious that Annapolis was an objective. The only detail missing was how large a force should go by sea.

"Now that we know we're limited to three hundred bodies, we need to make sure we have enough bicycles and get the Marine company that's going tucked away ASAP so the main force can get moving."

With those few words, Andy had set things in motion. The fate of the nation would be settled in the next twenty-four to forty-eight hours.

"Are there any questions? Does everyone know what to do?" added Andy.

Detweiler opened his mouth as if to say something but then stopped himself.

"OK, then, let's get it done," Andy said, concluding the meeting.

The tent emptied. Everyone had been issued their orders, so it was just a matter of carrying them out. The main force would advance to fight their way to the airport. The amphibious force would take the barge and tug to Annapolis, conduct an assault, secure the prisoners being held there, and then hold until relieved.

"Dr. Detweiler," Andy called out to stop Detweiler from leaving. "You had a question?"

A DAY LIKE ANY OTHER

Detweiler stopped, as did Cummings. They were a team now—at least, that's how Cummings saw it. He wasn't going to let Detweiler out of his sight—he was too important.

"Well," Detweiler began, "bicycles? Why bicycles?"

"Ha!" Andy let out a little chuckle. "The bicycles. Well, we're pretty sure there's a drone watching us right now. So sending a convoy of vehicles over to the coast would surely be noticed. We were going to just march over there. It's fourteen miles, so it's not very far, but it would take time and a lot of energy. Squatch saw a couple of our knuckleheads racing bicycles down the street, which gave him the idea to ride bicycles to the port."

"I have a good idea every now and then. We had to scour the whole neighborhood to find enough bikes," said Squatch as he walked past, carrying a large table out to the truck used to transport the command tent and equipment.

"So we're going to let the convoy move off toward Baltimore," Andy continued. "Once they're gone, we'll come out of hiding and head for the shipyard in small groups. Motorcycles would have worked too, but unfortunately, most of those got cooked when The Event hit us. The ones the scouts are using were all in a Philly PD impound in a metal shipping container. The metal must have protected their electronic components from getting fried. Apparently, and luckily for us, Philadelphia has a problem with illegal motocross bikes."

"Fascinating," Detweiler began. "That actually makes perfect sense, due to the lack of any sort of metal shielding on a motorcycle. I would think it similar in regards—"

Cummings interrupted Detweiler before he really got going.

"Hold on. You said we'll get going once the convoy is gone. Are you guys going with the assault force?"

Andy looked over to Cummings just in time to catch a dirty look from Squatch, who was passing behind him at that moment.

"Just me," Andy said in a low tone so as not to get Squatch riled up again. It had been a major argument in which Squatch, Wally, Dmitry, and David had all started yelling at him all at once.

"It was my idea, Mr. Director, so if it goes badly, I need to be there," Andy continued.

"It's bullshit and you know it," said Squatch, passing by again, this time carrying a radio set.

"They're pretty pissed off, as you can imagine," said Andy, giving Squatch a dirty look. "I get that they want to go, but their place is here with the main force, and I made Dmitry promise to get David home if I don't come back because there's no way in hell he's coming with me—not this time."

"No need to explain, Andy," replied Cummings. "I get it. Good luck. We'll see you in Annapolis."

With that, Director Cummings shook Andy's hand and left the tent, taking Detweiler with him, who gave Andy a nod as he left.

For a moment, Andy felt as though he'd never see either one of them again.

Squatch shouted as they were about to take the tent down around him and snapped him out of it. "Are you staying or going?"

Andy wasn't having it; he needed his friend's head in the game.

"I'm going, I'm going! Being pissed at me isn't going to change anything. Get over it, and just make sure you guys get there ASAP. Focus on that, OK?"

"We'll be there," Squatch began, still with an edge to his voice. "Just don't die before we get there."

"Thanks for the advice," Andy replied.

That was the end of that conversation, and they both went about their tasks. This was how it was with hard men. In normal-people language, it would sound more like, "Hey, I'm worried, so be safe," to which the reply would be, "That's nice of you, and I appreciate it." The truth of it was that the level of danger and the probability of death weren't lost on either one of them; this was just the only way they knew how to express it.

1221 HOURS, THE WHITE HOUSE, WASHINGTON, DC

ADMIRAL KANE AND Master Chief Norwood arrived at the White House to find a scene of utter panic. The CAT-MAN officers there were frantically filling and stacking sandbags all around the perimeter of the building. The stark contrast between the activity around the building and the still peaceful and unblemished landscaping of the grounds was surreal. The normal police and Secret Service security were nowhere to be seen; there were only CAT-MAN officers. Kane and Norwood gave each other a look after the guard, who couldn't have been more than eighteen years old, cleared them through without searching the car or even running the little mirror on wheels around under the car to check for explosives. Their appointment was at 1300 hours, and they had arrived early expecting security to be more thorough and time-consuming.

A DAY LIKE ANY OTHER

The lack of security was off-putting for both of them, and they wondered separately how that could be.

They were met by an aide to the president's chief of staff and a CAT-MAN officer who apparently was nothing more than a valet, as he took the keys to their vehicle and drove off. Master Chief Norwood thought to himself, *This is some serious* Keystone Cops *shit goin' on here.*

They were led through the confusion that was apparently consuming the White House presently to the Oval Office. The aide opened the door, poked his head in, and announced that the Special Operations folks were here. He gestured to them to go in and closed the door behind them.

"Gentlemen!" said Keller as they entered, rising to his feet. "Come in, come in, please, have a seat," he added, gesturing to the sofa.

Kane and Norwood both hesitated at first, slightly put off that the commander in chief would so obviously be kissing their asses the moment they entered the room. They made their way to the sofa, taking notice of the man seated on the opposite sofa. They both recognized him as CAT-MAN Director Sykes. The hair on the back of Master Chief Norwood's neck bristled at the sight of him. He knew enough about him to know that he didn't like him. *This is gonna suck. Stay calm and go along with whatever these two have up their sleeve, then get the hell out of here,* he thought as he took a seat.

Sykes didn't bother to address them or even look up at them; he just kept flipping through the folder of papers on his lap. After a long, awkward silence, he looked up at the two of them and then at Keller and said, "You should probably tell them what it is you need them to do." Then he went back to his papers. Norwood couldn't help but notice that Sykes had a number of scratches on his face and several busted knuckles. *That's how I look after a combat operation,* he thought, squinting his eyes slightly, then looking over at Keller, who was seated now and grinning at them. *Did Sykes just tell the president what to do?*

"Yes, well," Keller began, "I'm sure you're both aware of the fact that an insurrection has started in Philadelphia. What you may not know, or maybe you do, is that a group of traitors, quite a large group actually, is headed this way."

Norwood was trying to focus and pay attention, but his mind was busy analyzing not only what Keller was saying but how he was saying it. *He's nervous*, Norwood thought.

"What we need is for you to take a team and"—Keller hesitated, clearing his throat—"find this group, locate its leadership, and eliminate it. Immediately."

Norwood said nothing. He understood why Keller was nervous now.

Admiral Kane said what they were both thinking. "Just so I'm clear, Mr. President, you're asking us to find and kill American citizens on American soil."

"Yes, I'm afraid that's exactly what we're asking," replied Keller, staring blankly at Admiral Kane.

Sykes looked up from his papers, giving his full attention to whatever the admiral was going to say next.

"With all due respect, Mr. President, what you're asking is illegal. The Posse Comitatus Act prohibits the military from becoming involved in civilian law enforcement matters. I would imagine local law enforcement or CAT-MAN would have jurisdiction here," Kane said, measuring his words and cadence to ensure he was understood. He knew about the force headed toward DC and imagined that was why they had been summoned to the White House. He also knew that under certain circumstances, the military could be used domestically, but he wanted to make it clear that he didn't want any part of what they were asking.

Sykes shifted in his chair, and Keller's face went pale and then beet red. Norwood thought, *The admiral struck a nerve—score one for Kane.*

Sykes thought for a moment, then leaned forward and said, "I understand it's an unorthodox request that we're making, but these are unorthodox times—"

Kane cut him off. "Unorthodox and illegal are two different things, Director."

Sykes continued, ignoring Kane's comment. "Unfortunately, it's evident that local law enforcement isn't equipped to deal with this, and, for the most part, Catastrophe Management teams aren't trained for this sort of thing. So you see, we need professionals. That's why you're here."

Kane and Norwood both sat silently, looking at Sykes, imagining themselves knocking his teeth out. They both knew what CAT-MAN had done to civilians on countless occasions. Now there was someone who could actually fight back, and they were scared.

Keller broke the silence. "Admiral Kane, if you need a congressional declaration, I'm sure we can get one today authorizing what we're proposing."

Kane smiled and said, "A congressional declaration would be just fine, Mr. President, thank you. The master chief and I will get a team together immediately. If you can get us whatever intel you have on this group, we'll get a plan together and have at them."

With that, Admiral Kane stood, and Norwood stood as well, following his boss's lead.

A DAY LIKE ANY OTHER

Keller and Sykes were both surprised that Kane had been placated so easily, and they both just sat in stunned amazement until Norwood spoke.

"The intel? Do you have intel for us?"

"Ah, yes," Sykes said, closing the folder on his lap and handing it over to Norwood. "This is everything we know about them at present."

"OK, thank you," said Kane as he faced Keller and saluted smartly. "We'll be on our way then, lots to do. I'll have my people looking out for that declaration, Mr. President."

Kane turned and exited with Norwood on his heels. As the door shut behind them, Norwood said in a firm whisper, "What the hell was that, sir?"

"Yeah, I know, Master Chief," Kane replied as they walked toward the exit. "There was no point in arguing. I just needed to get out of there."

As if from nowhere, the First Lady appeared in front of them, causing them both to stop short.

"Admiral Kane, it's so good to see you again," said Joyce, taking the admiral's hand and gaining his full attention, thus distracting him from seeing that Special Agent Billings had handed Norwood a folded piece of paper and quickly whispered, "Your eyes only, Chief."

Admiral Kane and Joyce exchanged pleasantries, and a few minutes later, Kane and Norwood were getting back into their vehicle.

Norwood was the first to speak. "What in the name of Christ?"

"Yeah, let's just get out of here before we're contaminated with the crazy that's taken over this place," replied Kane.

CHAPTER 39

1915 HOURS, SPARROWS POINT SHIPYARD, MARYLAND

IT HAD TAKEN until almost noon for the main force to get completely clear of the I-95/I-695 encampment. Andy had waited a good hour and change before sending the first group out from hiding. Andy left with the second group, leaving the company commander to space his men out as he saw fit. Andy was anxious to get to the port and see the vessels they'd be using. Reports had been coming in from the lead units on I-695 that they had been meeting light resistance, but the scouts were reporting that the CAT-MAN force in the city was starting to move out to the north in front of their advance.

The tug and barge combo had been about what Andy had expected. The crew had already started stacking bags of concrete around the wheelhouse and had created firing positions on either side of the bridge. The sides of the barge were low enough that the troops on board could climb over without needing ladders, but ladders had been collected from around the shipyard in the event they were needed once they reached Annapolis. Satisfied, Andy sent word for the assault force to start boarding just before sunset. They had been coalescing in a warehouse not far from here as they arrived, which they all did with only minor crashes and mechanical issues. A box van had been the last to leave, carrying machine guns and extra supplies; this vehicle was also responsible for picking up the stragglers.

With everyone accounted for and the sun setting, it was time to get going. The plan was to set sail into the middle of the channel and allow the receding tide to pull them out into the Chesapeake Bay and south toward their objective. The tug would keep its engines running but only make course corrections when necessary. They were to appear as just another drifting wreck abandoned following The Event. The Marines on the barge were to stay under the cover of large tarps that had been found in the shipyard. When the sun had fully set, the Marines would come out of cover, and the tug would pick up speed and head for Annapolis. The helmsman had been issued night vision goggles to ensure they wouldn't hit any floating debris and to make the approach and landing at Annapolis as precise as possible.

As they got underway, Andy's radio operator, who had been monitoring the main force's frequency, informed him that CAT-MAN resistance had stiffened. Their tactics were to block the road then hit and run. They were using Javelin and AT4 anti-tank rockets effectively, and the lead units were taking casualties. Two of the Strykers were hit, and Colonel Reynolds had ordered the Bradley Fighting Vehicles to deploy. Andy thanked him and said to keep him posted on any new information. The main force had to still be somewhere north of Baltimore, and they were already getting held up. *This is not good*, he thought as he looked at his AAA atlas map of Maryland.

Andy turned to Captain Williams, the company commander in charge of the assault force, and asked, "Did you catch all that?"

Captain Peter Williams was a Naval Academy grad, so his company was an easy choice when selecting which of the Marine companies would conduct this assault. He had resigned his commission when given the choice of that or attending retraining. Something about the idea of some CAT-MAN–sanctioned training that was somehow going to make him a better officer just didn't sit right. He had left the Marine Corps and spent the winter with his extended family on his grandfather's farm in upstate New York. He, like everyone else here, had heard Andy speak on the radio and answered the call. Now he found himself leading a reinforced rifle company destined to attack his alma mater and liberate his fellow officers being held there.

"Yeah, I was listening in," replied Captain Williams. "We have to follow the same game plan, though, even if it means we have to wait longer than we like."

"The plan stays the same," Andy began, looking back at his map. "We don't have a choice. Have your boys sweep the campus, deal with any guards, get our people gathered up and tucked away in the field house by the marina, and wait."

"I'll put patrols out to give us a heads-up if we get company, and we'll fight a delaying action until help arrives. If we get backed up, we'll occupy the buildings around the field house and dig in for the long fight," said Captain Williams, pointing to the rough map of Annapolis he had drawn when they were finalizing the plan.

"You're sure the field house is big enough for whatever we might find?"

"Yeah, yeah, it's an indoor track and field stadium. It's plenty big. Plus, it's right up against the marina on one side, and there are wide-open practice fields on the back end that go down to the water."

"No one is gonna sneak up on us, but we're also not going anywhere if we get boxed in there."

"Nope, not unless this old tub we're standing on grows bigger."

"I guess we'll just have to hold until relieved then, won't we?"

"Annapolis is beautiful this time of year," replied Williams with a smile.

1700 HOURS, THE WHITE HOUSE

SYKES HADN'T LEFT Keller's office all afternoon, and Keller was clearly ready to snap.

"Mr. President, I understand you've requested the Second Marine Division and Eighty-Second Airborne Division to get moving this way, but it's time to give them a direct order or start replacing generals," said Sykes.

For the first time, he was showing signs of the stress he was under. Mr. X had called three times—three times Keller had ignored it, and three times Sykes's phone had immediately rung. The usual tension between Sykes and Keller had escalated to new heights.

"You know, I'm finding it strangely satisfying to hear you call me 'Mr. President,'" Keller said with a smile. "I mean, now that you need desperately something, that is."

Sykes looked down at the floor, then up at Keller, then down at the floor again, contemplating what to say or what violent thing to do to Keller. At that moment, Keller believed Sykes would kill him right there on the spot, and he didn't care. Sykes's satellite phone buzzing broke the silence.

Sykes answered, "Yes, sir." Keller could only hear Sykes's side of the conversation. "Yes, sir . . . Yes, sir . . . I'll explain it to him, yes, sir . . . Thank you, sir." With that, Sykes hung up and took a deep breath.

"So, what words of wisdom did his excellency the evil emperor have for you this time?" asked Keller, leaning forward, pretending to be excited.

The thought that Keller was drunk flashed through Sykes's mind for a moment, but he refocused and spoke calmly and with a sincerity that Keller had never heard from him. It rattled him slightly.

"Mr. President, I understand your frustration with the position we've put you in, and I honestly don't blame you for being obstinate and actually reveling in the chaos. Mr. X asked me to calmly explain the reality of the situation at hand plainly so there's no confusion and no doubt about what's coming."

A DAY LIKE ANY OTHER

Sykes paused for a moment to ensure he had Keller's attention. Satisfied, he continued.

"As far as we can tell, the force headed this way consists of active-duty military, retired military, and recently separated military from all service branches who, for the most part, are combat veterans. They are led by some anonymous person who captivated them to the point that they will fight their own government regardless of the odds. They are highly skilled, highly motivated, and very well armed, and they very obviously are headed here.

"On our side, we have brought together as many CAT-MAN personnel as we can as quickly as possible, and we outnumber them probably twenty to one. We're also well armed, and we've even gotten our hands on a few anti-tank rockets. The trouble is that one of their troops is worth twenty of ours. You are well aware of how and where we recruited all of our people. They are not trained, not motivated, and stand for nothing. Most of them lived in their mom's basement before and got paid to protest the police at best, or at worst, we sprung them from jail or got them out of otherwise sticky situations. They're only here because we paid them or they hate America. My guys from our international connections are the only military-trained fighters we have, and there is maybe one of them for every two or three hundred of the minions—because that's what they are: minions."

Keller sat back in his chair and exhaled. He knew everything Sykes was saying was true.

Sykes continued, "We've sent everything we could to meet them in Baltimore, but that's only to slow them down. We're using up the few rockets we have very quickly. Whenever they actually go head-to-head with us, they beat us mercilessly to the point that our troops are trying to run away, resulting in my guys having to shoot a couple of the deserters to keep the rest from running. It's a very ugly situation up there. The bottom line is that they are going to get through, no matter how many we kill or how long we delay them. This is their next stop, and they especially want your head on a pike. The only hope of turning this around is to get the Second Marine Division and the Eighty-Second Airborne Division with all their firepower up here from North Carolina as quickly as possible."

Keller exhaled deeply and said in a defeated tone, "I'll go down to the Situation Room now and get them on the radio."

"Thank you, Mr. President," replied Sykes, sounding equally defeated.

TOM OLIVA

2021 HOURS, CHESAPEAKE BAY
THE MOUTH OF THE SEVERN RIVER,
ONE MILE FROM ANNAPOLIS

The trip down from Baltimore was tediously slow. Drifting with the current in the sea air was glorious at first, but it quickly became uncomfortable for all concerned—the barge was not built for passengers. Once the sun fully set, they started making good headway, and before long, they were lining up to make their approach to Annapolis. About a mile out, they would put swimmers into the water to go ahead and scout the landing site that lay directly ahead in the darkness.

Andy went down to see the Marine Force Reconnaissance off and go over the plan one last time.

"You boys all set?" asked Andy as he walked up. They had found a good amount of gear in a scuba shop not far from the I-695 encampment—enough to outfit six swimmers who, up until today, had been riding dirt bikes and scouting ahead of the main force. The recon Marines were satisfied with the equipment and confident that the mile swim was not an issue. The tide was coming in now, there was no moon, and the waters were calm.

"Piece of cake," replied the team leader.

"One last time, what are the signals?" asked Andy.

"If it's an unopposed landing, we flash an infrared strobe—three flashes, pause, then three more flashes," the team leader replied.

"And we come in nice and quiet and get everyone off the barge real low-key," said Andy.

"If they're all alert and watching the waterfront and we can't deal with them quietly, we give you two flashes followed by one flash," the team leader said, tightening the straps on his scuba tank rig.

"And then we come in fast and hard, and we get everyone off the barge as quickly as possible and assault through whatever resistance there is," Andy replied. "If that's the case, you boys get your heads down. We can't afford to lose you."

"We're all expendable, boss man," the team leader replied with a giant smile.

"Ha, not today. We can't afford to lose anyone," replied Andy. "Take a good look around—we have plenty of time. As long as we make the final run while it's still dark, we'll be OK. If we don't get a signal within an hour of sunrise or if we hear shooting at any point, we're coming in full assault mode."

"Sounds good, boss man."

With that, the team leader put his mouthpiece in his mouth and slipped backward into the water, giving Andy a salute as he did.

"OK, now we wait, again," said Andy to Captain Williams and anyone else within earshot.

CHAPTER 40

DAY 9

0030 HOURS, US NAVAL ACADEMY, ANNAPOLIS, MARYLAND

MOMENTS AGO, AFTER another painstakingly long wait, they received the signal that the CAT-MAN guards were not a threat to the assault force making its initial landing. Andy had encouraged everyone to eat and try to get some sleep since they might not be getting either anytime soon. Now all his men were focused only on getting their gear on and checking their weapons. There had been no rest for him, though, and food felt like a giant lump in his stomach. It was game time.

Andy had spent the hours since the recon team had left alternating between pacing the barge among the Marines and pacing the bridge of the tug. Though the plan was simple—get in, secure the friendlies, and wait for the main force to arrive—the hundreds of little things that needed to happen and the fact that the CAT-MAN force in Baltimore was putting up a real fight were wearing on Andy's mind.

None of that mattered at the moment. Andy could feel them picking up speed. It would take no more than ten minutes for them to cover the distance from where they had been waiting and land on the sea wall opposite the field house. Andy hurried down from the bridge to join the Marines who would go over the side first. It was important that he led the way, or at least to him it was.

As he arrived, a whispered "Lock and load" was passed down the line, and rifle and machine-gun actions could be heard chambering a round. At this moment, all Andy could think of was not falling in the water as he got off the barge. In the moments that followed, his adrenaline levels increased, and Andy went over in his mind what he was to do in the assault: get off the barge, collect the command team, head straight to the marina, turn left along the docks, turn right at the field house, follow to the end of the building, turn left, set up security with the three radio operators, enter and clear the field house with the other six members of the command element, send the signal to the main force that they had landed, and stand by to start receiving liberated prisoners. Everything after that would be dictated by the gods of war. *May they be merciful.*

The barge made a scraping sound and then a crunch as the tug pushed up against the concrete seawall, and with that, all motion stopped.

"Let's go!" said Andy as he went over the side in a forceful whisper that came out louder than he planned. He took several steps, glanced to his left and right, and saw that his command team was right with him, so he continued on toward the marina. As he made the left turn along the docks, he saw a figure coming toward him with his hands in the air and assumed it was a member of the recon element.

In the darkness, Andy could barely tell that it was the recon team leader. Captain Williams joined them, and the three of them went into a crouch. Captain Williams directed the assault force to stop and get down and directed his Marines to provide security to the left, all with hand signals.

"Whaddya got?" said Andy.

The recon team leader spoke quickly—he was all business, and the clowning from before was gone. "We swept all the grounds this side of Route 450 and King Street. Most of the place is asleep, but we did find a few buildings with guards actively walking the perimeter. I have my guys watching them. I suggest we hit them first. The bars on the windows led us to believe that where the prisoners are."

"OK, so we hit them first, as quietly as possible, then clear the rest of the buildings methodically," Andy said, nodding his head first at Captain Williams and then at the recon team leader.

Captain Williams turned to his platoon leaders, who had joined them as the recon team leader was giving his brief, and gave them his orders quickly. The plan had changed in the first moments of the assault—such is war. Two hundred Marines would move to the perimeter of the grounds to provide security and await further orders while the target buildings were assaulted. It was the reverse of the original plan, essentially. The remainder would follow Captain Williams and the recon team leader to the buildings they were to assault first.

Satisfied, Captain Williams gave Andy a thumbs-up and then signaled the assault force to move out again. With that, Andy stood and headed for the field house. Other than the sound of three hundred pairs of boots hitting the ground, the air was silent. Andy thought, *We need to run quieter. We'll wake the dead—we sound like a herd of buffalo.* He quickly realized the absurdity of that notion and just focused on getting where he needed to be.

Andy's team reached the field house a few moments later, and soon after that, they were exiting the building, which was clearly empty. Andy took the handset to the radio, tuned to the main force's frequency, and transmitted the code word.

"Blueberry, blueberry. I repeat, blueberry."

After a few moments, a reply came back. "Copy blueberry, repeat, copy blueberry, out."

Andy keyed the handset twice to acknowledge the receipt of the reply and handed it back to the radio operator. One word conveyed that they had landed safely, unopposed, and were conducting the sweep of the facility. Nothing else needed to be said at this moment.

It wasn't more than five minutes later that a message came from Captain Williams for Andy.

"Alpha-Six, this is Redbone."

Andy had been monitoring Williams's frequency and replied, "This is Alpha-Six Actual. Go ahead, Redbone."

"Alpha-Six Actual, stand by for visitors," Williams replied.

Andy picked up an edge of excitement in Williams's voice. "Visitors" was the code word for liberated prisoners, the first group of which was headed to Andy's position. *We've done it*, Andy thought, a smile forming on his face.

"Copy, visitors, Redbone," Andy replied.

The smile left Andy's face. In the distance, he heard a long burst of automatic weapon fire, followed by a low-grade explosion, which could only be a hand grenade detonating. The element of surprise was gone, but they were in, and Andy knew that once they were in, there was no throwing them out.

Captain Williams's voice came over the command net radio. "All units prosecute original objectives."

The time for quiet was over, and it was time to take down the objective as quickly as possible. One by one, platoon leaders acknowledged the message, and within moments, sporadic gunfire could be heard in the distance from all over the Naval Academy grounds.

The next message from Williams was for Andy.

"Alpha-Six, original objectives secure, visitors inbound."

A DAY LIKE ANY OTHER

The buildings that the recon team leader had suggested were secure, and the prisoners held there were on their way to Andy.

"Copy that, Redbone. Well done," Andy replied.

"Click-click," was the only reply Andy got, and it was all he needed.

0055 HOURS, THE WHITE HOUSE

THE CHILDREN'S DOSE of cold medicine had kicked in quickly, but that had been hours ago. Joyce was starting to have a real fear that the girls would wake up too soon. Billings had said he would return when the way was clear. It was approaching one o'clock in the morning, and he had not yet returned.

Joyce had been sleeping in the girls' room for several months, so it hadn't raised any eyebrows when she had settled in with them earlier this evening. What had not been noticed was the three small backpacks she had packed for her and her daughters. She had seen enough and was ready to get out. Billings had assured her that he and his agents could get her and the children out, and she trusted him. What she was attempting was extremely dangerous, but she feared staying was even more dangerous. She knew what had happened in Philadelphia and what was at this moment happening in Baltimore. She didn't want her children to be here when the battle arrived in Washington.

Billings returned moments later, unflappable as always, and calmly said, "My guys have located all the cameras along our exit route. We can go now."

Joyce simultaneously breathed a sigh of relief and felt a wave of terror flood her mind. "OK, let's go before the medicine wears off."

Joyce and Billings each scooped up one of the twins, who stirred slightly but were still knocked out, much to Joyce's relief. As they exited the girls' bedroom, Joyce glanced briefly at the master bedroom door, where she knew her husband was presently sleeping. Sadness gripped her, but she carried on, determined to get her children out of the obvious target the White House had become.

As they made their way toward the exit Billings had prepared, they walked past one of Billings's agents holding a rectangular box about the size of a box of kitchen matches. Joyce wondered why it was being pressed up against the corner of an ornate painting frame. Around the next corner was another agent who was holding a similar rectangle against a light fixture. Finally, a third agent was holding his rectangle against the exit sign above the door they were headed for.

Suddenly, the agent by the exit sign turned and tucked the rectangle into his pants pocket, turning again and crossing his arms. Billings quickly ducked into a maintenance closet, and Joyce followed. Billings shut the door quietly and gestured to Joyce to stay silent.

Sykes strode past the Secret Service agent standing by the exit sign without even giving him a glance. He had other concerns at the moment. Sykes stopped directly outside the closet that Billings and Joyce occupied. Another man had approached from the other direction with concerning news.

"What the hell is going on now?" Sykes said, sounding exasperated.

"I'm sorry to wake you, Director Sykes, but this couldn't wait," the man began, breathless. "We just received word that Annapolis is under attack."

"Under attack?"

"Yes, sir. We don't know who is attacking them or how bad the damage is. We lost contact."

Sykes blinked hard a few times, then replied, "Who the hell do you think is attacking them? And if you lost contact, I'd say it's pretty bad! Go wake the rest of the team, genius."

Just as Sykes began to move away, he heard what he thought was a soft cough from behind the door beside him. Sykes stopped and turned his attention to the maintenance closet door, reaching his arm out to the doorknob.

"Director Sykes! Should I wake the president?" The same man who Sykes had just talked to was calling from the end of the corridor.

Sykes spun toward the man and snapped, "No! I'll wake him! Now get on with it!"

Sykes turned his attention back to the doorknob, and, grasping it, he began to turn it slowly.

"Excuse me, Mr. Sykes." It was the Secret Service agent who had been standing by the exit. "Is there something going on? Is there a problem? Shall I alert Agent Billings?"

Sykes looked up from the doorknob, his patience clearly stretched. "No, nothing you should concern yourself about."

For the next few moments, the two men stood staring at one another in awkward silence. Finally, Sykes glanced at the doorknob, then looked back at the agent and then at his watch. Deciding he was wasting precious time, he moved on to go wake Keller.

A DAY LIKE ANY OTHER

On the other side of the door, Agent Billings was holding one of the Keller twins with his left arm and pointing his pistol at the door with his right. *That was close,* he thought.

0113 HOURS, THE WHITE HOUSE

PRESIDENT KELLER WOKE up with a start. Sykes was standing over him shining a flashlight in his face.

Keller sat up, throwing his hands out to shield his eyes from the light.

"What the fuck? How dare you come into the residence uninvited! My family lives here, you son of bitch!"

Sykes, as usual, could care less about what Keller thought, said, or felt.

"Well, for one, they're not here, which raises other questions, but we'll deal with that later."

Sykes had popped his head into the girls' bedroom on his way past. He was sure he had heard something coming from that maintenance closet and needed to check on his hunch. He didn't know what Joyce was up to and frankly didn't really care. It was one less headache for him to deal with.

"What do you mean they're not here?" Keller was wide awake now. "What have you done with them?"

"I haven't done anything, and like I said, we'll deal with that later," Sykes said, handing Keller a pair of sweatpants. "Right now, we have a bigger issue. The retraining camp at the Naval Academy in Annapolis is under attack."

"I know where the Naval Academy is," Keller replied as he dressed. "Have the insurgents broken through in Baltimore already?"

"No, they're still in the suburbs of Baltimore, headed south along the I-695 corridor. This is a different force that appears to have come in from the Chesapeake Bay," replied Sykes. "You need to get up and go get a hold of that SEAL team and tell them that their targets will no doubt show up there at some point. They'll want to see their prize once they break through in Baltimore."

"Um, OK, if you say so," replied Keller, who was at the moment more concerned about where his family was.

"I'm not kidding. Go make that call right now. I'm sure your wife and children are in the building somewhere," Sykes said impatiently. "I have to get going now, so don't piss me off and just do it."

"I'll do it, Sykes, calm down," replied Keller. "Where are you going?"

"To Baltimore."

CHAPTER 41

0800 HOURS, US NAVAL ACADEMY, ANNAPOLIS, MARYLAND

THE SATISFACTION ANDY felt looking out over the now packed field house at the 7,533 prisoners they had liberated was tempered by the poor condition most of them were in. They had arrived for what they thought was retraining to prepare them for domestic disaster relief efforts. What they had found instead were CAT-MAN goons locking them up and brutalizing—or even murdering—anyone who resisted in any way. They had survived the winter on moldy bread and a weak soup that was nothing more than flavored water. They had soon realized that the point of all this was to either break them, turning them into useful tools of the CAT-MAN machine, or to kill them. They had survived mentally and emotionally by looking after one another and resisting in any way they could. Some had become sick from abuse and malnourishment, and some had died, but they had always held out hope that someone would come for them and set them free. Today, their hopes were realized.

From the first radio call that visitors were inbound, Andy and his team had received a steady stream of survivors right up until sunrise. Those who weren't in terrible shape had helped the ones who were worse off, and in some cases, they had carried them. Andy had been humbled by their gratitude and their strength of spirit. Some had even asked for weapons to help man the perimeter. Andy had politely thanked them, encouraging them to help their weaker comrades and prepare them for the next leg of their journey, wherever that might be.

A group of sailors who were stationed at the Naval Support Activity across the river from Annapolis had approached the northern perimeter asking what was going on. Upon learning what had taken place, they had offered to start taking survivors to the base clinic, which, although small, was still better than any of these people had seen in some time. Andy agreed, but not until the main force arrived from Baltimore. He wasn't taking any chances and didn't want these survivors getting strung out and caught in the open if they were attacked before help arrived. The sailors agreed and returned to the other side of the river to muster more help and prepare for the transfer, which they all hoped would occur sometime this morning.

Captain Williams, who had been organizing the perimeter defense and dispatching foot patrols from his command post near the base chapel, had just arrived to debrief Andy for the first time since they landed.

"The boys kicked some ass last night, captain," said Andy, shaking Williams's hand.

"That they did. I couldn't be prouder," replied Williams. "I lost track. What's the final count?"

"7,533 prisoners liberated," Andy began, "and 135 CAT-MAN captured. We're not sure how many we killed—at least a dozen—and the docs tell me we have seven casualties, none of which are life-threatening."

"Yeah, three of those are from the initial firefight right after we liberated that first batch of prisoners," Williams replied, pointing in the direction where that firefight had occurred. "One of the CAT-MAN overseer guys was stepping out for a smoke and came face-to-face with a squad of our guys headed to set up on the perimeter."

"No shit," Andy said. "Surprise, surprise."

"It was his last surprise," Williams continued. "He cut loose with a full auto burst from an MP5 and hit the three closest Marines to him. Lucky for them, an MP5 shot a 9-millimeter, and the rounds exploded on their ballistic plates. They took a bunch of shrapnel 'n' shit from it, though. The CAT-MAN dude backpedaled inside, but one of our guys got a frag in just as the door closed. That was the end of that, but it woke up his buddies, and it was game on from there. Turns out that guy was former KGB, and a few of the folks we liberated recognized him as we were dragging his carcass out of that building. They said he was particularly sadistic, and the whole group spit on him as they passed."

"No shit. KGB. Who are we gonna find next?" Andy said sarcastically. He directed his attention to the tourist map he had open on an ammunition crate in front of him. "How are we looking on the perimeter?"

"We're tucked in nice and tight between Dorsey and Spa Creeks," Williams began, pointing to each feature as he mentioned it. "Our guys are positioned in buildings all along the Naval Academy boundary wall with views over the wall. The visitor center and attached buildings are the base of the defense.

We're spread thin, but we have decent fields of fire, and, at the very least, no one is getting in without us knowing it."

"What about a reserve force if there's a breach?" asked Andy.

"I have one squad with me at the chapel. That's all we can spare from the main line of defense," replied Williams, looking up from the map.

One squad as backup for over half a mile of ground should there come a need was not very comforting.

Sensing Andy's concern, Williams asked, "Have we heard from the main body yet?"

"We should be hearing from them any minute," replied Andy. "They're late, actually. They should have called while we've been talking."

As if on cue, the radio operator monitoring the main force's frequency gestured the radio handset toward Andy and said, "It's Silverback for Alpha-Six." Silverback was the callsign for the main column and very much Squatch's idea.

"Go ahead, Silverback. This is Alpha-Six," Andy said, putting the handset to his ear.

"Alpha-Six, the comms guys tell me that the encryption is solid, so I'm just gonna lay it out there." It was Colonel Reynolds, and he sounded frustrated.

"Copy that, Silverback. Send your traffic," replied Andy.

"Alpha-Six, we've encountered very stiff resistance. CAT-MAN is using delaying tactics very effectively. They had roadblocks to stop us, and then they hit us with anti-tank rockets and small arms fire. It's been like that all night. Four of the Strykers are a total loss, and both the Bradleys are heavily damaged—one's engine is destroyed, and the other's tracks and transmission are toast. We've recovered them, and I'm told the weapons are still functional. We're taking casualties at every turn, but CAT-MAN is sacrificing so many of their people that we don't know how they haven't run out yet. It's a bloodbath up here. What's your situation?"

"Copy that, Silverback," Andy began, trying to sound upbeat. "We have secured the package—it was worth the trip—and await your arrival."

"Alpha-Six, be advised that at the rate we are going, we won't arrive there until sometime tomorrow morning," replied Reynolds.

"Copy that, Silverback. We'll get comfortable and keep an ear out for you," Andy replied, still trying to sound upbeat.

"Listen, Alpha-Six," Reynolds replied, sounding even more dire than he did before, "sometime early this morning, about the time the resistance got stronger, a scout team spotted a large number of CAT-MAN vehicles depart their headquarters area and head your direction."

Andy's stomach clenched. Captain Williams, who had been listening on another handset, gave Andy a look.

"Copy that, Silverback. CAT-MAN force headed this way. What is the estimated strength of that force?" Andy replied, forgetting to sound upbeat.

"Best guess would put the enemy force headed your way anywhere from twenty-five hundred to three thousand bodies. Expect anti-tank rockets and crew-served weapons as well," replied Reynolds. "Wish I had better news for you, Alpha-Six."

"No worries, Silverback. We'll dig our heels in and keep the package safe until you get here," replied Andy.

"Copy. Silverback out," replied Reynolds, who then smashed his fist down on the hood of his HUMVEE with a curse.

Andy turned to Williams and said, "Push those patrols out as far you dare and have them start using delaying tactics of our own. We need to keep that force far away from here for as long as possible."

Williams gave Andy a nod and started issuing orders into the command net radio.

Andy then turned to his command team and said, "Get the word out to everyone that a fight is coming."

Hold until relieved, Andy thought, overlooking the frenzy of activity his command post had just become, then gazing into the field house. *They won't touch you again.*

0816 HOURS, SOMEWHERE ON INTERSTATE 95 HEADED TOWARD WASHINGTON, DC

AN EXHAUSTED SYKES was headed back to DC now after a very hectic few hours. Sykes had rushed to Baltimore after he had watched Keller contact Special Operations Command. He had promised Mr. X that he'd make sure Keller did it before he left. Satisfied that Keller had made things clear to Admiral Kane, Sykes got on the road.

He arrived at the CAT-MAN command post just outside of Baltimore to find organized chaos. His orders were being carried out to the letter. As busloads of CAT-MAN officers arrived, they were immediately organized into a new line of defense in front of the advancing insurgent force. His men, the foreign mercenaries, had orders to lead the hordes of expendables to their fighting positions, fire a rocket or two, and shoot anyone who tried to retreat. When it was obvious the insurgents would break through, they were to fall back, saying they were going to bring up the reinforcements waiting out of view, and leave one of the minions in charge. Of course, there were no reinforcements, and this group, just like the ones before, was to buy as much time as possible with their lives.

Sykes had gathered "his" men to him, as far away from the masses of CAT-MAN expendables as possible. He explained the situation as he knew it and instructed several of his most trusted men to take whatever bodies were available and go crush whoever had just attacked Annapolis. The Naval Academy was one of their largest and most brutal reeducation camps. What went on there could never come to light, and having a force come and capture it was an opportunity to liquidate the prisoners held there. Sykes always felt that the reeducation concept would never work and that they should have just eliminated any military officers who didn't follow orders, regardless of the legality of said orders.

It was all water under the bridge now, and Sykes felt it would all work out now that there was an insurgent force to blame for whatever bloodshed was to come. Before he left the command post, he had witnessed dozens of buses departing to the east and was satisfied that they would get the job done. He was also confident that the vast majority of them would not survive. *Less mouths to feed*, he thought.

1156 HOURS, THE CAPITOL BUILDING

"LOOK, MAN, I know you all are on high alert, but I need to get these parts cleaned or my tanks won't be firing a shot."

Sergeant Maddox wasn't going to be turned away. He needed to get into those showers again. He had been paid a visit by a Master Chief Norwood and now found himself deep in a thriller of a plot that he saw no way out of. Norwood had approached him, stating that they apparently shared a mutual friend who needed a favor from the both of them. Now, Sergeant First Class Maddox was carrying out his part of the plan.

A DAY LIKE ANY OTHER

Norwood had introduced himself and showed him the note Agent Billings had handed him at the White House following his and Admiral Kane's meeting with the president. All it said was, "Go talk to the lead tanker at the Capitol and tell him Joyce needs him to get the woman out of the duct and get her into this man's care. Sergeant Maddox, meet Chief Norwood." (Joyce was referring to Norwood, but she knew Maddox would have no idea who Norwood was and wanted to keep the note short as trying to explain would require several sheets of paper. She instead opted for an awkward introduction via crumpled note.) Norwood had asked, "What the hell is going on here?" Maddox had pondered if he should trust Norwood or not. Seeing that they were both equally vexed by the drama they had both been drawn into, he had decided to explain what he knew and to get the congresswoman out of the building. Norwood, looking irritated that he was now a part of this, had shaken his head and then explained where to take the congresswoman if he succeeded in getting her out. They had agreed that getting involved was extremely stupid, but, nevertheless, they were going to do it. Early this morning, Maddox had once again been awakened by the First Lady. She had wanted to know where Norwood told him to take Congresswoman Dreyfus. He had known then that he was doing the right thing.

So here Maddox stood, with four of his men holding a large duffel bag full of random tank parts he had gathered from his spare parts inventory and dumped in the nearest mud puddle. He had chosen now to carry out his plan since he knew the prisoners had already been counted this morning and wouldn't get counted again until the evening. The activity around the building was at a fever pitch, and he hoped that all the confusion would get him past the guards that much easier. The CAT-MAN sentry he had in front of him had fear in his eyes, and Maddox would play on that fear to get himself in.

"I don't know what the hell is going on, but it seems to me like you're gonna want some tank support real soon. If I don't get these parts cleaned, greased, and reinstalled, we're all up shit's creek, my man," Maddox said, forcefully enough that he almost believed it.

"Why the hell did you take them apart to begin with?" replied the CAT-MAN sentry, sounding nervous and angry simultaneously. "That was a stupid thing to do at a time like this!"

Maddox stifled the urge to chokeslam the CAT-MAN sentry for speaking to him as he had.

"Hey, man, I get it, but these tanks sat all winter. They need a thorough cleaning. We need to wash these parts in hot water to break up the crud."

The sentry sounded more desperate than angry with this response.

"I'll see if I can get you a bucket of hot water. No one is supposed to get in or out. We're on high alert—there's a force of terrorists headed this way."

"I thought of that, my man. We'd need dozens of buckets, not to mention what we really need is the water pressure," Maddox replied, trying to sound as friendly as possible.

The CAT-MAN guy turned and looked behind him. Maddox assumed he was looking for anyone who could tell him what to do. He then keyed the mic of his radio and spoke. "This is post seven. I need a supervisor." After three more attempts with no reply, his frustration building, he finally said, "OK, go ahead, but be quick."

Maddox said, "Thank you. We'll be in and out."

As he and his men began to move, the CAT-MAN sentry said, "Wait!"

Maddox stopped and wondered what his chances of success were if he knocked this dude unconscious and hid his body. Maddox turned, wondering if this was the end of his little caper, and said, "What's up?"

"I need to look in the bag," replied the sentry, who had remembered suddenly that checking bags coming into the building was one of his jobs.

"That's not a problem, my friend. Open the bag, boys," Maddox replied cordially.

Satisfied that the bag was full of nothing but dirty tank parts, he sent Maddox on his way.

Maddox was surprised to find the hallways nearly deserted. *They all must be outside filling sandbags*, he thought.

They walked quickly to the showers, Maddox wondering all the while if the woman in the ducting would be there and how long he would have to wait if she wasn't. It wouldn't take long before they were discovered and tossed out, and Maddox knew he wouldn't be able to talk his way through like he had on the way in.

After checking that the showers were empty, Maddox posted two of his men at the door with instructions not to let anyone in. He then moved to the vent where the voice had come from.

"Ma'am, you in there?" Maddox whispered into the vent.

Maddox was about to ask again when a voice answered, "Yes, I'm here."

Maddox was shocked. "How'd you know when we'd be here?"

A DAY LIKE ANY OTHER

"I didn't. I've been coming and sitting here for weeks after morning roll call. That's how you found me the first time," replied Congresswoman Dreyfus.

"Well, let's get you out of there, ma'am," Maddox said as he began removing the screws holding the vent grate on.

Four screws later, the vent grate came loose, and for the first time, the voice from the ducting had a face. Congresswoman Eleanor Dreyfus began exiting the duct headfirst, and Maddox and his men reached up and pulled her the rest of the way out. It was obvious why she was the only one who would fit in the vent. Her tiny frame was exaggerated by the baggy orange coveralls she wore.

"It's very nice to meet you in person, ma'am, but we've got to get moving. I'm sorry, but you're not going to like your ride out of here," Maddox said as his men started removing tank parts from the duffel bag and placing them in the vent.

Maddox was impressed at how the duffel bag looked much the same with a person in it as it had with the parts in it. The heavy canvas hid the contours of Eleanor's body perfectly. As they made their way back toward the doors they had entered through, it seemed there were more CAT-MAN officers in the hallway than before. Maddox started feeling increasingly nervous every time a passing CAT-MAN officer gave them a sideways look, though he didn't show it. He was less concerned about what might happen to him if he were discovered than he was about failing in his mission to deliver Eleanor to Chief Norwood.

As Maddox and his men carrying the duffel bag neared their exit, he noticed there were now three CAT-MAN officers in the doorway: the one who had let them in and two others, one of whom seemed to be a supervisor by the way he was talking to the first CAT-MAN guy. *Here we go*, thought Maddox.

"Here they come now," said the guy who had let Maddox in.

"Hey, we're all done. Thanks again, we really had a dilemma on our hands," Maddox said as he went striding out the door right past the three officers, his men and the duffel right behind him.

"Hold on!" said the CAT-MAN supervisor.

Maddox kept walking but said over his shoulder, "No time to waste. We gotta get these parts installed."

"I said stop!" the supervisor said more forcefully, raising his weapon.

Maddox stopped, as did his men.

"What's the problem?" Maddox replied matter of factly.

"What's in the bag?" asked the supervisor.

Maddox glanced over at the guard who had let them in and replied, "Tank parts, didn't your man here tell you?"

"There are parts in there. I checked the bag when they came in," replied the first guard, feeling the need to defend his actions.

"Well, I need to see them now," replied the supervisor, giving the first guard an angry look. "What part of 'no one in or out' did you not understand?"

"These parts are all clean and ready for installation," Maddox replied, holding his hands up in front of him.

"Open the bag!" replied the CAT-MAN supervisor. He was not going to be put off.

"'Open the bag,' he says. I'll open the bag," Maddox said to no one.

Maddox unzipped the bag and stood back with his hands up.

"What the hell is this?" the supervisor half shouted.

"I told you these parts were cleaned and ready for installation," Maddox replied.

"It's a fucking bag in a bag? Stop screwing around and show me these parts!" The supervisor was getting frustrated.

"That's preservation paper. We need to keep these parts clean until we can grease and install them." Maddox sounded like a mechanic explaining why a customer's car is spewing black smoke.

"That's the stupidest thing I've ever heard. It's a friggin tank. You mean to tell me these parts are that delicate?" replied the supervisor in disbelief.

"Hey man, welcome to my world. Take it up with the engineers who designed it. I'd like to catch those nerds and give 'em a piece of my mind. Can we go? We're burnin' daylight," Maddox replied, sounding amused.

"I don't have time for this! Get the hell out here!" The CAT-MAN supervisor sounded completely exasperated. "Don't come back here again until this thing is all over!" he shouted as Maddox and his crew walked away.

Maddox felt enormous relief—his ruse had worked. He wasn't sure what he'd have done if the guards had persisted and found Eleanor in the preservation paper bag.

The duffel bag was taken directly to a waiting HUMVEE and gently placed in the back seat. Maddox slid into the passenger seat, and one of his men got in the back next to the bag. Not until they turned the corner and were out of sight of the Capitol Building did Maddox say, "OK, get her out of there."

Eleanor emerged from the bag with a gasp. Although they had cut holes in the sides of the bag and hadn't sealed it shut, she had still endured the claustrophobic experience and was relieved to be free of it. She realized she was out in the sunshine and fresh air after having had neither all winter and was grateful for another kind of freedom. This was nothing, though, compared to how she felt seeing Joyce Keller smiling at her as she exited the HUMVEE beside what she assumed was the Potomac River.

2100 HOURS, US NAVAL ACADEMY, ANNAPOLIS, MARYLAND

IN THE HOURS following the news of a large force headed their way, Andy and Captain Williams had set to work developing a new defensive strategy. Instead of tucking everyone within the Naval Academy boundary, it was decided that they would find defensive positions as far out from there as possible and fall back street by street as necessary.

It was decided to put the first line of defense about a mile out from the Naval Academy, centered around a middle school, an art school, a hotel, and a condominium complex since those were the strong points. These all overlooked open areas that provided clear fields of fire. A large apartment building that overlooked College Creek secured the northern flank. This building also overlooked a large power substation that had caught fire during The Event and now looked like a twisted metal modern art display. One Marine machine gunner was noted as saying, upon seeing this site from the roof of the apartments, "Oh, yeah! I can do a lot of killin' from here."

The gaps in the defense would be covered from other positions set back from the main line, mostly from single-family homes. It was these parts of the line that were most vulnerable. If these were neutralized, the other parts of the line would be cut off from support and, more importantly, cut off from returning to defend the Naval Academy and from protecting the men and women they had just liberated. Andy stressed to all the platoon leaders that when they were given the order to fall back, they had to comply regardless of how secure their position felt. Andy gave a passionate explanation.

"It's not in the DNA of warfighters to move backward in the face of the enemy, but the mission is to delay the CAT-MAN advance and keep the Naval Academy safe until the relief force arrives. We have to fall back in good order, making them bleed for every street, and when we've fallen back to about five hundred yards of the main gate, everyone will return to the positions they were in this morning and make our stand. I know it's cliché, but I have to say it: good luck and good hunting."

With that, handshakes and back slaps were exchanged among the Marines present as they departed to join their men in their assigned fighting positions. It was at this point that Andy understood what Squatch and Wally had felt when he told them they wouldn't be coming with him on this operation.

Captain Williams insisted Andy return to the command post at the field house.

"On that radio and with the officers we liberated is where you're needed. You'll have to decide if and when we start getting them over to the NSA side of the base. There's only one bridge that crosses over there. It'd be easier to defend if we get overrun on this side of the river."

It was a sobering thought, but Williams was right. There was a chance that at least part of the CAT-MAN force would get through the perimeter, and it was Andy's responsibility to keep those people in the field house safe. He didn't like splitting them up, but the change in the situation gave him little choice. He had already ordered the worst of the prisoners to be transferred to the NSA base clinic and permitted a doctor and several Navy corpsmen to come into the field house and provide aid. He had also issued what captured rifles they had to all the volunteers from the NSA side and told them to protect that bridge at all costs. If CAT-MAN got past the front line, they'd be all there to stop them.

Just after sunrise, the CAT-MAN force sent from Baltimore had started arriving at the Naval Academy stadium to the northwest of the initial defensive line. Captain Williams had recognized the stadium as an excellent place to coalesce forces and manage an operation and had sent the recon team to keep an eye on it. Buses were arriving in one long convoy after another, and it was obvious Captain Williams was correct that CAT-MAN would make this their base of operations.

The recon team was reporting via command network radio so everyone in the landing force would hear what he was saying. As the CAT-MAN force accumulated, the buses emptying sixty to seventy CAT-MAN officers at a time. After watching the numbers swell, the recon team leader made a request.

"Alpha-Six, this is Fig Leaf." The recon team leader, being a character, had come up with his own callsign. "Yeah, now all you jokers can imagine me wearing nothing but a fig leaf when we chat on the radio," he had said with a giant smile.

A DAY LIKE ANY OTHER

"Go ahead, Fig Leaf," replied Andy.

"Enemy force has coalesced. Lead elements preparing to move off to the southwest. Additional enemy transport continues to arrive. Request permission to engage lead element. Troops congregating in the open."

Troops congregating in the open, he had said. Andy knew that meant a juicy target that could not be passed up. The recon team leader was requesting permission to compromise his hidden position in order to take out a large number of enemy combatants before they even had a chance to move on foot toward the Naval Academy.

Andy didn't even have to think about an answer.

"Fig Leaf, Alpha-Six. Engage targets as you see fit and fall back to new overwatch position."

"Redbone copies. Engage and fall back to new overwatch. We'll be looking out for you," Williams chimed in.

"Copy. Engage and fall back," replied Fig Leaf. "Let's get this party started."

A few moments later, even from over a mile away, Andy could hear the recon team engaging the CAT-MAN force—small arms fire and the thumping of MK-203 grenade launchers firing followed by the low-grade explosions of the projectiles detonating. Andy was not prepared for the roar of gunfire that followed a few moments later. The CAT-MAN force was returning fire en masse, and it was deafening. The next sound Andy heard sent a chill down his spine—the thump and whoosh of a rocket being fired, and then another. Upon hearing the detonations, Andy was sure the entire recon team was dead, so when the radio crackled to life and the recon team leader's voice came over the net, Andy felt a slight relief.

"This is Fig Leaf." He was clearly running and talking quickly; his breathing was rapid, but his tone was steady and professional. "Multiple tangos down. Enemy firing AT-4 rockets. Team falling back to new overwatch. Out!"

It was another two hours before any of the other defensive positions saw any CAT-MAN soldiers. The recon team's attack had knocked the CAT-MAN force back on its heels and caused a much-needed delay. "We're off to a good start," Andy said multiple times after checking his watch.

The next time the CAT-MAN force was seen, it was from multiple defensive positions at once. The CAT-MAN leaders had waited until their full force had arrived before trying to move out again, and now they were all moving at once.

The recon team had fallen back and taken up a new observation post atop the Annapolis Police Department.

"Hey, this is Fig Leaf. Strong enemy force approaching from north, south, and west—"

The transmission was cut off, and a moment later, the sound of multiple explosions explained why. For whatever reason, the police station was the target of multiple rockets. There were no further communications from Fig Leaf or anyone else from the recon team.

The volley of rockets must have been a signal to start the attack, and that's just what happened. The command net went crazy with units reporting large numbers of CAT-MAN infantry approaching their position.

Captain Williams broke in on the chatter. "This is Redbone. Wait until they are close before you fire. Hit them hard, then change position. Don't let them zero in with any fire, but especially not those rockets."

The first bursts of fire from the defensive positions cut down probably a hundred CAT-MAN officers, but Captain Williams knew his stuff, and the CAT-MAN overseers were waiting. Using the lives of their people as bait, when the defenders fired and revealed their positions, the CAT-MAN overseers fired their rockets at where the fire had come from. Those defenders who had not moved quickly enough were caught in the blast of an exploding rocket warhead.

That is how it would go all day. The CAT-MAN overseers would marshal a couple hundred of their troops together, then send them all at once in a human wave attack toward the defensive line. The defenders would cut all or most of the attackers down, then have to move quickly to avoid being hit by return fire. It took several hours and four human wave attacks before Captain Williams gave the order to fall back to the next line of defense. Andy had been sending vehicles to evacuate the wounded and dead and to resupply the forward positions. It was obvious they had held this line as long as they could.

At first, the defense was an organized line of resistance as it had been before, but the constant attacks by the CAT-MAN force had driven deep wedges into the defense. It became a chaotic brawl where squad leaders and fire team leaders were making tactical decisions based on what was in front of them. The true strength of this force was its ability to think and fight independently. They all knew what the objective was—to buy time and bleed the CAT-MAN force at every turn. They didn't need any additional orders; they knew what to do. Firefights were sometimes between neighboring houses, and the defenders would narrowly avoid being surrounded only to fall back fifty to a hundred yards and start the process of fighting for their lives all over again.

A DAY LIKE ANY OTHER

About an hour ago, Captain Williams had seen with his own eyes a CAT-MAN overseer shoot his own men who were trying to retreat. Captain Williams had muttered, "Oh, fuck no," and shot the overseer twice in the chest and once in the head at a range of over two hundred yards. Immediately following, a rocket slammed into the building, and Captain Williams could no longer be reached on the radio.

Andy had been to the front line several times throughout the day to get updates and lead counterattacks. But after learning of Captain Williams being at the impact point of a rocket and being unable to reach him on the radio, he went forward to assess the situation and make a decision on what to do next before it was completely dark out. Williams had been Andy's eyes and ears, as well as his tactician. *Guess I'll have to figure it out on my own from here*, Andy thought as he set off at a trot toward the sound of gunfire.

A few minutes later, after dodging CAT-MAN fire from somewhere down the street, Andy was at the Maryland State House. The governor was not home, so Andy felt this would be the best place to gather his platoon leaders and get a no-bullshit assessment of the situation. It didn't take long for him to realize that though they were holding their ground, the situation was untenable, and it was inevitable that some part of the line would soon break. Andy decided, based on the fact that they had more dead, wounded, and missing than able-bodied fighters, that they should fall back to the Naval Academy grounds. After further consultation with his platoon leaders, it was decided to consolidate in the buildings closest to the field house, issue the last of the ammunition, and then send small teams out to ambush the CAT-MAN forces as they approached.

The sun had set now, and an eerie silence had fallen over the entire scene. Clouds had gathered, blocking out the moon and stars, compounding the silence with an equally eerie, pitch-black darkness. Everyone was placed and resupplied. Andy had relented and issued what weapons they had available to the most able-bodied of the officers they had liberated. After being confronted several times, one of them had said, "We're commissioned officers in the service of this nation. Afford us the ability to protect our nation or, at the very least, go out fighting." Andy couldn't argue with that. They were now posted on the top floor of the building directly adjacent to the field house.

The radio crackled to life. "Alpha-Six, this is Silverback."

"Go ahead, Silverback," replied Andy.

"Relief force headed your way. ETA not known at this time," replied Silverback.

"Copy. ETA not known," replied Andy.

The Militia had left the airport. The trip from the airport was only sixteen miles, a thirty-minute drive under normal circumstances. Tonight, however, there was no way to know how long it would take the relief force to reach Andy and company.

Before Andy could sign off with Silverback, an illumination flare was fired skyward somewhere to Andy's right. Someone had sensed movement and fired a flare to have a look. The flare burst, bathing the area in a creepy glow, revealing a large group of CAT-MAN infantry approaching in the darkness. They were close. Simultaneously heard and felt, several large explosions ripped the night air. The homemade Claymore mines had been detonated on the perimeter, filling the air with thousands of bits of metal. The combat engineers had fashioned them from the little bit of C-4 explosives they had brought using nails, screws, and any other sharp metal objects they could find. The result was dozens of CAT-MAN bodies and body parts strewn about. The brutality of it would haunt the dreams of many for years to come, but tonight it was either CAT-MAN or them. It was about survival.

In the long moments following the blasts, Andy knew this was the end, either for him and his force or the CAT-MAN force opposing them. He picked up the radio handset and transmitted to his teams an order he never imagined himself giving.

"All units, this is Alpha-Six. All units fix bayonets. I repeat, all units fix bayonets." Andy handed the handset to his radio operator, drew his bayonet, and fixed it to his rifle. Then he shouted with all he was worth, "Bayonets!"

From all over the perimeter, the call "Bayonets!" was repeated until it combined into one giant, raucous roar of voices.

The bayonet essentially turned a rifle into a spear and dated back to the origin of the gun. Armies would blast one or two shots at each other at short range then charge forward, bayonets fixed, to disembowel the enemy in a melee of bloody carnage. In modern times, the bayonet was seldom used. It was more of a way for a commander to send a clear message to his troops that they were staying put, there would be no retreat, there would be no surrender, and they were to fight to the end. Along with Kevlar body armor and helmets, all the members of the assault force had been issued bayonets, whether they thought they needed them or not. Tonight, with ammunition low, their backs to the river, thousands of lives to protect and their own numbers dwindling, Andy

A DAY LIKE ANY OTHER

meant to use the bayonet the way it was originally intended and end this fight right here and now.

Andy took the handset back, keyed the mic, and said, "All units, attack! This ends right now!"

Andy gave the handset back to the radio operator and said to those around him, "Follow me." He jumped from cover and ran off into the darkness, yelling as he ran, "Aagggghhhhhh!"

The first enemy he encountered was a CAT-MAN overseer staggering about, disoriented and stumbling over dismembered bodies. *Good,* Andy thought as he closed the distance, plunging his bayonet into the man's chest. Andy's momentum carried him forward and right on top of the now motionless overseer. Andy had no doubt his order would be followed, but the rumbling of running feet and shouting voices confirmed that his Marines were on the attack.

Andy gained his feet just as his command team caught up with him, and they charged on together toward the enemy. Ahead of them, a group of CAT-MAN officers appeared out of the darkness, backpedaling away from the oncoming attack. They were bayoneted and left bleeding where they fell. A few feet farther ahead, a CAT-MAN overseer was shooting at his own troops as they rushed past him, not knowing why they were running. Andy solved that mystery with a single shot from his rifle, shooting from the hip as he ran up on the man and hitting him in the face. Andy made sure he was down with a second shot to the chest. Andy's group pressed on, running and killing as they went. A group of CAT-MAN officers attempted to stop them and fired their weapons without aiming, missing with every shot. Terrified, they tried to run, but it was too late. Andy's command team set upon them in an instant. In the ensuing melee, Andy came face to face with a CAT-MAN officer who couldn't have been more than twenty years old. Andy bayoneted him in the chest as the man screamed like a woman, then continued forward with his men. Of all the horrors Andy would see that night, it was this one that would haunt him for the rest of his days. The image of this young man, eyes filled with terror, stabbed in the chest and left calling for his mother in the darkness as he bled out.

All along the perimeter, the CAT-MAN force was broken and retreating. Exhausted and outmatched already and now confronting wild-eyed lunatics rushing toward them with bayonets, they broke and ran for their lives, some dropping their weapons along the way. It was over in under five minutes. It was obvious that many of them had run. All who remained were dead, wounded, or wanted desperately to surrender—desperate to the point that they begged they be taken away from here.

About two hours later, Squatch and Wally arrived with the relief force. They found Andy at his command post beside the field house, rifle (bayonet still fixed) in one hand, radio handset in the other, and a lit cigarette in his mouth. He was covered in dried blood and grime; one of his pant legs was torn at the knee. A quick glance around and one would see that all those who had fought the Battle of Annapolis looked pretty much the same.

Upon seeing his friends, radio handset still to his ear, Andy said only, "Welcome to Annapolis."

CHAPTER 42

DAY 10

SUNRISE, US NAVAL ACADEMY, ANNAPOLIS, MARYLAND

THE DAY'S FIRST rays of sunlight revealed a surreal scene of carnage and violence. One could follow the path of the battle by simply following the path of destruction and gore. Andy knew it was bad, but actually seeing it shook him, though he did not express it outwardly. *How did anyone survive this?* he thought.

Andy had quickly brought Squatch and Wally up to speed on how things had played out since they had landed so many hours ago. The former prisoners were once again being transported to the NSA base clinic and other facilities on that side of the river. Patrols had been sent out to locate any dead or wounded who were still in the battlespace.

The recon team leader was brought in on a stretcher, his head and both legs bandaged.

"Where ya been, Fig Leaf?" Andy said upon seeing him.

Fig Leaf replied, "Buried in the police station, boss man. I miss anything important? Other than you boys trashing the place, that is. Can't leave you all alone for a minute."

"You didn't miss much; we just redid the landscaping," replied Andy with a smile, giving Fig Leaf a fist bump as he was carried to the field house–turned–aid station.

"I'm not diggin' it, Alpha-Six," replied Fig Leaf unapprovingly.

The rest of Fig Leaf's team was also buried in the wrecked police station, two of whom were killed. It was a miracle any of them had survived.

With the sun rising, it was considered safe enough for David, Dmitry, Director Cummings, and Detweiler to drive down from the airport. Andy was shocked by the sight of all four of them. All had bandages on their hands and arms, and their clothing seemed charred superficially.

"What the hell happened to all of you?" asked Andy as they approached.

"Dad!" was all David could say, embracing Andy forcefully.

"Zis one is very brave," said Dmitry, grabbing David's shoulder with a squeeze.

Director Cummings stepped up, shook Andy's hand, and said, "We could say the same to you, Andy."

"Yeah, well, things got a little hectic," replied Andy. He noticed Detweiler staring at a pile of CAT-MAN bodies. "Is he OK?"

"Not sure yet," replied Cummings, turning to look at Detweiler. "We were in the middle of the column, and a group of CAT-MAN with anti-tank rockets managed to slip through and ambush us. The Stryker right in front of us got hit and went up in flames. David here was the first out of the car; he rushed over and started pulling guys out of the fire. We all did, but he was the first one there. Next thing we know, we're being shot at—even the good Dr. Detweiler took cover and returned fire."

"You guys got your own fire team goin' here, don't ya?" replied Andy, putting his arm around his son's shoulders. He was trying to make light of the very concerning situation and his horror that his son had had to deal with that when he should have never been here to begin with.

Andy's radio operator interrupted.

"Alpha-Six, the lookouts on the tugboat say there's something you need to see over there."

"Tell them I'm on my way," replied Andy. He turned back to the group. "Let's take a walk. I'll show you guys the field house on the way back," he said, gesturing toward the river.

As they began walking, Cummings quickened his pace so as to catch up to Andy and said quietly, "I'll keep an eye on Detweiler; you keep an eye on your boy. They saw some things that they weren't the least bit prepared for."

Andy looked at Cummings, then glanced back at David, who was walking a bit behind them, blankly staring ahead of him. "I'll keep an eye on him. Thanks."

"No problem. It got bad on the road back there," replied Cummings.

"Who's gonna keep an eye on us?" replied Andy.

"I hear that," said Cummings. "I guess we'll have to keep an eye on each other."

A DAY LIKE ANY OTHER

"Fair enough," replied Andy with a nod.

THE GROUP APPROACHED the seawall cautiously. If the lookout had seen something he needed to look at, then there was no telling what it could be. The Coast Guardsman who had piloted the tug and barge met them at the corner of the marina that Andy had only recently learned was the sailing club.

"Whaddaya got?" asked Andy, noticing the bloody bandage wrapped around the man's head.

The bridge of the tug had taken a direct hit the night before. The machine guns positioned there had engaged a large group of CAT-MAN trying to move up along the seawall. A couple of rockets had been fired, and one had hit the bridge, killing two sailors and a coastie. The other had hit the barge near the water line and must have cracked the hull, and it had been taking on water slowly since. It would have probably sunk by now if it weren't securely tied off to the still-seaworthy tug and to the mooring points along the seawall as well as the Triton Light (a navigational beacon marking where the Severn Creek meets the Spa River, essentially the spot they had come ashore).

The Coast Guardsman, noticing Andy looking at his bandaged head, reached up and touched it reflexively, then said, "We noticed a small craft moving up from the south just before sunrise. With night vision, we couldn't tell if it was drifting in with the tide or not. Once the sun started to rise, it started heading this way, dead slow."

Andy looked through a set of binoculars at the craft and could see a man dressed in camouflage and woman dressed in civilian clothes standing up on the bow of the craft.

"That looks like one of those special ops boats the SEALs use," said Wally, also looking through binoculars.

"Can I have a look?" asked Cummings. The detective in him wanted more information.

Andy handed him his binoculars, and a moment later, Cummings said, "Signal them to come in—they're no danger to us."

LUCE HALL, IT was decided, would be the place to receive their visitors. The closest undamaged building to the marina, it was an easy choice. The visitors were searched for weapons, then led to an empty office by a dozen Marines and told to make themselves at home. A short time later, there was a knock on the door, and Andy, Squatch, and Wally entered.

They had debated covering their faces, but Director Cummings assured them once again that these people were no threat. Nevertheless, Andy insisted that only he, Squatch, and Wally enter the room at this time. Regardless of what Cummings felt, Andy wanted to feel them out before he showed all his cards and too many faces to these people.

As Andy looked around the room, he saw that Cummings was correct. Of the two men, one had the look of law enforcement, and the other was clearly a Navy SEAL; Andy had seen enough of both over the years to be able to pick them right out. There were two women, one of whom he recognized and the other a tiny person who wasn't more than five feet tall and a hundred pounds. There were two young children as well—twin girls. Andy smiled at the twins, took a seat across from the seated women, and spoke softly.

"You're absolutely the last person I expected to see here, Madam First Lady," Andy said sincerely.

"This is the last place I ever imagined finding myself," Joyce Keller replied. "I didn't catch your name, though."

"My name is . . ." Andy began before being interrupted by Squatch and Wally both making *mmmmmmmggghh* sounds in unison.

Andy blinked slowly, then continued, "My name is Andrew, and that will have to do for now."

"Fair enough, I suppose," replied Joyce.

"I recognized your daughters from TV, ya know, back when we had TV. Who else have you brought with you today?" Andy said politely, though the burning question was why *she* was here. Andy refrained from asking it. *We'll get to that.*

"Yes, my brave girls. This is Abigail, and this is Aimee," replied Joyce, embracing her daughters tightly. "Say hello to Andrew, girls," she added.

"Hello, Andrew," the twins said in unison.

"Hello, girls, it's very nice to meet you," Andy replied happily. For a moment, he was far away from the previous night's horrors.

"We went on a boat!" exclaimed Abigail (or was it Aimee? Andy couldn't tell the difference yet). At that moment, everyone in the room was taken away from the stress and turmoil and permitted themselves a smile.

"I saw! It's a really cool boat too," replied Andy, glancing up at the man he presumed was a Navy SEAL and the owner of said boat.

A DAY LIKE ANY OTHER

"We went really fast, and then it got dark, and Mama said we had to stay really quiet, and that was no fun," replied Abigail/Aimee.

"Yeah, that part probably wasn't much fun," replied Andy. He could go on like this all day, but all eyes were on him, and he sensed Squatch was getting impatient by the heavy exhale he heard over his shoulder.

"I'm gonna talk to your mom now, OK, sweetie?" Andy said politely.

"Yes, she's a great conversationalist, I'm sorry," said Joyce with a smile.

"No problem," replied Andy. "She's a lovely child."

"Thank you so much," replied Joyce. She liked Andy—he surely wasn't the monster he was being made out to be back in DC.

Joyce began with the introductions again.

"This is Congresswoman Eleanor Dreyfus seated next to me," Joyce said, gesturing toward the tiny woman.

Andy glanced over his shoulder at Squatch, who gave Andy a nod in response. Joyce continued, not noticing the exchange.

"This is Special Agent Billings, head of my security detail," Joyce said, gesturing toward the man Andy had pegged for law enforcement.

"And this is . . ." Joyce paused. "I'm sorry, in all the excitement I never got your name. Master Chief, correct?"

"Yes, ma'am," replied Master Chief Norwood, "and for now I'd like to just go by 'Master Chief.'"

"Oh, OK, I guess that's a thing today," replied Joyce, well aware of the need to protect identities at this point but still not quite comfortable with it.

"That's a nice boat you've got there, Master Chief," Andy said with a half-smile.

"What makes you think it's mine?" replied Norwood, expressionless.

"Well, the fact that it's a riverine assault craft that the SEALs use, and you're a Navy SEAL. I kinda put two and two together," replied Andy, raising his eyebrows.

It was at that moment that Norwood knew he was dealing with another military man. Knowing what an assault boat was was one thing, and identifying him as a SEAL was another, but it was the way Andrew carried himself, the way he wore his equipment, that gave him away. He was probably a Marine by the respectful way he addressed him as "Master Chief"; Marines were big on using proper rank and titles. What convinced him most of all was his calmness in dealing with the situation at hand—they called it deliberate calm.

"You wanna take her for a spin?" replied Norwood. The game of sizing one another up was over as far as Norwood was concerned.

"Maybe later, Master Chief," replied Andy with a smile. He continued, turning his attention back to Joyce. "It's been very nice meeting everyone, but the question we're all dying to ask is, why are you here?"

"That's understandable," Joyce began, shifting in her seat and visibly uncomfortable with the reality she must now speak to. "In short, I've come here today, with my children and the congresswoman, because, well, there's no other way to say it—evil has taken hold of our government, and you and your people are the only ones doing anything about it."

"Stop right there," Andy interrupted. He could feel his blood pressure rising and needed to speak while he could still speak calmly. "You are aware that your husband is the head of that government, right?"

"Yes, I am very aware, but—" Joyce began.

Andy wasn't done. "And the congresswoman here is part of that same government, correct?"

"Yes, I am, we are aware of that." Joyce's tone was still polite but markedly more forceful. "That's why we have come here, into obvious danger with unknown individuals whose intentions we can only assume are good, because what we left in DC is worse than the unknown."

Andy could appreciate what she was saying, but the past eight days and the months leading up to it were the making of the imbecilic leaders in DC. Having two of those leaders here in front of him, presumably looking for his help somehow, was too ironic to pass up the opportunity to rub it in their faces a little.

Andy spoke calmly and precisely. "I just want to make perfectly clear what I'm seeing here. Your husband and his government have overseen the destruction of the national power grid, the suspension of Constitutional law, the incarceration of military officers, and the systematic starvation and deprivation of tens of millions of ordinary citizens in CAT-MAN–run FEMA camps. Now, you come here looking for what? Protection?"

"What you say is true, though I don't know about incarcerating military officers, and I've heard the camps are bad, but I've never actually seen one. My husband is not an evil man, just a weak one, as I'm finding out," Joyce said softly, humbly.

"Well, you're going to get an education on all of that here in a few minutes," Andy replied, then turned his attention to the congresswoman.

A DAY LIKE ANY OTHER

"And you," he began, "we know who you are. For years, you've been railing against private gun ownership. Going on and on about assault weapons and ghost guns and weapons of war on our streets, the whole time not having any idea what you were talking about. Then most recently, we hear you on the radio praising President Keller for his banning of all firearms. That was you, right? I've got the right person?"

"Yes, that was me," replied Dreyfus, trying to sound assertive but coming across as arrogant.

Andy didn't like her tone and leaned forward in his chair, for the first time since entering the room displaying the anger he was feeling inside. He remained calm, but his tone was much firmer now.

"With all due respect, congresswoman, none of this would be possible without guns—this force, these men and women who you've come seeking. All of them, when they joined us, brought their own firearms—AR-15s mostly—and their own ammunition and food and medical supplies. It wasn't until later that we started capturing CAT-MAN equipment. You do understand that? It's important that you understand that."

Congresswoman Dreyfus, seeing that her previous statement was more combative than she intended, changed her tone and said, "I understand that, and it's clear now that I was wrong. No one ever anticipated something like this happening. We just wanted people to be safe."

Andy sat back in his chair and exhaled through his mouth.

"It's been a crazy few days. We're going to take you around and let you see for yourselves the full reality of all this. But to say no one anticipated something like this happening just isn't true. Every law-abiding citizen who has armed themselves since the founding of this country anticipated this. It just fell to this generation to finally see it through."

Andy sat quietly for a few moments, as did everyone else in the room, except the Keller twin girls, who continued coloring and quietly bantering with each other.

"Why have you come here, Madam First Lady?" Andy said, finally.

Joyce thought for a moment, choosing her words carefully.

"We are here because our government has been overthrown; my husband is nothing more than a figurehead. CAT-MAN Director Sykes and whoever he is on the phone with all the time are in charge. Congress, all the Supreme Court justices, the Joint Chiefs of Staff—they've all been locked up in the Capitol Building for months as prisoners. They are being kept there to give credibility to all the terrible things that are going on in the name of Catastrophe Management. The congresswoman escaped to tell the story, and now we are here. All I ask is that you spare my husband's life if you are to encounter him."

Andy said nothing for a few moments, contemplating his next move. Satisfied that the First Lady had come here with good intentions, he felt it safe to bring in the rest of the team.

Andy stood and said, "If you'll excuse us, my colleagues and I are going to step out for a minute."

With that, Andy, Squatch, and Wally exited the room and made their way to an adjoining room where Cummings and Detwiler were listening through the wall.

"You guys get all that?" Andy asked quietly.

Cummings and Detwiler both responded in the affirmative.

"What's this about Sykes being on the phone?" asked Squatch.

Detwiler cleared his throat and replied, "Well, it would have to be a satellite phone."

"Wouldn't the satellites have been cooked during The Event?" asked Wally.

"One would assume so, but we also believed so many other devices would have been cooked, but they are still functioning. I imagine if a satellite was properly shielded and in an appropriate orbit, it could have survived The Event," replied Detwiler.

"OK," Andy began, "the two of you go in there. I'm sure the First Lady will be happy to see the both of you. Find out how the congresswoman escaped and what's going on in the Capitol Building that she needed to escape from. Pretty much find out everything you can, really."

Cummings and Detwiler gave a nod and exited the room.

Andy turned to Squatch and said, "Send a runner to Colonel Reynolds and let him know about this. He's gonna be itching to move south, but we need to get what intel we can from these people before we move. Then find whatever former SEALs we have with us. I know there are at least two, so get them over here if they're still alive. Maybe they know this master chief. I want to know if we can trust him."

"Got it," replied Squatch, then exited the room.

Finally, Andy turned to Wally and said, "Get your girlfriend over here. Someone is going to have to stay with the twins while we give the First Lady a quick tour of the mess out there and introduce her to some of the survivors from the camp here and from the big camp in Philly. If your girl is not

A DAY LIKE ANY OTHER

available, then get another female—girls that young will be more comfortable if a woman is with them. Then get a few of those survivors over here to meet with the First Lady and the congresswoman."

"Will do," replied Wally. Before leaving the room, he added, "She's not my girlfriend."

THE WHITE HOUSE

"WHAT DO YOU mean you can't find them?"

Keller was livid. His wife and daughters hadn't been seen since the night before. He knew she was pretty mad at him and had been giving her as much space as he could, but the fact that Sykes was telling him she was gone was extremely concerning. He knew Sykes had his people watching his wife night and day, and if they didn't know where she was, then she was gone to who knows where.

Sykes's usual amusement from Keller's outbursts was not present, as he had an even more serious development to drop in Keller's lap.

"Your wife and kids disappearing is one thing, but we've got a bigger problem," Sykes began. "One of the congresswomen was missing from the head count this morning—Eleanor Dreyfus. Do you know her?"

"Yes, I know her. Of course I know her," Keller snapped back. "My wife and kids disappearing is not 'one thing.' It's the only thing at this point." Keller could feel his blood pressure rising even further than it already was. "My wife has been slipping in and out of here for months, and your people couldn't keep track of her. She could be anywhere. And as far as the congresswoman, I'm honestly not surprised you lost her. She's probably hiding somewhere in the Capitol Building, or maybe she's gone too, given the incompetence your people have shown."

Sykes was in no mood for one of Keller's tantrums.

"Look, the fact that your wife has been a nuisance since this began is completely on you, and the fact that she's gone is on you too. It's not up to me and my people to babysit your wife because you can't keep her in line yourself."

"Keep her in line? You don't know Joyce very well," Keller shot back, almost amused at the thought.

"As for the congresswoman, she's either in that building, or someone helped her get out. If she's in there, we'll find her. If she got out, we'll find who helped her and deal with them, then we'll go find her," Sykes shot back.

"It's just mind-boggling that the two most protected places in Washington can't keep a couple of women and two children from disappearing," Keller replied, rubbing his temples.

"That's the situation at this point." Sykes needed to change the subject. "We took a real beating in Baltimore and Annapolis. What forces are left are setting defensive positions along I-95. That's the path we believe the insurgents will take, given the fact that that's the route they've been using. Have you heard from the Second Marine Division and Eighty-Second Airborne? When are they going to get here?"

"What a waste of human life, all of this," Keller said, sounding exhausted. "The Eighty-Second began arriving at Camp Lejeune this morning. Both divisions assure us they're departing sometime tomorrow morning. Then it's only a few hours before they start arriving here."

"For your sake, you better hope that's not too late," Sykes replied, leaning forward in his chair.

0921 HOURS, US NAVAL ACADEMY, ANNAPOLIS, MARYLAND

"WHAT IN THE holy fuck is going on over here? We are burning goddamn daylight! I got patrols out on the march route. Those sons of bitches are diggin' in all along I-95. It's gonna be another day like yesterday, goddammit."

Those had been Colonel Reynolds's exact words upon his arrival at Andy's headquarters. After receiving Squatch's message, Reynolds had immediately jumped into his HUMVEE and driven down from the airport.

Andy took several minutes bringing Reynolds up to speed concerning the arrival of their visitors. After a happy reunion with Cummings and Detwiler, the First Lady had gone into detail about how she and the congresswoman had managed to escape Washington. Andy conveyed the story to Reynolds, who, at first, listened impatiently, but as the story went on, became more and more of a believer in their good fortune.

Master Chief Norwood, after meeting with the former SEAL team members marching with the Militia, had also disclosed that CAT-MAN forces

A DAY LIKE ANY OTHER

were expecting them to march along the I-95 corridor and had focused all of their remaining strength there. He had suggested taking Route 50 into DC since that route was undefended. Andy had dispatched patrols immediately upon learning of this, and Norwood had been correct: the scouts radioed that they were on the outskirts of the city and had encountered no CAT-MAN personnel whatsoever along the way. Though it still felt odd issuing orders to a Lieutenant Colonel, Andy instructed Reynolds to begin moving the force at the airport down to Annapolis and have the scout teams to the north continue to monitor CAT-MAN troop movements and report any changes.

The Militia units already located in Annapolis would move out along Route 50 immediately, and all units coming down from the north would fall in behind. Reynolds agreed that Route 50 was the better option and sent word to have Andy's plan carried out. Before their meeting was done, Militia units were already moving toward Washington.

The next order of business was to gather the command team and figure out exactly what they were going to do once they got there. The first team would be arriving there, if unmolested, in approximately three hours. As Andy exited the headquarters tent to go find Squatch and Wally, he noted that a steady rain had begun falling.

0930 HOURS, UPSTATE PENNSYLVANIA

"I HAVE TO go. My being here is putting you all at risk."

John Redstone had stayed by Ryan's side since he had come out of surgery. Dr. Taft had worked on Ryan for hours and was confident he had repaired all the damaged blood vessels. He had wanted to give Ryan another blood transfusion but could only give him two pints since María and Mrs. Taft were the only compatible blood type matches. Ryan's blood pressure had been stable, and color was coming back into his face. The increasing CAT-MAN activity on the road at the end of the Tafts' access road was starting to concern John, and he felt it was time for him to leave and maybe draw CAT-MAN interest away with him.

"There's no guarantee they'll leave if you go. They've had an interest in this place ever since . . . well, you know," replied Dr. Taft.

"I'm sorry about that," John replied. He regretted what they had done with the CAT-MAN bodies. At the time, it had seemed like making a statement was the thing to do. It had brought entirely too much attention to the Tafts' little homestead. If he had to do it over, he would have disposed of the bodies and vehicle and left it a mystery as to what had happened to them.

"It's all water under the bridge at this point," said Dr. Taft. There was nothing they could do about that now, and for John to try and just drive off right in front of the CAT-MAN officers parked out on the highway was ludicrous. He'd be followed and arrested immediately, and with no witnesses, who knows how that would end.

"If you feel you have to go, walk out and go over the mountain on one of the logging trails," Dr. Taft said, pointing toward the hillside that rose in the distance. "When you get to the other end, there'll be a house. The owners are the Prescotts. Tell them I sent you and that you need a ride to get back to your family. They'll help you; they're good people."

"Thank you, Doctor, and thank you for looking after Ryan," John replied, shaking Dr. Taft's hand.

"Don't worry about Ryan. His gunshot wounds don't look as much like gunshot wounds since the surgery. If anyone asks, he lost his footing and fell down a ravine and was impaled on a tree branch," replied Dr. Taft with a smile.

"I won't forget what you've done for my family," replied John.

An hour later, John was long gone, having said goodbye to Ryan, who was still in and out of consciousness. John had slipped out the back door and headed for the logging trail, and the CAT-MAN guys on the road were none the wiser. Dr. Taft was glad John had gotten out clean. Part of him wondered if they were being paranoid, and another part was wishing he had taken Ryan with him. His house was still being watched, and he knew it was only a matter of time before he received another visit from CAT-MAN officers.

0945 HOURS, US NAVAL ACADEMY, ANNAPOLIS, MARYLAND

"I'M NOT GOING to the hospital. I'm able to stand, I'm able to walk, and I'm able to lead my troopers. So that's the end of that," said Ramirez adamantly. He had sustained burns and shrapnel injuries when his Stryker had been hit. The blast had blown him out of the commander's hatch and onto the ground, which most certainly saved his life. The rest of his crew had not survived. He had made it very clear in response to the suggestion that he report to the makeshift hospital on the NSA side of the base that he was going to see this through.

"We get it," Andy began, "but if you feel like you're gonna fold, you need to pass the reins, OK?"

"Fair enough," Ramirez replied.

It was obvious he was in a great deal of pain, but Andy knew they needed him and that Ramirez wasn't going to sit by and watch his troopers go without him.

"OK, now that we've settled that, let's get down to the business of figuring out what we're actually going to do once we get to DC, being as we're almost there," Andy said, changing the subject back to the issue at hand.

The objective had always been to capture the Capitol Building, where Congress was said to have sequestered themselves. The mission had changed since learning that Congress was actually imprisoned there; it went from capture and arrest to a rescue mission. The second objective was to capture Keller if possible. With units already heading toward DC and Tenth Mountain units heading to Annapolis, Andy called for a meeting of the minds to nail down some specifics. Present were Andy, Squatch, Wally, Reynolds, Ramirez, Dmitry, Cummings, and Detweiler. Andy had asked David to come with him, but he chose not to. He was not dealing well with what he had seen and had been keeping to himself most of the time since he had arrived with the main column.

"So far, we have a march route and two objectives when we get there. We're here now to fill in the blanks, so we need to get all the ideas on the table right now," Andy said, pointing to the map of Washington, DC, he had laid out on the table in the center of the room. He had highlighted Route 50, the Capitol Building, and the White House. "We need to know what we have left to put into this operation, what we're up against, and what they might do once we arrive."

"The answer to the 'what do we have' question is as follows," said Squatch. He, Wally, and the command staff had tallied the numbers, and they weren't pretty. "Both the Bradleys are unable to move with their own power. The crews say their turrets and guns still work, and with the help of a bulldozer, they were able to get them back onto the flatbed trailers. So we can use them; we just have to drive them around with tractor trailers. Four of the Strykers are fully operational, along with the MEV.

"As far as manpower goes, including the truck drivers, support folks, and walking wounded who can go with us, Tenth Mountain can muster out a total of 2,523, down from 3,212. The Militia head count is 2,107, down from 3,025.

Keep in mind that number includes everyone, even a few hundred walking wounded, some of whom probably should be staying here, but resources here are already overwhelmed, and we need everyone we can get."

After doing some quick math in his head, Andy was nauseated at how many casualties they had taken. He knew his Annapolis force had taken a beating—only 185 out of three hundred would be making the trip. Hearing the totals brought home what a bloody day yesterday had been for all of them, and the knowledge that thousands of the CAT-MAN soldiers they had faced were now dead brought him no solace.

"Colonel Reynolds, what are your thoughts on taking down the objectives?" Andy asked.

Reynolds cleared his throat and began to speak while pointing at the circled objectives on the map.

"Well, what you can't see on this map is that the buildings around the Capitol Building are multistory fortresses all on their own. We're gonna have to surround the Capitol Building by securing all of those buildings. I'm suggesting Tenth Mountain go straight into the attack once we arrive, and once we secure a perimeter, the Militia can then assault the Capitol Building. You're gonna need ladders to get up the ends, which is where I suggest you assault—both ends, north and south, at once. The White House is gonna have to wait. We're gonna need all our people to secure the Capitol. All we can do is try and keep anyone from getting in or out until we can get a force over there. That's my opinion. We'll fill in the details once we get eyes on the building. We're gonna need a base of operations somewhere close to the targets as well."

"I think we can all agree with the Colonel's plan—the simpler the better. Wally, what's the latest from the scout teams?" Andy asked, turning his attention to Wally.

Wally stepped forward, looking at his notes, and said, "Scout teams report that the CAT-MAN forces digging in along I-95 are still there, so they haven't figured out that we aren't going that way yet. The scout teams in DC think they found a good place to coalesce and launch our attacks from. It's a college campus right off of Route 50, so it's got the space for all our vehicles, and it's only about a mile and a half or so from the Capitol Building. They've also made contact with some locals who are eager to help us—a reverend and his parishioners who say they've been harassed by CAT-MAN all winter to report to a FEMA camp, but they've refused. They say they've been pretty much in hiding for the last month or so. Scout teams also confirm that CAT-MAN activity is centered around the Capitol Building and the White House, and they also confirmed the presence of six M1A2 Abrams main battle tanks at the Capitol Building."

"Excuse me, can I say something?" Director Cummings said, raising his hand.

"Of course, Mr. Director, that's why you're here," replied Andy.

"Thank you," Director Cummings began. "The First Lady and Congresswoman Dreyfus have both stated that they had been assured that those tanks wouldn't be a threat. A Sergeant First Class Maddox, the commander of those tanks, told both of them separately, and they believe him since it was him and his troops who got the congresswoman out of the Capitol Building. I see them as being on our side already. At the very least, they took a huge risk in getting her out of there."

"Thanks for bringing that up, Robert. I don't think everyone was aware of that," Andy said. "Director Cummings spent some time with our guests earlier. He's convinced that their intentions are sincere, and that's good enough for me."

All assembled nodded in agreement.

"While we're on the subject of the First Lady and the congresswoman, I feel that they should both come with us so we can keep an eye on them, as well as have them there when we liberate Congress. They can testify as to what they've seen and put their pals' minds at ease that we are actually the good guys," Andy said, putting his idea out to the group since he still wasn't sure if he could keep them safe. He needed his compatriots on board with whatever the decision was.

"I'm OK with that, provided the little kids stay here. I can't have something happening to them on my conscience," replied Reynolds.

"I'll stay with the First Lady and congresswoman," Cummings said, raising his hand, "Billings, Detweiler, and I will keep them safe."

"OK, I'll arrange for someone to babysit the twins, providing the First Lady agrees to it. If not, we'll just bring the congresswoman. She doesn't have a choice," Andy replied, watching as Militia trucks passed by, headed for Route 50. "We need to start wrapping this up, boys."

Wally raised his hand and began to speak. "We can surround the White House, block the gates, and keep Keller trapped there only until he calls for HMX to come evac him out."

Wally was correct. The moment they got the call, helicopters would launch from Quantico, Virginia, just a few miles away, and Keller would be whisked away by some of the Marine Corps's best pilots and crews.

"It's a chance we're gonna have to take, Wally," Andy replied. "Let's hope all their birds aren't operational, because if they are, we'll have to shoot them down if we can."

Andy didn't like the idea of firing on other Marines, but the stakes were too high at this point. Too much blood had been spilled to let Keller get away so easily.

"There may be another way," Wally replied. "I'll talk to you about it after this. Everyone needs to get moving, and if you agree, it'll only really involve me."

"OK," Andy began, looking at Wally quizzically. "I guess we'll wrap this meeting up and meet again at this college the scouts found. By then we should have the assault plans finalized."

"Wait," Cummings said, sounding a little concerned, "what about the two divisions the First Lady told us about? The ones coming up from North Carolina?"

Reynolds was the first to answer.

"Yes, Mr. Director, we haven't forgotten. From what it sounds like, they've been dragging their feet until now. We can only hope we beat them to DC and march the Speaker of the House out to them and order them to help us. My thinking is that they don't know what we're all about, but they don't trust CAT-MAN either and are staying out of it as long as they can."

Reynolds had said what they all knew. Basically, if the Second Marine Division and the Eighty-Second Airborne Division showed up with the intent of fighting, then it would be the end of Andy's little revolution.

After a long silence, Andy said, "Alright, we'll just have to get there first. Let's get there and get it done." He then turned to Wally and said, "OK, what have you got in mind?"

As the group began to disperse, Andy heard Reynolds tell Squatch, "At least with all this rain, we won't have to worry about drones eyeballin' us every step of the way."

CHAPTER 43

DAY 11

0445 HOURS, WASHINGTON, DC

THE TRIP FROM Annapolis had been a somber one. The rain had continued the entire trip, and everyone and everything was soaked. It seemed, thankfully, to be letting up.

The scouts had found that the Gallaudet University campus was unoccupied and large enough to accommodate the entire force while still providing a defendable position if it came to that. The wounded were to be housed in the sports facility adjacent to the Bison's football field, which would host the encampment for everyone else. The vehicles would form a laager around the camp with the Strykers interspersed to provide solid cover and to spread their firepower around. More importantly, the campus was only a few blocks from the National Mall and their final objectives, the Capitol Building and the White House.

The plan was already in motion. It was a long shot, but it was all they had. The next few hours would decide the future of this country. For Andy, the future of all these courageous souls concerned him more. They had all followed him, trusted him to lead them. They could have left at any time; nothing was keeping them here. There was no pay, no contracts to honor, no threat of court martial. They stayed, every one of them. Who were these people? So many of them were wounded, and with medical supplies running short, Andy wondered how many more they would lose. How many had they buried along the way already?

He felt that creeping doubt again, the fear that had plagued him the entire time since leaving the farm eleven days ago. Had it only been eleven days? It felt like years. They had been successful, victorious, every time. At what price? Would he put all these good people in their graves? Then that voice came to him again: *They trust you more than you trust yourself.* The voice was always right. He hadn't noticed the rain had stopped.

"Take it eeeaaaaassy, take it eeeeaaasssy, don't let the sound of your own wheels make you craaaazy . . ."

Was that music playing? A guitar and a male voice singing sounded familiar. He knew the tune. He found himself humming along as he looked over the map of DC.

The National Mall, the White House, the Capitol Building—it was a lot of ground to cover, but also a lot of ground for CAT-MAN to defend. Upon arrival at the university grounds, Andy had called for one last meeting before Reynolds's troops began clearing a path to and around the Capitol Building. Joyce had decided to come with them after getting her girls settled with the base commander's family, so she and Congresswoman Dreyfus were in attendance as well.

Eleanor had said there were about three hundred CAT-MAN defenders at the capitol building and another hundred or so at the White House. Andy was sure there were more by now. He remembered how Squatch had pounced on her with his trademark impoliteness: "About three hundred? One hundred or so? Man, why are we listening to this bitch? She don't know." Andy had to laugh a little even now at the look on her face. It was as if Squatch had slapped her squarely across the mouth, which was what he had really wanted to do, but for Andy's sake, he had controlled himself. He guessed she wasn't used to being called a bitch, at least not to her face anyway. Eleanor had also said that the six Abrams tanks positioned at the Capitol Building would not be a threat and repeated the conversation she had had with Sergeant Maddox.

He chuckled again, recalling the way Squatch had scoffed, making a half-choking, half-laughing sound as he stood up and said, "You've got to be shitting me. We're basing an assault plan on this bitch's fairy tale? Bro, I'm gonna go find me some body armor and write my will or something, man. This shit is crazy!"

As he left, Eleanor, visibly distressed by how she was being referred to repeatedly as "this bitch," spoke up and said, "You know I'm trying to help you!" Squatch, still within hearing distance, had responded, "Yeah, where were you last fall?"

Andy knew where his friend had been coming from and hadn't disagreed with him. Had Eleanor and her peers done their jobs in the opening hours of The Event, how many thousands would still be alive? And that was why he had let him speak his mind. She now knew she was in a whole new world, and Andy needed her to understand that. He agreed with Squatch that her story of estimates and cryptic promises from Army tankers was thin, but he also knew that what she was saying made sense.

The music was still playing. He knew it was his imagination; he really needed to get some sleep. However, that was out of the question for the foreseeable future. As he stared at the map, he kept going over the plan in his mind. Colonel Reynolds and the Tenth Mountain, under the cover of darkness, would secure a perimeter around the Capitol Building and secure key structures to ensure the assault force had sufficient cover to get into position.

Once in position, the Capitol Building would be peppered with a volley of high-explosive mortar rounds. Rounds were in short supply and were needed to support the first assault waves that were to attack the north and south sides of the building simultaneously, so they would be used sparingly and precisely. The mortars would continue to bombard the west side of the building as well as the roof, where Eleanor said there may be some of those "weird tube gun things," referring, of course, to mortar tubes. Everyone hoped she was wrong on this one. For assaulting troops in the open, a mortar bombardment is about as bad as it can get, and unlike an M1A2 Abrams main battle tank, it did not take much instruction to drop a mortar round down the tube and ruin someone's day.

With the mortars suppressing the west side of the building and the roof, the east side was the responsibility of the Strykers. They would use their .50-caliber machine guns to hammer the fortifications and hopefully keep the north and south walls from being reinforced. The Bradleys would be driven into position opposite the north and south fortifications and would pound the sandbag defenses with high-explosive rounds. The hope was that they would blast breaches in the sandbags. If that didn't work, the engineers had prepared demolition charges to do the job. The trouble with that was that someone would have to climb a ladder and place said charges. The goal was to create two breaches on each side of the building for the Militia to assault through.

If Eleanor was right and there were only three hundred CAT-MAN officers, then it would make sense that the longer walls would have more defenders. The west wall looked out over the Reflecting Pool and was far too open and far too long to make any assault feasible. The east wall was the back door to the Capitol Building. It was a short distance from the buildings behind it, so from there, the Strykers would suppress, then assault the east wall once the north and south forces had breached the fortifications. The key to success was accomplishing the breaches quickly before the CAT-MAN force could react and reinforce.

Andy would lead the southern assault force, Squatch would lead the northern force, and Lieutenant Ramirez would lead his Strykers and accompanying infantry on the east. If the first assault waves reached the fortifications and the position was untenable, then the assault would be aborted. The radio code word "Doris" would be transmitted, and the assault waves would fall back and regroup. If the assault was to continue, the first-wave commanders would fire red aerial flares, and all other commanders would answer with red flares.

The plan was simple enough and had a good chance of success—if there were only three hundred defenders, if the M1s were out of action, if CAT-MAN didn't have mortars, and if they moved fast enough to keep the CAT-MAN force off balance and unable to react. Not to mention the fact that there were not enough troops to surround the White House to prevent reinforcements from coming to the aid of the Capitol Building as well as prevent President Keller from escaping. No word had come from Wally either—that part of the plan was a gigantic "if."

"That's a lot of 'ifs,'" Colonel Reynolds had said, rubbing his neck.

He was correct, of course, and when it came right down to it, it was going to fall to Andy to fire that first flare and commit the whole force to the unknown.

He was snapped out of his thoughts by the sound of people clapping and cheering. Then he heard more music, but this time it was a female voice. It wasn't his imagination after all. He stepped outside to find Squatch cleaning his pistol, smiling from ear to ear and singing along. It was a song popular with the preteen-girl crowd. The giant man sang like some kind of adolescent schoolgirl, "And you're gonna hear me roooarrr!"

Andy couldn't resist ribbing his old friend. "Sing it, Squatch!"

Surprised and just a little embarrassed, Squatch jumped to his feet, waving a cleaning brush in one hand and the pistol slide in the other.

"You want me to shut them up? Someone found a music store that still had some instruments intact. I'll go shut them up!"

"Hold up, Sasquatch," Andy said, looking around. Andy was watching a pretty young woman with blonde hair in a ponytail singing in the prettiest voice he thought he'd ever heard. There was a large man with a scruffy beard playing the guitar. The woman was singing, the man was playing, and for the first time in days, Andy saw smiles and heard laughter. The camp was starting to buzz, and a crowd was forming in a circle around the band.

A DAY LIKE ANY OTHER

Andy turned to his friend and said, "This is exactly what we need."

"It is?" Squatch replied. "I'd rather have some gunships, bro."

Andy said, "You know the words to that song pretty well, big guy." Andy was grinning from ear to ear, and Squatch could see it.

"Hey, man!" Sasquatch began. "I got daughters, bro. I gotta stay hip, ya know!"

Andy gave his giant friend a playful backhand to the ribs and said, "I know, I love that song. It's just strange seeing a man-ape sing it with such vigor."

Squatch slapped his friend on the back, nearly knocking him into the mud and said, "It's a lucky thing you're my bro. Otherwise, I'd have to hurt you."

"I know, Sasquatch," Andy replied, still grinning.

Just then, Andy heard an out-of-breath voice shouting, "Don't stop them! Don't stop them!" It was Andy's intelligence officer from his command staff. He was shuffling toward the music show, unraveling an extension cord that was plugged into the generator providing power to the aid station, which had been receiving wounded for hours now. Behind him were several troopers carrying a pair of speakers, a keyboard, and what looked like enough percussion instruments to make a full drum set.

"We wouldn't think of it," replied Andy with a smile.

As the band equipment entourage passed, Andy noticed that more and more Militia members were emerging from whatever cover they had found to shelter from the rain. All were in full battle gear, as the order had been passed about two hours ago to be ready to move at any time. Some were lighting cigarettes; others were stretching, happy to be moving about; but most were headed toward the impromptu concert.

Director Cummings, Detweiler, Joyce Keller, Congresswoman Dreyfus, and Special Agent Billings joined Andy and Squatch in watching the performance. The drum set and speakers were almost ready, and the intelligence officer was conversing with the singer and the guitar player, handing over a microphone.

"I'm no expert on military tactics, but having a concert right now seems like a bad idea," said Detweiler. "Won't that tell them where we are?"

"It's a terrible idea, and they've known where we are since we got here," replied Andy.

Just then, as if on cue, thumping sounds echoed somewhere off in the distance. It was different from the sounds of battle emanating from Reynolds's operations around Capitol Hill.

"Incoming," Andy said calmly.

A moment later, the tell-tale sound of ripping air let all present know that mortar shells were headed their way, and everyone threw themselves to the ground. Billings grabbed the First Lady and rolled both of them onto the ground, covering her body with his. Squatch did likewise with the congresswoman. The rounds impacted nearby, throwing up mud and dirt, but no one was hit. Somewhere outside the perimeter, an Air Force forward controller turned Militia member saw the flashes of the rounds launching and quickly called for mortars to fire at those coordinates. A moment later, Militia mortars were firing, and a moment after that, secondary explosions were heard off in the distance. Andy could hear the controller over the radio say, "Target destroyed, good shootin'."

With that, the Militia started shouting and talking trash to the now very unhappy and probably dead CAT-MAN mortar teams, which in the distance probably sounded more like a rowdy crowd at a sporting event. The guitar player took the microphone and started saying "Assssss-hooooole" over and over as if a referee had made a bad call in a hockey game. He was joined in his chant by all present, and soon one could hear the chant echoing out into the DC streets.

As Billings helped the First Lady to her feet, Squatch did the same for the congresswoman.

"Thank you," said Dreyfus, brushing mud off of her clothes.

"This doesn't mean we're friends," replied Squatch.

The impromptu music festival had its newly acquired set of drums pounding a heavy beat. The "lead singer" was now singing into a microphone that the intelligence officer had just handed her. "Thun-der ahh-ahh-ahh-ahhhh-ahh-ahh, Thunder-ahh-ahh-ahh-ahhh-ahh-ahh, You've been thun-der-struck!" The amplifiers carried the sound even louder out into the streets, the echoes of which were reverberating off the downtown buildings perfectly, causing the intelligence officer to smile broadly.

"Isn't that woman singing your friend Wally's girlfriend? Jessica Adams is her name. What a lovely girl. The twins took right to her. When they asked her why she had blood on her clothes and hands, she told them her friend got a boo-boo and she put a Band-Aid on it for him," said Joyce. The truth of the bloody clothes was that she had tried to plug a bullet hole in one of her platoon member's chests to no avail—he had died in her arms.

"Yeah, that is her. I'll be damned. That's one talented young lady," Andy replied.

A DAY LIKE ANY OTHER

She had been there to see Wally off at the marina in Annapolis. He had questioned if Wally's idea was even feasible and still had some regret in letting him go, but Wally had insisted, so Andy had agreed. Watching his friend speed off with the SEALs in their little boat had left Andy feeling very sad, like he would never see him again. It was a long shot, but Wally was so sure of his plan that Andy couldn't say no. So Andy had watched as Wally, the two SEALs from their own ranks, and Chief Norwood's team headed off south into the Chesapeake Bay. The last anyone had heard from them was a radio call from Chief Norwood stating that Wally had been taken into custody by CAT-MAN guards while trying to enter the objective. It seemed Wally's plan wasn't off to a very good start.

The band was really getting into it now. Jessica had handed the microphone over to another female trooper, who was singing a song Andy recognized as a newer release.

Jessica and another woman were skipping and clapping their hands over their heads in time with the drum beat, as backup dancers would at a concert, getting everyone into the song. The fact that they were in full combat gear made it all the more impressive.

David and Dmitry arrived at Andy's little group of spectators, having just come from getting their burns cleaned and redressed. David was covered in red mud from head to toe, causing Andy to do a double take and ask, "What the hell happened to you?"

David, without expression, pointed to Dmitry and said, "When the mortar rounds came in, he pushed me into a giant mud puddle."

Andy grinned, trying not to laugh, and turned his attention to Dmitry, who was laughing quietly. "I did not mean to push him so far, but za boy is not as heavy as he looks," replied Dmitry.

Andy nodded and smiled, satisfied with Dmitry's answer, then turned his attention to David and said, "Let's go have a chat, son." He put his arm around his son's shoulders, leading him away from the group.

"What's up, Dad?" asked David.

"I'm really sorry," Andy began. "I should have never let you come along. You've seen things that you never should have. I put you in great danger, and the danger is only getting greater."

"Dad—" David began, but Andy stopped him, raising his index finger, and continued speaking.

"You are not coming with me; you will not be part of the assault force or any other force. I need you to stay with Cummings and Detweiler. They will go with us to Union Station. When we secure the Capitol Building, they will bring the First Lady and the congresswoman there. Then, and only then, will you go there." Andy spoke forcefully but not with anger. "Is that clear?"

"But Dad—" David tried to speak again, but beginning the sentence with the word "but" was a mistake. Andy cut him off again.

"No 'buts.' If things go badly, you're to stay with Director Cummings. I've already talked to him. He's going to take Detweiler back to Philadelphia, so you'll go with them. When he thinks it's safe, he'll get you back upstate to the farm. None of this is open for discussion. Am I making myself clear? Your mother can't lose both of us."

"I understand," replied David, tears welling up in his eyes.

Andy put his hand on David's shoulder and said, "If it goes that way, I need you to tell your mother and sister that I love them and that I'll always be with them. Can you do that for me?"

The tears were flowing down David's face, clearing a path through the mud.

"I can do that, Dad," he replied, giving Andy a hug.

"Thanks, buddy. I love you, kid," said Andy, squeezing his son tighter.

"I love you too, Dad," replied David, wiping muddy tears from his face.

Andy noticed that a runner had arrived from Colonel Reynolds and said, "Let's go see what Reynolds has to say," giving David one last hug.

The band had noticed the runner as well and stopped playing, as did the assembled spectators. All attention was on Andy and the runner. The intelligence officer, other members of Andy's staff, and all three battalion commanders were making their way over as well.

The runner was soaked with sweat and grime, and one eye was just about swollen shut.

"What happened to your eye?" Andy asked.

"Oh, it's pretty swollen, ain't it?" the runner, a good ole boy from Alabama, replied, touching it with his index finger. "The colonel did it. Well, he didn't mean to. We were clearing a stairwell, and a grenade came bouncing down the stairs, so the colonel pushed me back into the rest of the stack. We all tumbled backward, with the colonel landing on top of us all."

"Why am I not surprised Reynolds was leading a stack, clearing buildings?" replied Squatch.

"Well, is he OK?" asked Andy.

A DAY LIKE ANY OTHER

"He took a piece of shrapnel in his butt cheek—man, did he cuss up a storm—but he's OK," replied the runner.

"Tough old bastard. What's the message?" Andy said, feeling like he had already wasted too much time on small talk.

"Colonel Reynolds says, 'I don't know what in the ever-living fuck you yahoos are doing back there, but it's scared the piss out of these bastards, and we're not going to get a better opportunity to get the assault force into position,'" replied the runner, then added with a smile, "The colonel has a way with words, don't he? It's true I seen some of them surrender. Their crotches was all wet—they is scared scared."

Andy looked over at the intelligence officer responsible for the speakers and instruments, and he was smiling from ear to ear and giving Andy two thumbs-up. The impromptu concert had turned into a psychological warfare operation. The fact that the Militia was having a party before going into battle while the CAT-MAN defenders were fighting for their lives was a total mind game, and it had worked. The CAT-MAN force was in disarray, and Reynolds had secured a perimeter. It was time.

Andy turned from the runner and said, "OK, Squatch, let's get weapons company and the Bradleys movin'."

Squatch nodded in the affirmative, then in a booming voice, shouted, "Weapons company, fall in. Bradley crews, saddle up!"

This set off a flurry of activity in the camp as the machine gun teams and mortar crews began to assemble.

Andy turned back to runner and said, "Let the colonel know that Plan X-Ray is in motion as agreed upon."

The runner said, "Will do, Plan X-Ray is in motion as agreed upon." He shook Andy's hand and said, "Good luck." Then he turned and headed toward a pickup truck standing by to carry him back to Reynolds.

Plan X-ray was the final assault plan. Weapons company, basically all the .30-caliber machine gun teams and the Bradleys on their flatbed trailers, were to take up firing positions to support the assault force and provide security to prevent the objective from being reinforced. Ten minutes later, the assault force would step off to take up their positions at the north and south sides of the Capitol Building. Once the assault force was in position, Andy would give the signal, and all the supporting arms would begin firing for twenty seconds. When the firing stopped, the assault force would charge the building.

Andy then turned to his radio operator and said, "Transmit the code word 'X-ray.'"

This would let Ramirez, the snipers watching the White House, and any other elements know that the assault was about to happen.

As the weapons company assembled, Reverend Earl James, the pastor of the church that had been so helpful since Andy's little army had arrived, began leading his parishioners in prayer. He was a Black man in his mid-sixties, lean and handsome with thick white hair and beard. His parishioners loved him, and he loved his community. When The Event had turned the world dark, he had opened his church to any and all in need. As the winter had dragged on, more and more desperate people had begun accepting his help instead of going into FEMA camps, and he had begun getting visits from CAT-MAN officers trying to convince him that he was merely keeping people from getting real help and protection at the government camps. After several of such visits, each one more forceful and intimidating than the last, it was clear he had been in the way of some CAT-MAN plan to get as many people into camps as possible. Doing what he saw as the Lord's work had become dangerous. He had moved the operation underground and watched as CAT-MAN patrols began rounding people up who would have otherwise preferred to be on their own.

When the scout teams had entered DC, Reverend James had seen it as deliverance and had immediately offered his assistance. When he had been asked to help by having some of his people act as guides around the city and help isolate the White House, he had agreed immediately. It was his people who had pushed disabled cars for blocks in order to blockade all the entrances to prevent anyone from coming or going. Sniper teams had covered them as they did their work, and the CAT-MAN officers on the White House grounds had made no effort to stop them as the snipers shot anyone attempting to approach them. With the White House secure and his people helping in the aid station, and with all of the different elements of the attacks now in process, he had decided his place was now at the university. He now gathered a group to him and began to pray aloud.

"Heavenly Father, we gather here this morning to ask that you watch over and protect these warriors who go forth now and who have been fighting all night to free this nation from the evil and the treachery that has infected it, enslaved its people, and murdered untold numbers. Thank you, Lord, for bringing deliverance at last. Amen."

A DAY LIKE ANY OTHER

Andy had been making his way over to address the weapons company but paused while the reverend was speaking. He now stood in front of twenty machine gun teams and three mortar teams, as well as the Bradley crews. As he positioned himself in front of them, all eyes turned his way and all chatter stopped. He had their undivided attention.

"OK," Andy began, making a point to look those he could directly in the eyes, "you all know the plan. Cover us for twenty seconds, and the Bradleys will use their infrared sights and mark targets with green lasers, then shoot anyone trying to get behind us when we go in. If we have to fall back and regroup, you'll cover us again. If you see red aerial flares, we're going over the top, so don't shoot us. Any questions?"

There were no questions—everyone knew their job.

"OK then, no questions. Let's get it done."

As machine gunners hoisted their M240G machine guns onto their shoulders and assistant gunners picked up ammo cans, the rest of the assault force started shouting and encouraging them. "Shoot straight, ya bastards!" was heard more than a few times. The drummer started another heavy beat: *Boom-boom boom, boom-boom boom, boom-boom boom*. One of the singers started a chant in time with the beat: "We will, we will rock you. We will, we will rock you."

As the weapons company and the Bradleys drove off, Squatch shouted, "OK, assault force, get on your gear. We step off in ten minutes!"

This created a flurry of activity as the members of the assault force began moving to the assembly area, donning helmets and equipment as they went. Andy returned to the command tent to look over the map one last time and gather what gear he had left there when he had gone to investigate where the music was coming from. He also retrieved four letters he had written to be opened in the event that he didn't survive the day—one each for Melissa, Kathryn, and David, as well as one to be delivered to Tommy Rye in Philadelphia to read on the radio program. He planned to hand them to Director Cummings before heading off with the assault force.

Andy took one last glance at the map and scanned the tent to ensure he hadn't forgotten anything, then turned and exited, wondering if it was for the last time. Standing outside were David, Dmitry, Cummings, and Detweiler. David was holding a cardboard box in front of him and handed it over to Andy.

He said, "They found something else in that music store and thought you'd appreciate it."

Taken slightly aback by this very nice but out of place gesture given the fact that he was probably going to die in the next half hour or so, Andy accepted the box, trying not to show his irritation, and opened it. Inside was a set of bagpipes. Andy's irritation turned to gratitude—his son knew how he loved bagpipe tunes.

Then, with disappointment in his voice, he said, "Ah, thank you guys, really, but I can't play the bagpipes, and I don't think I'll have time to learn anytime soon."

From his right, a voice with a heavy Scottish accent said, "Aye, that'll be why I'm here, laddie."

Andy recognized the man though he hadn't had an opportunity to speak with him as of yet. Andy knew he was the one everyone called "The Scotsman."

William Robert Craig had been born in Glasgow, Scotland, his father a policeman and his mother a nurse. He and his brothers had been raised with the belief that there was no higher service than protecting and caring for others. He had joined the Army at age eighteen and had served with the Second Battalion of the Black Watch Regiment in Iraq. As part of his duties, he had been one of the unit's bagpipers, having learned to play as a boy. After meeting an American servicewoman in Iraq and subsequently falling in love, he had immigrated to the States and settled in Ohio. When the world had turned upside down, he had done his best to protect his new family, but as winter had dragged on, he had relented to the hunger and moved to a FEMA camp. Quickly realizing what a mistake that had been, he had escaped with his family as part of a larger group, using a food riot as cover to make good their getaway. He had been in hiding with other survivors when he heard Andy's voice on the radio. Leaving his family, he and a small group had driven through the night to join the resistance in Philadelphia. He had proven himself several times in the past eleven days, and when the call had gone out this morning for someone who could play the pipes, all eyes had turned to him. He set off to meet his destiny at the side of their leader, Andrew Lemon.

"It's a pleasure to meet you," Andy said, shaking the Scotsman's hand.

"Likewise," replied the Scotsman.

"Will you pipe us into battle?" asked Andy.

"Aye, that I will. I'd be honored," replied the Scotsman.

"Good then. Stay by my side, and when I ask you to play, you pick the tune," Andy said with a smile, somehow feeling there was no way they could lose now.

A DAY LIKE ANY OTHER

"That sounds like a good deal to me," replied the Scotsman, who then began inflating the set of pipes Andy had just handed him.

"Alright then, let's go get this done," said Andy as he started walking toward the now assembled assault force. Standing in company formations four columns deep, festooned with all their equipment, they looked imposing.

As Andy approached, Sasquatch faced the formation and shouted, "Assault force, AAA-TTEN-TION!"

Instantly, a thousand troops snapped to attention.

Sasquatch about-faced, saluted Andy, and said, "Sir, the assault force is formed."

Andy returned Squatch's salute.

"What's the final head count?"

"1,023. Right around five hundred for each side, north and south." Andy gave his friend a nod and said, "Post!"

With that, Squatch repositioned himself just behind and to the right of Andy, facing the formation.

Once Squatch had stopped moving, Andy said, "Assault force at ease!"

The assault force that had been at the position of attention went to a more relaxed stance, their attention still focused on Andy.

Andy gestured for a pickup truck that was standing by, loaded with ladders for the attack, to pull up to him. He climbed up onto the hood, where he could be seen and heard better.

"Can everyone in the back hear me?"

After seeing a few thumbs-up signals from the back of the formation, Andy continued.

"I know you all have been briefed by your company commanders, but I just wanted to give it to you one last time before we move out."

Andy paused and looked over the assembled force. They were an impressive sight—warriors all armed, supplied, armored, and ready for battle. There was no fear in their eyes.

"We're going to make our way to the Capitol Building via Union Station. From there, we'll split into two groups, half with me to the south side of the building and half with Sasquatch to the north. When we're in position, I'll give the signal, and the weapons company, all the armored vehicles, and the mortar platoon will hammer the defenses for twenty seconds. When they stop, we go. Everyone knows their job. Those carrying ladders will get us into position, so be ready to put them up when we've established breaches in the sandbag walls.

Engineers will blast those breaches open if the Bradleys' fire doesn't. When it's decided that we can get in, I'll fire a red star cluster aerial flare. All the other elements will answer with red stars of their own, but don't wait for that. Once you see a red star, go up those ladders and over the top.

"The call sign for the operation are as follows. White Horse, that's us. White Horse One and Two are on the south side, and White Horse Three and Four are on the north side. The weapons company, the Bradleys, and the Stryker force are Red Horse. Tenth Mountain is Black Horse, and the sniper teams watching the White House are Pale Horse."

Andy paused to let that information sink in, then continued his briefing.

"Keep in mind that once we are inside, there will be noncombatants—that's to say the entire legislative and judicial branches of the government as well as the Joint Chiefs, and who knows who else is in there. We need to confirm our targets before we fire. Once we've secured and safeguarded all those folks, we will quickly assemble a force to go take down the White House. Things will be happening quickly, and we may have to improvise and adapt. Oh, there are also some tanks at the Capitol Building. I'm told they're not a threat, but let's get past them as fast we can and keep an eye on them after that just in case. I tell you all this again because if you find yourself holding a radio handset or in possession of a red star cluster aerial flare, then that means you're now in charge and you need to know."

Andy took a long pause at this point to let his last statement sink in. It was going to be tough getting through those defenses. Leaders were going to die, and someone was going to have to take charge.

"We all know what needs to be done," Andy continued, "so let's get it done. Good luck, and I'll see you in the fortress."

Andy climbed down from his field-expedient podium and directed the driver to pull away. Once the truck pulled away, Andy came to the position of attention and, with a booming command voice, said, "ASSAULT FORCE . . . AAA-TTEN-TION!"

The assault force came to attention as one as if one brain controlled a thousand bodies.

Andy, again in a booming command voice, said, "When I give the command, the assault force will fix bayonets! FIIIIIXXX BAYONETS!"

Again, as one, the assault force drew bayonets from the scabbards on their equipment belts and fixed them to end of their rifles, then returned to the position of attention.

A DAY LIKE ANY OTHER

Andy's next command was, "Battalion commanders, take charge and carry out the battle plan!"

The battalion commanders saluted and replied either, "Aye aye, sir" or "Yes, sir" depending on their branch of service, then about-faced toward their respective battalions and gave the command, "Right face! Forward march!"

The final assault was in motion. Andy exhaled forcefully, turned to his new bagpiper, and said, "Pipe us a tune, Scotsman. Something befitting a march to battle."

Men have marched into battle to the sound of bagpipes for centuries as replacements for drum and bugle calls. All Andy knew was that the sound of bagpipes got his blood going and made him feel ten feet tall.

"Aye, your wish is my command," replied the Scotsman.

Moments later, the distinct sound of the pipes was rising above the line of march. Andy recognized the tune as "Scotland the Brave," and though he was not one bit Scottish, it gave him chills, and he honestly felt that there was no way they could lose. Watching the expressions of the faces that marched past him, he saw that he wasn't the only one. They were a cross section of America—every race, every color, every creed, men and women—marching forward into battle as one. Andy felt pride he hadn't ever felt in his life, and he was humbled.

What happened next both shocked him and filled him with pride.

David looked at his father and said, "Dad! Isn't that the Scottish national anthem or something?"

Andy looked at his son and said, "You have been paying attention! I'm so proud of you, son. Remember what I told you."

Then, Andy, Squatch, Dmitry, and the Scotsman stepped out in front of the marching column headed for Union Station. The Scotsman gave David a wink and a smile as he marched past, his pipes blaring.

SYKES, WHO HAD come over to the Capitol Building to ensure their defenses were ready and had been trapped there all night, looked in the direction of the bagpipes. He said to all those around him, "They're coming." What he didn't say out loud was, *And we're fucked.*

CHAPTER 44

SUNRISE, UPSTATE PENNSYLVANIA

CAT-MAN VEHICLES HAD been gathering on the highway for over an hour. With the sun rising, Dr. Taft could see that there were at least eight. He had noticed all the activity while checking on Ryan. Feeling as though his patient was in danger, he had woken his wife and María, and together they had carried Ryan on a litter to Melissa's house. With Ryan being a large man, this had proved an exhausting task. Twice along the way, Ryan, though still somewhat sedated, had asked them to just put him down—he feared they would all have heart attacks at any moment.

Melissa had been awake and ran out to help them the last several yards. She was now looking through a pair of binoculars at the CAT-MAN vehicles on the highway.

"Yeah, they're all moving up the driveway now," Melissa said, still looking through the binoculars.

"We've got to get him out of here, up the mountain into the woods, or we're all finished. They'll recognize bullet wounds right away," said Dr. Taft, sounding concerned.

He had told John that the wounds wouldn't be recognized as bullet holes, but that was not true. He had needed John to escape and had told him what he thought would get him to go.

"OK," Melissa began, putting the binoculars down, "you guys all take him and the children and get out the back door. I'll stay here and buy time if needed."

"No, no," Dr. Taft wasn't having it. "I'll stay and you go."

"Dad! We don't have time to argue," Melissa said with force. "You're his doctor, and he clearly still needs one. I'll give you guys a head start then catch up. I can still run pretty fast, even through the forest. They'll probably go to your house first anyway. Now go!"

A DAY LIKE ANY OTHER

"Fine, but you'd better be right behind us," replied Dr. Taft as he lifted his corner of the litter, feeling helpless at the thought of leaving his daughter in obvious danger.

As they piled out the door, Melissa picked up her AR-15 and looked after them as they headed off into the woods. Kathryn, who had taken her mother's corner of the litter, looked back at Melissa with tears in her eyes. Melissa thought, *Well, this was a great idea.*

Then she said out loud, "Where are you, Andrew?" For a moment, she thought she heard bagpipes in the distance, causing her to scoff and chuckle simultaneously. "Well, either you're dead or about to do something ridiculously macho and reckless."

As she anticipated, the CAT-MAN vehicles stopped at her parents' house, which they quickly surrounded, then entered. *Here we go,* she thought as she sighted in on the CAT-MAN officer who looked to be in charge.

THE US CAPITOL BUILDING

SYKES HAD GATHERED his CAT-MAN overseers about an hour ago, out of earshot of any of the rank-and-file CAT-MAN officers—he didn't want them to hear what he was about to say. He informed his overseers—fellow mercenaries—that the force coming was better trained, more disciplined, and more experienced than the force defending the Capitol Building. Not to mention that it was very highly motivated, which in a fair fight could mean the difference between winning and losing. Clearly, this was not a fair fight.

He told them that if the assaulting force succeeded in breaching the defensive barricades, then they should consider the battle lost and make their way to the tunnel that led to the Senate office building, from there making their way back to friendly forces. He also told them that they were to do this quietly and leave the minions to buy time with their lives since they were very much expendable.

Sykes wished them good luck and set off to try and make his way back to the White House. His last order was to get Sergeant Maddox and his men out of the tanks and replace them with CAT-MAN officers.

"They'll need a crash course, but it doesn't take much to pull a trigger and rotate a turret."

TOM OLIVA

THE WHITE HOUSE

KELLER WAS IN a panic.

"What the fuck do you mean we can't leave?"

"We can't leave," the CAT-MAN overseer who Sykes had sent to watch Keller replied matter of factly. He hadn't told Keller his name, and Keller hadn't asked. He continued, seeing that Keller wasn't going to let it go. "They've blocked all the gates with cars and blown all the tires. Every time we send someone out to try and move them, they get shot in the face by snipers. That's why."

"Can't we use the Beast and push our way through?" Keller replied, referring to the heavily armored presidential limousine.

"The Beast could possibly bash its way through, but we don't know if they've rigged any explosives or any other surprises for us in that mess they've created. We're just going to have to wait and see how things play out at the Capitol Building and hope your helos can get you out if things go badly," replied the nameless CAT-MAN overseer.

"This is bullshit! I'm the president of the United States!" replied Keller, his face turning red with indignation.

"That's nice, but you're still stuck here," he replied with a shrug.

UNION STATION, WASHINGTON, DC

A DOZEN OR so Tenth Mountain soldiers were guarding approximately two hundred CAT-MAN prisoners on F Street near Second Street beside Union Station, where the buildings provided shelter. The once distant sound of bagpipes was clearly getting closer, grabbing the attention of guards and prisoners alike. The sound continued getting louder as it came closer, echoing off the buildings along Second Street. When the music sounded as if it were right around the corner, one of the Tenth Mountain soldiers guarding the intersection came running toward the group of guards and prisoners, waving his arm and shouting, "Clear the way! The Militia is coming!"

With that, the guards started shouting at their prisoners, "Get on your feet!" With their hands zip-tied behind their backs, many of the prisoners, already exhausted and disheartened, had a difficult time standing up from their seated position. This prompted the guards to start pulling some up by their clothes and pushing them against the wall of the Securities and Exchange Commission. One guard shouted, "Move your ass, didn't you hear? The Militia is coming!"

As the Militia passed—Andy in the lead, Squatch to his right, David to his left, and the Scotsman, bagpipes blaring behind Andy—the Tenth Mountain guards stood a little taller, and the CAT-MAN prisoners slumped a little lower. Some cowered, already broken, the sight of this new force overwhelming them. Some burst into tears knowing the friends they still had in the Capitol Building were about to die.

As Andy passed Union Station and entered Columbus Circle, he saw Colonel Reynolds by the fountain and had the Scotsman stop playing. He told Squatch to halt the formation once they were all on Columbus Circle, then headed over to consult with Reynolds.

"Hey, Colonel, heard you got clipped in the ass," Andy said in a low tone as he approached Reynolds.

"Yeah, word gets around, I guess," Reynolds replied, turning to show Andy the bloody and torn seat of his pants, a fresh bandage visible through the tear.

"That doesn't look so bad," Andy said, trying to sound positive.

"Luckily, they didn't hit anything important. Why the hell are you whispering?" Reynolds said, changing the subject away from his buttocks. "After all the racket you guys have been making back there, now you want to whisper?"

"Kind of ironic, isn't it?" replied Andy.

Squatch joined them, along with David and the three Militia battalion commanders.

"Hey, Colonel, I heard you got shot in the ass," Squatch said.

Reynolds let out a low growl and said, "Did you two rehearse giving me shit before you came up here?"

Andy and Squatch looked at each other and shrugged.

Reynolds nodded his head, then began to speak. "There's thick fog forming over the whole area, all that rain, and now the sun is starting to rise. This can work to our advantage. We've got all the strong points occupied, and we're ready to cover your attack. The northern force will leave here, move down Delaware Avenue, and set up for your assault along Constitution Avenue. The southern force will leave here along Massachusetts Avenue and turn right onto Second Street. I would double-time it from there until you reach Independence Avenue since you have twice as far to go; we want to use this fog to our advantage. You set up for your assault, and when you're ready, give the word and the rest of us will cover you. The trucks with the ladders are already in place in the north and south, as are all the supporting guns." Reynolds took a moment to look each of them in the eye. "Good luck boys, give 'em hell."

Reynolds shook each man's hand and, when he came to Andy, said, "No bagpipes on the way in, OK?"

Andy replied with a smile, "There's a stiff in every crowd."

Andy turned to David, put one hand on his shoulder, and said, "Remember what I told you."

Andy then turned and walked back toward the waiting Militia with Squatch by his side.

"Don't get killed, ya big idiot," Andy said, shaking his friend's hand.

"No guarantees, little buddy. You watch your ass," replied Squatch with a smile.

THE CAPITOL BUILDING

IT HAD TAKEN less than fifteen minutes for the northern and southern forces to get into position. The ladders were where Reynolds had said they would be, and Andy now stood, radio handset in hand, looking into the fog at the giant shadow that was the United States Capitol Building. *Well, here goes nothin'*, he thought to himself. Then he raised the handset to his face and said the code word for the preparatory fires to begin: "Nuisance, all units, nuisance."

The early morning silence was instantly shattered by deafening gunfire. The Bradleys on the north and south sides of the building were pumping the last of their high-explosive rounds into the sandbag barricades. The goal was to punch through at two locations on each side. The Strykers were firing their .50-caliber heavy machine guns at the eastern side, and the mortar crews were firing high-explosive rounds into the western side and onto the roof. Some in the assault force covered their ears, and others smiled and laughed, the sound of which was lost, of course.

Andy had begun counting out loud the moment he gave the order, "One one thousand, two one thousand, three one thousand . . ." No one could hear him counting, of course, but it wasn't for anyone else—it was just for him. As he reached ten one thousand, the Bradley to his right rear shifted its fire to the eastern end of the barricades. All the while, the machine gun teams in the buildings behind him were raking the top of the barricades—at least, what they *thought* were the tops, as it was difficult to know for sure through the fog.

A DAY LIKE ANY OTHER

"Twenty-one thousand . . ." The Bradleys and Strykers were the first to stop shooting; having some of the last working timepieces, they knew exactly when twenty seconds had elapsed. (Any watch run by a battery had immediately ceased working the moment The Event had occurred, likewise for any cellular device.) Moments later, the rest of the covering force stopped firing and began quickly reloading should their covering fire be needed again.

As the firing stopped, Andy said only, "Let's go!" as he began to sprint off into the fog. Five hundred warriors rose with him, plunging off into the fog toward the hulking shadow in the near distance. Likewise on the north side, Squatch had only stood and waved his arm forward, and his five hundred warriors were also in motion.

Andy could see flashes and hear booms as the mortar crews continued firing at the west side of the building. He could also hear the Strykers firing at the east side. The intent of those sustained fires was to keep reinforcements away from the north and south. As Andy got closer to the building, he could see off to his left the distinct outline of an M1 main battle tank, and, to his horror, the turret began rotating in his direction. *Maybe they'll miss,* Andy thought as he ran.

Andy's attention turned from the tank to what seemed like black baseballs arching up from behind the barricades that he was now only a few yards away from. He realized in the next moment that they were not baseballs but hand grenades, and a moment after that, they began exploding among the charging Militia. One of them exploded behind Andy, throwing him to the ground. Disoriented, he raised himself up to kneel on all fours and lingered there as the world spun wildly around him.

To his front, a Militiaman lay in a heap, the holes in his back still smoldering where the grenade fragments had imbedded in his vest. Jessica, who less than an hour ago had been singing and performing like a rock star, came sliding up next to the man and rolled him over. He instantly sprang back to life with a "What the fuck!" She shouted in his face, "Get up and go!" as she pointed toward the barricades. There was blood on her hands and her face. Andy thought, *My God, Wally can't lose her too.* She then turned her attention to Andy, making eye contact.

Suddenly, Andy felt himself flying through the air and thought, *Well, this is how it ends.* He watched the ground drift past him in silence, and he saw Jessica turn her attention to another Militiaman who was down. Andy thought, *Yes, move on to someone you can help . . .* He felt totally at peace.

Andy's peaceful escape ended abruptly as he landed in a heap at the base of the barricades. Dmitry and the Scotsman had been to Andy's left and right when the grenade had gone off, throwing them all to the ground. They had recovered themselves, but seeing Andy on all fours had thrown them both into a panic. They had scooped him up by his armpits and run as quickly as they could to the cover of the barricades, nearly running Jessica over.

Dmitry was bleeding from his shoulder above the triceps of his left arm. The Scotsman's right trouser leg was torn below the knee, and he was bleeding from a laceration to his calf. Andy was bleeding from his ears, but luckily for all three of them, their body armor and helmets had taken most of the shrapnel.

Andy sat for a moment collecting his thoughts and taking in the scene around him. The Scotsman was firing up at a CAT-MAN officer who had just shot one of the engineers off a ladder to Andy's immediate right. Dmitry caught the engineer and, in one motion, laid the man on the ground and picked up the entrenching tool he had been using to dig at the sandbags. Apparently, the Bradleys' fire had not broken completely through, and now it was necessary to dig a small hole into what remained and place explosives to finish the job. Dmitry went bounding up the ladder at what seemed like far too fast a pace for a man of his size and began digging at the sandbags. This time, the Scotsman and others were covering the top of the barricades, and any heads that popped up to fire at Dmitry were quickly dispatched to the hereafter.

Grenades were still being thrown from the other side; some were landing and exploding, causing casualties, and others were being caught midflight and thrown back over. The tank Andy had taken notice of moments ago was still pointing its main gun right at them but was not firing, nor was its coaxial machine gun. Had either gun been firing, this attack would already be over. Even without the tank shooting at them, casualties were mounting, and to say the scene was chaotic was an understatement.

Dmitry was done hacking at the barricade, and a block of explosives with two wires hanging out of it was handed up to him. He placed it in the hole he had just created and started packing sandbags on top of it.

Andy had to decide if the assault would continue or if they should fall back and regroup. His ears were ringing, and all the sounds around him were muffled. A grenade exploded, and a body fell at his feet. The Scotsman fired his rifle, striking a CAT-MAN officer in the head, who fell backward with blood spurting from the wound. Andy looked to his left, where his radio operator, handset to his ear, blood dripping from a gash on his forehead, was shouting in Andy's face.

"All assault teams pinned down at the barricades! Casualties mounting! Barricades are not breached! Sasquatch is down!"

Andy looked up from his seat against the barricade to see two figures standing upright and without concern. They were dressed differently—they wore no body armor, nor were they wearing the CAT-MAN urban camouflage. Then Andy recognized the uniforms. They were the standard Marine combat uniforms from World War II and Vietnam. He had seen both enough times, so it was obvious.

One of the men crouched to get closer to Andy's face and said, "Boy, you've got to shake it off and get your shit together."

Then the other figure spoke.

"You're the one who has to make the call here. Only you."

Andy was stunned as both figures instantly disappeared. He snapped back from the semi-stupor he was in. He was now keenly aware of the situation and knew what he had to do. Andy reached down, grabbing the red star cluster flare from his equipment belt, and fired the flare directly overhead.

He then turned to his radioman, whose face was bleeding from what looked like being dragged across cement, and said, "All units, attack the fortress!"

Dmitry came tumbling down the ladder and landed at Andy's feet. He had been trying to move a little too quickly again, but this time he had lost his footing and fallen pretty much from the top. The engineer who had handed Dmitry the explosives shouted, "Fire in the hole! Fire in the hole!" then pressed the actuator, triggering an instantaneous and deafening explosion that sent sandbags hurtling skyward.

Before the debris even stopped falling, Andy was headed up the ladder one-handed, his other hand holding his rifle with the bayonet fixed and pointed toward the top of the ladder. Andy did not see all the other units responding with red stars in reply, nor did he hear three other detonations blasting holes in the CAT-MAN defenses. He was concerned only with being the first man into the defenses.

Andy topped the barricades not knowing what awaited, but what greeted him was not what he expected. The explosion had torn open (or thrown) hundreds of sandbags. The CAT-MAN defenders opposite the blast were covered in sand and half-buried in sandbags, and all of them were down. They were a writhing mass of bodies. One defender was up against the building, folded into the fetal position and sobbing uncontrollably. These people were not a threat, but the defenders who weren't in either blast radius were, and they began firing. Andy was quickly joined by Dmitry, the Scotsman, and dozens of others, and all returned a devastating fire. Andy could see through the smoke and dust that the other breach was now pouring attackers into the fight. Not wanting to hit his own people, Andy charged forward, followed closely by the ever-growing mass of Militia coming up the ladders behind him.

CAT-MAN resistance collapsed, and the remaining defenders quickly surrendered or retreated into the building, barring the doors behind them. This had been anticipated, and the majority of both Andy's and Squatch's forces had already secured the main entrance to the building. They had gone up the ladders and directly to the doors overlooking the reflecting pool, mowing down anyone in their way. They had been inside the building just seconds after coming up the ladders. Lieutenant Ramirez and his Stryker force had secured the back doors. With all the attention being paid to the assaults on the north and south while the east and west were under fire, the attackers moving quickly and with purpose had simply overwhelmed the CAT-MAN defenses.

Andy turned to his radio operator and said, "Tell Cummings to get the congresswoman and First Lady up here ASAP. I want Congress to see friendly faces when we liberate them."

Andy then headed for the main entrance. Adrenaline still pumping, he felt like he was walking on air. The pain of the many tiny pieces of shrapnel embedded in his skin hadn't kicked in yet.

The Scotsman slung his weapon and began to pipe a tune. Andy recognized it as "The Gael."

UNION STATION

SYKES HAD LEFT for the White House before sunrise to try and get back before the insurgents' attack, intending to get Keller out. He had been shot at several times and had had to change direction. He found himself approaching Union Station. The sun was rising and the fog was clearing. Feeling desperate to at least get out of what was clearly a perimeter around the Capitol Building, he attempted to move quickly past the building and broke into a full-on run.

As he got within thirty feet of the station, he saw a vehicle parked near the western end of the building. It was running. He thought, *That's my way out.*

A DAY LIKE ANY OTHER

Sykes was sprinting now. Seeing this as his last chance to break out, he prepared himself to fight and kill anyone he encountered at the vehicle.

Just as Sykes arrived at the front of the vehicle, two men appeared, moving as fast as he was in the opposite direction. The collision was epic. The two men went tumbling backward, one bashing into the grill of the vehicle, the other stumbling backward and ending up flat on his back. Sykes went skidding across the pavement and ended up on his stomach facing Union Station. Sykes looked up to see Special Agent Billings shuffling the First Lady and some other person back into the building. Sykes quickly realized it had been Cummings and Detweiler he had run into, neither of whom were back on their feet yet. Sykes sprung to his feet, swinging his rifle up to fire at Cummings first. He would put Detweiler down once and for all next.

Several shots rang out in rapid succession: *Bang bang bang bang bang!* Sykes spun around, falling sideways, having been hit in the torso. His armor had failed to save him this time. As he hit the ground, a rifle, its barrel still smoking, was pointed at his face.

David shouted, "Don't move, or I'll shoot you again!"

Sykes put his hands up and said in a fading voice, "A fucking kid . . ."

Cummings, back on his feet now, quickly rolled Sykes over, handcuffing his hands behind his back. Several Tenth Mountain soldiers and Colonel Reynolds arrived moments later, having heard the shooting right outside his headquarters.

Cummings looked up at Reynolds and said, "This is CAT-MAN Director Sykes!"

"I'll be damned, it sure as hell is," replied Reynolds, lifting Sykes's head by the hair to get a good look.

"We have to go. Andy is waiting to open the chambers where Congress is being held. Will you take charge of my prisoner?" Cummings asked, sounding out of breath. The collision with Sykes had stunned him.

"We can do that," replied Reynolds as he gestured for his soldiers to take Sykes away.

"Don't let him die, if you can," Cummings said as he opened the back door for the First Lady and congresswoman.

TOM OLIVA

THE CAPITOL BUILDING

ANDY WAS STANDING outside of the House Chamber with about fifty of the Militia. They were waiting for the First Lady and Congresswoman Dreyfus to arrive before attempting to enter. The occasional sound of a grenade detonation or gunfire was sporadically heard echoing through the halls of the Capitol, but for the most part, the building was secure.

Squatch joined them, bleeding from both of his shins, having been on the receiving end of a CAT-MAN grenade, and said, "Cummings and crew are here. They ran into Sykes, literally. David popped him. Reynolds took him into custody—that should prove an interesting interrogation. If Sykes survives, of course."

"David popped him?" Andy replied.

"Yup. Four, five shots, center mass at close range," replied Squatch, looking around at the CAT-MAN bodies strewn about the entryway of the doors. "Did we do all this?"

"No, not us. We found them like this," Andy replied as he gestured toward a dead CAT-MAN overseer with a large folding knife sticking from his chest.

A few moments later, Cummings's little entourage arrived. Joyce was practically running. She went straight for the doors and would have opened them had Andy not stopped her.

"We don't know what's waiting for us in there," Andy said calmly yet with a firmness that stopped her in her tracks. "How about we stand off to the side and call to them through the door that you're here with friends?"

"Yes, of course," Joyce replied, stepping to one side of the doorway. She then called through the doors, "Hello, anyone in there? This is Joyce Keller. I'm here with Eleanor Dreyfus and some others. We came to free you."

After a few moments, the sound of furniture being removed from blocking the doors was heard. Then the door began to crack open. Everyone with a rifle outside the door quickly sighted in.

Sergeant First Class Maddox opened the door slowly and said jokingly, "It's about time you all got here."

Everyone relaxed as Joyce spoke.

"I'm sorry it took so long."

"There she is!" Maddox said in a booming voice as Eleanor came toward him, extending her arms with tears in her eyes and embracing him.

A DAY LIKE ANY OTHER

"Can we go inside, Sergeant?" Eleanor asked.

"Yes, ma'am, I know they'll be happy to see you again," Maddox replied, gesturing her into the House Chamber.

Andy interjected. His mood was dampening the more the adrenaline wore off and the pain of his injuries became more prevalent.

"Remember, we need the Speaker of the House, president pro tempore of the Senate, all the Joint Chiefs, and all the Supreme Court justices."

"I remember, Andrew," replied Joyce, "and thank you."

Andy instructed his radio operator to request that Colonel Reynolds come over from Union Station, then turned his attention to Maddox.

"You guys responsible for these?" Andy said, pointing to the dead and dying CAT-MAN soldiers littering the hallway.

"That would be us, yup. Hey, that's where my knife got to," Maddox replied, focusing on the CAT-MAN with the large folding knife protruding from his chest.

"Nice work. I'm guessing those are your tanks outside. I imagine you had something to do with them not blasting us to pieces," Andy said with a smile.

"Sergeant First Class Maddox at your service," Maddox began. "I told that tiny woman that my tanks wouldn't be hurtin' no one, and I keep my word."

"So what happened here?" asked Andy.

The low din that was coming from the House Chamber was gradually rising to the level of celebration as the reality of their liberation began to set in. Andy could hear Joyce and Eleanor speaking as they explained what had been going on since those present had been imprisoned here. In ones and twos, they started filtering out past Andy and Maddox. Medical personnel were entering as well. There was a great deal of activity now in what just a few minutes ago had been a very contentious situation.

Sergeant Maddox nodded, then replied, "We were in our tank, all buttoned up, waitin' for you guys to arrive. The closer you got, the more nervous the CAT-MAN folks became. Then about the time they figured out you had them surrounded, they came, got us out, and put their people in. They rounded us all up and put us in here. They searched us, but not real good, and we got a bunch of knives and a few pistols in here."

"They didn't leave any guards? How'd you get control?" Andy asked in disbelief.

"They did," Maddox began. "They had guards up in the gallery, but they kept pullin' more and more out to replace people they were losin', I guess, until they were all gone. We got people up there, and they barricaded those doors real good, so if they wanted back in, they'd have to come through these doors right here. When all the explosions outside stopped, we figured you were in the building and the CAT-MAN folks would come back. See, back when they first put us in here, one of my guys overheard the CAT-MAN overseers talkin' about leavin' no one alive if things went bad. So we got ready, and when they opened them doors, we jumped 'em. They weren't expectin' that, and we killed a bunch of 'em. Some of the congressmen joined in too. The rest ran off when one started yellin' about gettin' to the tunnel."

"You saved a lot of lives today, Sergeant, inside and outside this building," Andy replied, shaking Maddox's hand.

"I suppose we did."

"I'm guessing those tanks can be back in action pretty quickly?"

"Yes, they can if need be. It's just a matter of reconnecting a few wires in the right places," Maddox replied with a smile.

"We're marching on the White House ASAP. Are you with us? We sure could use the firepower," Andy asked, returning Maddox's smile.

"Oh, I'm in, and my tankers are in too. When do we roll out?" Maddox replied with a grin.

Colonel Reynolds appeared through the mass of humanity, radio operator in tow, and said, "Are you throwing a party in here?"

"Colonel Reynolds, meet Sergeant First Class Maddox. He has some main battle tanks and has agreed to join us," replied Andy.

Andy had sent for Reynolds in the event Maddox needed some persuading to join them. Andy thought that seeing another active-duty soldier, a high-ranking one, would be helpful. As it turned out, Maddox was eager to join the fight.

Maddox snapped to attention, saluting Reynolds, and said, "Good morning, sir."

Reynolds came to attention and returned Maddox's salute.

"Welcome to the team, son."

US SENATE OFFICE BUILDING, SUB-LEVEL

THE DARKNESS WAS almost absolute. The only light present was from emergency exit signs that apparently ran on battery power. Reynolds had cut the power to all of Capitol Hill in the opening hours of his assault. The

A DAY LIKE ANY OTHER

twelve-man team sent to watch the Capitol Building tunnel exit had one of the few sets of night vision goggles left, and there was just enough ambient light for them to function.

They had been there for several hours, silently watching the darkness. At first, they thought they had imagined the sound of footsteps, an illusion fueled by boredom over time. They listened harder and squinted into the blackness. The team leader, speaking in a barely audible whisper, said, "Get ready." The team members quickly brushed away their boredom as their adrenaline spiked.

Through his night vison goggles, the leader saw the group of CAT-MAN soldiers quickly walking toward them. He waited until the CAT-MAN guys were within fifteen yards. He knew the rest of the team could see the shadowy outlines of their targets at that distance. He took a breath and quietly said, "Now."

The two M249 Squad Automatic Weapons erupted in fully automatic fire. The team leader and two other soldiers began throwing grenades, and the rest of the team was firing their weapons as quickly as they could.

It took only moments. The entire group of CAT-MAN soldiers were down. The team leader shouted to call a ceasefire several times. Then only the moans of several CAT-MAN wounded in the tunnel were heard. The team leader felt a twinge of sadness and nausea—the CAT-MAN soldiers had never had a chance, and his team had slaughtered them. The feeling passed, and he was back to business. He sent two of his men forward to start checking for survivors, then picked up his radio handset to make his report.

"This is Team Seven. Forty to forty-five tangos down in the tunnel. Team intact. Send medical aid for enemy WIA."

UPSTATE PENNSYLVANIA

MELISSA HAD BEEN alternating between looking out the back door at the stretcher bearers' progress into the forest and the activities of the CAT-MAN officers at her parents' house. She felt the knot in her stomach growing tighter every time she looked out the back door. They were barely fifty yards away with the stretcher, and there remained at least another fifty yards before they were in thick enough brush to no longer be seen from the house. *Come on, hurry up*, she thought to herself.

She could see that CAT-MAN officers were now exiting her parents' house, and the officer she felt was in charge was now pointing and gesturing for his people to start moving toward her house. They fanned out in a line and began moving toward her, their vehicles moving along with them. She could also see more vehicles, more than a dozen at least, turning off the highway and heading up the driveway. *Well, I guess this is how it ends,* she thought as she raised the rifle and sighted in on the CAT-MAN leader, this time intent on squeezing the trigger once she was sure of the shot. As the CAT-MAN leader grew larger in her sight, she felt strangely at peace.

WASHINGTON, DC, PENNSYLVANIA AVENUE HEADED TOWARD THE WHITE HOUSE

IT TOOK ANDY standing on an ammunition crate and shouting at the top of his lungs to get the pandemonium that possessed the Capitol Rotunda under control. Those of the Militia were stunned silent; they had never heard Andy raise his voice outside of a firefight. Everyone else was stunned silent by his sheer projection and commanding voice.

He had Congress vote on removing Keller as president and witnessed the swearing-in of the Speaker of the House as the new president. He then informed the new president that he and the Militia, supported by elements of the active-duty forces present, were marching on the White House to apprehend and arrest William Keller.

Andy was going to the White House regardless of whether the new president objected or not. However, having his blessing made it much cleaner when it came to how history would view it, as well as avoiding any legal ramifications should the ever-changing political winds turn against him and his troops sometime in the future.

Now, Andy, Maddox with four of his tanks, and about two hundred Militia and Tenth Mountain troops (pretty much a gathering of who could be spared from other duties) were now on the march toward the White House. Maddox's tanks were in the lead, driving down the middle of the street in a wedge formation. The infantry was behind them in two columns on either side of the street, walking along the curbside. Andy was on one side, the Scotsman by his side playing "The Black Bear." ("It's a fine tune for just such an occasion," the Scotsman had said.) They were joined by Dmitry and Jessica, whom Andy had told, "You stay by my side. Wally would kill me if anything happened to you." It was a fantasy, of course, that being close to Andy was any safer than being anywhere else today.

On the other side of the street, Squatch and Reynolds marched at the head of their column. Andy could see that Reynolds was irritated by the bagpipe's tunes, which only amused Squatch to the point of a grin he couldn't wipe from his face interspersed with open laughter.

On two separate occasions, Maddox had stopped his tanks to rake the street ahead with machine gun fire. He had seen something or someone he didn't like and had decided they needed to die. On a third occasion, a CAT-MAN soldier had fired a rocket from a third-floor window that bounced off the lead tank and went careening down Pennsylvania Avenue, eventually exploding somewhere behind the formation. The turret of Maddox's tank had rotated and fired one high-explosive round through the window, exploding that corner of the building. There had been no more resistance after that.

The White House had appeared in front of them, and they started the process of encircling it. Suddenly, from the west, three helicopters appeared from between the buildings on E Street. One flared back on its tail violently, then settled on the White House's south lawn, while the other two took up overwatch positions about one hundred feet off the ground. Andy saw they weren't the usual helos with white-painted tops and forest-green fuselages that they were used to seeing pick up the president. These were olive, drab, Sikorsky UH-60 Black Hawks. Andy knew they were still HMX-1 aircraft, the president's usual ride—these were considered green-side aircraft—piloted and crewed by Marines. Wally had told him that following The Event, HMX-1 had acquired the three combat aircraft in order to have less flashy and more combat-capable aircraft should they be needed. These aircraft were armed and ready for a fight.

Andy's radio operator said, "Overwatch sniper teams are requesting permission to fire."

"Tell them to hold their fire. We're not going to risk killing any members of the military," Andy replied calmly.

The helicopter on the ground was there for no more than a few seconds before it lifted off as aggressively as it had landed, turned north, and disappeared down Sixteenth Street. The two overwatch aircraft followed moments later. Andy's radio operator spoke again. "Sniper teams report that former President Keller and two CAT-MAN boarded the helo."

Squatch's voice came over the radio. "And away he goes..."
Andy looked across the street to see Squatch flapping his arms like a giant bird.
Just for now, Andy thought.

CHAPTER 45

THE WHITE HOUSE

AT FIFTEENTH STREET, the formation split, one half moving north, and the other half continuing on. Within five minutes, Andy had units positioned to essentially surround the White House, one tank conspicuously positioned on each side so anyone inside could see. No activity could be seen whatsoever—whoever was left inside wasn't moving.

Andy was handed a bullhorn, which he raised and spoke into.

"Attention in the White House." Andy paused to ensure he had their attention, then continued, "We have the building surrounded." Andy paused again to let the visual set in. "The person you were protecting is gone; he left you here to die. You're defending a building now. If you come out unarmed, you will not be harmed. If not, we will flatten the building with all of you inside, I promise you."

Andy put down the bullhorn, took the radio handset, and said, "All units prepare to open fire on my command. Team leaders, call out any activity."

One by one, they acknowledged the orders.

No sooner had Andy handed the handset back to the operator than the radio operator said, "Rhino on the guard frequency sends code word 'raspberry.'"

Andy smiled and said, "Tell Rhino to stand by and await further instructions."

After what seemed an eternity, Andy could see CAT-MAN officers exiting the White House. Team leaders began reporting that the CAT-MAN were coming out to surrender.

Andy took the radio handset again and said, "OK, all units proceed with caution. Move onto White House grounds by whatever means necessary, receive prisoners, and secure the building."

The relief Andy felt was euphoric. He didn't have to order another bloody assault, and his relief was noticeable in his voice.

He turned to his radio operator and said, "Tell Rhino we need fifteen minutes, then we'll be ready for them." He almost sounded gleeful.

Fifteen minutes later, with seventy-five CAT-MAN prisoners secured and most of the White House having been swept by teams, the hum of rotor blades could, again, be heard echoing down the concrete canyons of DC.

Andy took the radio handset once again.

"OK, everyone, let them come in. We need to clear the South Lawn, please."

No sooner had Andy issued his orders than three helicopters appeared over the White House. This time all three landed, and the landing was much different than before. This time, instead of aggressively flaring and landing in an instant, they came into a hover and gently began to settle.

In one of the gunner's windows, Andy saw a sight he was all too familiar with. The crewman had his torso outside of the aircraft through the gunner's window and was making bodybuilder poses. Wally was back with a tale to tell.

WHEN WALLY HAD left Annapolis with the SEALs, Andy had wondered if he'd ever see his friend again. Wally had offered a solution to the problem of Keller being evacuated by helicopter. He and the SEALs would leave on the assault boat from Annapolis and travel to Marine Corps Air Facility Quantico, the home of HMX-1, an approximately 150-mile trip by sea. Once there, Wally would simply walk through the front gate; HMX had been his last unit before he left just after The Event. He would tell the guards that he had reconsidered and wished to return to active duty. He hoped to at least speak to his former commanding officer to try and convince him to help them. Worst case would be that he'd end up in CAT-MAN custody or the commanding officer says he wouldn't help. In either of the latter scenarios, or if they failed to receive word from Wally that he had succeeded, the SEAL team would destroy any HMX aircraft present at the air station.

At first, the CAT-MAN sentries at the front gate took Wally as one of the insurgents attempting to gain access to the base. Of course, they were correct in their assumption and began pummeling Wally with their rifle butts. However, the Marine sentries posted not far away responded to the commotion and quickly recognized Wally as one of the crew chiefs at HMX, putting a stop to the beating and bringing him to the HMX hanger.

A DAY LIKE ANY OTHER

After a brief argument with the CAT-MAN officers, the commanding officer, Colonel Wilde, was successful in running them off on the pretense that Wally was one of his Marines; he vouched for him.

A no-nonsense leader, Colonel Wilde had achieved an impressive service record both in and out of combat. Combined with his connection to more than a few political acquaintances, he was awarded command of one of the most prestigious units in the Marine Corps. His Marines feared and respected him for his plain speech and sensibility.

His first words to Wally were, "What the fuck are you doing back here, Staff Sergeant Childs? Especially right now! All hell is breaking loose out there! Fuck, we're on strip alert to evac the president out of DC."

"Yes, sir, I understand, and that's why I'm here. Is this a safe place to talk?" Wally said, looking around the room as if it might be bugged.

Wally took the next thirty minutes to explain the things he had seen and the events that had brought him back here. He said nothing of the SEAL team waiting to destroy Wilde's aircraft should he decide against helping.

Colonel Wilde listened intently, expressionless and without reaction. When Wally finished, Colonel Wilde stood and walked to the window. He peered out for a few minutes, causing Wally to start becoming uncomfortable. Finally, he turned to Wally and said, "Wait right here." He was gone, again, for what seemed way too long to Wally, who was starting to think Wilde had gone to fetch the CAT-MAN guards to take him away. Wally started imagining how he might slip away before the colonel returned.

Colonel Wilde returned a few minutes later with the squadron sergeant major and who Wally assumed were all the pilots and crewmen who remained with the unit. The room filled quickly with people, all of whom knew Wally, and brief greetings were exchanged before Colonel Wilde closed the door and said, "OK, tell them what you just told me."

After listening to Wally's tale, followed by a spirited debate, it was agreed that they would help him. Normally, Colonel Wilde would not base his decisions on a majority consensus, but in this case, considering they were about to execute a coup d'état, he felt he should give his Marines a say. Wally assured everyone present that if it came to them flying Keller out, the Speaker of the House would already have been sworn in by then, and they would be doing nothing more than apprehending a criminal.

Together they formed a plan. The part that involved a SEAL team brought an immediate angry reaction from Colonel Wilde, as he was just now learning of their presence in the area.

"When the fuck were you gonna mention that, Childs?" he had asked.

Over the next several hours, things were quietly put into action so as not to arouse suspicion from the CAT-MAN soldiers assigned to the squadron. They would smuggle the SEALs onto the base, open the armory to draw weapons for the mission, and quietly arm all of the maintainers. They, under the sergeant major's command, would take control of the base away from the CAT-MAN officers once they got word the mission was a success.

When the call came, everything was ready and everyone knew what their role was to be. They were airborne within five minutes, and with it only being thirty miles away as the crow flies, they were performing a combat landing just a few minutes later. Wally barely had time to enjoy the exhilaration he always got from crewing these amazing machines.

Keller was hustled out of the Beast, which had raced out to meet them. In moments, Keller and two CAT-MAN overseers scrambled on board, and the aircraft was airborne and on its way before Wally could even get the door closed.

Somewhere over the Potomac River, near the Virginia/Maryland border, the two SEALs posing as door gunners drew their SIG Sauer 9-millimeter pistols and shot each of the CAT-MAN overseers twice in the head. Keller sat stunned, a pink mist of CAT-MAN blood lingering just for a moment in front of his face before dissipating. Wally pounced on him and had his hands bound with zip ties before Keller even knew what had happened, while the SEALs ensured the CAT-MAN overseers were dead.

They sent the code words, then orbited over a wooded area that must have been a national park of some sort until they were clear to return.

After a few minutes, Keller recovered enough to utter the words, "What will become of us?"

Wally replied, "Good question."

CHAPTER 46

UPSTATE PENNSYLVANIA

MELISSA GLANCED OUT the back door one last time. Her parents, María, and Kathryn seemed only a few yards farther along than the last time she had looked. They weren't going to make it. Even if she ran up there right now and helped, her parents looked as though they would have a heart attack at any moment. She settled in behind her rifle; this would be her last stand. She had set herself up as Andy had instructed, a few feet back from the window so her targets wouldn't see her until she began firing. She had spare magazines beside her and a shotgun by the door as a backup. On her hip, she had her 9-millimeter handgun as a last resort.

Her heart nearly stopped as a dark form suddenly appeared beside her. The last time she had seen Gomer, he had been out back beside the slow-motion stretcher team. She didn't bother trying to shoo him back outside—it was too late.

The line of CAT-MAN soldiers moving across the field stopped about fifty yards away. The person who Melissa presumed was the leader confirmed her assumption when he took cover behind a vehicle and began calling to the house.

"We have reason to believe the house contains contraband weapons and may be harboring fugitives," the CAT-MAN leader began, looking from side to side, ensuring his people were in position. "We will be entering the house. Any resistance will be met with overwhelming force."

Melissa saw that the line of vehicles driving up from the highway was now turning into the field as well. There had to be twenty vehicles. *It's now or never*, she thought.

"It's you and me, buddy," she whispered to Gomer, who emitted a low growl.

She sighted in again on the CAT-MAN leader's face and began taking up the slack on the trigger.

Just then, she heard police sirens wailing, breaking her focus. She looked up from her rifle to see that the source of the sirens was Sheriff Dunlop's police cruiser, the light bar on the roof flashing wildly. He was followed by a line of civilian vehicles. The cruiser and probably half the vehicles pulled out in front of the CAT-MAN force while the rest pulled in behind them.

Sheriff Dunlop's voice came over the cruiser's PA system.

"This is an unlawful assembly, and all CAT-MAN personnel will lay down their arms immediately and put their hands on their heads."

Before Sheriff Dunlop finished speaking, John Redstone exited the passenger side of the cruiser, rifle in hand. Likewise, from all the other recently arrived vehicles, armed individuals exited and sighted in on the CAT-MAN officers.

With the tables being turned so suddenly, the CAT-MAN officers were confused as to what they should do, and an awkward pause lingered for a few moments as what was happening began to sink into their CAT-MAN skulls.

Sheriff Dunlop snapped them out of their stupor with his next words: "Lay down your weapons immediately, or we will begin firing."

The words themselves, combined with the force in Dunlop's voice and the multitude of guns pointed at them, showed the CAT-MAN force the reality of the situation. They began dropping their weapons.

Dunlop's people pounced on the CAT-MAN officers and began taking them prisoner, grabbing them and pushing them against their own vehicles to be searched. John Redstone gazed upward and gave a nod to Melissa, now visible in the window she had been about to start ending lives from moments ago.

John had made it over the mountain and back into town. Knowing Sheriff Dunlop to be a good man, he had sought him out and explained what he had witnessed going on to the south—what Andy and the others were involved in. He had beseeched the sheriff to intervene in what he assumed was about to happen at the Tafts' farm. Dunlop had agreed to help and had proceeded to round up as many of the townspeople he could find.

The relief and gratitude Melissa felt nearly brought her to tears, but then she suddenly remembered her parents were about to go into cardiac arrest somewhere in the woods behind her house. She scrambled off into the woods, calling for John to follow with help.

THE WHITE HOUSE'S SOUTH LAWN

ANDY AND SQUATCH arrived at the helicopter's door just as Wally slid it open.

Wally shouted over the turning rotor blades, "Do I deliver, or do I deliver?"

A DAY LIKE ANY OTHER

Andy and Squatch smiled widely while moving aside for the two SEALs, who were dragging the bodies of the CAT-MAN guys they had killed, to get out of the helo. Andy took a long look at Keller, savoring the moment until Wally handed him a headset and said, "Colonel Wilde wants a word with you."

Even after all he'd been through, Andy felt a twinge of *Oh shit* at the statement. Old conditioning dies hard, he figured.

Andy donned the headset and said, "Good morning, sir. Thanks for the help."

"Yeah, look, I need to get moving," Colonel Wilde began. "The sergeant major says my boys have most of the base secured, but there're a few tough firefights in progress. So I need to get back. We've done the right thing here. Don't let them screw it up again."

"Aye aye, sir," Andy replied.

He removed the headset and turned to help Wally and Squatch get Keller out of the helicopter's door. As they cleared the rotor arc, the bird lifted off, and moments later, all three helos were headed off to the south at top speed.

The walk back to the White House felt like a parade to Andy. Chief Norwood and his SEAL team, having flown in on the other two aircraft, had quickly surrounded them as they walked, providing security. A group of Militia joined them, and they all moved as a group. The CAT-MAN prisoners—on their knees, hands on their heads—looked on, under guard. As they entered the building, Militiamen and soldiers who had just completed sweeping the building had gathered by the entrance and cleared a path. To Keller, they must have looked like a gauntlet of bearded, dirty, bloody men, all of whom looked on silently, their eyes telling the tale of hardships they'd endured under his tyranny. Keller walked with his eyes ahead, focusing on nothing. He just walked on, a man resigned to his fate.

Ahead, Andy saw Jessica seated at a grand piano and recognized the song she was playing. *Heavy metal in a classical key? Very nice.* Andy snapped himself out of his own thoughts and began wondering if he had a concussion. Jessica stopped playing when she noticed the activity behind her. Her eyes met Wally's, and they both smiled widely.

Reynolds met them and said, "Oval Office." He gestured for them to follow him.

As they entered the Oval Office, Andy saw that Ramirez (looking as if he were in a great deal of pain), Dmitry, Cummings, Detweiler, Maddox, David, and the Scotsman were all already there.

349

Cummings leaned over and said quietly to Andy, "Billings had his guys sweep the room. They found cameras and listening devices. It's clear now. They're working on clearing the rest of the building. He also sent a team to guard the new president."

Keller, who had been silent until now, spoke up forcefully as if he had just been awakened.

"Billings! Billings! Where is my family? Are they safe?"

Seeing Keller so helpless and desperate made Andy feel sorry for the man. Andy said, "They're fine. You'll see them again soon."

Keller visibly relaxed and asked if he could sit.

Squatch, not feeling the least bit sorry for Keller, replied, "No! You stand."

Reynolds, being the highest-ranking officer in the room, stepped forward and began to speak.

"William Keller, you have been charged with treason, genocide, dereliction of duty, failure to uphold your oath, and a dozen other charges that will be made known to you later. Congress has impeached you and removed you from office. The Speaker of the House has been sworn in and has assumed the duties of president of the United States."

Keller listened and thought for a moment. His shoulders relaxed, and he exhaled deeply and said, "Thank God. What a relief..."

Andy fought the urge to laugh, convinced now that he had a concussion. A few moments later, the phone Cummings had taken off Sykes began ringing. Simultaneously, the phone Wally had taken off Keller began ringing as well.

Keller closed his eyes and said, "How does he always know?"

Cummings answered, looking confused and sounding puzzled, putting the phone on speaker for all to hear.

"Hello?"

"You bunch of rabble! Peasants!" Mr. X was livid. Keller sat now, oblivious to anything going on around him. "What is it exactly you think you've accomplished?"

Andy couldn't help but reply in a smart-ass fashion.

"Yes! Hello! To whom am I speaking?"

"You insolent bastard, who the hell do you think you are?" Mr. X replied. It sounded as if he were pounding on a desk with his fist. "You don't know what you've done! You don't know who we are?"

"Yes, exactly. Who are you? That was my question before you started flipping out," Andy replied with a smile.

A DAY LIKE ANY OTHER

Squatch grinned from ear to ear, and Wally covered his mouth to stifle a laugh. Even Keller looked up from his despair and smiled for a moment, apparently enjoying someone finally giving it back to Mr. X after all those months of being his puppet on a string.

"You want to know who I am, who *we* are?" Mr. X's tone was more measured now. "Kings rule through us—that's who we are. For centuries, we've been the ones pulling the strings, boy. The rest of the world has fallen into line. The United States now stands alone. Good luck going forward. This isn't over."

The phone went dead.

Andy said, "He hung up on us." This prompted measured laughter from the room. "What an unpleasant man."

Keller replied, "You have no idea. And I'd believe him when he says this isn't over."

THAT NIGHT, TOMMY Rye began his program with these words: "Hello, America. Today freedom was once again ensured with the blood of patriots..."

EPILOGUE

Upon exiting the Oval Office, Andy was met by his radio operator and informed that the new president, the secretary of defense, the Joint Chiefs of Staff, and several members of Congress had gone out and met with the commanding generals of the two divisions approaching from the south. The situation was made clear, and units were deployed to neutralize the CAT-MAN forces approaching from the north and west. The sound of helicopter gunships pounding the CAT-MAN columns in the distance was a soothing sound to Andy.

By nightfall, the Secret Service and Capitol Police, reinforced by active-duty units, had secured the Capitol Building and White House. Andy, after consulting with all parties involved, deemed the mission complete and ordered all Militia units back to the college base camp. The camp was somber as all took stock of the events of the last eleven days.

The next day was spent getting an accurate casualty count and recovering the bodies of the fallen, including those lost in the battles in Baltimore and Annapolis. The following morning, all the units involved in the march from Philadelphia gathered in Arlington National Cemetery to lay their comrades to rest. The names of the fallen were read aloud, and the entire force listened and reflected. The Scotsman played "Amazing Grace" and other appropriate tunes for such a somber occasion.

Andy made a brief speech before the rifle salute and the playing of taps.

"You swore an oath to defend this country, and when the country was in need, when freedom was repressed, when its people were suffering, you responded. Marching with you has been the honor of my life. I am proud to have served with you. You should be proud of what you've done. We gather today to lay our brothers and sisters to rest. I charge all of you to carry on with your lives and honor them in your actions every day. Remember them and honor them until we meet them again in Valhalla."

Over the following few days, groups of Militia from the same geographical areas were encouraged to return home. Dmitry's brothers and grandmother showed up one day. She got out of the car, hugged Dmitry, and said, "Vee vill go now." With that, Dmitry headed back to Philadelphia.

Before she got back in the car, she turned to Andy and said in very broken English, "Yes, zat vas your father and grandfather you saw. Zey came to help you ven you needed help za most."

This left Andy strangely comforted and a little freaked out at the same time.

Lieutenant Ramirez was taken to Walter Reed Medical Center, along with all of the seriously wounded, where he spent three months and received several surgeries for his burns. He was promoted to captain and, due to the terrible shortage of junior officers, offered a position in the active-duty Army, which he accepted.

Lieutenant Colonel Reynolds received a promotion to full colonel and was given command of an infantry brigade within the Tenth Mountain Division. He remained a cantankerous old grouch.

Sergeant First Class Maddox eventually returned home as well, with a crazy story to tell. In the end it was his decision to disable his tanks' fire control systems that most likely saved the country from descending into a fascist nightmare for good. When asked about that decision, he would always just say, "It seemed like the right thing to do."

Congresswoman Dreyfus, like all the rest of the members of Congress, returned to her district after passing sweeping legislation meant to get the country back on its feet again. She returned home an ardent Second Amendment supporter and made the trip with an AR-15 by her side. The weapon had been gifted to her by Sasquatch himself.

Joyce Keller and her daughters were put up at the vice president's residence to afford her access to her husband, now being held at FBI headquarters. (Cummings had said, "I want him somewhere I can keep an eye on him.") She kept herself involved in the relief effort, especially with those who had been held in the camps and the military officers who had endured the "retraining" facilities. That part of the CAT-MAN "program" had come to be known as "The Great Purge," and many officers would never recover, physically or emotionally.

Andy saw all of them off and thanked each trooper individually. Not until all had gone and Andy was satisfied that the wounded were in good hands did he gather his things and make his rounds of goodbyes to his new friends in DC, then head home with Squatch and David.

Wally, taking advantage of the new president's first executive order recalling all military personnel who were able back to active duty, returned to

Quantico. His love of flying was rekindled and his love for life reawakened. Jessica returned to her home in Delaware, and the two vowed to meet up again soon.

Melissa and María were tending the farm when they saw Andy's truck coming up the driveway. Melissa called to the house, "Hey kids, your dads are home."

The initial joy and relief of being together with his family again was increasingly interrupted by thoughts and memories of the events of those eleven days. The intense labor of keeping the farm going and preparing stores for the winter occupied most of Andy's waking hours; the work created a very needed distraction. At night, Melissia would find him standing by a window, rifle by his side. At first, she'd convince him that he should come back to bed, but in time, she found that she felt safest knowing he was on watch, something she felt real guilt about. They'd find a way to get through it all, she told herself.

Some nights, he would awaken having heard something outside. Other nights, the sight of his first radio operator dying in front of him, the screams of a bayoneted CAT-MAN officer, or a thousand other sights or sounds would awaken him. He felt ever-present guilt over all of the losses they had suffered as a result of orders he had issued. What bothered him the most, however, was that he had survived when so many others had not. Some nights, he would awaken to the sound of David walking the floors, no doubt beset by some of the same torments as his father, and this troubled Andy greatly.

Cummings (with the help of the CIA, NSA, NASA, and Homeland Security), using the two satellite phones they had taken from Keller and Sykes, had managed to track down the calls' origins to a residential compound in Costa Rica. Chief Norwood's SEAL team was dispatched and inserted via a HALO parachute jump. After watching and monitoring communications for forty-eight hours, the decision was made using voice analysis programs that the owner of the compound was Mr. X, verified by Keller himself. It was also determined that Mr. X, whose real name was Xavier Lehner, was a multi-billionaire who had been implicated in several schemes that resulted in currency crashes in multiple countries spanning many years before The Event.

Norwood's team got the go-ahead to apprehend Lemmond and captured him eight hours later after a very brief firefight with the small security force present. Sixteen hours after that, he found himself sitting in front of Cummings and a room full of interrogators. Always the smug one, Mr. X started the session with, "You've made a big mistake."

A DAY LIKE ANY OTHER

Detweiler put all of the biggest minds he could find to work trying to get power back to the country. A young scientist commented that he had seen a television program before the lights went out around the world about devices that could produce energy from Earth's magnetic field. He also mentioned a conspiracy theory that all of the patents and technical data were deemed classified and locked up somewhere in the patent office.

Detweiler sent a group to ransack the patent office and there, low and behold, they found volumes of information on this technology. A prototype was tested a few weeks later, and a few weeks after that, the first production models were being delivered. Andy, Squatch, and the Tafts received some of the first units. To save on construction time and materials, old transformers that had blown but not burned up during The Event were repurposed for the units. One community at a time, the lights started coming back on.

Internationally, Mr. X's statement about the US standing alone started becoming true. The United Nations was disbanded and reconstituted as the League of Free Nations in Brussels, Belgium. The name was only a name. Without the means, the arms, or the will to counter their governments and the trampling of their personal freedoms, the other nations of the world became tyrannical oligarchies. Any citizens with the guts to speak up, much less stand up, against the tyrants were rounded up and sent away as enemies of humanity. These governments, under orders from their masters, voted the United States a rogue state and its government, having been installed by a violent insurrection, illegitimate.

While this was concerning to Andy, he paid it little mind. He had his life at home to tend to. The farm kept him busy—hunting when he could, teaching the younger children to shoot and survive, loving his family. For Andy, each day was a day like any other, and he needed to get on with it.